W9-CTE-402

Praise for WYRMS

"The plot is complex but without any flaw in conception or resolution. The prose is a model of narrative clarity; the author never says more than is needed or arbitrarily withholds information, yet even the simplest declarative sentence carries a delicious hint of further revelation."

— *The New York Times Book Review*

"Card takes the reader from the complex and hair-trigger world of court diplomacy to a mountaintop where a monstrous creature awaits his victim/lover. Beautiful, thought-provoking, and compulsively readable."

— Ellen Datlow, fiction editor of *Omni*

"Card looks deep, where others take much for granted. [*Wyrms*] has moments of great eloquence, humanity, and wisdom...like his worthiest characters, Card has the strength to forgo glamor in favor of truth."

— *Locus*

"When I published Orson Scott Card's first stories in *Analog* magazine, I predicted he would become one of the most important writers in the field of speculative fiction. *Wyrms* proves that I was right. And more. Card is not only one of the most important writers in the field — he is one of the absolute best!"

— Ben Bova

"The fine, detailed writing style of this marvelous story finally convinced me that Card is one of the three or four top SF writers of our time."

— A.E. van Vogt

Tor books by Orson Scott Card

Ender's Game
The Folk of the Fringe
Future on Fire (editor)
Future on Ice (editor)*
Hart's Hope
Saints
Maps in a Mirror:
   The Short Fiction of Orson Scott Card
Songmaster
Speaker for the Dead
The Worthing Saga
Wyrms
Xenocide

THE TALES OF ALVIN MAKER

Seventh Son
Red Prophet
Prentice Alvin

*forthcoming

ORSON SCOTT CARD

WYRMS

A TOM DOHERTY ASSOCIATES BOOK

WYRMS

Published by arrangement with Arbor House

Cover art by Dennis Nolan
Book designed by Sheree L. Goodman

A Tor Book
Published by Tom Doherty Associates, Inc.
175 Fifth Avenue
New York, N.Y. 10010

Tor ® is a registered trademark of Tom Doherty Associates, Inc.

ISBN: 0-812-52136-6
Library of Congress Catalog Card Number: 87-1323

First Tor edition: August 1988

Printed in the United States of America

0 9 8 7 6 5 4

To Mark and Rana,
for greatness of heart

1 | THE HEPTARCH'S DAUGHTER

HER TUTOR WOKE HER WELL BEFORE DAWN. PATIENCE FELT the chill of the morning through her thin blanket, and her muscles were stiff from sleeping on a hard mat on the floor. Summer was definitely over, and she allowed herself to wish, however briefly, that the north-facing window of her room might be glazed—or at least shuttered —for the winter.

It was all part of Father's training, to harden and toughen her, to make her despise the luxuries of court and the people who lived for them. She assumed that Angel's ungentle hand on her shoulder was a part of the regimen. *What, did I smile in my sleep? Did it look like my dreams were sweet? Thank you, Angel, for rescuing me before I was corrupted forever by some imaginary delight.*

But when she saw Angel's face, his worried look told her that something was quite wrong. It was not so disturbing that he worried, as that he let her see he worried; ordinarily he could hide or show any emotion at will, and had trained her to do the same.

1

"The King has a task for you," whispered Angel.

Patience cast off her blanket, took up the bowl of icy water on the windowsill, and poured it over her head. She refused to let her body flinch at the cold. She toweled herself roughly with burlap until the skin all over her body tingled.

"Does Father know?" she asked.

"Lord Peace is in Lakon," said Angel. "Whether he knows or not is no help to you here."

She knelt quickly beneath the ikon that was her room's only decoration. It was a shimmering engraving of the starship *Konkeptoine*, cut into bright green crystal. It was worth more than the price of a poor man's house. Patience liked the contrast between the deliberate poverty of her room and the opulence of her religious display. The priests would call it piety. She thought of it as irony.

Patience murmured the Come Kristos in eight seconds— she had it down to a science—kissed her fingers and touched them to the *Konkeptoine*. The crystal was warm. Aker all these years, still alive. No doubt it was almost hot when her mother touched it, when she was a girl. And long before Patience would have a daughter, it would be cold and dead, the light gone out of it.

She spoke to Angel over her shoulder. "Tell me the task King Oruc has set for me."

"I don't know. Only that he called for you. But you can guess, can't you?"

Angel was testing her, of course. It was the story of her life, test after test. She complained about it, some- times, but the truth was she enjoyed it, took pleasure in solving the diplomatic puzzles that Father and Angel constantly put to her.

So—what could King Oruc want her to do? The Heptarch had never called for her before. She had often been in Heptagon House, of course, but only when summoned to play with one of the Heptarch's children, never to perform a task for the Heptarch himself. Which was to be expected. At the age of thirteen, she was hardly old enough to expect a calling from the King.

Yesterday, though, an embassy had arrived from Tassali, a kingdom in the East which, in ancient times, had once been under the suzerainty of the Heptarch of Korfu. That meant little: All seven parts of the world had once been ruled by the Heptarchy, and Tassali had been free of Korfu for a thousand years. Prekeptor, the only prince and heir presumptive of Tassali, a sixteen-year-old boy, had come with an array of high-ranking Tassaliki and very expensive gifts. From this information Patience had already concluded the obvious—that the embassy was there to conclude a marriage treaty with one of King Oruc's three daughters.

The dowry had no doubt been negotiated a year ago, before the embassy set out. One does not send a royal heir to meet the bride until most of the details of the treaty are set. But Patience could guess easily enough that one remaining point of negotiation was bound to be the question: Which daughter? Lyra, the eldest daughter, fourteen years old and second in line to the Heptarchy? Rika, who was only a year younger than Patience and easily the brightest of the Heptarch's children? Or the baby, Klea, now only seven years old but certainly old enough to be married off if politics demanded it?

Patience could think of only one task she might perform in connection with this visit. She was fluent in Tassalik, and she seriously doubted that Prince Prekeptor spoke a word of Agarant. They were quite provincial in Tassali and clung to their dialect tenaciously. If a meeting were to take place between Prekeptor and one of Oruc's daughters, Patience would be an excellent interpreter. And since Klea was an unlikely candidate and

Rika could speak passable Tassalik, it was most likely that the chosen daughter was Lyra.

All this reasoning took place while Patience pulled on her silk chemise. She turned to face Angel then, and smiled. "I'm to be the interpreter between Prekeptor and Lyra, when they meet today so they can decide whether they detest each other so much it is worth causing an international quarrel to avoid being married."

Angel smiled. "It seems the most likely thing."

"Then I must dress to take part in an official meeting between future sovereigns. Would you call Nails and Calico to me?"

"I will," said Angel. But he stopped at the door. "You must realize," he said, "that Prekeptor will know who you are."

It was a warning, and Patience understood very well that King Oruc was playing a dangerous game, putting her in the middle of a political situation so closely involved with royal succession. Especially with Father away. Oruc must have planned this for some time, to have Father away on a trivial matter. Ordinarily, Lord Peace would have been at the heart of the negotiations over such a vital alliance.

Nails and Calico, her dressing maids, came in, trying to seem light and cheerful, when obviously they had been aroused from deep—and, in Calico's case, drunken—slumber. Patience selected her gown and wig and endured their ministrations as they turned her into a poppet.

"Called to the King," Nails kept saying. "What honor, for a daughter of a slave."

It was annoying to have her father called a slave over and over again, but she knew that Nails was not being malicious, merely stupid. And as Father always said, Never be angry when fools behave like fools. It's better when fools identify themselves, Patience reminded herself. It removes so much uncertainty.

When the women were finished, the sun was just coming up. She dismissed them and opened the small brass case that contained the diplomatic equipment Father and Angel had decided she was old enough to use discreetly.

For self-defense, a loop, of course. It was a long strand of incredibly strong plastic, so fine that it was almost invisible. It could cut through flesh with only a little pressure. It had knobs of plastic on both ends, so Patience could grasp it without slicing off her fingers.

And for attack, a glass pendant which contained a swarm of pinks, almost invisibly tiny insects that homed in on human eyes and in a matter of minutes would build honeycomb nests that always resulted in blindness within hours. If the eyes were not removed quickly, the pinks would bore through to the brain and cause chronic, permanent palsy. A vicious weapon, but Angel always said that a diplomat who is not prepared to kill had better be prepared to die. She tipped back her head and put drops in her eyes, of a liquid that would kill pinks on contact. It would stay in her eyes for hours. As Father said, Never carry a weapon that can be used against you.

As she prepared herself, she tried to figure out what King Oruc had in mind for her. There were other interpreters he could use. The choice of Patience was fraught with implications, especially if Prekeptor knew who she really was. There was no circumstance Patience could think of where anything would be helped by using *her* as interpreter; and she could think of dozens of things that might go wrong, to have the daughter of Lord Peace standing beside the daughter of King Oruc, when the heir to a powerful kingdom came to meet his possible wife.

Patience had been aware throughout her childhood that

she was not an ordinary slave in the Heptarch's household. One of the first lessons a child in King's Hill had to learn was to treat each slave according to the strictest protocols of rank. Whores and chamberslaves needed no more respect than dogs; ambassadors and ministers of state, like her father, Peace, were treated with as much honor as any lord except the Heptarch himself or the heads of the Fourteen Families.

But even among the children of the most noble of the King's slaves, Patience was given special treatment. Adults whispered when they saw her; many of them surreptitiously found opportunities to touch her lips with the back of a hand, as if in a symbolic kiss.

She had told Father of this one day when she was five. He immediately grew stern. "If anyone does it again, tell me at once. But better than tell afterward, try to stand away from them, and not give them an opportunity."

He was so serious that she was sure she had done something wrong.

"No, child," said Father. "First, do not show me that you are afraid and ashamed. Your face must never show such things."

She relaxed her face, as her tutor, Angel, had taught her.

"And second," said Father, "you have done nothing wrong. But for these adults, who should know better, to do such things is—"

Patience expected him to say something like "wrong" or "sinful," because the priests had been hinting about certain things that people did with children's bodies that were very bad.

So she was startled when he said, "Treason."

"Treason?" How would it injure the Heptarch to touch the lips of the daughter of a slave?

Father studied her calmly, then said, "I have decided

you can know, now, or else you won't be able to protect yourself against these thoughtless traitors. Your grandfather was Heptarch until the day he died. I have no brothers or sisters."

She was only five. She knew something of the laws of succession, but it did not occur to her to apply them to herself. Father pointedly glanced toward the parlor, where the servants would be listening. All the servants except Angel were chosen by the King, and frankly spied for him. Father smiled at her and said, "How is your Geblic?" Then he wrote in Geblic on a piece of paper:

Compose a brief letter to this person:
Agaranthamoi Heptest

She had been trained in the protocols of names and titles from her first words. The labyrinthine network of precedence, rank, and royal favor was second nature to her. So were all the ins and outs of the royal titles. The surname of the ruling Heptarch's family was always rooted in Hept; the forename of any person of royal blood was always rooted in Agaranth.

She also knew that only the ruling Heptarch could bear the surname Heptest, and Agaranthamoi meant "eldest son and only child." Thus, Agaranthamoi Heptest by definition meant the Heptarch, who had no brothers or sisters. Since Oruc, the ruling Heptarch, had several siblings, his dynastic name was Agaranthikil. This could not possibly be his name, and to call any living person *but* Oruc by the surname Heptest was treason.

But the test was not merely to decipher the meaning of the names, she knew. Father had just told her that her grandfather was ruling Heptarch all his life, and Father was his only child. Therefore Agaranthamoi was a perfectly proper forename for him. Father was telling her that he was the rightful King of Korfu.

So she wrote a short letter:

Agaranthamoi Heptest, Lord and Father:
Your unworthiest daughter begs you to be discreet, for to utter your name is death.
Humbly, Agaranthemem Heptek

Her hand trembled as she signed this strange name for the first time. Agaranthemem meant "eldest daughter and only child." Heptek meant "heir to the reigning Heptarch." It was a name as treasonable as the one her father had written. But it was her true name. Somehow, in the movement of history, her father had been deprived of his throne, and she of her place as his heir. It was a staggering burden for a child of five to bear. But she was Patience, the daughter of Lord Peace and pupil of Angel the Almost-Wise, and in the eight years since then she had never once uttered either name, or given the slightest sign to anyone, by word or act, to show that she knew what her rank and birthright ought to be.

Father burned the paper with their names on it, and combed the ashes to dust. Ever since that day, Patience had watched her father, trying to determine what his life meant. For King Oruc had no more faithful and loyal slave than Lord Peace, the man who should be Heptarch.

Even in private, even when no one could hear, Father often said to her, "Child, King Oruc is the best Heptarch the world could hope for at this time. In the five thousand years since the starship first brought human beings to the world Imakulata, it has never been more important to maintain a King on his throne than it is, today, to preserve King Oruc."

He meant it. He did everything he could to prove to her that he meant it.

It caused her untold agony of heart, trying to discover why Father gave such love and loyalty to the man who exercised power and received honor that by rights should have belonged to Lord Peace. Was Father so weak that he could not even reach for what ought to be his own?

Once, when she was ten years old, she hinted to him of how this question perplexed her. And his only answer was to place his fingers on her lips, not as some traitors had done, to receive the kiss of blessing from the mouth of the King's daughter, but to silence her.

Then, gazing intently into her eyes, he said for the first time: "The King cares only for the good of the King's House. But the King's House is all the world."

That was the only answer she got from him. In the years since then, though, she had begun to grasp what he meant. That the Heptarch, the true Heptarch, always acted for the benefit of the whole world. Other lords could act to preserve their dynasty or enrich themselves, but the true Heptarch would even give up the Heptagon House and let a usurper rule in Heptam, the capital of Korfu—if, for some unfathomable reason, such a thing was to the greater benefit of the whole world.

What she could never understand was how her father's displacement from his proper place benefited anyone. For as she grew more learned and skillful in the arts of diplomacy and government, observing the great public councils and hearing of the delicate negotiations and compromises that gathered ever more power to Heptagon House, she saw plainly that the most brilliant mind, the prime mover in consolidating King Oruc's hold on Korfu, was Lord Peace.

As always, she had finally had to conclude that her education was not complete. That someday, if she learned enough and thought enough, she would understand what Father was trying to do by working so loyally to keep the usurper in power.

Now, however, she did not face so theoretical a problem. She was thirteen years old, far younger than the age at which a diplomatic career usually began, and King Oruc had called her to begin service. It was so obviously a trap that she almost believed his purpose might be innocent. What good could possibly come to King Oruc by inserting the rightful heir to the throne into the middle of a delicate dynastic negotiation? How could it help Oruc to remind the Tassaliki that his own family had held the Heptagon House for a mere fifty years? That there was a marriageable daughter of the original ruling family, whose claim to the Heptarchy went back hundreds of generations, five thousand years to the first human beings to set foot on Imakulata? It was so reckless that it was hard to believe Oruc stood to gain anything that might offset the potential risk.

Nevertheless. I will go where the King requests, do what the King desires, to accomplish the King's hopes.

He did not receive her in the public court. It was too early for that. Instead she was led to the Heptarch's chambers, where the smell of the breakfast sausage still spiced the air. Oruc pretended not to notice her at first. He was engaged in intent conversation with the head of Lady Letheko, who had been his Constable until she died last year. She was the only one of the King's household slaves who understood as much of the nuances of protocol as Lord Peace did; in his absence, it was not surprising that King Oruc had ordered her head brought in from Slaves' Hall to advise him during the visit of the Tassal embassy.

"There may be *no* wine served," Letheko insisted. She moved her mouth so vigorously that it set the whole jar moving. King Oruc let go of her air bladder to steady the jar. No sense in spilling the gools that kept her head alive, or slopping messy fluids all over the fine rugs of the chamber floor.

Deprived of air, she nevertheless kept moving her mouth, as if her argument was too important to wait for such a trifle as a voice. Oruc resumed pumping.

"Unless you want them to think of you with contempt as a winebibber. They take their religion seriously, not like some people who act as if they thought Vigilants were mere . . ."

Again Oruc let her bladder run out of air. He waved a servant to take away Letheko's head, and turned to Patience. "Lady Patience," he said.

"The Heptarch is kind to speak so nobly to the daughter of his lowest slave." It was pro forma to talk that way, but Patience had her father's knack of making the trite phrases of diplomatic speech sound sincere, as if they had never been spoken before.

"How lovely," said King Oruc. He turned to his wife, who was having her hair brushed. "Hold up your mirror, my love, and look at her. I heard she was a pretty girl, but I had no idea."

The Consort lifted her mirror. Patience saw in it the reflection of the woman's pure hatred for her. Patience responded as if it had been a look of admiration, blushing and looking down.

"Lovely," said the Consort. "But her nose is too long."

"The Lady Consort is correct," said Patience, sadly. "It was a fault in my mother's face, but my father loved her anyway." Father would have been annoyed at her for reminding them, however subtly, of her family connections. But her tone was so flawlessly modest that they could not possibly take offense, and if the Consort continued in trying to provoke her, she would only make herself look increasingly boorish, even in the eyes of her husband.

Oruc apparently reached the same conclusion. "Your

hair is sufficiently beautiful for the needs of the day," he said. "Perhaps, my love, you could go and see if Lyra is ready."

Patience noted, with satisfaction, that she had guessed correctly which daughter was meant to be the price of the Tassal treaty. She also enjoyed watching the Consort's attempt at seeming regal as she stalked out of the room. Pathetic. King Oruc had obviously married beneath the dignity of his office. Still, she could understand the Consort's hostility. By her very existence Patience was a threat to the Consort's children.

Of course she showed none of these thoughts to King Oruc. He saw nothing but a shy girl, waiting to hear why the King had called her. Especially he did not see how tense she was, watching his face so carefully that every second that passed seemed like a full minute, and every tiny motion of his eyebrow or lip seemed a great flamboyant gesture.

He quickly told her all that she had already figured out, and ended with the command that she had expected. "I hope you'll be willing to help these children communicate. You're so fluent in Tassalik, and poor Lyra doesn't know more than ten words of it."

"You do me more honor than I can bear," said Patience. "I'm only a child, and I'm afraid to put my voice into such weighty affairs."

She was doing what her father said a loyal slave must do: warn the King when the course he had chosen seemed particularly dangerous.

"You can bear the honor," he said drily. "You and Lyra played together as children. She'll be much more comfortable, and no doubt so will the prince, if their interpreter is a child. They'll be, perhaps, more candid."

"I'll do my best," Patience said. "And I'll remember

every word, so that I can learn from my mistakes as you point them out to me afterward.''

She did not know him well enough to read his calm expression. Had he really been asking her to spy on Lyra and the Tassal prince? And if so, did he understand her promise to report afterward all that they say? Have I pleased him or offended him, read too much into his commands, or not enough?

He waved a hand to dismiss her; immediately she realized that she could not yet be dismissed. "My lord," she said.

He raised an eyebrow. It was presumptuous to extend one's first meeting with the King, but if her reason was good enough, it would not harm her in his eyes.

"I saw that you had the head of Lady Letheko. May I ask her some questions?"

King Oruc looked annoyed. "Your father told me that you were fully trained as a diplomat."

"Part of the training of a diplomat," she said softly, "is to get more answers than you think you will need, so you'll never wish, when it's too late, that you had asked just one more question."

"Let her speak with Letheko's head," said Oruc. "But not in here. I've heard enough of her babbling for a morning."

They didn't even give her a table, so that Lady Letheko's canister sat directly on the floor in the hallway. Out of courtesy, Patience stepped out of her skirt and sat cross-legged on the floor, so Letheko would not have to look up to see her.

"Do I know you?" asked Letheko's head.

"I'm only a child," said Patience. "Perhaps you didn't notice me."

"I noticed you. Your father is Peace."

Patience nodded.

"So. King Oruc thinks so little of me that he lets children pump my sheep-bladder lung and make my voice ring out harshly in this shabby hallway. He might as well send me out to Common Hall on the edge of the marsh, and let beggars ask me for the protocols of the gutter."

Patience smiled shyly. She had heard Letheko in this mood before, many times, and knew that her father always responded as if the old lady had been teasing. It worked as well for her as it had for Father.

"You are a devil of a girl," said Letheko.

"My father says so. But I have questions that only you can answer."

"Which means your father must be out of King's Hill, or you'd ask *him*."

"I'm to be interpreter between Lyra and Prekeptor at their first meeting."

"You speak Tassalik? Oh, of course, Peace's daughter would know everything." She sighed, long and theatrically, and Patience humored her by giving her plenty of air to sigh with. "I was always in love with your father, you know. Widowed twice, he was, and still never offered to take a tumble with me behind the statue of the Starship Captain in Bones Road. I wasn't always like this, you know." She giggled. "Used to have such a body."

Patience laughed with her.

"So, what do you want to know?"

"The Tassaliki. They're believers, I know, but what does that mean in practical terms? What might offend Prekeptor?"

"Well, don't make jokes about taking a tumble behind the statue of the Starship Captain."

"They don't think he was the Kristos, do they?"

"They're Watchers, not Rememberers. They don't think

Kristos has ever come to Imakulata, but they watch every day for him to come.''

''Vigilants?''

''God protect us from Vigilants. But yes, almost. More organized, of course. They do believe in warfare, for one thing. As a sacrament. I do protocols, you know, not theology.''

''Warn me of whatever I need to be warned of.''

''Then stop pumping.''

Patience stopped pumping air, and lay supine before the severed head in order to read its lips and catch the scraps of sound that an unbreathing mouth can produce.

''You are in grave danger. They believe the seventh seventh seventh daughter will bring Kristos.''

Patience wasn't sure whether she had heard correctly. The phrase meant nothing to her. She let her face show her puzzlement.

''No one told you?'' asked Letheko. ''God help you, child. An ancient prophecy—some say as old as the Starship Captain—says that the seventh seventh seventh daughter will save the world. Or destroy it. The prophecy is vague.''

Seventh seventh seventh daughter. What in the world did that mean?

''Seven times seven times seven generations since the Starship Captain. Irena was first. You are the 343rd Heptarch.''

Patience covered Letheko's lips with her fingers, to keep her even from mouthing such treason.

Letheko smiled in vast amusement. ''What do you think they can do to me, cut off my head?''

But Patience was no fool. She knew that heads could be tortured more cruelly and with less effort than would ever be possible with a living human being. If she were wise, she would stop this dangerous conversation with

Letheko at once. And yet she had never heard of this prophecy before. It was one thing to know she was in the dangerous position of being a possible pretender to the throne. But now to know that every true believer in every human nation of the world thought of her as the fulfiller of a prophecy—how could Father have let her go on for so many years without telling her all of what others thought she was?

Letheko wasn't through. "When you were born, a hundred thousand Tassaliki volunteered to form an army to invade Korfu and put you on the throne. They haven't forgotten. If you gave the Tassaliki so much as a hope that you would join them, they would declare a holy war and sweep into Korfu in such numbers and with such fury as we haven't seen since the last gebling invasion. King Oruc is insane to put you in the same room with a young Tassal prince who wants to prove his manhood."

Again Patience covered Letheko's mouth to stop her speech. Then she lifted herself on her hands, leaned forward, and kissed the wizened head on the lips. The stench of the fluids in the canister was foul, but Letheko had risked great suffering to tell her something far more important than how one behaves properly with a devout Tassal prince. A gool sloshed lazily in the canister. A tear came to the corner of the old woman's eye.

"How many times," mouthed Letheko, "I wanted to take you in my arms and cry out, My Heptarch, Agaranthemem Heptek."

"And if you had," whispered Patience, "I would be dead, and so would you."

Letheko grinned maniacally. "But I *am*." Patience laughed, and gave Letheko air to laugh aloud. Then she called the headsman to take the old lady back to Slaves' Hall.

Patience walked through the great chambers of the

court, seeing the people on their errands there in a different light. Most of them wore crosses, of course, but that was the style. How many of them were believers? How many were Watchers, or even secret Vigilants, harboring mad thoughts of her saving—or destroying—the human race, ushering in the coming of Kristos to Imakulata? More to the point, how many of them would die in order to bring down King Oruc and restore Peace to Heptagon House as its master, and Patience as his daughter and heir?

And as thoughts of bloody revolution swam through her head, her Father's cool voice came to the surface and said, through a hundred memories, "Your first responsibility is the greatest good for all the world. Only when that is secure can you care for private loves and comforts and power. The King's House is all the world."

If she was the sort of woman who would plunge Korfu and Tassali into a bloody religious war, she was too selfish and mad for power to serve as Heptarch. As many as a million could die. Perhaps more. How could anything ever surface from such an ocean of blood?

No wonder Father never told her. It was a terrible temptation, one she could never have faced when she was younger.

I am still young, she thought. And King Oruc is putting me alone in a room with Prekeptor and Lyra. We could talk in Tassalik and never be understood. We could plot. I could commit treason.

He is testing me. He is deciding whether or not I will be loyal to him. No doubt he even arranged for Letheko to be available, so I could learn from her what he no doubt knew she would tell me. My life, and possibly Father's life, is in my own hands right now.

But Father would say, What is your life? What is my life? We keep ourselves alive only so we can serve the

King's House. And he would *not* say, but I would remember, The King's House is all the world.

Patience tried to figure out whether the world most needed her alive or not. But she knew that this was not a decision she was capable of making, not yet, not now. She would try to stay alive because it was unthinkable to do anything else. And to stay alive required perfect, absolute loyalty to King Oruc. She could not even appear to consider a plot to take the throne.

One thing was certain. After this was over, if she pulled it off, Father's and Angel's simple little tests would never frighten her again.

2 | MOTHER OF GOD

LYRA WAITED IN THE GARDEN OF HEPTAGON HOUSE. OBVI-
ously, her mother had dressed her. Her gown was a
bizarre mixture of chastity and seduction, modest from
neck to floor, with just a touch of lace at her throat and
wrists. But the fabric was translucent, so that whenever
she was backlit her voluptuous shape was perfectly
silhouetted.

"Oh, Patience, I was so glad when Father said I could
have you interpret for me. I begged him for days, and he
finally relented."

Could it be that her presence here was only the result
of Lyra's pleading? Impossible—Oruc was too strong a
man to let his daughters endanger his throne on a whim.

"I'm glad he did," said Patience. "I'll be sorry if you
have to leave Heptam, but at least I can tell you whether
I approve."

This was obviously a joke, spoken by a thirteen-year-
old slave to the daughter of the Heptarch, but Lyra was
so tense she didn't notice the impropriety of the remark.
"I hope you do. And oh, if you see something in him

19

that I don't see, please let me know. I want so very much to please Father by marrying this prince, but if he's really awful, I can't possibly go through with it."

Patience showed nothing of the contempt she felt. Imagine—a daughter of the Starship Captain's blood even thinking of refusing a marriage, not for reasons of state, but because she found the suitor unattractive. To put one's personal pleasure ahead of the good of the King's House was proof of unfitness. You should be out in a country house, said Patience silently, the daughter of a country lord, going to country dances and giggling with your girlfriends about which of the country boys had the fewest pimples and the least repulsive breath.

Neither her words nor her face betrayed her true feelings. Instead she made herself a perfect mirror, reflecting back to Lyra exactly what Lyra wanted to see and hear. "He won't be awful, Lyra. The negotiators would never have come this far if he had a second head growing out of his shoulder."

"Nobody gets second heads anymore," said Lyra. "They have a vaccine for it."

Poor child, thought Patience. She was usually bright enough to understand such an obvious irony as that.

It did not seem incongruous to Patience that she was thinking of Lyra, three years her senior, as a child. Lyra had been pampered and spoiled, and despite the evidence of her body she was not a woman yet. A thousand times in their years as children together in King's Hill, Patience had wished for just one night a year in the soft bed of one of the Heptarch's daughters. But now, seeing the poor result of a gentle upbringing, she silently thanked her father for the cold room, the hard bed, the plain food, the endless study and exercise.

"You're right, of course," said Patience. "May I kiss you for luck?"

Lyra distractedly held out her hand. Patience knelt before her and reverently kissed Lyra's fingertips. She had learned years ago what a soothing effect such obeisance had on Oruc's daughters. As Angel always said, Your own humility is the best flattery.

The far door to the garden opened. A white hawk flew out the door into the open air. It immediately flew straight up and began to circle. A white songbird, already perched on a low branch, began to sing sweetly. Lyra cried out softly, hiding her mouth behind her hand, for it was obvious the hawk had seen. It plummeted downward directly toward the songbird—

And was caught by the swift motion of a net. It struggled, but the young falconer who had caught the hawk reached deftly past the jabbing beak and brought the bird upside-down out of the net. The falconer was dressed all in white, a perfect, dazzling white that hurt the eyes when the sun was reflected in it. He whistled; the door opened behind him and two servants came out, bearing cages. In only a few seconds, the falconer had put the two birds into the cages.

Through it all, the songbird had not missed a note. Obviously, thought Patience, this scene has been rehearsed so often the songbird has lost its fear of the hawk.

Then she looked more closely and realized that, quite to the contrary, the songbird remained perfectly placid because it was blind. The eyes had been put out.

The servants stepped back toward the door as the falconer sank to his knees in front of Lyra and began to speak in Tassilik.

"Me kia psole o ekeiptu," he whispered.

"So will I protect you always from the despoiler," said Patience. Her inflection was, as far as possible, a perfect mirror of Prekeptor's.

"It was beautiful," said Lyra. "The song, and you to save the bird."

"Iptura oeenue," said Patience, mimicking Lyra's breathless delight. "Oeris, marae i kio psolekte."

"Oh, you sound just like me," whispered Lyra.

Prekeptor spoke again, and Patience translated. "I have brought a gift for the Heptarch's daughter."

He reached out his hand. A servant placed a book in it. "A copy of the Testament of Irena, the Starship Captain's Daughter," he said.

He held the book out toward Patience. Patience was annoyed, since it was more proper for the suitor to ignore the interpreter and place the book directly in the hand of his intended. But perhaps in Tassali a servant was used to pass even intimate gifts between lovers. There were stranger customs.

Lyra pretended to be thrilled when Patience gave her the book. Quietly Patience pointed out to her that the pages of the book were unfinished paperleaf, which had grown in such perfectly uniform shape and size that no trimming was needed to make a perfect book. "It took great effort in breeding the paperleaf," said Patience. She did not point out that it was about as stupid a waste of time as she could imagine, since processed paperleaf was much better for writing and lasted longer, too.

"Oh," said Lyra. And she managed to come up with a gracious little speech of thanks.

"Don't think that I pride myself on my technique with plant husbandry," protested the Prince. "It has often been said that the plants and animals of Imakulata seem to understand what traits we are trying to develop, and they change themselves to cooperate. Even so I shall gladly be and do exactly what the Heptarch's daughter desires of me."

Patience was growing uncomfortable with the way

Prekeptor looked directly at her instead of at Lyra when he spoke. The interpreter is furniture; every diplomat was taught that. Except, obviously, Tassal princes.

Prekeptor came up with another gift. It was a small glass rod, hollow and filled with flowing light. Even in broad daylight it glowed; when he shaded it under his hand, it was positively bright. Again he smiled modestly and made a little speech about his own poor skill at husbandry. "If there were any Wise left in the world, I might have done this far more quickly, by altering the genetic molecule, but as it is I turned the great shipeater weed into something quite useful." He smiled. "You can read the Testament in bed after your father has commanded you to blow out the candles."

"I never read in bed," said Lyra, puzzled.

"It was a joke," said Patience. "At least smile."

Lyra laughed. Too loudly, but she was obviously *trying* to please the fellow. And for obvious reasons. His white clothing showed his body to be lithe and strong; his face could have been the model for a statue of Courage or Manhood or Virtue. When he smiled, he seemed to be making love with his eyes. And Lyra didn't miss any of it.

Except that Prekeptor never took his eyes off Patience. And now she realized what a dangerous game the Prince was playing.

"The Heptarch's daughter will find that the prophecies of joy in the Testament will all be fulfilled in her life," said Prekeptor. Patience dutifully translated, but also realized now that the Prince was saying every word to her, the *true* Heptarch's daughter, with the meaning doubled. The prophecies in the Testament no doubt included some of the mumbo-jumbo about the seventh seventh seventh daughter. He was urging Patience to accept the prophecies.

The Prince had still a third gift. It was a plastic sheath that fitted over the glass rod. Within the sheath were constantly shifting flows of bright-colored but transparent animals. With the light inside, the display was fascinating and beautiful. Prekeptor handed it to Patience.

"The Heptarch's daughter will see that it can be worn, if she chooses, like a crown, for all the world to see and admire," said the Prince. "It's like the future—you can choose any color and follow it wherever it goes. If the Heptarch's daughter chooses wisely, she'll take a path that leads to the restoration of all that was lost."

Subtly, in mid-speech, he had ceased using double meanings. Now he was clearly speaking only to Patience, and offering her a restoration to the throne.

Patience could not possibly translate Prekeptor's last sentence. Lyra would insist on an explanation. However, Patience could not leave it out of her translation, either, or change its meaning, because that would alert Oruc's listeners that she was conspiring with the Prince to conceal his treasonous offer.

So instead she stood silent.

"What did he say?" asked Lyra.

"I did not understand him," said Patience. To Prekeptor she said, "I'm sorry my understanding of Tassalik is so poor, but I cannot understand anything that is said on this subject. I beg the Prince to converse on matters that this poor interpreter can comprehend."

"I understand," he answered, smiling. His hands were trembling. "I, too, feel fear, here in the heart of Heptagon House. What you do not know is that all of our party are trained soldiers and assassins. They are prepared to penetrate to the deepest recesses of Heptagon House to destroy your enemies."

Anything Patience answered could be her death sentence. In the first place, she herself had been trained as an assassin, and she knew that if Prekeptor's plan had any chance of working, he had just destroyed it by saying it out loud in the open garden. No doubt throughout Heptagon House all the Tassal embassy was now being placed under irresistable arrest, with the words of their own prince as their indictment. That he did not know that he would be listened to here in the garden told Patience that Prekeptor was too great a fool for her to entrust her life to him.

But there was nothing she could say to stop him and clear herself. If she said, I have no enemies here in Heptagon House, she was admitting that he was somehow correct to call her the Heptarch's daughter. She had to go on pretending that she had no idea of why he was speaking to her, and to do that she had to pretend not to understand the plainest-spoken Tassalik. It wasn't likely anyone would believe it, but it was not necessary to be believed. It was necessary merely to make it possible for Oruc to *pretend* to believe it. As long as they could both pretend that she didn't know she was the rightful Heptarch's daughter, she could be allowed to live.

So she put on her most baffled expression and said, "I'm sorry, I guess I'm out of my depth. I thought I spoke Tassalik well enough, but I see that I don't."

"What is he saying?" asked Lyra. She sounded concerned. As well she might be, since Prekeptor, far from coming to marry her, had come to kill her father and, no doubt, her as well.

"I'm sorry," said Patience. "I understood almost nothing."

"I thought you were fluent."

"So did I."

"Mother of Kristos," whispered Prekeptor. "Mother of God, why don't you see the hand of God in my coming? I am the angel that stands at the door and knocks. I announce to you: God will fill your womb.''

His words were frightening enough, but the fervency with which he said them was terrifying. What role did he have in mind for her in his religion? Mother of God— that was the ancient virgin from Earth, and yet he called her that as if it were *her* name.

Still, she showed nothing of the surprise she felt. She kept the vaguely puzzled look on her face.

''Holy Mother, don't you see how Kristos has prepared the path for his coming?'' He took a step toward her. Immediately she hardened her expression, and he stopped, retreated two steps. ''No matter what you think, God is irresistible,'' he said. ''He has devoted seven times seven times seven generations to create you to be the fit mother of the incarnation of Kristos on the planet Imakulata. This is greater than the number of generations down to the time of the Virgin of Earth.''

She let the helpless, puzzled look return to her face, even as she tried to plan a course of action. In a way, this was just like one of Angel's favorite games. He would give her a complex mathematical problem—orally, so she had no written guide to help her concentrate—and then immediately launch into a complex story. Five minutes or ten minutes or half an hour later, the story would end. At once he would demand the answer to the mathematical problem. When she had answered it, he would ask her to tell him the entire story. In detail. Over the years she had become adept at concentrating on two things at once. Of course, her life had never before depended on the outcome of the game.

''They have not taught you, I see. They have kept you ignorant of your true identity. Don't pretend not to understand my language, for I know you do. I will tell you. God created Imakulata as his most godly planet. Here in this world, the powers of creation run fast and deep. On Earth it took thousands of generations for evolutionary change to take place. Here, in only three or four generations we can breed major changes into any species. Those trifles I brought as gifts—they are new species, and it took only four generations to perfect them. It is as if the genetic molecule understood what we wanted it to become, and changed itself. This is as true of species that came from Earth as it is for the native species. It is only here on Imakulata, God's World of Creation, that every creature's genetic molecule, which is the mirror of the will, obeys the slightest command to change. Does giving off more light increase the plant's chance of reproducing? Then immediately every plant gives off *far* more light—even plants that did *not* take part in the experiment, plants as much as a half-mile away. Do you see what this means? God had given us here on Imakulata a taste of his power."

Patience toyed with and then rejected the idea of killing the Prince. If he had been an ordinary subject of the Heptarch, it would have been her duty to kill him for what he had said already, if only because he represented a clear danger to Lyra. But it was not the prerogative of an interpreter to kill the heir to the throne of Tassali. King Oruc might regard it as an unfortunate intrusion into his foreign policy.

"But to himself God has reserved the breeding of humanity. Alone of the life forms of Imakulata, human beings remain unchanged. For God is performing the creation of man. And the crowning achievement is you— for God will cause you to give birth to Kristos, the only perfect man, who is the mirror of God, just as the genetic molecule is the mirror of the will, the cerebrum is the mirror of the identity, and the limbic node is the mirror of the passion. The Wise thought they could meddle with the genetic molecule directly, that they could alter the plans of God by making your father incapable of bearing daughters so the prophecy could not be fulfilled. But God destroyed the Wise, and your father *did* bear a daughter, and you shall bear the Son of God no matter what you or anyone may do to try to prevent it.''

Patience could not leave, either. She needed to show a decisive rejection of what he had said, not just a desire to run from it. Besides, she wasn't sure Prekeptor would let her leave. The madness of his faith was on him; he trembled, and there was such fire in him that it was beginning to kindle a response in her. She dared not listen to more, for fear she might begin to doubt her own skepticism; she dared not leave; she dared not kill him to silence him. Therefore she had only one choice.

She reached into her hair and carefully drew out the loop.

''What are you doing?'' asked Lyra, who had been taught, as a child of the heptarch, to recognize all the known weapons of assassination.

Patience did not answer Lyra. She spoke instead to Prekeptor. ''Prince Prekeptor, I believe I understand enough to realize that you believe my very existence is somehow a reason to bring down my noble Heptarch, King Oruc. Now that I see what a danger my very life causes to my King, I have no alternative, as a true servant of the King's House, but to end my life.''

In a quick motion she passed the loop around her own throat, drew it tight, and gave a tiny jerk that caused the loop to cut into the skin to a depth of about two millimeters all the way around her neck. The pain was surprisingly slight at first. The cut was not uniform—in some places it cut quite deep. But it had the effect she intended. Immediately blood streamed thick as a bright red collar around her neck.

The look of horror on Prekeptor's face was almost fun to watch. "My God!" he cried, "My God, what have I done!"

Nothing, you fool, thought Patience. *I've* done it. And silenced *you*, too. Then the real pain came, and dizziness from the sudden loss of blood. I hope I didn't cut too deeply, thought Patience. I don't want to leave a scar.

Lyra screamed. Patience felt her legs giving way under her. Ah, yes. I must collapse as if I were dying, she thought. So she let herself slump down to the ground. She clutched at her own throat—carefully removing the loop in the process—and was surprised at the great amount of blood that was still flowing. Won't I feel foolish if I cut myself too deeply and bleed to death right here in the garden.

Prekeptor was weeping. "Holy Mother, I meant no harm to you. God help her, O Lord of Heaven, who sent away the Wise in their blasphemy, forgive now this Fool who gave himself to your service, and heal the Mother of Thy Son—"

The sides of the world closed up; she could only see in a tunnel straight ahead of her. She saw hands come and take Prekeptor and carry him away from her. She heard Lyra's screaming and weeping. She felt gentle hands take her and lift her up, and someone whispering, "No one has ever been so loyal to a heptarch as to take her own life rather than hear treason."

Is that what I've done? thought Patience. Taken my own life?

And then, as they carried her out of the garden, she thought: I wonder if Angel will approve of my solution to the problem. As for the story, I remember every word of it. Every word.

3 | ASSASSIN

PATIENCE WAS ALREADY WEARY OF LYING IN BED AFTER THE
first day. Visits from people with nothing intelligent to
say made her even wearier.

"I don't think there'll be a scar," said Lyra.

"I wouldn't mind if there were," said Patience.

"It was the bravest thing I ever saw."

"Not really," said Patience. "I knew I wouldn't die.
It was the only way to silence him."

"But what was he *saying*?"

Patience shook her head. "He wasn't the ideal husband for you, believe me."

Lyra looked profoundly worried. Well she should be,
thought Patience. Maybe Lyra is realizing for the first
time that her dynastic rights might be in danger from me,
however loyal I try to be.

"Was he trying to—to arrange to—you know. With
you."

Oh. Of course Lyra wouldn't have dynastic worries.
She had never been taught responsibility. "I can't talk
about it," said Patience. She turned her face away,

though, so Lyra would convince herself that the answer was yes.

"Right in front of me, wanting to—but why you? I know you're pretty, everyone says so, but *I'm* the Heptarch's daughter—and I'm not ugly, either. I'm really not. I'm very objective about that."

"The only men who wouldn't be glad to have you as their wife are the victims of terrible pelvic accidents," said Patience, smiling.

After a moment, Lyra understood and blushed. "You mustn't talk that way." But she was flattered. And now that Patience had succeeded in convincing her that she didn't owe some debt of guilt for Patience's wound, Lyra left.

At least I didn't come here yesterday as ignorant of the truth as Lyra still is. Someday, though, someone will tell her who I am, and why my father's ancient claim is seen by some as a bit more valid than Oruc's. Then she'll understand what was really going on today, and perhaps realize that it was my survival I was working for, not my death.

What worried her was not Lyra's reaction. It was King Oruc's. He was the only audience that Patience's performance was designed to please. If he saw her gesture as a desperate effort to prove her loyalty, then she would survive. But if he actually believed she was trying to kill herself, he would believe her insane and never trust her with anything. Her career would be over before it began.

The doctor had her wound clamped shut with the jaws of hundreds of tiny earwigs. "Not like regular earwigs, though," the doctor said. "These were bred to provide a powerful and continuous pincer movement until I squeeze their abdomens in a certain way. They respond to the flexing of your skin and promote the healing process. *Without* excessive scar tissue."

"Very clever," murmured Patience. Everyone assumed she didn't want a scar. But she wasn't sure. It wouldn't hurt to have a visible reminder, every time people saw her, of how loyal she was to King Oruc. She was tempted to squeeze off the earwigs herself, or readjust their position so the scar would dimple and twist. But no, it would be too obvious if she deliberately left a scar herself. It would diminish some of the power of her act.

For it *was* a powerful act. Oruc gave her a room of honor in Heptagon House during her convalescence, and many adults stopped to wish her well. Few of them were skilled at the diplomatic arts, and so she could easily see that most of them were at once drawn to and repelled by who she was. She was a young girl, after all, with only the first bloom of womanhood on her, of an age that often caused wistfulness in adults who ache for their youth and beauty, even though they know perfectly well that they were never really as young and beautiful as she. She was also the true Heptarch's daughter, the legendary seventh seventh seventh daughter of the Starship Captain. Until now, they could never openly seek her out, for fear of arousing King Oruc's suspicions. But who could criticize them for paying their respects to a young girl who had performed heroic service for the King's daughter?

So she received them as they visited in ones and twos, to say a few words, touch her hand. Many of them tried to touch her with gestures of respect that properly belonged only to the Heptarch's family; she rejected those gestures by subtly replacing them with her own. Always she explicitly honored her visitor as being someone far superior to her in rank. Some saw this as a clever disguise; others as true humility; to Patience, it was survival.

For she noticed that Angel did not come to visit her, and that Father did not seem to be hurrying home. It was unthinkable that they would not come to her if they could. Therefore someone must be forbidding them to come. And the only one who could do that was King Oruc. Something in her performance had bothered him. He still wasn't sure of her.

At last the stream of visitors stopped. The doctor came with two orderlies. Gently they lifted her into a litter. They did not have to tell her where she was going. When Oruc summons, there is no need for discussion in Heptagon House. One simply goes.

They set down the litter in Oruc's chamber. His Consort wasn't there, but three unfamiliar heads were. She did not recognize them. And she had spent enough time in Slaves' Hall to know all the faces there. So either these were not former ministers of state, or they were so important to King Oruc that he kept them out of Slaves' Hall, so no one else could talk to them. Each head's canister rested on its own table, with a dwelf seated behind it to pump the air bladder.

"So that's the girl," one of them murmured when she came in. Because the dwelfs weren't pumping right then, he did not make a sound, but she saw his lips move. And though she wasn't sure, another might have mouthed her true name, "Agaranthemem Heptek."

The doctor fussed and preened, showing off his excellent skill at healing her wound. Without, of course, a scar.

"Very good, Doctor," said Oruc. "But then, I expect my technicians to perform their tasks well."

The doctor was miffed at being called a mere technician, but of course he tried to conceal his annoyance. "Thank you, Lord Heptarch."

"No scar," said Oruc. He peered at her neck critically. "None at all."

"But a string of bugs around her neck. I think it would

be a hard choice, between a scar and a necklace of
earwigs."

"Oh, no," said the doctor. "The earwigs will come
off very soon. Now, if they displease you, sir."

Oruc looked weary. "What you heard, Doctor, was
not my stupidity, but my sense of humor."

"Oh, of course, I'm such a fool, forgive me, I'm a bit
tense, I—" and then, realizing his talking was making
things worse, the doctor burst into artificial laughter.

"Enough. Fine work. I commend you. Go away."

The doctor scurried out the door.

Oruc exhaled wearily. "Surely there has been a de-
cline in the quality of court life since the Flight of the
Wise."

"I wouldn't know, sir," said Patience. "I wasn't born
then. I've never known any of the Wise."

Oruc raised an eyebrow. "By heaven, neither have I."
Then he shook his head. "No, it's not true to say that.
I've known some Wise among the dead." He did not
need to glance back at the three heads behind him. "And
one wise man among the living, one man among all my
ministers who gives me counsel worth hearing, who
cares as much for Korfu as I do."

"My father," she whispered.

"A most unlucky situation, isn't it?" said Oruc. "Even
the wisest King needs good advice, and there's little of
that left in the world. I would give half my kingdom to
know what became of the Wise when they left here, and
how to bring them back."

One of the heads behind him spoke up. Apparently the
dwelfs were pumping again. "Oruc, you're likely to lose
half your kingdom because you *don't* know."

Another head gave a crazed old man's giggle. "So it's
a bargain for him, to give it up and get back the Wise in
the bargain."

"You know where the Wise went," said the third, a grim face with no teeth. "Cranning. And there's no bringing them back from *there*."

"It's the dilemma of our times," said Oruc to Patience. "We're long overdue for another gebling invasion. Twelve times in seven thousand years they have poured out of their vast city Cranning, out of the caverns of Skyfoot, and each time all of human civilization has been broken under their onslaught. Then they go back to their caverns or back to being somewhat pitiful merchants and voyagers and wanderers through the world, while human beings struggle back, rediscover what science they can. Only one human institution has outlasted it all, a single bloodline of power from the first moment mankind set foot on Imakulata until it was time for the thirteenth gebling invasion." He did not say it, but of course she knew he was referring to the Heptarchy. To her family.

"And then," said Oruc, "instead of an invasion, all the Wise, all the men and women of learning—no, not of mere learning, but of true understanding—all of them, one by one, felt the Cranning call. An unbearable, undeniable, irresistible urge to go somewhere. They were never sure where, they said. But they were followed, and they all went to Cranning. All of them. Statesmen, generals, scientists, teachers, builders—all the men and women that a King must rely on to carry out his rule, they all left. Who could stand then, when the Wise were gone?"

"No one," whispered Patience. She was truly afraid now, for he was speaking so frankly of the fall of her family's ancient dynasty that she could not help but assume he intended to kill her after this conversation was over.

"No one. The Cranning call took them, and the Heptarch

fell. He wasn't much of a Heptarch, your great-grand-father."

"I never knew him," said Patience.

"A beastly fellow. Even discounting the propaganda my father put out, he was unspeakable. He used to preserve the heads of his former lovers and put their canisters around his bed, to watch him make love to his latest creature."

"I should think," said Patience, "that was more of a torture to the current lover than to the former ones."

Oruc laughed. "Yes. Though you're only a child, so you shouldn't know about such things. There are so many things you shouldn't know about. My personal physician—who is *not* Wise, I suspect—examined you before the earwig man sewed you up. He tells me you could not possibly have done a more perfect job of cutting yourself to draw the most possible blood without causing any permanent or even dangerous damage."

"I was fortunate," said Patience.

"Your father didn't tell me he was training you in the arts of murder."

"He has trained me to be a diplomat. He has often told me of your maxim, that one well-placed assassination can save untold numbers of lives."

Oruc smiled and spoke to the heads. "She flatters me by quoting my own words back to me, and telling me that the great Lord Peace repeats them often."

"Actually," said the dourest head, "I said those words to you first."

"You're dead, Konstans. I don't have to give you credit."

Konstans. Eight hundred years ago there had been a Konstans who restored Korfu to hegemony over the entire length of the Glad River, only ten years ater a gebling invasion, and without a drop of blood being shed. If it was the same man, it would explain the decrepit condition of the head. Few heads ever lasted as long as a thousand years—this one was nearing the end of its function.

"I still have my vanity," said Konstans's head.

"I don't like it that he has taught her how to kill. And so deftly that she can create death's illusion on herself."

"She is her father's daughter," said another head.

"That's what I'm afraid of," said Oruc. "How old are you? Thirteen. How can you kill besides the loop?"

"Many ways," said Patience. "Father says I'm not strong enough to pull the bow properly, and casting a javelin isn't much use in our trade. But poisons, darts, daggers—I grew up with them."

"And bombs? Incendiaries?"

"The duty of a diplomat is to kill as quietly and discreetly as possible."

"Your father says."

"Yes."

"Could you kill me now? Here, in this room, could you kill me?"

Patience did not answer.

"I command you to answer me."

She knew too much of protocol to be drawn into the trap. "Sir, please don't toy with me this way. The King commands me to speak about whether I could kill the King. Whether I obey or not, I commit terrible treason."

"I want honest answers. Why do you think I keep these heads around me? They can't lie—that's what the headworms do to them, they make sure that they can never answer dishonestly, or even withhold part of the truth."

"The heads, sir, are already dead. If you wish me to behave as they do, it is within your power."

"I want truth from you, and never mind protocol."

"As long as I am alive, I will never speak treason."

Oruc leaned close to her, his face angry and dangerous. "I am not interested in your determination to survive at all costs, girl. I want you to speak honestly to me."

Konstans chuckled. "Child, he can't kill you. You're safe to speak to him, for now, at least."

Oruc glared at Konstans, but the head was undeterred.

"You see, he depends on your father, and he believes your father will never serve him faithfully unless you're held hostage here. Alive. So what he's trying to determine now is whether you can also be useful to him, or whether you will remain nothing more than a constant temptation to his enemies."

Konstans's analysis made sense, and Oruc didn't argue with him. It seemed absurd to her, to have the most powerful human being in the world treating her like a potentially dangerous adult. But her respect for Oruc was rising in the process. Many a lesser ruler would have destroyed her and Father, fearing the danger of them more than any possible value they might have.

So she made the decision to trust him. It frightened her, because that was the one thing Father and Angel had never taught her: when to trust. "My Lord Heptarch," said Patience, "if the thought of killing you could live for a moment in my heart, then yes, I could do it."

"Now?" There was an expression of veiled triumph in his eyes. Had he won a victory, then, by convincing her to trust him?

I have begun; I will not retreat. "Even now, even if I told you I was going to do it, I could kill you before you raised a hand to defend yourself. My father knows his trade, and I have studied with the master."

Oruc turned to one of the dwelfs. "Go fetch my guards and tell them to come arrest this girl for treason."

He turned to Patience and calmly said, "Thank you. I needed a legal basis for your execution. These heads will be witnesses that you claimed in my presence to be able to kill me."

It shook her, how calmly he betrayed her. And yet she could not wholly believe the betrayal. No, this was just another test, another move in the game. He really did need Peace—he proved it by the fact that he took no major action without consulting Peace first—and so he really did fear to kill Patience. Nothing had changed that.

And if it was a test, she would win. She nodded gravely. "If I can best serve my Heptarch by dying through legal process, I'll confess to that or any other crime."

Oruc walked to her, touched her hair, stroked her cheek with the back of his fingers. "Beautiful. The Mother of God."

She endured it placidly. He wasn't going to kill her. That was victory enough for the moment.

"I wonder if someone *is* breeding humans, as the Tassaliki claim. Not God—I doubt he bothers much with the mating of humans on Imakulata—but someone. Someone with the power to call the Wise." He took her chin, not gently, and tipped her face upward. "If someone wanted to breed magnificence, I could believe you as the result of his work. Not right now, you're still a child. But there's a translucence to you, a lightness in your eyes."

Until this moment, it had never occurred to Patience that she might be beautiful. Her mirror did not reveal the soft and rounded features that were the fashion of beauty these days. But there was no hint of flattery or deception in Oruc's words.

"As long as you're alive," he whispered, "anyone who sees you will want me dead, so you can take my place. Do you understand that? Me and all my family, dead. Whether or not someone bred you to be what you are, you *are*. And I will not have my children destroyed for your sake. Do you understand me?''

"Your children have been my playmates all my life," said Patience.

"I should kill you. Your father even advised me to kill you. But I won't do it."

But Patience knew that there was an unspoken word: *yet*. I will not kill you *yet*.

"What maddens me is not that I choose to leave you alive, for in truth I rejoice in you as surely as any Vigilant. What maddens me is that I don't remember deciding to leave you alive. I don't remember choosing. The decision was simply—made. Is it you? Is it some trick of manipulation your father taught you?''

Patience didn't answer. He didn't seem to expect her to.

"Or am I being twisted as the Wise were twisted? The decision made for me because whoever it is wants you, wants you alive." He turned to the heads. "You—you have no will anymore, only memory and passion. Do you remember what it is to *choose?*"

"A dim memory," said Konstans. "I think I did it once or twice."

Oruc turned his back on them. "I have done it all my life. Chosen. Consciously, deliberately chosen, and then acted upon my choice, regardless of passion. My will has always been in control of my triune soul—the priests know it, that's why they fear me, why there is no revolution in your name. They believe that whenever I choose to, I can and certainly will kill you. They don't know. That on this matter I have no will."

Patience believed that he believed what he was saying. But it was still not true. There would come a time when he feared her more than now, and he would kill her. She could feel that certainty lying beneath everything he said. For that was the foundation of his power, that he could kill anyone when he chose to. "Father told me once," she said. "There are two ways to rule human beings. One is to convince the people that if they do not obey, they and those they love will be destroyed. The other is to earn the love of the people. And he told me where these two ways lead. Eventually, the course of terror leads to revolution and anarchy. Eventually, the course of flattery leads to contempt and anarchy."

"So he believes no power can last?"

"No. Because there is a third way. It looks like the course of love sometimes, and sometimes it looks like the course of terror."

"Back and forth between the two? The people wouldn't know you then, and none would follow you."

"No. It isn't back and forth between anything. It's a straight and steady course. The course of magnanimity. Greatness of heart."

"It means nothing to me. One of the cardinal virtues, but the priests don't even know what it means."

"To love your people so much that you would sacrifice anything for the good of the whole. Your own life, your own family, your own happiness. And then you expect the same from them."

Oruc looked at her coldly. "You're repeating what you learned by rote."

"Yes," she said. "I will observe you, though, my Heptarch, and see if it is true."

"Magnanimity. Sacrifice anything. What do you think I am—Kristos?"

"I think you are my Heptarch, and you will always have my loyalty."

"But will my children?" asked Oruc. "Can you tell me that?"

She bowed her head. "My lord, for your sake I would die for your children."

"I know. We've had theatrical proof of that. But I know better than you do. You are loyal to me because your father taught you to be, and he is loyal to me because he loves Korfu as much as I do. He's a wise man, your father. The last of the Wise, I believe. I think it's only because of his bloodline that he hasn't heard the Cranning call. When he is dead—that old man, I can see death in him now already—when he is dead, how can I trust you then?"

The guards he had sent for were waiting in the doorways. He beckoned them in. "Take her back to the physician and have those bugs removed. Then give her back into the custody of her father's slave. Angel. He's waiting in the garden." He turned to Patience. "He's waited there for days, never stirring. A most devoted servant. By the way, I've ordered a medal struck in your honor. Every member of the Fourteen Families will wear it for this week, as will the Mayor and Council of Heptam. You handled the situation with the Tassali brilliantly. Perfectly. I will have occasion to use your talents again." He smiled gruesomely. "*All* your talents."

This had been her final examination, then, and she had passed. He intended to use her as a diplomat, young as she was. And as an assassin. She would wait now, as her father had always waited, for the knock on the door in the night, and the shadowy messenger with a note from King Oruc. She would read the note, as Father did, to learn who it was who should die. Then she would burn it and comb the ashes into fine powder. Then she would kill.

She almost danced down the corridors of Heptagon House. She needed no litter now. She had faced the King, and he had chosen her as her father had been chosen.

Angel took up her education where it had left off only a few days before, as if nothing had happened. She knew enough not to speak of these matters inside King's Hill, where everything was overheard and reported.

Two days later, Angel recieved a message late in the afternoon and immediately closed his book. "Patience," he said. "We will go down into the city this afternoon."

"Father is home!" she cried in delight.

Angel smiled at her as he put her cloak around her shoulders. "Perhaps we could go to the School. We might learn something."

It wasn't likely. The School was a large open place in the middle of Heptam. Years ago, the Wise of the world had come here to teach to all comers. Because of Crossriver Delving and Lost Souls' Island, Heptam was known as the religious capital of the world; the School made it the intellectual center as well. But now, a generation after the Flight of the Wise, the School was no more than a gaggle of scholars who endlessly recited dead and memorized words that they did not understand. Angel took great delight in teaching Patience to go to the heart of an argument and find its weak place. Then she would confront the would-be philosopher and skewer him publicly. She didn't do it often, but enjoyed knowing that she could, whenever she liked. Learn something? Not at the School.

It wasn't learning she was after anyway. It was freedom. Whenever Father was away, she was forced to remain within the high walls of King's Hill, among the same nobles and courtiers and servants. She had long since explored every corner of King's Hill, and it held no surprises for her. But whenever Father came home, she was free. As long as *he* was behind the walls of King's Hill, Angel could take her wherever he wanted in the city.

They used these times to practice techniques they could never use in King's Hill. Disguises, for instance. They would often dress and talk as servants, as criminals, as merchants, pretending to be father and daughter. Or, sometimes, mother and son, for as Angel said, "The most perfect disguise is to change from one sex to another, for when they are searching for a girl, all boys are invisible to them."

Even better than the disguises, though, was the talk. Switching from language to language, they could freely converse as they walked along the bustling streets. No one could stay near them long enough to overhear an entire conversation. It was the only time when she could ask her most difficult and dangerous questions and voice her most rebellious opinions.

It would have been completely joyful, this trip down the hill to Heptam, except for one constant sadness: Father never came with her on these trips. Oruc never let them leave King's Hill together. So all her life, all her conversations with her father had been guarded, careful. All her life, she had had to guess what Father really meant, discern his true purpose, for as often as not he could never say in words what he wanted her to know.

Their secrets could only be passed back and forth by Angel. He would take her out into the city, and she would talk with him; then he would leave her in King's Hill and walk in the city with Peace. Angel was a good friend, and both of them could trust him implicitly. But in spite of Angel's best efforts, it was like conversing through an interpreter all the time. Never in her life had Patience known a single moment of true intimacy with her father.

As they walked through King's Gift and High Town, descending long sloping roads toward the School, Patience asked Angel why the King forced them to be separate this way. "Doesn't he know yet that we are his most loyal subjects?"

"He knows you are, Lady Patience, but he misunderstands why. In treating you and your father this way, he says nothing about you, but much about himself. He believes that by keeping one of you hostage at all times, he can guarantee the loyalty of the other. There are many people who can be controlled that way. They're the people who love their families above anything else. They call it a virtue, but it is nothing more than protecting one's own genes. Reproductive self-interest. That is the thing that Oruc lives by. He is a great King, but his family comes first, so that in the final crisis, he could be held hostage, too." It was treason to say such a thing, of course, but he had split the sentence into Gauntish, Geblic, and the argot of the Islanders, so there was little chance of a passerby understanding any of it.

"Am I Father's hostage, then?" Patience asked.

Angel looked grim. "Oruc thinks you are, Lady Patience, and any assurance Lord Peace gives him that he would be loyal even if you were free seems further proof to the Heptarch that your father is desperate to win your freedom. And mark me well, little girl. Oruc thinks you are obedient in order to protect your father's life, as well."

"How sad, if he believes that everyone who says they love and serve him willingly is a liar."

"Kings have found they live longer when they assume the worst about their subjects. They don't live more happily, but they tend to die of old age rather than the abrupt disease called treachery."

"But Angel, Father will not live forever. Who will he think is my hostage, then?"

Angel said nothing.

For the first time, Patience realized that there was a

good chance she would not outlive her father by many years. Patience was the daughter of his second wife, whom he had married late; he was near seventy now, and not in the best of health. "But Angel, all the reasons the Heptarch has now for not killing me will still be in force then. If all the religious fanatics think I'm to be the Mother of Kristos—"

"Not just the fanatics, Lady Patience."

"What will it do to the legitimacy of his rule if he kills me?"

"What will it do to the legitimacy of his children's rule if he does not? *He* can keep you under control, but when he dies, you'll be young, at the peak of your powers. And now he knows that you are a dangerous assassin, a clever diplomat, with a powerful will to survive. It will be dangerous to Korfu, perhaps to the whole world, if he kills you; it will be dangerous to his family if he does not. Look for an assassin in the days following your father's death. If all goes well, your father will know he is dying soon enough to send me away. You are expected to know how to deal with any assassins and get out of King's Hill. At sunset on the day of your father's death, meet me here, at the School. I will have a way to get you out of the city."

They walked among clusters of students. The nonsense being spouted by the sophists on every side seemed a bitter contrast to the thought of her future after her father died. "And where will I go?" asked Patience. "I'm trained for the King's service. If he's trying to kill me, I can hardly do that."

"Don't be such a fool, Lady Patience. Never for an instant were you trained for the King's service."

In that moment, Patience's understanding of her whole life up to now turned completely around. All her memories, all her sense of who she was, what she was meant to become, changed. I am not meant to advise and serve a King. I am meant to *be* the King. They do not mean me to be Lady Patience. They mean me to be Agaranthemem Heptek.

She stopped. People walking behind them pushed past. "All my life," she said, "I have learned to be loyal to the King."

"And so you should be, and so you shall be," said Angel. "Walk, or the spies who frequent this place will overhear us, and we're speaking treason. You are loyal to King Oruc for the very good reason that for the good of Korfu and all human nations at this time, he should remain as Heptarch. But the time will come when his weakness will be fatal, and then for the good of Korfu and all human nations, you will need to assume the throne and bear the scepter of the Heptarchy. And at that day, Lady Patience, you will be ready."

"So when Father dies, I go to Tassali and raise an army? Invade my own land and people?"

"You'll do what is necessary for the good of the whole people at that time. And by that time you will know what that good must be. It has nothing to do with what is good for you or your kin. You know that your duty comes before any private emotion or loyalty. That is why King Oruc does not really hold you or your father hostage. If the good of the King's House required either of you to take an action that would certainly result in the death of the other, you would not hesitate. That is true magnanimity, to love the whole, and therefore to love no part greater than the whole. A daughter no more than a stranger, where the good of the King's House is concerned."

It was true. Father would let her die, if the good of the King's House demanded it. Angel had first said it to her when she was only eight years old. On the day of her formal baptism, he took her out King's Creek to the

Binding House on Lost Souls' Island—the King's private and loyal monastery, not that nest of sedition at Heads House in Crossriver Delving, where the priests prayed openly for Oruc's death. As Angel rowed the boat, he told her that Father would certainly let her die and make no effort to save her, if it was for the good of the King's House. It was a cruel thing, and she felt it like a knife through her heart. By the time her baptism was over, however, and they were again on the water returning to King's Hill, she made her decision. She, too, would have greatness of heart. She, too, would learn to love the King's House more than her own father. For that was the way of it. If she was to become like her father, she would have to reject her love for the old man. Or, perhaps, merely keep it in abeyance, to be discarded easily if it were ever necessary for the good of the King's House.

Despite that decision, though, she still longed, just once, to have the opportunity to speak freely and fearlessly with Peace. Even now, walking through the School with Angel, speaking to him about her greatest fears for the future, she was keenly aware that he was not her father.

She did not want to discuss anymore what would happen when Father died. So she rattled on for an hour about everything that had happened in the garden of Heptagon House, and later, in the King's chambers. She explained how she had unraveled the puzzles. She even repeated almost verbatim the strange doctrines that Prekeptor had set forth about her destiny.

"Well, as far as it goes," said Angel, "he tells a reasonably true story. The Wise were playing with genetics in a way never before possible. They had developed living gels that read the genetic code of foreign tissues and mirrored the genetic molecule in slowly shifting crystals on the surface. It enabled the scientists to study the genetic code in great detail, without any magnification at all. And by altering the crystals in the gel, the tissue samples could also be altered. Then they could be implanted in the host's reproductive cells. It was a similar technique that kept your father from having a daughter for so many years. And a similar technique that changed him back, so you could be born."

Patience answered scornfully. "So God didn't like them meddling with the mirror of the will, and took them away?"

"The mirror of the will, the triune soul—you shouldn't scoff at it, even if you *have* decided to be a Skeptic. This religion has lasted pretty well over the years, and partly because some of the ideas work. You can live with the triune soul as a model for the way the mind works. The will, contained in the genetic molecules—why not? It's the most primitive part of ourselves, the thing that we can't understand, why we finally choose what we choose— why not put it in the genes? And then the passions—the desire for greatness on the one side, and all the destructive desires on the other. Why not put them in the limbic node, the animal part of the brain? And the identity, the sense of self, that *is* our memories, the cerebrum, all that we remember doing and seeing, and what we conceive it to mean. There's a certain power in conceiving your own self in that way, Patience. It allows you to separate yourself from your memories and your passions, to impose discipline on your life. We are never deceived into believing that either our environment or our desires cause our behavior."

"More to the point, Angel. What happened to Prekeptor, with or without his religion?"

"He was sent home. Though I must tell you that you put the fear of God in him."

"He was already trembling with it."

"No, that was the love of God. Fear was your contribution. They had to wash his clothes after he saw you slit your own throat. All his sphincter muscles released."

She let herself laugh, though it wasn't kind to be amused. Still, he had been so fervent that she couldn't help laughing to think of the crisis of faith he must have had, to see the Mother of God apparently dying before Kristos could make an appearance.

They stayed in the city for hours, talking and playing until the sun set behind Fort Senester in Gladmouth Bay. Then Angel took her home, to see her father.

Never before had he looked so old and frail to her. A strange hollow look to his eyes, a sunken look to his skin. He was wasting. She was only thirteen years old, and her father was already beginning to die, before she ever had a chance to know him.

He was stiff and formal with her, of course; deliberately, so she would be sure to know that this was for an audience, and not particularly for her. He commended her, commented on her behavior, criticizing freely some of the things she had done that she knew perfectly well he approved of completely.

And when it was over, he handed her a slip of paper. On it was the name of Lord Jeeke of Riismouth, a marcher lord, one of the Fourteen Families. She was to visit him with her tutor as part of an educational tour of the kingdom. Lord Jeeke was to die no sooner than a week after she left, so that no one could connect her with his death.

It was surprisingly simple. The journey took three days. On her first night there, she shared a wine glass with Lord Jeeke, which was filled with a nonhuman hormone that was, by itself, harmless. Then she infected Jeeke's mistress with spores of a parasitic worm. The spores were passed to Jeeke through intimate contact; the hormone caused the worms to grow and reproduce rapidly. They infested Jeeke's brain, and three weeks later he was dead.

She was already back in King's Hill when the news reached them. She wrote letters of condolence to Jeeke's family. Father read them and patted her shoulder. "Well done, Patience."

She was proud to have him say so. But she was also curious. "Why did King Oruc want him dead?"

"For the good of the King's House."

"His personal pique, then?"

"The King's House isn't Heptagon House, Patience. The King's House is all the world."

"For the good of the world? Jeeke was a gentle and harmless man."

"And a weak one. He was a marcher lord, and he had neglected his military duties. The world was more pleasant because he was a good man. But if his weakness had led, as was likely, to rebellion and border war, many would have died or been left crippled or homeless by the war. For the sake of the King's House."

"His life against the possibility of war."

"Some wars must be fought for the good of the King's House. And some must be avoided. You and I are instruments in the hands of the King."

Then he kissed her, and as his mouth rested by her ear he whispered, "I'm dying. I won't live three years. When I die, cut into my left shoulder, midway along and above the clavicle. You'll find a tiny crystal. As you live, cut it out and keep it, whatever the cost." Then he pulled away and smiled at her, as if nothing strange had been spoken.

You cannot die, Father, she cried out silently. In all my life we've never spoken. You cannot die.

She performed four more assassinations for King Oruc, and a dozen other missions. She turned fourteen, and then fifteen. And all the while Father waited back in King's Hill, growing weaker and older. On her fifteenth birthday he told her she didn't need a tutor anymore, and sent Angel away to be overseer of some lands he held outside the city. Patience knew what it meant.

Not long after, Father woke up too weak to get out of bed. He sent the nearest servant to fetch a physician, and for a moment they were alone. Instantly he handed her a knife. "Now," he whispered. She cut. He did not even wince from the pain. She took from the wound a small crystal globe, beautiful and perfect.

"The scepter of the Heptarchs of Imakulata," he whispered. "The Usurper and his son never knew what or where it was." He smiled, but in his pain his smile was ghastly. "Never let a gebling know you have it," he said.

A servant came in, realizing they had been left alone too long; but she came too late and saw nothing, for towels covered the slightly bleeding wound, and the tiny amber-colored globe was in Patience's pocket.

Patience fingered it, pressed on it as if to squeeze some nectar from it. My father is dying, Father is dying, and the only thing I have from him is a hard little crystal I cut from his flesh, covered with his blood.

4 | FATHER'S HEAD

THE HEADSMAN STOOD OUTSIDE THE DOOR AS PATIENCE waited for her father to die. He lay on the high bed, his face grey, his hands no longer trembling. Yesterday, the day before, as word of his final disease spread through King's Hill and down into King's Gift and High Town, a steady stream of visitors had come to say good-bye, to receive a final benediction. They all murmured some excuse to Patience as they left: We were friends in Balakaim. He taught me Dwelf. But she knew why they came. To touch, to see, to speak to the man who should have been Heptarch. There was blessing in the breath of the dying King.

Now Patience, who had heard nothing but wisdom and brilliance from him all her life, watched the old man's lips move in the forms of two dozen languages, babbling the empty phrases of courtesy that had been his stock in trade. It was as if Peace had to purge himself of all the words of grace before he died.

"Father," she whispered.

The door opened suddenly. The headsman peered inside.

55

"Not yet," she said. "Go away."

But the headsman first waited until he saw Peace's hand move a little. Then he closed the door again.

Father lifted his hand to touch his collarbone, where a small wound was still unhealed.

"Yes," she said. His memory was going.

He murmured.

"I can't hear you," she said.

"Patience," he whispered. She was not sure if he was saying her name or giving her a command.

"Father, what should I do now? How should I use my life, if I can keep it?"

He murmured.

"I can't hear you, Father."

"Serve and save," he said in Dwelf. And then, in Gauntish, "The King's House."

"Oruc will never let me serve him as you did," she said in Geblic.

He answered in Agarant, the common speech, which the headsman could surely understand. "The King's House is all the world." Even as he died, he had to make sure that the story of his loyalty reached Oruc's ears. Patience saw what it was for: so Oruc would begin to doubt that Peace ever was disloyal to him. Let him wonder if he misjudged the both of us all along.

But Patience knew it also had another meaning for her. Even though in her life she might never bear the title, she nevertheless had the Heptarch's responsibility. She was to serve the world. She was to have universal magnanimity. "You taught me to survive," she whispered. "Not to be a savior of the world."

"Or a sacrifice," said his breathless lips.

Then his lips were still, and his body shuddered. The headsman heard the squeak of the bed and knew. He opened the door and came in, the headpot in his left hand, the long wire of the scalpel in his right.

"Miss Patience," he said, not looking at her, "it's best you not watch this."

But she watched, and he could not stop her, since he had not a second to lose if he was to have the head alive. The scalpel was nothing but a coarser and stronger version of Patience's own loop. He passed it around her father's neck and locked the end of the wire in place. Then he whipped left and right, severing all the loose flesh and muscle instantly. It took a moment longer to work the wire through the cartilage and nerves between the vertabrae. Peace had been dead scarcely ten seconds before the headsman lifted the old man's head by the lower jaw and laid it gently in the headpot.

The headpot rocked a few moments as the gools that lived inside jostled for position on the veins and arteries of the open throat. They would keep the head alive until it could be installed in Slaves' Hall.

Of course they did not leave her the body, either. Lord Peace may have been the King's ambassador in life, but in death his body was the corpse of the Last Pretender, and if the priests of Crossriver Delving or Lost Souls' Island got their hands on it, there'd be no end of trouble. So the diggers took him away to the King's Boneyard, and she was alone in the house.

She wasted no time—Father had told her long ago how dangerous would be the moment of his death. First protect secrets, he had always taught her. He had never kept many written documents. She found them all in moments and without hesitation she quickly burned them and raked the ashes into dust.

Then she took the tiny amber globe that had dwelt in her father's flesh and swallowed it. She wasn't sure whether the crystal it was made of could survive the process of digestion, but she didn't know what it was or how to implant it in her own body, and she didn't want it found if she were searched.

She had already prepared her traveling bag. It was filled with the tools of survival. Masks and makeup and wigs, money and jewels, a small flash of water, pellets of sugar. Not much, so it wouldn't encumber her. But enough. Her weapons were concealed in the open, where she could reach them easily. The loop in her hair. The glass blowgun in the cross that hung fashionably between her breasts. The poison in a plastic pellet between her toes. She was ready to survive, had been ready throughout the deathwatch, knowing the Oruc would surely arrange for her to die at the same time as her father, if not of the same disease.

She waited. The house was empty, the servants gone. They had been there, watching, spying all her life. If she had harbored any hopes that Oruc would let her live, the absence of the servants dispelled them. He wanted no witnesses, especially not witnesses whose tongues were professionally loose.

There was a knock on the door. It was the bailiff. It would be the bailiff, then—he was one of the many King's slaves trained to kill at the King's command. He apologized and presented her with papers of eviction. "It's a house for a King's slave, Miss Patience," he said, "and the King's slave is dead, you see." He stood between her and the other rooms of the house; she would not be allowed to take any of her belongings, he explained. They had known it would be this way, of course. Angel had taken everything of consequence with him some time ago. She would get it when she left King's Hill and joined him.

She smiled graciously and walked slowly toward the door. The bailiff made no sound that she consciously

heard, nor was there a shadow. Perhaps it was the faint-
est trembling in the stone floor, or the slightest pressure
of moving air on her hair. Without knowing how she
knew, she knew that he was about to kill her. She
lurched to the right, shifted her weight, and twisted and
kicked all in a smooth motion. The bailiff had just begun
to lunge with the dagger he held in his left hand, and
now he had time only to show the surprise on his face as
her foot caught him in the knee, bending it sideways.

He gasped in agony and dropped the dagger. Some
assassin, she thought with contempt. Did Oruc think that
such an oaf could kill the daughter of Lord Peace? It was
not even a struggle. She left the dagger in his right eye.

Only when the bailiff lay on the floor with the dagger
sticking up like a jaunty decoration did she realize that
this was the first time she had ever acted against the will
of the King. It was surprisingly easy, and she enjoyed
thwarting him even more than she had enjoyed serving
him. King Oruc, you have made a foolish mistake by not
trying to use me in my father's place. I have a certain
flair for government work. And now it will work against
you.

Then she reminded herself that she was still not Oruc's
enemy, even if he had chosen to be hers. She was the
servant of the King's House, and she would do nothing
to weaken his reign unless she knew it would bring about
a greater good.

She went to the door and opened it at once. There
would be soldiers all around, of course, but it was likely
that they did not know she was supposed to be killed.
There was too much lingering support for the ancient
bloodline. So as long as she seemed calm, she could
probably get by. No, not calm. Grief-stricken.

She wept as she left the house. It was the cry that
Father had insisted she learn, the soft, feminine sobbing

that roused the pity of men and made them feel strong and protective.

"Damned shame," one of the soldiers whispered as she passed.

And she knew that all of them were thinking: She should be Heptarch. She should be in Heptagon House, and now they won't even let her stay in King's Hill. But she was thinking that she would be lucky to live till morning.

Angel had told her to go to Admiralty Row at once, as soon as they tried to kill her. They had developed three separate escape plans. But she did not intend to use any of them. After all, she knew at least as much about the ways in and out of King's Hill as he did. As a child, permanently trapped within the walls of the King's quarter, she had been free to explore as she liked, and she knew ways over and under walls, through hidden passages in buildings, and though she had grown too large to fit through some of them now, she could still get from here to there in many different ways. And she was not going to leave King's Hill until she had spoken to her father's head. He had been so distant, so subtle in his life, but she would get some secrets from him now. He would talk to her now as he had never talked to her in life. It was a simple matter to dodge into the well-tended gardens of King's Wood. The ground was soft, taking footprints easily, but she was soon clambering from limb to limb among the trees. These giants had been old trees when her great-grandfather ruled in Heptagon House and the Fourteen Families had offered their heads to him forever. Now their leaves concealed her and their branches were her highway to the south wall of the garden. They could not follow her footsteps in the air.

She paused once in a safe cluster of branches to strip off her women's clothing. Underneath it she wore the short breeches and long shirt of a common boy. She was almost too large now to play the part, since boys took to long pants or professional gowns as soon as they could these days. At least her breasts were not too large yet, and Father had been gracious enough not to die when it was her time of month. She smudged her face, pulled off her wig, and tousled her short hair. She decided to keep the wig—it was a perfect match for her hair, and she'd be hard put to find another. She stuffed it into her bag. The dress she jammed into the crook of a branch. It was black, of course, and it wouldn't be easy to see it from the ground.

It was already dusk when she got to the wall and dropped to the ground on Granary Row. No one saw her. She appropriated one of the drawcarts and pulled it by its rope to Larder Row. After years of practice with Angel, her boyish stride was utterly convincing. No one took a second look at her. She had no trouble leaving her cart and walking, as so many servants did, to pay her respects to the dead in Slaves' Hall. If those who saw her had thought to examine her face, they might have known her—the daughter of Lord Peace had the best-known face in King's Hill. But the essence of disguise, Angel had always said, is to avoid close examination. The clothing, the walk, the dirt, the coarseness kept them from noticing her at all.

The doorkeeper wasn't there. He rarely was, and would have caused her no problem if he had been. He was almost blind.

She wandered among the shelves of living heads. She had spent many hours here, and knew most of the faces, had talked to many of them. Long-dead ministers of long-dead kings, they had once wielded vast power or influenced monarchs or served as the King's voice in hundreds of foreign courts. As usual, most of the eyes were closed, since few of the dead took much pleasure in living company. Instead they dreamed and remembered, remembered and dreamed, calling up with perfect clarity all that they had ever seen and felt in their lives. Only a few of them watched her pass; even if one of them had been able to muster up some curiosity, he could not have turned his head to see where she would go.

Father would not be here, of course, not upstairs among the favorites. It would be too soon for that—his head had to be trained and broken to the King's will first. So Patience made her way to the place under the stairs where a wooden louver in the heating vent was missing. The weather was warm enough that none of the ovens was alight; the air was cool in the stone passageway. She climbed downward into the darkness. At the bottom she turned—left?—yes, left, and crawled until she came to a wooden grating on the floor. It was dark under her. They had not yet started on Father, then.

So she lay near the grating, absolutely still, listening to the sounds that funneled through the heating system. There were places all over Slaves' Hall where conversations could be heard distinctly in these passages. A good part of Patience's self-education in politics had taken place here, as she listened to the cleverest ministers and ambassadors pry for information from the dead or conspire for power with the living.

To her surprise, they did come to Slaves' Hall looking for her—she heard the soldiers ask the gatekeeper and search the public floors. But they were searching in a desultory way, not because they expected to find her here but because they had been told to search everywhere. Good. They had lost her in King's Wood and had no idea where she had gone from there.

Later, the headkeeper came into the cellar room, lit the bright oil lamps, and began to work on her father.

She had heard and seen the process often enough before. It took less than an hour to link the headworms with the nerves in her father's spine. She watched coldly as her father's face sometimes writhed in agony, for most nerves caused pain when they were awakened by the headworms. Finally, though, the headkeeper dismissed his apprentices. The physical process was finished.

His neck bones were attached to a rack, his windpipe was attached to the breath bladder, and his neck was just touching the gel that sustained the headworms that clung to his nerves and the gools that sent tendrils through his blood vessels. They would keep his head alive, his memories intact, for the next thousand years—or until a King grew tired of him and had his head thrown out.

The headkeeper talked to him then, asking him questions. He taught the headworms by dripping certain chemicals into the canister when Lord Peace's answers were forthright, and other chemicals when he hesitated or seemed agitated. The headworms quickly learned which of the head's nerves caused pleasure and which caused suffering.

In a short time they were ready, and needed no more stimulation from the headkeeper. Now the headworms would be agitated by the increased tension of resistance, of lying. Then they in turn would stimulate other nerves, so the head felt extremes of urgent needs—the bowel or bladder full, the belly famished, the throat dry with thirst, the nerves of sexual pleasure on the edge of orgasm but never quite there. When the head answered truthfully, it got some measure of relief. When it lied, the longings increased until they were agony. Isolated from their bodies, heads never had much stamina, and their will was usually broken in a single night, however much they might resist.

Patience calmed herself, prepared herself to listen to

her father endure much before the worms broke him. And at first it seemed his resistance might be long and painful. Then to her surprise he began to whine. It was a sound she had never heard before, and she thought she knew all his voices.

"No matter what I do," he said. "You can always make it worse and worse."

"That's right," said the headkeeper. "The worms will find the things you most long for, and you'll never be satisfied until you learn to speak the truth."

"Ask me again. Ask me anything."

They did, and he told them. No resistance at all. Intimate things, terrible things, secrets of state, secrets of his own body. Patience listened in disgust. She had been prepared for her father's pain, but not for his quick capitulation.

They thought he was resisting them when he said he didn't know where Patience was. But Patience knew that he had held nothing back. Perhaps he had known he would break this easily—perhaps that's why he had prepared so well for her escape. He must have known his own weakness, though he concealed it from everyone else until now.

"I knew that you'd ask me, and so I made sure I didn't know. I told Angel a year ago to make plans with her, and tell me nothing of them. Then when I felt death was coming on, I sent Angel away—I knew they'd kill her bodyguard first. Patience is on her own until she can meet him. But Angel and I trained my daughter carefully, gentlemen. She speaks every language that I speak, she is a more accomplished assassin than Angel himself, and she is cleverer by far than any adviser to the king. You will never catch her. She's probably gone already."

The headkeeper finally believed him. "We'll tell the King you're ready now."

"Will he come and talk to me?" asked the head.

"If he wants to. But no one else ever will. With the things you know, there's no chance he'll put you in a public room. Who knows? Maybe he'll install you in his private chambers." The headkeeper laughed. "You can watch every intimate moment of the King's life, and he can get your advice whenever he wants it. There is precedent, you know. Your grandfather—"

"My grandfather was a twisted wreck. King Oruc is not."

"You hope," said the headkeeper.

"King Oruc is a great Heptarch."

The headkeeper looked at him suspiciously. Then he smiled. "You really do mean it. And all this time everyone thought you served Oruc because your daughter was a hostage. Turns out you really were loyal. A weakling." The headkeeper slapped him lightly on the cheek. "You were nothing, and now you're less than nothing."

He doused the lights and left.

As soon as he was gone and the brass key turned in the lock, Patience lifted the grating and dropped into the room.

"Hullo, Father," she said. She fumbled in the darkness until she found his breath bladder. Then she pumped air so he could speak.

"Go away," he said. "I already taught you everything I know."

"I know," she said. "Now I want you to tell me everything you fear."

"I don't fear anything now," he said. "Right now I'm voiding my bladder, which I haven't done without pain in three years. Go away."

"You have neither bladder nor urine, Father. It's just an illusion."

"The only reality a human being ever knows, my

darling girl, is what his nerves tell him, and mine are telling me that—oh, you vicious and ungrateful worm of a girl, the headworms are torturing me again because I'm resisting you."

"Then don't resist me, Father."

"I'm not your father, I'm a piece of dead brain tissue kept alive by the probing tendrils of the gools and stimulated by trained worms."

"You never *were* my father." Was that a catch in his throat? A tiny gasp of surprise? "You always made speeches to me, for the servants to overhear. Angel was the only father I had."

"Don't waste your time trying to hurt me. I'm past hurting."

"Did you ever love me?"

"I don't remember. If I did, I certainly don't love you anymore. The only thing I desire now is to urinate forever. I would gladly trade a daughter for a decent prostate."

She found the matches where the headkeepers had set them down, and lit a single lamp. Her father's eyes blinked in the light. She smiled at him. "You're going to tell Oruc everything, but you're going to tell me first. All my life you've been able to keep secrets from me. But not anymore."

"You don't need to know any of the secrets. I saw to it you knew everything. I thought you were intelligent enough to know that every word Angel spoke to you came originally from my lips."

"He told me that you would willingly let me die if it would serve the best interests of the King's House."

"What would you rather? That I tell you that I thought your life was more important than the whole world? What sort of egomaniacal monster are you?"

"A human being," she said.

"The worst kind of monster," he said. "We're all monsters, living in utter isolation, sending out words like ambassadors that beg for tribute, for worship. Love me, love me. And then when the words come back, 'I love you, I worship you, you are great and good,' these monsters doubt, these monsters know that it's a lie. 'Prove it,' they say. 'Obey me, give me power.' And when they are obeyed, the monster grows hungrier. 'How do I know you aren't manipulating me?' cries the monster. 'If you love me, die for me, kill for me, give all to me and leave nothing for yourself!' ''

''If human beings are all monsters, why should I sacrifice anything for them?''

''Because they are beautiful monsters,'' he whispered. ''And when they live in a network of peace and hope, when they trust the world and their deepest hungers are fulfilled, then within that system, that delicate web, there is joy. That is what we live for, to bind the monsters together, to murder their fear and give birth to their beauty.''

''That's as mystical as what the priests babble about.''

''It *is* what the priests babble about.''

''You have sacrificed the possibility of power, you have made us strangers all these years, and all for some invisible, nonexistent connection between human beings you've never even met?'' She tried to put as much contempt as possible into her voice.

''You're fifteen. You know nothing. Go away.''

''I know your life has been a deception and a disguise.''

''And when I dropped the disguise and told you what I have lived for, you mocked me. The babble of the priests! Do you think that because something is invisible, it doesn't exist? There is nothing but empty space between the infinitesimal pieces of matter; the only thing connecting them is their behavior, their influence on each other, and yet out of those empty, invisible connections is built all that exists in the universe. Most of it empty, the web insensible. Yet if for a single moment the web broke down, everything would flash out of existence. Do you think it's any different for us? Do you think that you exist independent of your connections with other people? Do you think that you can ever serve your own interest without also serving theirs? Then I should have killed you in the cradle, because you aren't fit to be Heptarch."

She saw in his face the same fervency she had seen in Prekeptor. Father, too, was a believer. But she could not believe that this was a belief that anyone could sacrifice for. "Was this the secret you hid from me all these years? Was this what you would have said to me if for one single moment we could have been alone and honest with each other? Was this what I yearned for all my life?" He had taught her how to show devastating contempt, as a diplomatic tool. She used it now: "I could have learned as much from any teacher in the School."

His face went slack again, went back to the neutral expression that he cultivated when he wished to show nothing. "If you don't get out of here at once, before Oruc or his men get here, you're quite likely to be with me in loving proximity for the next thousand years, getting sucked out by gools in a bowl of soup. I don't like you well enough to want your company. I used to think you were a well-behaved child, but now I see you're a slfish, inconsiderate brat."

"No," she said. "There are things I need to know. Practical things, that I can use to survive."

"Survival I taught you from infancy. You'll survive. Go away."

"What was it that you feared the most?"

His face took on a mockingly devoted expression. "That you would die. I did all that I did to keep you alive. Why else do you think I served the Usurper's Son so faithfully? He had you hostage here."

He wanted her to believe that he was lying. But she could also see that the headworms were not tormenting him. He had told her the truth. He simply didn't want her to know it was the truth. So she was asking the questions that would give her the answers she wanted. "Why were you afraid of my death?"

"Because I loved you. Back when I was alive. I remember it dimly."

But this was a lie. She could see the trembling around his lips; the headworms were in control of his nerves, and tortured him in unconcealable ways when he resisted. So it wasn't love. It was something else. And thinking of that took her back to a time in her early childhood, to the night that most haunted her nightmares. There was something in his face now that reminded her of his face that night. "You lied to me that night," she said. "I realize now, you lied about something."

"What night?" he asked.

"What was it you didn't tell me, Father, the night they brought you Mother's body in seven sacks?"

"You remember that?"

"For some reason it sticks in my mind."

He raised an eyebrow. "I don't remember it."

"Now more than ever you remember."

"God help me, if I must remember that night, then have the grace to take me from this rack and let me die."

"That night when you opened the first sack and saw what it was, you shouted, 'I'll never go, I'll never let you have her, not my daughter, not ever.' Who were you shouting at? What was it that made you so afraid? You trembled, Father. I never saw you tremble before or since."

"I was afraid of King Oruc, of course."

"You never were afraid of him. And lying does you no good—see what the headworms do with you?"

Abruptly he changed tactics. He smiled, and wryly said, "Even the headkeeper had some mercy. Now I feel like I've been constipated for a month and a diarrhea attack is beginning. You have no idea how bad these worms can be."

"Tell me now and have your ease."

Lightly he said, as if it didn't matter, "I feared the call to Cranning. It was the caller that I shouted at, whoever it was."

"Who else could it be but the gebling king?" asked Patience.

"Oh, you think you've solved it?"

"Angel told me that the gebling kings have always been able to command their people without a word. From mind to mind."

"Did Angel tell you that this power of the geblings has never touched a human being? We're deaf as a post when the geblings cry out to each other."

"The Cranning call—if it isn't the geblings, who is it, and why do you fear it?"

"I don't know who it is, but I fear him. I fear what he can do to people. The Wise of Grandfather's day were brilliant and strong, the greatest minds in the history of the world, working together, building on each other's learning, until they did things that had never been done on any world. Here, where iron is so hard to find that we can never rely on the machines that have always made humans powerful, they unlocked the powers of life. They weren't just petty breeders, like the Tassaliki, like the ancient scientists who created these headworms and gools four thousand years ago—those were mountebanks by comparison. The Wise of Grandfather's day had taught the chromosomes to name themselves in crystals, atom for atom, in patterns that could be seen and read by the naked eye. They had found how passion fish mate with clams to make cressid plants. And when I was born, they changed me so that I could never sire anything but sons.''

Patience thought about that for a moment. "They did it so the prophecy wouldn't be fulfilled. So there'd be no seventh seventh seventh daughter."

"That was the plan."

"Why did you change your mind? Why did you have Angel undo what they did? Surely you didn't become a Watcher."

"No, not a Watcher. The Wise did this to me when I was still a child. As soon as they had made my body incapable of siring girlchildren, the Cranning call began. One by one, the best of them began to leave. They would go off to teach somewhere. They would retire to a country home. They would be sent as ambassadors or governors. But they would never arrive at their destination. Instead they would be seen along the rivers and roads leading to Cranning."

"Your father was Heptarch then?"

"Not yet. My father watched what happened to the empire, as all the able men disappeared. He went to them and begged them not to go. The ones who hadn't yet felt the Cranning call vowed most solemnly to stay. The ones who *had* felt it, though—they promised anything but they broke all their promises. And Grandfather did nothing to stop it. It was a frightening time, with provinces in rebellion, the army in disarray. Father finally had Grandfather arrested and took over the government."

"So the Usurper wasn't the first to overthrow a Heptarch."

"For the good of the King's House, even treason. Yes. But it was too late. Even when he tortured some of them, even when he killed some as an example, they went. Even when he cut off their heads and put them here, in Slaves' Hall, the Cranning call was so strong in their minds that the headworms had no power over them. The Cranning call was more urgent than anything the headworms could do to them.''

"What were they wanted for?"

"Do you think Father didn't try to find out? But they themselves didn't know. And no one ever knew what became of them, once they got to Cranning. Father's spies never came back. And after a few years, the empire was lost. Twelve of the Fourteen Families were in revolt. Oruc's father led it. But he wasn't called the Usurper then. He was called the Liberator. He came, he said, to restore Grandfather to his rightful place on the Heptarch's throne.''

"Ah."

"Father should have killed Grandfather."

"As Oruc should have killed us?"

"Grandfather wasn't the—seventh seventh seventh daughter." Lord Peace closed his eyes. Patience knew that if he still had his body, he would put his fingertips together, then touch them to his mouth; she could almost see his hands rise. She felt the grief for his death well up in her for the first time, seeing him half-alive like this, remembering him whole.

She shook off the feeling. "How was I born, Father?"

"My father lost the city of Heptam before I came of age. I led one army, he led another. He lost and was captured and killed. I never lost. I wandered the wilderness with an ever-shrinking guerrilla band. One by one my sons came to adulthood. One by one they were killed. The enemy seemed to find my boys so easily—as if some traitor led them. It was as if some terrible invisible power guided them to destroy everyone but me. Everyone but me. My first wife, my father, my children, and I alone was alive.''

"So you could sire the daughter of prophecy."

"I studied the chronicles. I realized that my family's fall began almost the moment they undaughtered me. That was the crime for which the Wise were taken and the throne was lost. You see, Patience, the prophecies that these men of science had long thought were mere superstition—someone or something of great power meant to have them fulfilled. And we thought—perhaps if we find a way to undo what was done. Perhaps if I could have a girlchild, then the Wise would come home, and all could be restored as it was. Peace could be restored to the world. But how could we undo the work of the Wise, so my daughter could be born? Who would know how to do it, when the Wise were all gone?"

"Angel," said Patience. "I know this story."

"I was in my forties then. He came to me, a very young man then, and said he had been studying the journals of the great men, and he thought he knew a way to refresh and revivify my woman-making sperm. He explained, but I could not understand it—I know what every educated man knows about genetics, but he was deep in the chemistry and mathematics of it, catalysts and countercatalysts and inducers and blocks. I said to him, 'You know too much. You've become one of the Wise. The Cranning call will come to you.' He only smiled and said, 'Lord Peace, my Heptarch, if the caller wants you to have a daughter, then he will leave me here.' "

"So my birth . . . served the purpose of the Cranning call."

"Angel and I argued over it. Better to be castrated than to give in to what this enemy wants, I said. But it came to this: We didn't know what purpose the Cranning call might have for you, but we knew that as long as you remained unborn, the world was in turmoil. We were at

Ilium at the time, under the protection of Lady Hekat. She told us, 'The prophecies are ambiguous. The seventh seventh seventh daughter is called the destruction of the world, and the salvation of the world. Why not let her be born, and then teach her to be a savior?' So I took Lady Hekat as my second wife, and Angel made the change in me, and you were born."

"Lady Hekat." Patience saw her mother's face as it had been the last time she saw her. Weeping as the soldiers took Patience away from her. Crying out, My daughter, my daughter, my child, God be with you, always with you; and then the knock on Father's door, and the sudden cry of agony as father looked into the bag that was delivered there. I saw his face. His face, Mother's face, the same agony. "And you trained me to be an assassin," she said.

"I taught you to serve the King's House. However much you think you hate me now, I know you. You will always act for the good of the King's House. You are the hope of humanity. Not as the Watchers and Vigilants believe, as the mere mother of some imagined god. You yourself. I know it."

"I'm a child, fifteen years old. I'm the hope of nothing. I have no great purpose."

"If you have no purpose of your own, then you will fulfill the purpose of the Cranning call. It waits for you, Daughter. But Angel and I have done all we could to teach you what the Heptarch lives for. If you haven't learned it, we could do no more."

"You don't know anything Father. You don't know who is calling from Cranning, you don't know what he wants me for, and you don't even know me."

"How could I know you, Patience? I felt the Cranning call, too. Are you surprised? I never felt it until you were born, but then it began. A terrible urgency to take you there, to carry you to Skyfoot and give you—to whatever waits there. Whenever I was with you, all your life, I have felt a longing worse than anything these petty worms can do to me. So I have spent as little time with you as I could, for fear I would break under the pain of it, and carry you off before you were ready.''

"Ready for what?"

"To face whatever waits there."

"Am I ready now?"

"How can I know? But you're as ready as I could make you in my life. Trust Angel now. He is the last of the Wise, the only one who can protect you from the thing that calls. From Unwyrm.''

"You know its name?"

"One prophecy says that you will take the world into Unwyrm's lair and give it to him, and all mankind will die and be reborn. It's the only prophecy that gives a name."

"Who made the prophecy?"

"A prophet, I suppose. What matters is that the Cranning call is proof that the prophecies are true—or some undefeatable power wants to make them true, which amounts to the same thing.''

"There's no such thing as an undefeatable power," said Patience. "You always taught me that."

"Go now, Patience. I've told you everything. Now don't let them find you here, or my whole life was for nothing. And if they ask me, I'll have to tell them that I saw you. It'll give them a fresh trail."

Almost she obeyed him. But then she realized that he had not fully answered her. There was still a twitching in his face, a sign that he was resisting, that he had not told her all that she had asked for.

"One more story," she said.

"No more.''

"The one you don't want to tell me."

The face grimaced as the head tried to resist the urging of the worms. "Leave me in peace, child! Let my name be something more than a terrible irony."

"Whatever you want so badly not to tell, that is the thing I most badly need to know."

"You're wrong, you fool! If you needed to know I would have told you! Leave me this one secret to take to the grave."

"I'll have it from you, Father! I'll have it, or wait here until Oruc takes me!"

Finally, sweating and weeping, the head spoke. Patience pumped steadily, but the voice was high and strange.

"The priests say that the Starship Captain was taken in the spirit by God, made some prophecies, and then disappeared into heaven."

"I know the tales."

"I know the truth. The captain of the starship *Konkeptoine* went mad as our ancestors orbited the world. It's true that he wrote the prophecy with his right hand in the ship's log. He also drew the map of the world, showing all the great deposits of iron and coal, the stuff that steel is made of. Then he used the ship's powers to destroy those deposits. In that one act he determined the future of the world. Imakulata is not naturally poor in iron. Because of his insane act of destruction, we children of the great engine builders are deprived of steel. We have no great machines. We are weaker in this world than human beings have ever been before."

"If he was insane enough to do that, why did anyone think he was a prophet?"

"Because his map was more accurate than the one the ship's own mind drew. He knew things about the world that could not be known. They said at the time he seemed to be possessed. I who have felt the Cranning call know

now that this was probably true. Whatever controlled him in the ship, that compulsive power is still alive. He left the ship in a landing craft and was never seen again. His craft was never found.''

"If something like this happened, why isn't it in any of the histories?''

"There are stories passed from Heptarch to Heptarch that none of the historians know. I meant you to know this much, anyway; I told Angel, and he was to tell you. The priests know only of the map he drew with his right hand, and the words he spoke with his mouth. The words that his possessor wanted us to believe. Words about how Kristos would come to Imakulata and make the human race new and perfect. But his daughter Irena, the first Heptarch, she saw something that only the Heptarchs know: As he spoke the prophecy and drew the map with his right hand, his left hand slowly tapped out into the mind of the ship, 'Save my daughter from the lair of the wyrms, or they will devour all mankind.' ''

"His daughter—''

"Not Irena, child. You. His distant daughter. At first they didn't know how distant. There were prophecies that it would be the seventh seventh daughter. Magic numbers. Only in the last thousand years have there been prophets who said that the Daughter of Prophecy, the Mother of God, is to be the seventh seventh seventh daughter of the Starship Captain.''

"Then there's no reason to believe that the prophecy is anything more than the raving of a Vigilant.''

"Of course. Except that the Cranning call obviously intends to fulfill that prophecy. I have no doubt that you are the daughter that needs saving, as the Starship Captain warned.''

"But what is the lair of the worms—this? The head-worms?''

"He wrote a word that in Star Speech, the most ancient of languages, means 'monster,' and not just any monster, but the most dangerous and cunning and powerful of enemies. An enemy powerful enough to take control of the Starship Captain's mind while the *Konkeptoine* still orbited Imakulata. An enemy powerful enough to call all the Wise to Cranning. Do you understand the danger of the world, Patience? We are facing an enemy that formed its plans seven thousand years ago, when we first arrived here. Whatever ruled Imakulata before humankind came here wants to rule again."

"A gebling then. They were the highest native life, as intelligent as humankind—"

"Were they? Then why is Geblic merely another corrupt form of Star Speech? And Dwelf and Gauntish, why did they have to take their language from mankind? They rose to where they are when humanity arrived; there was something more powerful, an intelligence older than they. I meant for Angel to warn you of this. I didn't mean for you to be ignorant of it. But that's all now. That's all, now go."

But even now, there was more, she could see what the headworms told her, that he was hiding still another secret from her. The headkeeper hadn't broken him. His power of resistance was still strong. But she would do what the headkeeper had failed to do. She would break him and have from him the tale he didn't want to tell.

"I know you better than that, Father," she said. "If I am such a danger to the world, you would have killed me in my childhood."

"The Starship Captain didn't say to kill his daughter. He said to save her. And even if he had not said so, I could not have killed you. Anyone else could die, child, anyone at all, but you would live. To destroy mankind or to save the world, I cannot guess, but you would live, whatever the cost.''

''Why! Not because I'm your daughter—so why!''

His face twisted in agony. She had asked him the unbearable question, and the headworms would torture the answer from him. But even as she realized this, she also remembered something else. This was the expression on his face the night of Mother's death. This was the mask of pain he wore. ''In all your talking, Father, you never told me what you meant when you cried out on the night they brought Mother's body to you.''

His mouth opened wide to form a scream that never sounded.

''The Cranning call. For me, the need wasn't for *me* to come. It was to bring *you*. Whole and alive. When I wasn't with you, I felt no call at all.''

''That doesn't answer my—''

''Your mother was always with you. She was also called. She was weaker than I was. She tried to take you. That's why I carried you away from her. She vowed she would never rest until she had you back, that she would do anything to get you away from me.''

Even now, though the dread was thick within her, she could not bring herself to understand what he meant.

''Listen, foolish girl! Didn't Angel and I teach you how to listen? My father was weak enough to let Grandfather live, when he should have died. I was stronger than my father was. Hekat meant to take you to Cranning. I had no strength to kill *you*, against the Cranning call, but I still had strength.''

Patience stopped pumping breath for him.

''You,'' she whispered. ''You told me it was a group of soldiers trying to curry favor with Oruc. You told me—they were even executed for it—but it was you.''

His lips formed words as he ran out of air. I never

meant to tell you. His eyes accused her. You made me tell you, and you didn't need to know.

It was more than she could bear.

"Why didn't you let her take me to Cranning. I would rather have suffered anything, and have her live."

"The King's House is all the world," said his lips.

"You weren't the Heptarch! You didn't have any responsibility for the whole world! You didn't have to kill my mother!" And she swept him from the table, spilling him to the floor.

At once she rushed to him, to lift the head back to the table, restore the gel that would keep his gools alive.

But he looked at her steadily as she knelt over him, and his lips moved and said, Let me die.

So she did the only thing she *could* do. She took Lord Peace by the jaw and tore the head away from the rack that held it. The headworms wriggled in the open air and the gools slid off and slopped onto the floor. All the time her father's eyes looked at her in gratitude and love.

Then, gasping with grief and fury, she tossed the head through the open grate in the ceiling and climbed up after it. She carried it with her for ten minutes as she scrambled through the heating system to the vent by the garrison barracks. By then it was dead beyond reviving, and she thought of leaving it at the barracks door. Let the soldiers explain to King Oruc how she got it there without being seen.

No. She could not leave his head like the carcass of a cat in the street. Not that *he* would care—he was beyond such concerns as respect and dignity. It was herself she was concerned for, Patience who could not bear to treat even this fragment of her father's body with disrespect.

What she could not understand was why she did not hate him.

He had killed Mother. All his weeping when they

showed how she had been mutilated, all his grief, all his embraces as he tried to comfort his daughter—and he was the one who killed her. All because of some madness about an ancient prophecy. Seven thousand years ago their ancestor went mad, and a few hundred thinkers took unlicensed trips to the gebling city, and for that her mother was murdered by her own husband.

Yet it was this monster who had made her what she was. For her own honor, if not for his, she could not shame him in death. Not because she loved him. She certainly certainly did not love him.

As she made her way along the ledges of the cliff outside the wall of King's Hill, she filled her father's throat and mouth with rocks and tossed the cold, misshapen thing into the sea.

5 | HEPTAM

ANGEL WAS SUPPOSED TO BE IN DISGUISE, LECTURING ON astrophysics in the School. But he wasn't there. It didn't surprise her. She was supposed to have arrived almost as soon as word first reached the city that Peace was dead. Every minute she delayed made it more dangerous for Angel, who was not unknown and might be recognized despite his disguise.

Perhaps he had stayed until nightfall—but he would certainly not have dared to stay the night inside the city. There were too many tongues paid well to wag, too many eyes that would see and remember the new teacher who had not been seen or heard of before. Perhaps, though, he would return in the morning. So, still passing as a boy, she passed the early hours of day like the many students searching for a teacher whose haranguing was particularly pleasing. She was tired, after a night without sleep. But part of her regimen had been sleeplessness, from time to time, staying awake and alert against the urging of her body. Angel and Father had stretched her limits so far that she no longer knew where they were.

She quickly recognized the spies circulating through the crowd. They had not been trained by Father or Angel; they were not subtle, and Patience knew she was not the only one who could tell they were not earnest seekers after truth. Many a teacher became tongue-tied when a spy came near, and tried to purge his doctrine of anything that smacked of sedition. Patience also knew that the spies she saw were not the dangerous ones. It was the spies she could not discern who frightened her.

So she made her way into Kingsport, the warehouse and shipping district that had once been a separate town and still had its own council and made some of its own laws. Great Market, only a short way up from the docks, stank of fish and sausages, alcohol and spice. It would not do to linger too long without buying—the merchants hired their own spies to search for thieves. So she made her way to the tonguing booths. She stopped at the canopy of a man whose sign promised he could translate Agarant to Dwelf, Dwelf to Gauntish, Gauntish to Geblic, and then back to common speech without a word changed. It was so extravagant an impossibility that she liked the man at once. She leaned on his writing table. He looked up at her from heavy brows and thick moustaches and said, in Agarant, "Take your hands off my table or I'll cut them off."

Patience answered in Panx that she knew was accentless. "My hands for your mealbag, it's a fair trade."

He squinted at her. "Nobody ever needs Panx," he said. "Don't speak it myself."

She spoke now in Gablic. "Then perhaps you can use my services somewhere else."

"Didn't you understand me? I don't need Panx."

Now she spoke in common speech. "The last thing I said was in Geblic. So much for your sign."

"I've never known a gebling merchant who couldn't

speak Agarant, so no one needs it anyway. How did you learn Panx and Geblic?"

"I'm a gebling," she said.

"Your barber is very good." He smiled. "Listen, boy, as long as you're here, I could use a scribe. How's your hand?"

"Good enough, as long as I can sit there in the shade, with something to keep sun off my neck."

"And the common gaze off your face, is that it?"

"I'm not afraid of the *common* gaze, sir."

"Ah. It's the uncommon gaze you dread. Come, sit, what do I care whom you're hiding from, as long as you don't steal from me? Though by the grandmother of Kristos, there's not much to steal. My name is Flanner. At least that's what my merchant's license says."

So she sat through the day, writing out in her trained and beautiful hand what Flanner had scribbled. Often she corrected his tendency to translate idioms literally, giving the sense instead of the words; if he noticed, he didn't say. He sent a streetboy for dinner at noon, and shared the food with her. At day's end, when all the clients had come by and there was no work left except a book that wasn't due till spring, Flanner stood up and rubbed his hands together. "Still an hour till full dark. What do you plan to do now?"

"Help you pitch your canopy."

"And then?"

"Ask you for six coppers for my day's work."

"Let's start with the canopy." They took down the awning and the four posts. It all collapsed into sticks and cloth that fit inside his table; two of the sticks became axles, and the table was now a cart. "Now, boy, it occurs to me that three times today I had to step over there to the pisspit, and you not once."

"Some have larger bladders than others," she said.

But she knew he would not give her the money, and he was perilously close to guessing who she was, if he hadn't already. So she reached into her hair and took out her loop. She flipped it down across his wrist, caught the ends to form a circle around it, and smiled. "Twenty-five coppers with the other hand," she said, "or you lose this one."

He saw the wire more than felt it. With only slight pressure it had cut into the skin and blood was forming droplets. His other hand took a purse from his belt. "So you're a thief after all," he said.

"I did an honest day's work," she said. "But I charge extra when people try to cheat me. Spill the purse."

He poured out the coins on the tabletop.

"A silver and five coppers, count them out and put them back in the purse."

He did it, being careful not to move the caught hand any more than necessary. When he had pulled taut the string of the purse, she snatched it with one hand, letting the loop dangle from the other. He did not try to catch her, just held his bleeding wrist and panted in relief.

"And remember that *pleiok* can be future tense as well as past. It gets you into more trouble." She dodged away into the gathering dusk.

Another day was ending, another day of putting herself at terrible risk in a public place, and Angel hadn't found her. No doubt the rumor of the boy who could speak four languages and had almost cut off Flanner's hand would reach his ear before morning—it was the kind of tale that spread fast through the taverns. Unfortunately, the King's spies would also hear it, so she couldn't wait for Angel to find her from the tales.

Her purse bought her passage on an upriver boat. All the outbound boats were being watched closely, but the ferries that carried gamblers and gamers to the Cuts needed no supervision, apparently. The porter who took her three coppers looked at her with squinting eyes. "You know they put cutpurses in the river in three pieces," he said.

Patience looked at the planks to avoid his gaze. So she looked like a thief in this company. Shouldn't be a surprise. Only the well off could play the Cuts, and she didn't exactly reek of money. But as Angel left, he had jokingly said that he figured to spend his time getting rich in the Cuts, because he was mathematician enough to control the odds. It was the only hint she had of where he'd be, and so she acted on it.

She paid the extra copper to use the privy house on the boat. It was a long pole upstream when the tide was out, and there was a queue. A very fat, foul-breathed woman got in line behind her. Her belly and breasts kept bumping into Patience, as if to urge her forward. She didn't want to make a scene, though, and so bore it patiently. But when the man before her got out, to her horror the woman pushed her way into the privy behind her.

Patience had never pictured herself having to kill someone quite so grossly fat. How deep would a weapon have to pierce in order to touch something vital? It didn't matter—a throat was a throat. By the time the fat woman had the door closed, Patience had her loop out and easily cast it about the woman's neck.

"Make a sound and you're dead," said Patience.

The woman made no sound.

"I don't want to kill you," Patience said. "I don't know if you meant to rob me or what, but if you keep silent and say nothing, I'll let you finish this voyage alive."

"Please," the fat woman whispered.

Patience tightened the loop. A sudden slackening of

resistance told her that it had bitten flesh. "I said silence," Patience said.

"Angel," the fat woman squeaked.

She hadn't expected that. She was keyed up against enemies, and hadn't thought the woman might be a friend. "What about Angel?"

"He's coming on the next boat. In the name of Cleanliness and Holiness and all the Sweet Smells, take that thing from around my neck. He said you were dangerous but he didn't say you were insane."

"Who are you?"

"Sken. I own a boat. I think I wet myself."

"Good. Then you don't need the privy house. I do. Get out."

"You're all heart. And what will they think, when I come out with my throat bleeding?"

"That you made an indecent offer to a young man in the privy, and he turned you down with vigor. I'll meet you at the railing—now go."

"You're a little turd," said Sken. She left, holding her neck.

Patience barred the door and finally relieved herself. It had been a long day. Now she understood why the heads gave in so easily when the worms tortured them with these body urges. Angel had found her after all, apparently, had been watching her until he had a chance to send word to her. Whoever this woman was, Angel trusted her. No doubt the fact that she owned a boat played some part in his plans.

But will it play a part in mine? Patience wondered what Angel was to her now. Father's slave, and so now hers, technically. But she knew he didn't really belong to her. It wasn't just because she couldn't take him into court to enforce her claim. He had served her father, not from fear, but from love and loyalty. One of the lessons of statecraft, Father often told her, was that loyalty could not be transferred or inherited; it had to be earned by each new lord in turn. Angel might now feel no loyalty at all, or believe that he was still bound to carry out whatever Father's last instructions to him might have been.

Patience, though, didn't feel bound to obey Father. She obeyed him for the last time when she tore his head from the rack and cast it into the sea. His desires were not to be added into the balance anymore. She was not a child, now. She could decide for herself what to do with the burden of prophecy and doom that had attended from her birth, that had unthroned her grandfather and killed her half-brothers.

And killed her mother, too; dear Mother, who had died so cruelly at Father's hands, and for my sake, all for my sake, Mother, if I could have, I would have died for you but now your death has bought for me all that it could buy—the years to become dangerous, too, in my own right. Haven't I killed in the name of the King? Didn't I leave my own assassin with a dagger in his eye? Didn't I steal Father's head out of Slaves' Hall though all the soldiers in King's Hill looked for me? I am not a little child or a helpless Heptarch whose servants have made her soft. I will not refuse the path that prophecy has declared for me, but I will not be half so meek as prophecy thinks I'll be. I will be more than a match for Unwyrm, whoever or whatever Unwyrm is.

So she leaned on the gunnel of the boat as the oarsmen below decks swept the river, pushing the waves westward toward the sea. Glad Hell's high prison wall loomed in the gathering night; then the island was past them, and the lights of Heptam were visible far to the south, across the marshes. I am outside the prison walls now, she thought. I am outside King's Hill, and I'll never go back there, except as Heptarch. Inwardly she laughed at the thought. Whatever else she might be or do in her life, the Heptarchy was the thing furthest out of reach. She would set herself to other tasks, and let the Heptarchy come to her if it would.

King's Hill was not the only prison she was free of. Those walls had always been the least of her jails. The training regimen was over. The constant tests and problems were ended. Never again would others determine her present and future according to their own desires. Instead she would go where she was born to go. To Cranning, the great Skyfoot city at the center of the world. How could she, for a moment, think of going anywhere else?

She felt a tingling of her skin at the thought of Cranning, a trembling in her loins, a hunger deeper than any she had felt before in her life. Cranning. All roads go there, all rivers flow there, all time bends there, all life ends there.

It became a pounding rhyme in her head.

All roads go there.

(But Father killed Mother—)

All rivers flow there.

(—to save me from someone—)

All time bends there.

(—who waits there, calling, calling—)

All life ends there.

Over and over the rhyme, the need, filling her with a passion she had never felt before. She knew what it was. No one needed to explain it to her. The Cranning call.

6 | GLAD RIVER

THEY SPENT NO TIME AT ALL IN THE CUTS. THOUGH PATIENCE was fascinated by the glittering clothing and everyone's passionate urgency to spend themselves all in one night, Sken led her at once to a small riverboat, the kind with a mast to help upstream when the wind was good, or to go out to sea on short runs, if there was a need. The heavy oars explained why the fat woman's arms were thick and muscular. Patience began to suspect, as Sken pulled them away from the island, that there was less fat on her than she had supposed at first.

"We wait out here in the dark," Sken whispered, "until his boat comes. Then we go back in and get him."

It was only a few minutes later; this early in the evening, there was a lot of traffic from Kingsport up the Glad River to the Cuts. Angel's disguise was good enough that Sken recognized him before Patience did. She was looking for an aging scholar, or the gracious old woman he sometimes had mimicked in the past. Instead, he was an obvious male whore, slightly drunk, painted till his face fairly glowed in the torchlight.

"I thought the essence of disguise was to be inconspicuous," Patience said. The oars dipped into the water without a splash—Sken knew the river and had the strength to glide upstream without seeming to strain.

"The essence of disguise is to be unnoticed," said Angel. He dipped his hands into the river to wash his face. "You can do that by being so nondescript that no one notices you, or being so embarrassing that no one can stand to look at you. Either way, your disguise remains unexamined, and so you remain unrecognized."

"Why did you leave me in the tonguing booths all day?" Patience said. She didn't like it when Angel proved that he still knew more than she did.

"Where were you yesterday, little fool, when I stood there in the School with my face hanging out for any of the King's asses to see me?"

"Talk softer," Sken whispered. "The King's patrol are known to anchor their boats on the river and listen in the darkness for fools who think they're alone."

They fell silent then. They passed the eastern edge of Cuts Island and began to pass among the pilings on which houses perched precariously high above the water. It was a district called Stilts—the town of the river people, who it was said were born and died without ever setting foot on land. It wasn't true, of course, but they did spend most of their lives on the water. The story was they got seasick on land. If they had liquor in them, they couldn't even walk unless there was a shifting deck under them. Patience had always suspected they made up the stories themselves.

"At high tide," said Sken, "the water comes up to there." She pointed to a level on the nearest piling about a meter above the water. "But in spring flood, there are weeks when we live in the attics, because the water on the first floor is three feet deep."

Patience marveled at that—the houses were all a good four meters above the water level. The land on the left bank, where the new town was rising, was high enough that it might not flood in the spring. But the marshland of the right bank must be under water for a good long time. Patience began to understand how the river controlled the way human beings lived here. Korfu had risen and fallen many times in seven thousand years. Heptam had been a provincial town and the center of the world. Yet in all that time, the river still worked its will in this place.

As if he read her thoughts, Angel said, "There was a levee on the right bank for a thousand years, and the marshland was heavily populated. But about five thousand years ago it was breached and no one rebuilt it. Within fifty years it was as if it had never been there. Time is against us."

The boat bumped up against a large piling. A house was built on this single massive stilt, with stabilizing boards angling off to triangulate with the great beams. "Here," said Sken. She tied the boat to the piling and climbed with surprising ease up a series of boards that made a sort of irregular ladder into the house. Then, before Patience could walk to that end of the boat to climb up, a net dropped down like a heavy spider.

"She's going to lift us up?" asked Patience.

"I brought some luggage with me," said Angel. Patience recognized his small trunk. Of course. Her things he could leave somewhere in hiding, but his little trunk was never long out of his sight. She knew he kept his disguises in it, but there were other things, too, which he showed to no one.

The trunk rose quickly upward into the house. Then Angel motioned for Patience to climb.

The house swayed slightly when they walked from one end to another. To someone who lived on the river, it probably felt fine, but to Patience it was unnerving. It was like living in a constant earthquake, she thought. And when Sken moved from place to place, her great mass tilted it even more. She seemed not to notice it, and Patience said nothing.

"I'm sorry I didn't meet you on time," Patience said. "I had some questions I had to ask Father. Questions I could only ask him when he was dead."

"I guessed as much," said Angel. "Did you leave him there when you were through?"

"Oruc had enough use of him when he was alive," said Patience. "He'll have no use of him now."

Sken was horrified. "You killed your father's head?"

"Shut up and tend to the food," Angel said softly. Sken glowered but obeyed.

"He asked me to," said Patience.

"As any sane man would," said Angel. "Just because we *can* preserve them doesn't mean we should. Just one more abomination we'll have to answer for someday."

"To God? I don't think he cares what we do with our heads."

Sken couldn't keep her silence. "If I'd known you were blasphemers I would have put you at the bottom of the river."

It was Patience who answered this time. "And if I'd known you were unable to keep your mouth still I would have left your head in the privy hole."

Angel smiled. "So you did have your loop on you?"

"I needed it twice. I wasn't very subtle, either."

"God knows," muttered Sken.

"Well, what did your father tell you?"

Patience looked at him coldly. "He told me what he said you were going to tell me."

"What is that?"

"Tell me what you're supposed to tell me, and I'll see if it agrees."

"Patience, I know more games than I ever taught *you*. If you tell me what secrets he told you, then I don't have to go on lying to you for the next thirty years."

"Did you know about how mother died?" asked Patience.

Angel grimaced. "I see you didn't ask him easy questions."

"He broke in two hours. I thought he had more strength than that."

"He had more strength than anyone."

"He whined and whimpered—and when the worms punished him, he even wept."

Angel nodded gravely. "Of course."

"What do you mean, of course! He was the one who taught me endurance, who taught me that the emotion I showed should never be the emotion I felt, and there he was—"

She stopped, feeling stupid.

"Yes?" asked Angel.

"There he was, showing emotions and I fell for it."

"Ah. So perhaps he didn't break at all."

"He wasn't lying to me. I saw when he was lying, and I saw when he stopped. He can't hide everything. Can he?"

"No. I think he told you the truth. What else, besides your mother's death?"

"Wasn't that enough?"

"The prophecy?"

"I knew a little about that anyway. He told me what the Starship Captain did with his left hand."

"Mm."

"Angel, I've decided where I want to go."

"Your father left me strict instructions."

"My father is dead now, and you belong to me."

Sken was surprised. "You mean you're a slave? I've been taking orders from a *slave?*"

"I am the slave of a Slave of the King. That puts me so far above you that you're unworthy to inhale one of my farts. Now *will* you shut up, woman?"

Actually, thought Patience, I'm the Heptarch now. You're Slave to the King herself. Her *only* Slave. Much may it profit you.

"So," said Angel. "Where do you want to go?"

"Cranning," said Patience.

Angel was angry, though he answered with humor. "Stiff as steel, the girl has lost her mind."

Now Sken was livid. "Girl! Girl! You mean this snip of a boy is a *female?* It is an abomination for the woman to wear the clothing of the man, and the man to wear the clothing of a woman—"

"Shall I kill her to get us some silence?" Angel asked.

Sken fell silent, stuffing hardbread into sacks and spiced sausages into watertight pouches.

"Child," said Angel, "that is the one place you can never go."

"I'm sure of it," she said. "But it's the one place I have to go. I was born for it, don't you see?"

"You were born for something better than to go off fulfilling mad prophecies."

"How will you stop me. Kill me? Because it's the only way you ever will."

"It's the Cranning call. That's what makes you want to go. It comes this way, an insane determination to go there, for no reason at all, against all reason—"

"Don't you think I know?"

Angel chewed on that for a moment. "So you think that whatever it is, you're stronger."

"I think that if it can call the wisest men out of the world and force my mother to want to sacrifice her daughter, then someone needs to stop it. Why not me? Don't the prophecies say that mankind will be reborn?"

"When Kristos comes," muttered Sken.

"The prophets were given their visions and prophecies by whatever it is that calls," said Angel. "They might be lies, to entice you."

"Then I'm enticed. If you're so wise, Angel, why haven't *you* felt the Cranning call?"

Angel went cold, his face a hard-set mask. She had always had the gift of goading him. "No one ever proved that *every* wise one heard the call."

There was no need to hurt him; she was using diplomatic tricks on a man whose honest words she would need again and again. So she smiled and touched his hand. "Angel, you spent your life making me as wise and dangerous as possible. When will I be readier? When you're too old to come with me? When I've fallen in love with some cod and had three babies that I have to protect?"

"Maybe you'll never be ready for whatever waits."

"Or maybe now. When I'm willing to die. When I've lost my father for the first time and my mother all over again. Now, when I'm willing to kill because of the rage that burns in me for what has been stolen from me and my father and my mother, now is the time for me to face whatever waits for me there. With you or without you, Angel. But better with you."

Angel smiled. "All right."

Patience glared at him. "That was too easy. You intended to be persuaded all along."

"Come now, Patience. Your father warned us both that the worst thing in the world was waiting in Cranning. As well as we knew him, and as well as he knew us, don't you think he knew we'd come to this moment?"

Patience remembered her father's head. Was he scheming even then, letting her force from him the very truths that he most wanted to tell her? "I don't care if he was," she said. "Even if my father really wanted me to go, I'll go."

"Good. Tonight then. We don't want another day here." He took a purse from his belt and took out two large steel coins. "Sken, do you know what these are worth?"

"If they're real, then you're a damned fool for carrying them without a bodyguard."

"Are they enough to buy your boat?"

Sken squinted at him. "You know it's enough to buy ten of my boats. If they *are* steel."

He tossed them to her. She bit them and weighed them in her hand. "I'm not a fool," she said.

"You are if you think they aren't real," said Angel.

"I won't sell you the boat unless you buy me, too."

"Buy *you!* That's enough to buy your silence, and that's all we want of you."

"I said I'm not a fool. This in't the price a man offers for a boat if he means to leave the money behind. You plan to kill me before you go."

"If I say I'm buying, I'm buying."

"You've let me hear enough tonight that you daren't let me live behind you. A girl traveling in disguise with a man who tosses steel about as if it were silver? Her father recently dead, and them both afraid of the law? Do you think we of the river haven't heard that Lord Peace died today? And that the King looks for his daughter Patience, the rightful Heptarch, the daughter of prophecy? You didn't care if I figured it out because you knew I'd be dead."

Patience knew Sken was right—she knew Angel well enough for that. "I thought you were talking so openly because this woman was to be trusted, not because she was to die."

"And what if you're right?" asked Angel. "What if I did mean to kill you? Why should I change my mind now, and take you along?"

"Because I know the river and I'm strong enough to row."

"We can hire a rower if we feel the need."

"Because you're both decent folk who don't kill people who don't deserve it."

"We're not that decent," said Angel. "We leave justice up to the priests."

"You'll take me along because she's my rightful Heptarch, and I'll serve her to the end of my life. I'd die before I let any harm come to her."

The fervency of Sken's speech was convincing. Schooled in guile, they knew naivete when they saw it. Sken hadn't the art to lie to them even if she wanted to.

"Well?" asked Angel.

Patience was willing. Sken's loyalty appealed to her. It hadn't occurred to her until now that she might have more friends with her identity revealed than she could ever have in disguise. "I almost cut off her head before. It's the least we can do now."

"Until we have no more need of you, then," said Angel. "And your parting wages will be a good deal better than death."

"What about these coins?"

"Keep them," said Angel. "They're an earnest of rewards to come."

It took only a few minutes to load the boat. They sang ribald songs together as they passed among the guardboats, and Sken roundly cursed the guards by name. They knew her well, and let her pass. They rounded a bend and passed into the forest, where the river ran cool and deep. Heptam was behind them, and they had begun the long road to Cranning.

7 | TINKER'S WOOD

PATIENCE DID NOT ENJOY THE RIVER TRAVEL. NOT THAT the water made her sick—she had crossed seawater often enough between King's Hill and Lost Souls' Island that the river seemed calm. There were many things that contributed to her malaise. The death of her father, the loss of all that was familiar to her, and, on top of that, the ever-present Cranning call, urging her on; she felt she had lost control of things, and it made her anxious.

What made it worse was that she had genuine physical discomfort as well. Sken and Angel were frank enough about handling the elimination of waste; they hung over the gunnel and everyone discreetly looked away. But Patience had swallowed the scepter of the Heptarchs, and wasn't about to let it vanish in the depths of the River Glad. So she could only relieve her bowel on land, and they didn't stop every day, or even every other day. And when they did, she took no pleasure in searching for the crystal. Many times she wished it had been smaller, or that she hadn't swallowed it. Since no one searched her, it hadn't been necessary after all, and now all this annoyance was for nothing.

But she found it at last, and tucked it safely away, hoping she would never have to resort to her own alimentary system as a hiding place again.

They left the Glad River at Wanwood, where it bent north and west. They bought a half-open carriage with four horses; they wouldn't need to keep out the cold, only the rain. The roads alternated between ruts and mudholes, depending on the weather. On the worst roads, Sken climbed off the carriage and walked.

"I thought you were well enough padded to withstand a little bouncing," said Angel.

"Padded! This is all meat, and tender as veal today, after this pounding."

No doubt they seemed an odd family, if anyone on the road took them for father, mother, and son. Patience, still disguised as a boy, publicly referred to Angel and Sken as uncle and aunt, which annoyed them both. But on the highway, few people commented on oddities, not to their faces, anyway; and their money won them admirers wherever they went.

The roads were not as safe as the river, not for travelers without armed escort. They were careful to stop for the night well before dusk, and in every inn they stayed at, the three of them shared a room. More than once Angel had to persuade burglars to abandon their life of crime. Removing a few fingers usually did the trick.

At last they reached Cranwater, the great river that flowed from Skyfoot in a single stream to the sea. They reached it at Waterkeep, an ancient castle that once marked the northest boundary of Korfu. Now the castle was in ruins and the city had shrunk to a fair-sized market town. Two dozen inns and taverns, what with the intersection of the river and the road.

They chose an inn and stabled the horses. At supper, with bread and cheese and pea soup at the tavern table, and Sken's mug filled with warm ale, Angel and Patience discussed their plans for the morning.

"It's time we left the road," said Angel. "The river is here, our highway northward."

"The river's narrow here," said Sken. "The current's strong. I'd need two strong men to help me row against it."

Angel had already thought of that. "The prevailing wind in these latitudes at this time of year is from the west, and usually the southwest."

"You're going to buy a windsucker?" asked Sken.

"Do you know how to pilot one?"

"I was wrapped in sailcloth the day I was born," said Sken. "Long before I settled me on the river with my second husband, my family was a seafaring family. Left our stilts every spring with the floods and a cargo of such stuff as Heptam makes, then home again before summer with the earliest fruits from the islands. Never got rich, as I recall it, but we got drunk a lot."

"Then you know how to handle a sailing vessel."

"Never done it on a river this narrow. But no reason it can't be done. Just have to do things faster, that's all. Don't buy too big a boat, that's all. You'd better let me choose it, too."

"Is that all?"

"That's all. Are you two made of money?"

A dwelf stood by their table with a pitcher of ale. "More?" he asked.

"No," said Angel.

"Yes," said Sken, glaring at him.

"Are you two made of money?" asked the dwelf. He had Sken's intonation exactly.

"Now look what you've done," said Angel. "We'll have the dwelf repeating it all over the tavern."

"Repeat repeat," said the dwelf. Then he giggled.

Angel put a couple of coppers in his hand, turned him around, and pushed him toward the kitchen.

"Sorry," said Sken.

"Even if dwelfs have no brains, they still have ears, and they can repeat anything." Angel let his annoyance show. It could be intimidating, and Sken was silent.

"Dwelfs are a puzzle," said Patience. "They do have their own language. They must have some kind of brain, to hold a language."

Angel shrugged. "I never ponder the mental capacity of dwelfs. I just think of them as exceptionally stupid geblings."

"But they aren't geblings, are they?"

"Another indigenous species. Imakulata needed humans, whether the geblings and dwelfs and gaunts thought so or not."

The innkeeper came out of the kitchen carrying bread to another table. But when that job was done, he came over and pulled up a chair beside Angel.

"Everything is excellent," said Sken. She was beginning to be drunk. "Everything is perfect. More ale, please."

The innkeeper was not amused. "I don't know where you people are from—probably Heptam, since you seem to think nothing can harm you."

"There are plenty of things that can harm us in Heptam," said Angel.

"There isn't a tavern in Waterkeep where you can safely show as much money as you've shown, and talk as freely. I hope you aren't planning to travel from here by road."

"Shouldn't we?" asked Angel.

"Better hire a trustworthy guard. Preferably by arranging with the townmaster for some of the local police. Otherwise you won't get ten miles from here alive."

"What is the unbearable danger?"

"Robbers."

"Is that all?"

"All? There's plenty of trade through here, and not much protection. Officially we're part of Pankos, but we haven't seen a royal officer in thirty years. So the townmaster makes the law in Waterkeep, and Tinker makes the law in the woods."

"Tinker?"

"He used to be a royal governor, or maybe just a royal governor's son. They say he was caught sleeping in the wrong bed. That was fifteen years ago. He lives in the forest north of here. They say he has a whole city of robbers living in treehouses. We call it Tinker's Wood."

"Sounds like children playing," said Angel.

"If you go south or east or west they'll stop you, and as long as you give them everything you own without a fight, they'll usually let you keep your clothes and your lives. If you have enough money, even your horses and carriage."

"And if we go north?"

"Then take an army. A very large one. Or go by boat. Tinker figures anyone headed north by road has decided to die. And he believes that death can be a long and satisfying spectator sport."

"You've convinced us," said Angel. "And thank you for taking the risk of angering him, by warning us."

"Oh, he doesn't mind if we warn people. There's always plenty of fools who figure if they buy a few extra arrows they can go where they like."

"I can go anywhere," mumbled Sken. "I'll cut em in half, every last bastard of em."

"Go by boat," said the innkeeper. "And don't go anywhere near shore for at least thirty miles upriver. It's good advice. People who take it live to thank me."

The innkeeper went back to the kitchen.

"Back to the water," said Sken. "About time." She lifted her mug to salute the others and sloshed ale on Angel. They enlisted the help of the four household dwelfs to get her to her room.

On the dock the next morning they found a good many boats for hire, but not many for sale. "Doesn't matter," murmured Angel. "Any boat is for sale when the price is high enough."

"Our money isn't infinite," said Patience. "We may want some next year."

"Do you want to get to Cranning or not?"

Yes, she wanted to get to Cranning. Wanted to more than anything else in the world. The Cranning call was with her now as a constant hunger. As long as she was moving toward Cranning, it eased, and she felt satisfied. But when there were delays, like now, as they walked on the wooden wharf of the riverport, the need became quite intense.

Today, though, she noticed a subtle change. It wasn't just that she needed to get to Cranning. Now she felt a longing to be on the water, to travel up the river. The morning sunlight dancing on the water looked magical, the curve of the river enticed her.

And it occurred to her that she had never felt such feelings before. She hadn't particularly enjoyed the journey on the Glad River. Why should she long for water-borne travel now?

She thought of last night, when the innkeeper had come to them. Perhaps he advised everyone to avoid Tinker's Wood, but she doubted it. The people of Waterkeep had to have some working arrangement with the local highwaymen, especially since they had no protection from a larger government. If the innkeeper was free to warn away travelers, then the robbers must not be very dangerous after all. And if the robbers were as dangerous as he had said, then how did he dare to risk his life to warn a trio of rich and foolish strangers away from the road?

What could it be but the Cranning call, prompting the innkeeper and now making her long to go by water. For some reason, Unwyrm—whoever he was—wanted her not to travel on the forest road. Was it simply to keep her safe? Or was it because there was something in that forest, along that road, that she must not discover?

Am I not a trained killer? And Angel? Sken, too, looks like she could be dangerous enough. Even if the robbers are as vicious as the innkeeper said, we could probably get through. And if Unwyrm wants us not to go that way, then that is the way I will go.

In the moment she made that decision, she felt an agony of regret. How could she even have thought of doing such a stupid thing? Risking the lives of all three of them on some stupid whim. When the water looked so inviting, was so easy, just to sail upriver—

And now she knew, through the cloud of these passions, that Unwyrm wanted desperately for her to stay off the forest road. She also knew that regardless of the cost, she would travel by land. The gnawing hunger for Cranning and for the river only got worse, but hadn't she been schooled all her life in putting off her ease? Hadn't she gone without sleep, without food, without water, in order to stretch her limits, to toughen her resistance? She could ignore any of her body's hungers, especially when she knew that it was an illusion sent into her mind by an enemy.

Or was it an enemy? It didn't matter. She was determined not to succumb to the Cranning call in every particular. She would go to Cranning, but she would take any route she pleased. She would not be controlled.

"This one," said Sken. The boat was small, compared to some of the sailing vessels, but it looked clean and sturdy.

"All right," said Angel.

"No," said Patience.

Sken was annoyed. "What's wrong with it?"

"Nothing. Except that I'm not going by boat."

Angel drew her away from Sken. "Are you out of your mind?" he whispered.

"Probably. But I'm not going by boat. I'm taking our carriage through the forest road."

"It's suicide. Didn't you hear the innkeeper?"

"I heard him very well. I also hear the Cranning call. He wants me to go by water. Wants it badly. I'm going to find out what it is that he doesn't want me to find in the forest."

"Death, that's what he doesn't want you to find."

"Are you sure? I think he's a little too eager to get us off the road. This isn't the best place to begin a sailing voyage upriver—the current's too swift. Sken said so herself, didn't she?"

"It's better than dying."

"Since when have you been afraid of a few highwaymen, Angel?"

"Since I thought of dozens of them dropping out of trees onto our heads. I'm trained to kill unsuspecting people in subtle ways, not fight with a bunch of unmannered thieves."

"You haven't met them. You know nothing about their manners."

"Did it occur to you that maybe this is just what Unwyrm wants you to do? Maybe the creature knows that you're stubborn and rebellious. Maybe it wants you to go into the forest, and figured this was the way."

"A little far-fetched, Angel."

"Maybe it wants the robbers to get rid of your traveling companions."

He was as much as confessing that he feared for his own life. The Cranning call resonated with his words. The feelings welled up in her. How can you endanger them? What kind of person are you? Selfish, arrogant. Go by water, for their sake.

But the more the Cranning call pressed her, the more she resisted. "Go by boat, then. I'll meet you in the first riverport village upstream. I can handle the carriage alone. You can even take all the money—I trust you."

"No," said Angel. His hands were trembling. "No, I won't leave you."

He really is afraid, thought Patience. Almost she decided to give in, for Angel's sake. But the moment she thought that, the Cranning call redoubled its force, as if her thought of yielding had opened a floodgate. She winced from the pain of it. Then the longing subsided, as if it had taken a great effort from Unwyrm to call her with such power. Good, thought Patience. Wear yourself out with trying. I didn't go without comfort all that time in my childhood just to give in and take the easy way now.

"Good. We go by land."

Sken was no happier than Angel had been.

"You don't have to come with me," Patience said. "You've served me well and earned your passage home."

"We need all the help we can get," Angel said. "I'll double your payment, if you come with us."

Sken looked at him with contempt. "I'll come because of who she is, not what you offer."

Angel smiled. Patience knew perfectly well that Angel had expected Sken to react that way. The art of diplomacy, as Father had always said: to provoke your opponent into wanting to do what you planned. Angel was a diplomat. Unwyrm wasn't. Unwyrm was very blunt about what he wanted, and Patience was just as blunt about rejecting him. There was no subtle byplay in this battle.

They left the dock and went to the stable. Their horses had been well groomed—Angel had paid for the service, since he was expecting to sell them.

Patience prepared her blowgun with three dozen wooden darts. They were more visible than her glass darts, but they flew farther and carried as lethal a dose of poison. Angel grumbled about being an old man as he took a shortbow and a packet of arrows from his trunk. "I'm not very good with this," he said. "I'm better with knifework in close."

"From behind, too, no doubt," said Sken.

"I can poison them all, too," said Angel. "Provided they invite us to supper."

"Poison and a knife in the back. What a man."

"Enough," said Patience. "This will be dangerous enough without a stupid quarrel over nothing." She spoke sharply, letting her voice carry away some of the ever-increasing punishment the Cranning call was inflicting on her. Just climbing into the carriage made her feel ill; she was trembling and nauseated as Angel snapped the reins to start the horses out onto the cobbled lane. The stones were ancient and worn even and flat by years of traffic, but Patience felt the tiny breaks between them like ruts that jarred her until her head ached.

But she had learned all her lessons well. She kept her demeanor calm, managing to look slightly amused at moments that were far from amusing. She would not break under Unwyrm's twisting grip. She would not let Angel see that she suffered. If she could fool Angel, she knew she was still in control of herself.

The town was not very big, and soon the highway passed between fields of vegetables and orchards, where farmers hoed or harvested among the ruins of old mansions that had once been the pride of Waterkeep. It was part of the cycle of things, in the years of human life on Imakulata. Waterkeep had once been great; it would be great again, or it would disappear entirely, but nothing stayed. Even the religions had their changing fashions, the Keepers and the Brickmakers, the Rememberers and the Watchers, and, only in the last century, the Vigilants in their little hermit huts. They would also fall to ruin. Nothing lasted.

Except the bloodline of the Heptarchy, which had gone on unbroken, the only institution that endured through all the millennia of mankind on Imakulata. It was a thing unknown in human history. She tried to remember anything comparable. The Romans were only a thousand years by the most generous count; the Popes only lasted some 2500 years. Even the patriarchate of Constantinople was gone now, though it had lasted long enough in a perverse and polluted form to send this colony to Imakulata. The colonists on Imakulata were supposed to keep Greek religion alive, though none of them spoke Greek or cared much, in the end, about maintaining the forms of the old Greek church. Nothing lasted except the Heptarchy.

Until now, thought Patience. Now this distant being, this enemy, this Unwyrm tears at me. It is the end of the Heptarchy if he conquers me. And if I keep resisting him, it is the end of me.

Orchards began to give way to stands of wood. Here and there a tiny village interrupted the growing forest, with a few cows on the commons, a few farmers in the fields, and children who shouted at the carriage and ran alongside until they couldn't keep up any longer. Sken cursed them loudly, which delighted them, and Patience pretended to enjoy it, though she was beyond anything but the imitation of pleasure now. Angel, however, stayed glum, urging the horses on at a brisk pace.

Finally, in early afternoon, the trees won out entirely, as the road become closed in with thick underbrush and old giants ten or twenty meters round. It was a perfect place for ambuscade, and Patience felt a new wave of shame at having led them into such danger.

They came to a long straight lane through the densest part of the woods. At the far end of the lane they could plainly see a thick rope stretched across the road, at such a height that it would catch the horses' necks.

"Brazen, aren't they?" said Sken. "They give us plenty of time to see what's coming."

"I'm turning around," said Angel.

At his words Patience felt grateful assent well up within her. But she had learned discipline. And her resistance to Unwyrm had become a madness in her now, as the pain of it became greater. "Go back if you want," she said. "I'm going on."

She had her glass blowgun in the cross beneath her shirt; it and the loop were her weapons of last resort if she were captured. She carried a longer, more accurate wooden blowgun. The darts, all heavily poisoned, were in a pouch. She could handle them safely enough; her father had seen to it she was inured to the most useful poisons before she was ten years old. She swung down from the carriage and strode out boldly toward the waiting rope.

Sken cursed, but followed her with a hatchet in each hand. And Angel grimly brought the carriage along after. "They can kill us whenever they want," he said.

"Watch the trees," said Patience. "The innkeeper said they liked torturing people. They'll try to take us alive."

"Now I feel better," said Sken.

"The rope is yours," said Patience.

"It's as good as down."

Patience scanned the underbrush, the trees overhead. The leaves were sparse enough to allow plenty of light; there was a slight breeze, too, which concealed any signs of movement by the robbers. Patience saw only a couple of men high in the branches. Bowmen, no doubt. But it was not an easy thing to aim a bow to shoot almost straight down at a moving target; if the archers in the trees hit any of them, it would be more by chance than design.

What worried her were the men on the ground, no doubt dozens of them hiding behind trees. They could swarm out from any direction. She slipped a dart into the blowgun and held three in her right hand.

They were still a few meters from the rope when four men stepped out from behind a tree and stood in the middle of the road, behind the rope. They swaggered, they smiled, they knew their victims had no chance. One stepped forward, preparing to speak. Patience knew that as he talked, others would come out and surround them. So there would be no talk. She blew a puff through the pipe. She had aimed for the throat, but the dart went high and entered his mouth. He stood, transfixed, the dart invisible to his companions behind him. So she had time to load again and shook before they realized what was happening. The second dart struck its victim in the forehead; the first man finally gagged and choked and fell over, writhing from the poison that was already reaching his brain. The other two men backed away, surprised for a moment that the initiative had been taken from them.

Sken moved slowly, but with great momentum, and one blow with her hatchet split the rope. Immediately Angel urged the horses forward, Sken swung up onto the carriage, and Patience jogged alongside, then caught hold.

The carriage bounced over the bodies in the road. She heard a voice in the underbrush saying, "The boy got Tinker. With his mouth."

For a moment it seemed they might be allowed to pass. Then the men began to shout, to scream, and arrows began striking the carriage from behind. Angel urged the horses on, shouted at them, and then suddenly gurgled and choked. An arrow stuck out of the side of his neck. Many hands clutched at the horses; the carriage came to a stop.

Patience had no time to worry about Angel. Fortunately the robbers wasted time cutting the horses loose. Patience ignored the horses and shouted for Sken to do the same. Sken took the left side of the carriage, swinging her hatchets and spattering blood in every direction. They backed off from Sken, perhaps hoping an archer would take care of her, but Patience kept blowing darts with deadly aim—at this range, she could hardly miss—and those who weren't killed outright screamed in such agony at the poison that the robbers began to lose heart. After all, their commander had been killed, they had already lost a dozen men, with some vicious injuries from the hatchets, and every dart that hit home meant another death. They cried out terrible threats and oaths, but broke and ran as the darts kept coming.

Sken had a deep cut in the back of one arm. "I'm all right," she said. "We've got to get out of here. They'll be back, they'll follow us, we've got to keep moving."

"Can you pull the carriage?"

"Better to run; what good will all your money do you if you're dead?"

"Angel's still alive. The only way to bring him is in the carriage."

Sken looked at the arrow in his throat, grunted, then

took her place at the front of the carriage. "Just keep a good lookout," she said.

Angel's wound wasn't bleeding much, and Patience knew to leave the shaft in place until they had time to try surgery. Unless they could find a good-sized town with an expert physician, though, there wasn't much hope for him. She should go back, hurry back to Waterkeep, where there would be a physician. And they could continue their trip by water, after Angel was better.

But she recognized this thought, too, as coming from Unwyrm. Or did she? Maybe it was common sense, maybe what she was doing with this determination to resist was killing Angel. How could she push on, not even knowing if there *was* a village ahead, when this loyal man, her teacher, virtually the only father she had ever really known, lay dying in the carriage?

On. She held that single thought in her head, go on. Go on. She scanned the road ahead and behind, watching for robbers or for one of the horses. Once a man stepped into the road behind them, armed with a bow; he died before he could get off a shot. There were no others. Perhaps they had given up. It didn't matter. For Angel's sake there could be no slackening of the pace.

She tried to join Sken in pulling the carriage. "Go away," said the woman. "You break up my rhythm. Keep watching."

And finally the trees thinned, and there was an orchard, and after the orchard, a field; villagers shouted to each other and began to gather.

"Tinker let you through?" asked a child.

"Have you a healer!" called Sken.

"Not a village healer," Patience said.

"They sometimes know more than the town physicians," she answered. "And if they have one, so much the better for the old man."

"We have a healer," said a man. "A gebling. But a fine healer all the same."

"Can you pull this carriage?" asked Sken. "Can you pull this to the healer? We can pay."

"Tinker left you with money?"

Patience was tired of hearing his name. "Tinker's dead," she said. "Take us to the healer."

"The boy's a pretty one," said one of the girls, a snaggle-toothed wretch who was trying to flirt. Patience sighed and climbed onto the carriage. Angel's eyes were open now. She held his hand to ease the fear he no doubt felt. "We're with friends," she said.

The villagers took hold of the carriage leads, and some pushed from behind. Sken gratefully climbed aboard. A strange feeling came over Patience as soon as the carriage started to move again, a feeling of sweetness, of peace. All the resistance from Unwyrm was gone. And now the Cranning call was back again, a yearning to go on, to go north, to Cranning. Where her lover waited for her, with gentleness and tender kisses, her lover waited to fill her womb with life. Patience forced these new feelings into the background, just as she had done with the old, more vicious ones. Unwyrm now wants to hurry me on. So apparently I'm right where he didn't want me to be. Heading for a gebling healer in a village hidden from the world by a band of robbers. Unwyrm couldn't have guided her here more surely if he had given her a map. Have I done, after all, what my enemy wanted? Or have I defeated him?

"There," cried some of the villagers. It was a good-sized house at the far end of town.

"He lives there with his sister," said a villager.

"And a human, a giant."

"They say the geblings sleep together," said another.

"Filthy beasts."

"But he's a healer, a true healer."

"What is his name?" asked Patience.

"Ruin," said a man.

Sken snorted. "That's a promising name."

Smoke curled from the chimney. Pass it by, said the Cranning call. Hurry on. Angel will be safe. Go on, pass it by, pass it by.

The door opened and a gebling woman emerged, covered with fur. She was clean, not filthy at all, beautiful by gebling standards. There was an intelligence in her eyes that made Patience decided to be wary with her. No sense in letting her know that she could speak Geblic. This house was important enough that Unwyrm didn't want her there. So she would enter it as an ambassador, and learn all she could before committing herself to anything.

And in the meantime, she hoped against all likelihood that Angel could be saved. Blood oozed from the arrow's root as the villagers carried him in. Patience thought of scattering copper coins for them, but instead took a steel coin and handed it to the old man who seemed to be the village headman. "For the whole village, for your kindness to us." The old man smiled and nodded, and people murmured their thanks. It was more money than the whole village earned in a year.

8 THE GEBLINGS' HOUSE

RECK HEARD THE VILLAGERS COMING WHEN THEY WERE STILL well away from her little house. There was an excitement in the murmur that the wind brought. She cocked her head to hear better. Could it be a gobbing? No, there was no anger in it. This wasn't a village that was given to letting the priests stir them up against the geblings. Which was not to say that it wasn't always a possibility. One never knew when humans would get religion and start killing.

But why the excitement, if they were coming for a healing? Someone important needed physicking, then, someone unusual or powerful. A stranger, of course, since no one unusual or powerful had ever lived anywhere near Waterside Village—one of a hundred villages by that name along the shores of Cranwater alone. The stranger must also be injured, not sick, for disease never drew a crowd for long. Fear of contagion.

Reck went to the door and called to Will. He was in the field, hoeing out the potatoes. He heard her, waved, tossed the hoe onto the sledge and pulled the heavy burden along the ground toward the barn. He was a tall man, a giant even by human standards; to a gebling he was almost double size. He had once been an owned soldier, a slave in the service of a general officer in one army or another. He was an accomplished killer, and stronger than any other man Reck had heard of.

But Reck had no fear of him. She had found him as a runaway slave many years ago and offered him protection and a place to farm. It was enough for him. He and Reck made a pleasant enough life of it. Neither said much to the other, because neither had much to say. Both did their work dependably and well, and took pleasure in the labor.

Still, they were wise enough to be discreet. After all these years it was no secret in the village that there was a giant man living with the geblings near the forest's edge. But they didn't enrage the villagers by flaunting it, just kept Will out of sight when people brought their sick and injured to be healed. It was not a problem with them. Will got the sledge in the barn and no doubt climbed into the loft to sleep until the people went away. Will had a remarkable ability to sleep whenever he wanted, for as long as he wanted. Reck often wondered if Will was ever haunted by the dreams that kept her sleepless so many nights. She wondered, but did not ask. Dreams were not a subject that a gracious gebling asked about.

She saw the people drawing a carriage toward her house. No horses. That meant that the owners of the carriage had fallen afoul of the robbers—Tinker's men, no doubt. That was no surprise. The surprise was that anyone came out of it alive. Tinker was usually more careful.

She sniffed the air. Blood, but no bowel smell. Perhaps only a superficial wound, something she could clean and bind up without waiting for her brother to come home.

There was a young boy in the carriage, sitting up and conversing with the villagers. He seemed to be in charge of things. An old man lay with his head in the boy's lap. A coarse-looking fat woman rode in the driver's seat, calling to the villagers who drew the carriage, urging them on with curses and promises and taunts. It was the old man who was injured, then. Only the one? And a young boy like that—Tinker always had his eye out for a catamite. Something strange had passed in the forest. Unlikely that Tinker was alive, with an outcome such as this. Whatever they were, they must be more formidable than they looked at first. That was all right; Reck understood that. She, too, was more formidable than she seemed.

She met them at the gate. "Carry the man in, if he can't walk," she said. "Leave the carriage there, and the rest of you go home."

"They killed Tinker," one of the villagers said.

"And half his men."

The fat woman was feeling boastful. "I killed half of em myself, and you can trust there was a mark or two on every one!" Could be bluster, but no. Reck saw bloodstains halfway up her arms. Some of the blood was her own. "You can wash in the basin outside here. Get that wound clean."

The fat woman washed as the villagers brought in the old man and laid him on the physicking table. The boy and the fat woman came in to watch; Reck paid no attention to them. The man had an arrow in his throat, lodged well in. It had passed behind the windpipe, so he had pain but no blood in his breath.

Blood was still welling slowly from the base of the wound. Reck leaned down and sniffed it, then put forth her long tongue to lick it. She heard the fat woman grunt in revulsion. The boy said nothing. There's something wrong with the boy, thought Reck. But she couldn't place it. More important was the taste of the old man's blood.

"Poison," Reck told them. "A nasty one. This wound won't heal. The blood won't stop flowing."

"Then we don't take the arrow out?" asked the fat woman.

"You were right to leave it in."

"What will you do?" asked the boy.

"Nothing." Reck turned to the villagers. "Go away, I told you. You've done all you can!"

"You'll do nothing!" said the boy. "Then we'll go on to the next village, thank you." The boy spoke in a voice that said that he expected to be obeyed.

Hum, the blacksmith's boy, answered on the way out the door. "Oh, this one's the girl goblin. It's the brother that's the healer."

"A girl!" cried the fat woman. "How can you tell, with goblins?"

"When you see the brother, you'll know. He's got him a tine this long. Never wears nothing but his fur."

Reck was used to the way humans ridiculed geblings to their faces. If geblings had been larger than two-thirds the average human height, they might have refused to bear it. But as long as geblings wanted to live away from Cranning, out in the world of men, they had to accommodate the empty-minded cruelty of humans. Her brother, Ruin, had a harder time bearing it than most. He lived in the woods most of the time, to get away from them, and refused to wear clothing at all, as if to say that he'd rather be the animal they thought he was than pretend to be like them.

"When will your brother come back?" asked the boy.

Reck didn't answer the question. Instead she studied

the boy's face, then sniffed the air again. That's what was wrong. The boy had no ridge of bone above the eyes, like most human males. And there was the smell of menstrual blood on him; the living blood from the old man's wound had masked it. But there was no lying to Reck's nose.

The door closed behind the last of the villagers.

"I said, when will your brother come back?"

"First," said Reck, "tell me who you are, and why you're pretending to be a boy."

Suddenly she felt a strong hand gripping her wrist, twisting her around. It was the old man. She had thought him unconscious, but now he held her like the jaws of a purweck. She might have hit him in the groin and made him let go, but she saw no reason to add to the pain he already had.

"You can fool humans," she said, "but not a gebling with half a brain. What the eye can't see, the nose can smell."

"Let her go," the girl said. "It's my time of month, remember? I forgot that geblings could smell it. It's a gift I wish I had."

The old man's grip relaxed. Reck did not move until he pulled his hand away.

"The old man's name is Angel. He's my tutor and my friend. This magnificent woman is Sken. She included herself with the purchase price when we bought her boat to leave Heptam." The girl smiled. "I was going to tell you my name was Adam, but now that you know my sex, I won't tell you my name at all."

"How do you propose to pay us, if Tinker robbed you?"

"Tinker didn't rob us. He only proposed to rob us. His men ran our horses off, but we gave them more than they expected. We thought to buy more horses here. But it seems no one has horses to sell.''

"The army takes them," Reck said. "To humans, they leave one horse for farming. Geblings get no horse at all.''

"I don't want your horse. I just want Angel healed.''

"My brother is coming.''

"You haven't even sent for him.''

"I don't have to send for him. He knows the animals of the forest. They see all that happens here, and tell him.''

The girl looked over at Sken, as if to say, What kind of superstitious nonsense have we got caught up in here?

The old man murmured, "We aren't villagers. We know that geblings can call each other. You don't have to tell animal stories to us.''

"It's the animals of the forest," Reck said. "But I learned long ago never to argue with a man who thinks he's a scientist.''

"I'm a philosopher. This arrow in my throat hurts like bloody hell.''

"I'm sorry. My brother may be far away. He may be a while in coming. There's nothing we can do.''

"I'm thirsty.''

"The arrow may pass right through your swallowing throat.''

"It does.''

"Then you don't get a drink, either.''

The girl and Sken both sat, then, the girl on a stool and Sken on the floor, leaning against the wall. Reck went back to her work, feathering the arrows she had made yesterday. It was a fine and tedious job, made no easier by the labored, painful breathing of the man on the table.

Will came in soon after, carrying water. He did not

look at the visitors, except for a glance at the man on the table. He set one bucket of water by the fire, and poured the other into a large jar by the table. Only then did he face the visitors.

"Will," he said, introducing himself.

"Sken," said the fat woman.

The girl said nothing.

"You live here?" asked Sken.

Will nodded.

Sken looked from him to Reck and back again. "Abomination," she said.

Will grinned. "I'm her slave," he said.

Sken relaxed a little. "It's foul for a gebling to own a man, but as long as she doesn't get the pony ride—"

"I'd say it's none of your business," said Reck, "and that you have a strange way of talking when you want this man to live."

"I speak my mind," said Sken.

"Then your mind is manure," said Reck.

Sken took only one step toward her. Both Angel and the girl cried out for her to stop. Will cried out also, but to Reck. Despite the cries, however, it was no sound that stopped Sken. It was the sight of Reck with her bow already in place. Only a moment, and she was ready to put an arrow wherever she wanted.

"No, Reck," said Will.

"They come as beggars to my door, and then accuse *me* of letting a human mount me. Though if any human ever tried, you're the only one that might live through it."

Angel spoke weakly from the table. "Forgive this woman. She was raised on the river, and never learned to speak civilly to anyone."

Reck let the bow relax. Sken tugged at the neck of her dress and sat back down, looking into the fire. Goblinbaiting had never brought her so close to death before. The gebling merchants that bought river passage in Heptam were meek and never answered back. This wasn't the first time Sken had had to revise her understanding of the way the world worked. But she never liked it.

Will set about making supper, and Reck resumed her fletchery. Angel breathed ever more shallowly. The girl sat silent in the corner. They remained that way, word less and wary, until dusk, when Ruin came home

9 | THE HEALER

RUIN FELT THE PRESSURE OF UNWYRM'S HATRED LIKE A WIND in his face. He fairly leaned into it, and grimaced at the pain of moving on. Had there been anyone to see him, he would have looked ridiculous, a naked, filthy, ungroomed gebling struggling to move through flat and grassy meadows in bright sunlight, torturing himself to stagger between trees whose branches easily bent out of his way. But always, whenever Ruin set his face toward Cranning, there was a hurricane of resistance. He was the only gebling of all geblings who could not go home.

It was after two grueling days of this—pushing forward, stopping to rest, pressing on again—that he felt Reck's call to him. That loving touch that seemed to press like gentle fingers on his spine—Ruin had never told her how her call affected him; no other gebling had such power over him. Especially now, after days of Unwyrm's shout of rage: The whisper from Reck was unbearable. Ruin stumbled to his knees and wept. Wept in anger— furious at Reck for calling him, furious at himself for not having the strength to ignore her call and fight on.

But he could not fight on. And after he lay in the grass by the stream for a few minutes or an hour, he crawled to the water and drank, then arose. For a moment he faced Cranningward; but the thought of another step in that direction was more than he could bear. He turned and went the other way. His feet were light under him. He loped through the woods and meadows, covering in minutes the ground that he had struggled through for hours. All the while his sister was like a song in his mind, comforting him, calling him back to her.

Calling him, but not calling him home. There was no gebling alive who could call any of their humanlike houses "home." There was only one home for geblings: The great city in the cliff, the mapless tunnels and delvings that reached a mile deep from the face of Skyfoot. Cranning, a city with more inhabitants than most nations, peopled with men and dwelfs and gaunts but ruled by geblings, for only geblings held within their minds the indelible, unwritable memory of every turn of every tunnel in the place. Every stone in every cavern was familiar, even to geblings like Ruin, who had never set his foot on the stone, never tasted the cold water that flowed through the tunnels from the glacier above, never slept under the arch of darkness that was infinitely more comforting than the sky. Where Reck was, Ruin could be at peace; but outside Cranning, he could never be at home.

And while Unwyrm lived, how could Ruin ever get there? It was the quandary of his life, ever since he was a child and his mother explained who he was and what he had to do. "You are the most excellent of excellent blood, you and your sister, with the seeds of mastery in your souls. There is nothing you cannot learn, nothing you cannot do, no thought that cannot come into your mind like light out of the storm. You were born to be the best answer of the geblings to the terrible hatred of Unwyrm, our only hope to slay him, the two of you."

"Where do I find him?" asked the child Ruin.

"He lives at the heart of Cranning, where the lifeblood flows. He lives in the very womb of the geblings, the viper in our womb, to devour our babies as they are born."

"Then teach me the way to Cranning, Mother, so I can go and kill him!"

Then Mother wept, her long tongue hanging dejectedly from her mouth, its twin points glistening with her tears. "How can you, of all geblings, not already know the way? Ah, Ruin and Reck, my son, my daughter, we made you to be the downfall of our enemy, but already he knows you and hides Cranning from you in your own mind."

When Mother died, Ruin and Reck wandered aimlessly in the world for a time. Each of them at once rejected and prepared for the work their mother had taught them they must do. Reck learned the arts of archery and could kill anything that she could see—but she refused to search for Cranning, denying that the place meant anything to her. She mocked Ruin for his endless effort to reach the place. "All dreams and visions," she said, "all foolish prophecies." But still she practiced with the bow in all her spare hours, and studied all the lore of Unwyrm that she could find among the geblings who traveled the river and came to take the hospitality of her house.

Ruin, in turn, would not become a killer. Instead he learned the arts of healing. He wandered in the woods, testing the herbs that grew there, using them to heal the sick and broken animals, the wounds caused by men and other beasts. When an herb was promising, he grew and nurtured it, taught it more of what he wanted it to do, and soon he had herbs that could drive away infections, root powders that could cure disease, berries that took away all pain. And he knew the inward shape of every body just by looking at its outward lines. The lizard and the lyon, the rubin and the grouse, he knew them, could cut them open and set them to rights. He could never have set his knowledge down in books, like humans did. Poor humans—they lacked the othermind, the secret memory in which geblings hid their great learning even from themselves. If you asked Ruin what was wrong with one of his many patients, he could not tell you, for his manmind, his wordmind—it knew nothing of healing. His wordmind could only speak, could only remember sights and sounds; he had no use for it. It was his othermind that he trusted, his othermind that he let rule him, and his othermind that held all his greatest gifts.

Except it was also his othermind that Unwyrm had found and forced away from Cranning. Only his weak and hated manmind could drive him forward, again and again, struggling for control of his legs and arms, in the endless vertical climb to meet his enemy. And when I meet him, what will I do? What am I fit for, except to be the first of my people to be devoured?

It was near nightfall and Ruin was bitter with failure when he reached the house he shared with Reck. He knew from the smell that there were humans inside, knew also that it was the old man who was injured and the young woman who most loved and feared for him. The fat woman was just a pile of sweat; he disregarded her. There was also the smell of Will, but Ruin disregarded him, too. If his sister wished to keep a human instead of an ox, that was her prerogative. Ruin never spoke to Will, and Will returned the favor.

Reck greeted him without a touch or a smile. There

had been anger here. Ruin questioned her in Geblic. "Why do you let them stay, if they offend you?"

"The girl," said Reck. "Tell me you can't feel it, what she does to Unwyrm, being here."

Ruin strode to the boy-dressed girl, sitting on the floor in the corner. Yes, he could feel it too, like prickles on his spine. Near her, Unwyrm was not driving them away at all. He was calling. It was something Ruin had never felt before, though he had heard of it: the Cranning call. It was unbelievably strong, like the promise of sexual pleasure, like a mother's love for a child. Ruin knelt and put his face close to the girl's face. He ignored her revulsion, ignored the hand that went up to her hair.

The fat woman shouted from by the fire. "Keep that filthy beast away from her or I'll kill him myself!"

"Quiet," murmured the girl. "He has more to fear from me than I from him." Ruin felt her breath on his cheek, and it seemed to be a warm breeze from Cranning, which called him now for the first time in his life.

"A naked gebling coming at a girl like that," grumbled the reeking old dunghill. "Time was when goblins knew their place."

Reck called him back to duty. "The fat woman who loves geblings is Sken. The man who is dying is Angel."

Ruin pulled himself away from the girl. It was almost a physical pain, when the Cranning call receded. Standing well away from her, though, it still had power over him, for the constant pressure of Unwyrm's hate was slackened. Ruin had never realized how much of his othermind Unwyrm had been using up. Now as he examined the wound, the understanding of it came so quickly and clearly that he could almost—not quite, but almost—bring it into his wordmind and explain it to himself. For the first time he realized what he might become if Unwyrm were dead.

Angel was unconscious. It meant Ruin would not have to waste time drugging him to sleep. He tasted the wound, which was still oozing blood. He knew the poison—one of the childish weeds that the woodland robbers were so proud of. It was the arrow itself that worried Ruin more. It had done some tearing on the way in and would do more coming out. The man's eating throat would not heal well, and he might starve to death before he could swallow again.

"I'll have to cut him," said Ruin, again in Geblic. "To let him heal inside. You tell the humans." He knew enough Agarant to make himself understood, but it was easier to let Reck deal with the humans. He much preferred communicating with the animals that didn't think themselves intelligent.

While Reck told the others what Ruin would do, he found the fungus spores that would undo the poison, chose a thin brass knife from his toolbox, and gently drew a long, fine strand from the wireweed in the window planter. There had been no metal in the soil, so it was all organic, and would eventually dissolve inside the body. He put the blade and the wireweed in his mouth with a sprig of claffroot, to sterilize them. Then, in a swift motion, he cut deeply in the man's throat, above and below the arrow. Ruin dipped his tongue in the fungus spores and then inserted his tongue in the incisions, deep within the wound, where the arrow's poison still prevented the clotting of blood. It would take only a few minutes for the spores to do their work, feeding on the poison and then producing their own bloodbinder to help in the clotting of the blood.

While he waited, he talked to Reck—in Geblic, of course, so the humans wouldn't understand. "The girl—who is she, and why is Unwyrm calling her?"

"How should I know?" asked Reck.

"You're the one who knows all the wyrmlore. She's too young to be one of the Wise."

"Maybe she's wise beyond her years. I think she's more dangerous than she looks. She isn't afraid of anything. She said nothing of it, but I think she's the one who killed most of Tinker's men."

"With her bare hands?"

"You know the human woman that Unwyrm wants. The Vigilants tell everyone the prophecy of the seventh seventh seventh daughter—"

"I pay no attention to humans, least of all to their religions."

"The seventh seventh seventh daughter was born fifteen years ago, to the deposed Heptarch of Korfu, which claims to rule the world. She could be of that age."

"It's too much to believe that of all the ways to Cranning, he would lead her right to us."

The spores had done their work; the bleeding stopped. Ruin took hold of the arrowshaft and jerked it out. The man cried out in his sleep. More blood flowed, but again the spores sealed off the wound. Ruin hooked his finger around the tattered esophagus and pulled it to where he could see it. Then he deftly made vertical cuts, removing the torn edges.

While he sewed the wounds with the wireweed, he spoke to Reck in Geblic. "It doesn't matter if she's the one or not, though, does it? She won't go to Cranning without us."

"I have no interest in Cranning," said Reck.

"You're as much in this as I am," said Ruin. "He presses you away as much as me."

"Except I don't try to go there, so it doesn't hurt me. You shouldn't try either, Ruin. Why do you think our family has stayed in exile all these generations, if not to be far from Cranning at just this time?"

"But he wants us to stay away. That changes everything. Every other time, he wanted the king to be there with him."

"So we go just because he doesn't want us to? Then he controls us as surely as he ever did."

"Every other time, Sister, he wanted to use the geblings to destroy whatever it was the humans had been building. He hasn't the strength to compel us all, but he compelled the king, and the king called the others to the common task. This time, though, it's all different. He doesn't plan to have the geblings act together. Perhaps he plans for us *not* to act together. And that's why we have to go."

"Give up the governing purpose of our ancestors, on a guess?"

"The ancestor who first made this plan had been in Unwyrm's control. That's why he decided on exile. But how can we be sure our exile wasn't what Unwyrm wanted him to decide?"

"There's no way out of that circle, Brother. Who knows if anything we do will play into his hands?"

"You see? So we decide for other reasons. And here is one: without Unwyrm's breath in my face, Sister, I can finally breathe. Whether Unwyrm means it that way or not, she can take us through to him."

"Until the moment he stops calling her."

"It all depends on whether he wants her more than he fears us."

"So you believe she's the one."

"Maybe fortune smiles on us." Ruin finished with the esophagus and put it back in place. "Tell her that his throat will heal in a few days. It'll be tighter than it was. He'll have to chew his food."

Reck turned and, in Agarant, gave the news to the others. Ruin was still sewing up the outside wound, this time using common thread, when Reck finished and touched his shoulder.

"Does it make a difference to you whether the girl knows our plans or not?"

"How would she know?" asked Ruin, tying off the thread.

"Because I just discovered that she understands Geblic."

Ruin turned and looked at the girl. Her face was blank. "What makes you think so?"

"Because she was already relieved about Angel before I told her he would be all right. And then she pretended to be relieved again after I told her. But her sweat was all wrong."

Ruin grinned at the girl, letting his tongue hang out a little. He knew how the slender forked tongue of a gebling unnerved human beings, though in fact she showed no sign that it bothered her. He spoke to her in Geblic. "Never try to deceive a gebling, human. You're the true Heptarch's daughter, aren't you?"

The girl answered as smoothly and easily as if they had been conversing all day, and Ruin noticed that she spoke Geblic without a trace of the awkwardness humans often had in trying to form sounds with their blunt and stubby tongues. "No, sir. I am the Heptarch."

So her father was dead. Ruin felt no sympathy for the death of a human. Humans put on a good show of grieving, but they didn't really understand the bonding of a true family. They had no othermind, and could speak only in words. They remained strangers from each other all their lives. What was the life of a creature like this? So he offered no commiseration. "You know the payment that I want for your friend's life."

"He's my slave, not my friend," she said.

"You'll take me with you. You'll make no effort to go without me."

"Maybe I'm not going where you think I'm going."

"You're going to Cranning to destroy my people, and I'm going to save them."

"Then why not kill me now, and save us both a good deal of trouble?"

"He wants you, but if I killed you he might make do with someone else. At least we know who and where you are. So when Unwyrm brings you to his nest, we'll be there, too. I think that means that we're friends." He smiled at her and let the tips of his tongue show.

Reck stood by the stewpot, the tasting spoon in hand. "Why do you keep saying *we*, when I have no intention of going?"

Ruin did not look at her. "Because you'd never let me face Unwyrm alone."

Reck shrugged. "Will's stew is ready."

Ruin leaned closer to the Heptarch. Though she was sitting and he was standing up, he did not have to bend far for their eyes to meet. "Will you give me your word? In payment for your slave's life?"

"You have my word, but not in payment for anything. Angel's life is his own to repay, and my word is my own to give."

Ruin nodded solemnly. "Then come join us at table."

Reck laughed aloud. "It was worth all this trouble just to see this moment—you, Ruin, inviting a human to eat with you."

"But she's not a human, is she, Reck? She's Unwyrm's woman and the mother of death."

"I am no one's woman," said the girl. "And my name is Patience."

It was Ruin's turn to laugh. "Patience," he said in Agarant. "Come and eat, Patience."

The table was designed for the comfort of geblings. It was too low for Patience to sit on a chair, so she sat on the floor. She was the only human at the table. When Sken took a step toward them, Ruin's look was enough to drive her back to her stool near the fire. Will made no effort to sit. He served them, then took a bowl to Sken.

Ruin noticed that Patience observed all the proper forms of respect. She had been well enough taught that it seemed as natural to her as to a gebling, to offer every few bites from her dish to him or to Reck, and to nibble at the bites they offered her. On those rare occasions when humans were invited to share a gebling meal, they usually showed what a great effort and sacrifice it took to eat from a gebling spoon. But Patience showed nothing but deference and grace. Unwyrm's woman should be loathsome, not gracious, thought Ruin. But it makes no difference. Before all this is over, I'll probably have to kill her after all. What's the death of a human, if it might save my people?

When the food was finished off, they drank hot water from the pot by the fire. Ruin offered to take them through the forest, but Patience would have none of it. "I take my people with me," she said. "When Angel is strong enough, we'll take him in the carriage. If we can find horses to buy."

Reck shrugged. "Buy? Ruin can find your horses tomorrow. He can find anything in the woods."

"Not to pull the carriage, though," he said. "We'd spend all our time dragging it out of mudholes. We'll go to the next human town and sell it and by a boat. The wind is out of the west, and Cranwater is wide and flat. The roads are the worst way to Cranning."

So it was agreed. The only argument came later, in the darkness, when Ruin lay beside his sister and she told him she meant to bring Will along.

"What is he to you?" asked Ruin for the thousandth

time. "Is he your lover, now? Do you want to bear his little monsters?"

She never answered such accusations. She only said, "He is my friend, and if I go, he goes too."

"So the giant comes with us. We'd better buy a large boat. There are too many of us already. And too many humans altogether." Then he fell to making obscene suggestions about what Will and Reck did whenever Ruin was away. She didn't answer, and he only stopped when her breathing told him that she had fallen asleep. It was hardly worth trying to make her angry anymore.

10 | CRANWATER

THEY WERE NOT THE HAPPIEST PARTY EVER TO SET OUT FOR
Cranning. Angel was too weak from hunger and loss of
blood to do more than endure the jolting of the road.
Though he could, painfully, drink milk from the farm-
houses they passed, it would take time for him to come
back up to strength, and even when he was conscious, he
listened to the conversations of the others and almost
never tried to speak. When they stopped at inns along the
way, Patience fed him gruel in his room while the others
ate at the common table. And the geblings slept in his
room through the night, taking turns watching over him
when, asleep, he clawed at the pain in his throat.

If Angel was silent, then Sken seemed never to stop
speaking. She grumbled about everything that went wrong,
and though she never said a word to or about the geblings
if she could help it, she made it plain that she loathed
them. She had a way of sniffing the air when Ruin was
near. And whenever Patience and the geblings spoke
"that jabbering noise," she grew sullen and threw nut-
shells at the horses' backs with particular vehemence.

139

Not Sken's surliness, not even Angel's misery ever engaged Patience's attention for long, however. She was caught up in other concerns. The Cranning call grew stronger in her every day, often distracting her from whatever she was doing or thinking. And the call was changing form as well. It was no longer just an urgency in her mind. Now it was a hunger in her body.

Night, in an inn not far from the river Cranwater. She dreamed a deep and powerful and terrifying and beautiful dream.

"Patience," whispered Sken.

Sken was shaking her. It was still dark. Was there some danger? Patience reached for the loop in her hair.

"No!" Sken tried to push her back down onto her mat.

Sken's push, the physical restraint, gave Patience a new fear, that Sken herself meant her harm. Patience was trained to protect herself against just such an attempt at murder in the night. For a moment, because she was not yet fully awake, her reflexes controlled her, and she lashed out; then she came to herself and stopped, her fingers already hooking behind Sken's ears, her thumbs poised to gouge out the riverwoman's eyes.

"Sweet lass," said Sken. "Just what your mother hoped you'd grow up to be, I bet."

The condemnation in Sken's words, the residue of momentary terror in her voice, the loathing revealed by the scant light that crossed the woman's face—This is how they see me, thought Patience. The common people, the people who play with their children, dance at the festival until they're drenched with sweat, scream and whine and accuse each other in the market. To them, a child my age should be a virgin at heart. If I were wise in the ways of love, that would sadden them, yes, as it does all adults when a child's body comes awake. But to see a child so young already ripe in violence and murder—I am a monstrous thing to Sken, like the deformed babies who are strangled and burned by the midwives.

Almost she said this: I was trained to be what I am, and I'm the best at what I do.

Then Sken would accuse her: This is the second time you tried to kill me. Or perhaps ask a bitter question: Do you murder even in your sleep?

Then Patience would say: How do you think a king keeps the peace, if not with tools like me?

But she would not defend herself. She might sometimes wish that she were not her father's daughter, but wishing wouldn't change the past. She had no more need to defend what she was than a mountain had to defend itself for being tall and craggy, or worn down and knobby, or whatever other shape it might have. What I am is what was done to me, not what I chose.

So instead of answering Sken's ironic words, Patience lived up to her name, and quietly asked, "Why did you wake me?"

"You were crying out in your sleep."

"I don't do that," said Patience. Hadn't Angel schooled her to be utterly silent in her sleep? She remembered all too well the cold water dashed in her face to wake her each time she made a sound, until she learned habits of sleep that kept her still.

"Then it's a miracle, a voice coming out of the air above your bed, and sounding just like you."

"What did I say?"

"From your cries, girl, I could think only one thing. That a lover was prying at you as vigorous as a farmer rooting out a stump in a field."

Only then did the memory of her dream come back to her, and with it the Cranning call. "He does it to me," she whispered. "He sends me dreams. Waking, sleeping—"

Sken nodded knowingly. "You dream until your whole body's ready for him, but he never comes to you."

"I have to go to him."

"The curse of women," said Sken. "We know how they mean to use our love for them, we know the whole price of it is ours to pay, but still we go, and still we stay."

"This one's no ordinary lover," said Patience.

Sken patted her head. "Oh, true. True, the one you love is never ordinary."

What, did she really think Patience was lovesick like some village maiden, pining for the handsome farmboy? Because Patience had never had such a girlish feeling, she wondered for a moment if Sken might not be right. But that was absurd. Patience had seen young girls in many noble houses, had heard them gossip about their real and would-be lovers. Unwyrm's relentless calling was far stronger. Even now it stirred within her; it took effort not to get up from her mat, leave the shabby inn, and walk, run, ride, or swim to Cranning.

Still, Sken's ignorant assumptions were harmless enough. In other times, Patience would have seemed to accept Sken's attempt at consolation. But she was too weary, too edgy from the Cranning call to care to play the diplomat. So she answered with the nastiness she felt. "And if I wait long enough, will I get over it?"

Sken, of course, had no diplomatic instincts. "You *are* a little bitch. A body tries to be nice—"

Patience answered, as if to explain everything about herself, "I've faced death more times this month than you have in your life."

Sken was still a moment, then smiled. "But you don't know boats like I do."

"We're not on the water now," said Patience.

"Nor are we assassinating anybody," Sken answered.

Patience lay back on the mat and smiled icily. Sken had made her point. "Death and the river, we each know our trade," said Patience.

"This lover who makes you sweat and cry out in your sleep—"

"Not my lover," said Patience.

"He wants you, doesn't he? And you want him?"

"He wants me like a jackal hungers for a lamb. And I want him like—"

"Like a fish wants water."

Patience shuddered. That's how it felt, even now, like needing to take a breath, a deep long draught of air. But if she took that breath, it would be her last.

"Sken," said Patience, "I'm made of paper."

Sken touched her gently, stroked the cold damp flesh of her arm with a single dry finger. "Flesh and bone."

"Paper. Folded this way and that, taking whatever shape they give me. Heir to the Heptagon House, daughter of Peace, assassin, diplomat, give me a shape, I'll wear it, I'll act the part, fold me again, again, I'll be his lover, the one who calls me, and if he ever gets me, he'll fold me down so small I'll disappear."

Sken nodded wisely, her whole body jiggling just a little with the movement.

"What if someone unfolded me all the way? What would I be then?"

"A stranger," said Sken.

"Yes, even to me," said Patience.

"Just like everybody else."

"Oh, do you think so! Do you think something like a normal woman lives inside this lovely delicate murderer's body?"

"Don't take on such airs," said Sken. "We're all

folded up, and nobody knows what we really are. But I know. We're all identical, blank, empty pieces of paper. It's the folding that makes us different. We *are* the folds."

Patience shook her head. "No, not me. Probably no one starts out blank and smooth, but certainly not me. I'm more than what they've done to me. I'm more than the roles I have to play."

"What are you, then?"

"I don't know." She rolled over, faced the wall to end the conversation. "Maybe I won't find out until just before I die."

"Or maybe just after, when they take your head."

Patience rolled back, caught the folds of Sken's robe in her tight-clutching fingers. "No," she whispered harshly. "If they ever do that to me, promise you'll split my head in two, you'll pour out the gools, something—"

"I won't promise that," said Sken.

"Why not?"

"Because if you're in such a state that they *could* take your head, Heptarch, it means I'm already dead."

Patience relaxed her grip on Sken's clothing, lay back down. The knowledge of Sken's loyalty *was* a comfort. But it was also a burden. Patience was so tired.

"Go to sleep," said Sken, "and don't dream of love."

"What should I dream of, then, since you're the master of sleep."

"Dream of murder," said Sken. "Knowing you, you'll sleep like a baby."

"I don't love death," whispered Patience.

Sken patted her hand. "No, I didn't think so."

"I didn't want my father to die. Nor Angel to be injured, I didn't wish for it."

Sken looked puzzled. Then she understood. "I know you didn't wish for it, girl," she whispered. "But it means you're on your own now, doesn't it? For a time at least. So of course that feels good."

"Exciting, sometimes. Scary."

"And knowing you face the strongest enemy in the world, alone—"

"Doesn't make me feel good."

"Don't lie," said Sken. "You love it, sometimes."

"I hate him for what he's making me want—"

"But to stand alone against him, you want that, you want to face him alone and win."

"Maybe."

"It's perfectly natural to feel that way. It's also perfectly natural to be an idiot."

"I can kill anybody."

"Anybody you *want* to."

The words sank in. "You're right," said Patience. "How can I kill him, if he makes me love him?"

"You see? You can't do this alone," said Sken. "You need Angel. You need the goblins, disgusting as they are. Their pet giant, too. You may even need me."

"Even you," whispered Patience.

"Sleep now. We're all with you, you're at the center of everything, we're all with you. Plenty of time to unfold yourself when this is over, and your lover's plow is hung on a wall somewhere."

Patience slept. She never spoke of the night's conversation again, but things were changed between her and Sken. They bickered as always, because Sken hadly knew another way to deal with people, but things were changed. There were ties between them, ties between sisters, strange sisters indeed, but good enough.

In the morning they traveled again, a queer caravan. But Sken's words had made a difference in the way Patience saw the others, too. She looked at them with new eyes, thinking, How can I use him, Why do I need her, What is the strength he has that makes up for a weakness in me? They were all dangerous—to her, but also to Unwyrm. The geblings especially, they were a mystery. The more Patience watched them, the more she realized that they did most of their communicating without speech, each seeming to sense when the other was in need. She was jealous of their closeness; she even tried to imitate them, going to Angel now and then, whenever she felt he might need her. Sometimes he did. More often he didn't. Whatever the geblings had, she lacked it. No special sensitivity. Geblings are too different from us. This power of theirs is something of this world, not from ours. They're like Unwyrm. Both part of this place, and I'm a stranger here.

Then the days of land travel were over. The river stretched before them again, this time with a busy town along its bank. It was no trouble finding a merchant to buy the carriage and horses. This close to Cranning, all the buyers were geblings, of course. So Patience dressed herself as a wealthy young man, took Will with her so no one would try to rob her, and did all the bargaining herself, without Ruin or Reck present to foul the deal. Geblings had a way of giving gifts to each other instead of making a profit, and though Patience knew that Angel's small treasury had money enough to buy as many boats as she liked, she didn't want to waste their resources. When what he had was gone, it could not easily be renewed.

The carriage gone, the money in hand, Patience—still looking for all the world like a cocky young man—took Sken with her to buy a boat. Sken was a riverwoman, after all; who else could judge a boat's fitness for their upstream voyage?

"Not that one," said Sken, time after time. Too small, too deep a draft, in bad condition, doomed to sink, not enough sail for upriver travel, too hard to steer—reason after reason to reject boat after boat.

"You're too picky," said Patience. "I'm not planning to live the rest of my life on it."

"If you buy the wrong boat," said Sken, "that's *exactly* what you'll do."

As they walked the bustling wharf, Patience noticed that the boats were all being sold or hired out by humans. "It was a gebling who bought our carriage," she said. "Don't they travel by water?"

"Don't ask *me* about goblins," said Sken. "I hope those two *don't* travel by boat."

"They saved a life that's dear to me," said Patience.

"And if they *do* sail with us, I hope they remember who's captain of the ship."

"*I'm* captain of the ship," said Patience.

"Not any ship *I'll* sail on, nor any sane person neither," said Sken. "You've got the money, that makes you owner. I've got the knowhow, and that makes me captain."

"Supreme authority?"

"Not quite."

"Oh? Who's higher than the captain?"

It wasn't Sken who answered. The voice came from Patience's other side, and it belonged to a man. "Pilot!" he said.

Patience turned—and saw no one, just a monkey jumping up and down as it pumped at a bellows. The bellows was connected to a tube that ran down into a thick glass jar, then up into the windpipe of a head whose eyes just peered over the top.

"Pilot?" asked Patience.

Sken had not yet turned. "Yes, a pilot. Someone who knows the river. Every river is different, and different from year to year, as well." Then she saw the one who had spoken, the head perched in a thick glass jar. Sken wrinkled up her face. "A dead one," she said. "Lot of good *he'll* do."

"Been up and down Cranwater every one of the last two hundred years," said the head.

"Heads don't learn," said Patience. "Heads don't pay attention, and they forget too quickly."

The monkey kept jumping up and down. It was distracting.

"I pay attention," said the pilot's head. "I know this river. Some pilots, the river's like an enemy, they wrestle it up and down. Some, it's like a god, they worship, they pray, they curse. Some, it's a whore for them, they think they're in charge but she plays them for fools. Some, it's a lover, a wife, a family, they live and die for it. But me—"

"Come along, young sir," said Sken. But Patience stayed to listen.

"For me, the Cranwater's not *like* anything else. This river is myself. That's my name, River, as God gave it to me that's my name, the stream is my body, my arms, my legs."

The monkey stopped to pick a louse. The head grinned, but because the mouth was lower than the lip of the jar, the thick glass transformed the smile into a hideous leer. The monkey tasted the louse, swallowed, and went back to work. Again the breath came through the pilot's throat.

"My boat's good," said River.

"Your boat's a rotten old canoe," said Sken.

"So. *You're* the captain, you get a good boat, but you come back and buy me for pilot."

"We'll get a *live* pilot, thanks all the same," said Sken.

"That's right, walk away, you've got legs, you can just walk off, what's that to you?"

A hawk swooped low, circled, came back and landed on a small platform atop the pole where River hung. It held a squirming rat in one talon. It raked open the belly, spattering blood, snatched the guts into its beak, then dropped the rest of the carcass into River's jar. The jar lurched as the gools and headworms attached themselves and fed.

"Pardon my lunch," said River. "As you see, I'm a self-contained system. You don't have to feed me, though I'm glad if you can keep my jar full of Cranwater, and it's nice if you now and then wash my jar. Monkey's apt to smear it with a bit of his stuff."

"Where's your owner?" asked Patience.

Sken was irate. "You're not thinking of—"

"Go buy a boat, Sken. You have fifteen minutes. Choose the best, and I'll come negotiate the price."

"I won't have this *thing* as pilot!"

"If Ruin and Reck have to put up with you as ship's captain, you'll learn to live with River as pilot. Weren't you the one said the pilot was most important?"

"You're enjoying this," said Sken. "You're making sport, and I thought we were friends."

"You're not making a mistake, young master," said River. "A pilot has to know the sandbars, the currents, the fast places, the slow places, the shallow channels, the spring rises, I know them all, I'll get you through, provided you do as I tell you, up to and including that Queen of Grease you have with you, what do you do, harvest her sweat and sell it as lamp oil downriver?"

Patience laughed. Sken did not.

"Buy the boat," said Patience. "I want this pilot, for reasons that are good enough."

River cheered her on. "For reasons of wisdom, for reasons of—"

"Shut up," said Sken to River. Then to Patience: "Young sir, you don't know this man—"

"I know from how his face has aged and cracked that he's at least two centuries, in hard sunlight and bad weather much of the time."

"Ah, it's the truth, the torture of my life written on my face," said River.

"So he's old," said Sken.

"He's been a head at least a century," said Patience. "Plying the river all that time. And in those many voyages, he's never failed a customer. He's never broken up a boat on a sandbar or a rock."

"How do you know that?" Sken demanded.

"Because the young master's got the spirit of discernment of truth in him," said River.

"Because he's here," said Patience. "If he'd ever let an owner down, his jar would have been broken, and he would have been poured out into the river long ago."

Sken glared, but had no answer. So she went farther along the dock, examining all the boats with an even more skeptical eye.

"You've got wisdom," said River. "I hope that among the hundred sons I conceived when I could still do the mattress hornpipe, there's one as well-favored and intelligent and—"

"And rich."

"As your most gracious self. Though I could wish a son of mine might have more of a beard on him."

"As he would no doubt wish his father to have more limbs."

River giggled, an artificial-sounding laugh because it all came from his mouth. There could be no belly laugh, with the monkey pumping the bellows with the same steady rhythm. "Ay, there's something lacking on both of us, I can't deny it."

"When will your owner come back?" asked Patience.

"When I send the monkey to fetch him."

"Then send."

"And miss out on conversation with such a likely young man? I buggered a few as fair as you in my time, I'll have you know, and they thanked me afterward."

"As I'll thank you for mislaying your practical buggery tools before we met."

River winked. "Nothing shocks you, does it?"

"Nothing that lives in a jar, anyway," said Patience. "Send the monkey. If you want to talk, I can read your lips."

River made three sharp kissing noises. Patience realized that it was a sound he could make without the bellows. The monkey immediately dropped the bellows and clambered around to perch on the lip of the jar, pressing his forehead against River's. A few more chirping sounds, tongue clicks, lip pops, and the monkey dropped to the wooden dock and ran off through the crowd.

River made a single clicking sound, and the hawk took off and flew away.

Patience stood, reading his lips as he made jokes, told stories, and studied her with his eyes. All the while, Patience felt Unwyrm calling her. Come faster, I need you, you love me, I'll have you. Not in words, it was never words, it was just the need. Fly to me now.

I'm coming, said Patience silently, trying hard not to think consciously of the murder in her mind.

The head named River babbled on and on, looking less and less like her father the longer she watched. Good. She didn't need the distraction.

Once they were on the water, Sken was in her element, and lorded it over them all. Never mind River muttering commands from his jar, which dangled from a pole near the helm; Sken was glad enough to follow River's orders about where to steer, once he showed that he really did know the river. Steering was the pilot's business—everything else about the boat was Sken's to decide. Only Angel, lying in comfort at last, without the bouncing of the road, only he was exempt from her orders. All the others, Sken kept them hopping with the business of a boat making the tricky upriver passage under sail and oar.

She took particular pleasure in ordering Reck and Ruin to climb the mast and fiddle with the two sails—she watched with unbearable satisfaction on her face as they dangled over the water doing her bidding. The height didn't seem to bother them, nor the work, but the water itself seemed to make them uncomfortable. And credit Sken with this: she did not abuse her authority. Like any good captain, she knew that the geblings would obey her, but only as long as she ordered them to do what was clearly needful.

Patience did her part as well, a full share of work, like any of the others. At first Sken was uneasy ordering her about, but if she left Patience without labor, Patience would come and ask, until Sken barked out commands to her as easily as to anyone. Patience was grateful for anything that engaged her mind. The Cranning call was relentless, but it was easier to live with when she was busy. So she spent many an hour braiding lines, raising and lowering sail, or leaning on the helm as River ordered their way upstream, tacking across the current to keep the wind, easing into deep channels with oars or poles to get past the tricky places—it was a vigorous, hardworking life, and Patience came to love the river, partly because of the peace it brought to her, partly for the life itself. Sken's coarseness and crudity became vigor and strength, when seen within the river life.

For all that Sken was a good captain, though, she was not perfect. Patience noticed within a few days that Sken tyrannized Will without mercy, perhaps merely because he let her do it. No doubt they weighed about the same, but she was a good meter less in height. It was comical, watching him pull on a rope or haul something above or below deck, his massive muscles rippling along his body as he worked, while all the time the jiggling fat woman scolded and cursed him. Poor Will, thought Patience. All the pangs of marriage, and none of the conveniences. But he bore it well and didn't seem to mind. It became part of the equilibrium. Patience let it go.

It was early morning. Will was drawing up the anchor while Reck was raising the sail. Ruin sat in the bow, staring glumly ahead. Sken sent Patience to secure a line when Reck threw it down, and the task brought her near to Ruin, who was not working this shift.

She saw him shudder at her approach. "Is it that strong, when you feel him calling me?" she asked.

He nodded, not looking at her.

"Who is he, this Unwyrm?"

"Unwyrm. Himself."

"But what does he look like?"

"No one has ever seen him."

"Where did he come from?"

"He was born from the same belly as the geblings."

This was a religious language, of course, and Patience mentally deciphered it into her own version of reality. "He's a gebling, then?"

Ruin shrugged. "He might be. Only more powerful than any gebling. And he hates us. That's all we know about him." He raised a lazy hand to point at the river.

"This water—he fills it with hate and sends it down to freeze us."

"The call—does it work like the way that you and Reck call to each other?"

"We can't control each other, if that's what you mean," said Ruin. "We feel it, and that's all. We feel it best between siblings. The closer your blood. Reck and I are twins."

"But Unwyrm does it at will?"

"He even does it to humans. None of us can do that."

"So he's like a gebling, only more powerful."

Ruin seemed angry. "He's nothing like a gebling."

"Then why do you call him *he?* How do you know he's a male?"

"You know he is, too. Because he's looking for the seventh seventh seventh daughter, and not the seventh seventh seventh son." Ruin turned slowly to face her. He was smiling, and it wasn't pleasant.

"What good would it do him to mate with a human? The offspring would never be viable. Starborne and native life can't interbreed."

"You humans put such touching faith in your myths."

He was just trying to torment her. Patience had seen him do the same with Reck, and she refused to pay any attention to it. "Is he one of another species, then?"

"Perhaps. Or maybe he's the only one of his species that ever lived."

"That's impossible. Species don't come out of nowhere. They have parents. There are generations. I know enough science for that."

"The best thing about science," said Reck, walking up behind Patience, "is that it keeps fools from ever discovering the truth, or even discovering that they don't have the truth already."

Ruin frowned at her. "Maybe human science," he said.

Reck grabbed the fur of the back of his hand, then slapped his hand away. "Ow," he muttered. He cradled the hurt hand in the other, as if it were a deep injury.

Reck smiled sweetly. "You're no better a scientist than the humans are."

"I've seen what I've seen, and not what I wanted to see or expected to see, which is more than you can say for any of *them*." His gesture toward Patience was fluid with contempt.

Reck tossed her head. "If you asked the Wise among the humans, they'd say the same to you. You never see anything that you aren't prepared to see, and when you do, you name it with the old names and pretend you understood it all along. And then everybody tells everybody else what everybody has already agreed to say, and everyone feels reassured about the world."

"You're so *wise*," said Ruin nastily. His anger, Patience saw, was not all pretended.

"That's what Mother commanded me to be, when she named me. 'Reck, child, it means *think,* it means *calculate,* it means *wonder about the causes of things.'* "

"Your names are commands?" asked Patience. "Then your parents had sweet plans in mind for *you,* Ruin."

Ruin and Reck both looked at her as if they had forgotten she was there. They had shown her more of their private relationship than a human was supposed to see. Patience was ashamed of herself for making them feel embarrassed. She, too, had forgotten that she had to be diplomatic. A diplomat is always the wary stranger, never the intimate friend. To the surprise of all and the liking of none, they had forgotten, for a moment, that they were not and never could be friends.

Patience smiled ruefully and walked away, feeling their eyes on her back like knives. But not so sharp as the yearning that almost immediately swelled in her. Cranning.

Was this great need the torture that Father's head endured, when the headworms sparked all his longings? Did he break under this pressure, or was his much worse? Will I come before this Unwyrm, who wants a woman, not a man, and break under this need like a disbodied head that has lost all will to resist? Will I be so hungry then that whatever he wants me to do, I'll mindlessly do, with no thought of resistance?

With that thought in mind, she spent the morning making something for herself from the things she found in Angel's strongbox. A pellet of poison, which she could take if things went wrong.

"What a clumsy solution."

It was Angel's voice. At once she closed his box, like a little girl caught by her father.

"It belongs to you," said Angel, "because *I* belong to you."

"I don't feel like it does," she said. "Or you. I've never really owned anything."

"It's a very subtle thing. Most people think they own many things, and don't. You think you never owned anything, and yet you do."

"What do I own?"

"Me. This box. All of mankind."

She shook her head. "I may have responsibility for all of mankind, but I never asked for it, and I don't own them."

"Ah. So you think duty and ownership are different things. The mother and father care for the baby and keep it alive—do they own it? And if they don't care for it, is it truly theirs? The child obeys the parents, serves them, and as they depend on its service, the child comes to own them, also. Yet he deceives himself that he is owned."

"You're very subtle, but if you're trying to say that I owned Father, you really have no hope of being one of the Wise."

"In my way of thinking, what I said is true. But I confess that most people think of ownership another way. They think they own what they make part of themself. Like Sken, with this boat. She feels its parts as if they were part of her; she feels the wind on the sail as if the sail were her body and the wind tilted her forward; she feels the rocking of the boat as if it were the rhythmic beating of her own heart. She owns this boat, because this boat is part of herself."

"The way River owns Cranwater."

"Yes," said Angel. "He doesn't feel the loss of his body, because currents and flows, banks and channels, they're his arms and legs, his gut and groin."

Patience tried to think of something she owned as Sken owned the boat. There was nothing she felt was part of herself. Nothing at all. Even her clothing, even her weapons were not her own, not in that sense. To herself, she was always naked and unarmed, and therefore no stronger than her own wit and no larger than the reach of her own arms and legs. "If that's ownership, then I own nothing," said Patience.

"Not so. You own no one thing, because you have let nothing become part of you, except a few weapons and languages and memories. But you also own everything, because the whole world, *as* a whole, it is part of you, you feel the face of the globe as if it were your own body, and all the pains of mankind as if they were your own pains."

Let him think what he wants, but I know it isn't so. I don't feel all mankind as mine, though Father taught me often that that was what the Heptarch ought to feel. I am solitary, cut off from everyone and everything. But believe what you like, Angel. She changed the subject. "Are you sure you're well enough to be up? And walking?"

"I'm not walking right now, am I? I'm sitting. Actually, though, I've felt much better for days. I just enjoy being lazy."

"I've needed you so much, these weeks—"

"You haven't needed me at all, and you've rather enjoyed finding out that you could do things on your own. But I'm glad you didn't decide to jettison me. I can be useful to you, you know. For instance, you don't need that poison."

"I might."

"You have something better."

"What?"

"The globe you took from your father's shoulder after he died."

Father had told her that no one else knew he had it. "What globe is that?"

"For more than a week on the Glad River, every time we slept ashore you spent fifteen minutes sifting through your nightstools. There's only one thing you could have swallowed that was worth performing such a repugnant task."

"I thought you were asleep."

"Child, who could sleep through a stench like that?"

"Don't be foul, Angel."

"I assume you found it."

"Father told me to take it, but never what it did, or how to use it."

"Your father never used it. Or at least, not to its full capacity. To be fully useful, it must be placed somewhere else in your body. In the deepest place in your brain." Angel smiled. "And right now you have a very good surgeon."

"Father told me that I should never let a gebling know I have this."

"One must take risks in this world."

"What is it?"

He switched into Gauntish. "Your scepter, my beloved Heptarch. But few of your recent predecessors have had the courage to wear it in their brain."

She answered in the same language. "You're saying Father wasn't brave enough for such an operation?"

"The operation is safe enough. But it's had such varying effects on different Heptarchs. Some have gone quite mad. One of them even murdered all his children, except one. Another started simultaneous wars with all his neighbors and ended up with the kingdom reduced to Heptam itself and a few islands to the west. Other Heptarchs have said it is like seeing the world for the first time, and they ruled brilliantly. But the odds are against you. Still, planted in your brain, it responds to your desires. Once it was there, if you ever truly wanted to die, you would die. So you might want to take the risk."

"What if it drove me mad?"

"Then you would probably become obsessed with going to Cranning to face the enemy of mankind, unprepared, uninformed, and unlikely to do anything but fail."

"In other words, what I'm doing now?"

"How could you do anything more insane? Unless you decided to take along two geblings who no doubt mean to kill you as soon as you've got them safely to Unwyrm."

She remembered what he had said about geblings a moment ago. "Why am I forbidden to let a gebling see that I have this jewel?"

"Because it isn't a jewel."

"It isn't?"

"It's an organic crystal taken from the brain of the King of Cranning in the fifth generation of the world."

"The gebling king. What did he use it for?"

"The geblings were reluctant to discuss it with us. We

know how it works on humans, but who knows what it did for him.''

Patience nodded. "If it was stolen from the gebling king, I suppose by right it belongs to Reck and Ruin.''

An expression passed suddenly across Angel's face, then vanished. Not a grimace that anyone else could see, for Angel was skilled at keeping his face blank. But Patience saw it, and knew that he was surprised, perhaps even frightened. What had surprised him? Didn't he know that, together, the brother and sister were king of the geblings? Of course he didn't know. Ruin had been sewing Angel's wound when Patience overheard the geblings' conversation that revealed to her who they were. Angel had been unconscious, and no one had spoken of it since.

"I'm sorry," she said. "Didn't you know they were king? It's something I overheard when you were not yet healed.''

"No, I had no idea. I'll have to think about that,'' said Angel. "That might change things. It might indeed. It gives me pause.'' He smiled and patted her hand, looking mildly nonplussed.

But Patience was even more confused than before. For Angel was lying to her. She knew what he would look like if his words were sincere and he were hiding nothing. But he *was* hiding something—all he showed right now was his mask. He had not been surprised at all, and he did not have to think about anything or change any plans. He had known all along who the geblings were. And if that was so, then what he hadn't known was that *she* knew who they were.

There are two things to do with a lie: pretend you believe it, or confront the liar with your knowledge of the lie. The first is what you do with enemies; she could only think of Angel as a friend. "How long have you known?" she asked him.

He was preparing to lie to her again, then stopped himself. "No," he said. "You're the Heptarch now, and I can't hold back from you. Your father told me their names, many years ago, their names and where they lived. The Heptarchy has made it a point to keep track of the gebling kings."

"So you knew all along that they were in that village."

"Your father knew, and warned me. They add just one more uncertainty to the equation. It would have been better to pass them by. And I wouldn't have had an arrow in my throat, either." He chuckled. "But I don't mind."

She smiled at him, but he was still lying to her. Something was wrong with what he said. Perhaps he hadn't known who they were. Perhaps Father hadn't warned him. It was impossible to guess, and she couldn't very well ask him now. With his first lie, he might still be a friend. With the second lie, she could only treat him as an enemy. Let him think his lie has succeeded, Father taught her, and your enemy won't be driven to more desperate measures.

What bothered her most was that never before in her life had she thought of Angel as her enemy. "What did Father fear they would do, when he warned you?"

"I don't know. I thought at the time he feared another gebling invasion. But I don't think it's human blood these two are thirsting for. The other kings called the geblings to Skyfoot with a cry of war on their lips. These two are almost in disguise. No gebling king has ever traveled in the company of humans. Living humans, anyway."

The more she listened to him, the more obvious it became that it was all lies, and Angel was growing more and more confident that she believed him. Angel had a plan, no doubt something he and Father had worked out some time ago, and part of the plan required him not to tell her all he knew. She was still a child in Angel's eyes, still not to be trusted with the knowledge to make an intelligent decision on her own. Angel was determined to keep her blind and force her down the road he and Father had chosen for her. Well, Angel, you may find I'm not quite the helpless babe you think I am. I can't force you to confide in me, but when the time comes, you'll wish you had, because I'll do as I have decided for myself, whether you like it or not, and if you try to stop me, Angel, even you might find that I'm too much for you.

She didn't believe it, though. Her bravado was a sham. Never before had she felt so childish and weak as now. I am not Heptarch yet, she realized. I have no kingdom and no power, just the destiny that you and Father and Unwyrm and the geblings and the priests all have in mind for me. You have so many plans for me that no matter what I do, it's what *someone* wanted me to do. A single puppet with a thousand strings, and I don't know who is holding any of them.

Her face showed none of this to Angel. Instead she smiled wickedly, the way she did when she teased him. "So you think I'd be safe to let Ruin know I have the scepter that should be his, and then ask him to cut open my brain and put it in?"

Angel held out his open hands. "I didn't say it was without risks."

She poked him playfully. "Go back to spending the days asleep. You were more helpful then."

She could see his tension ease, as she pretended to be the lighthearted, trusting girl she had always been with him in private. He believed her. "I think Ruin wll agree," he said, "that the scepter is more human than gebling now. The Heptarchs have had it for more than three hundred generations. Still, I'm not saying you should up and tell him right now."

"It's impossible to know what to do," she said. "All the prophecies hint at disaster, but they don't tell me what causes the disaster. Anything I choose might destroy the world or save it, and I don't know which is which. And you aren't even going to help me decide."

He smiled. "You knew you might be leading the world to disaster when you decided to go to Cranning. I'm just going along for the ride. Been lots of fun, so far." He got up and walked weakly back to his pallet under the canopy.

Patience sat and watched the water for some time. Just when she had begun to feel confident, Angel turned out to be playing his own game. There was no one she could trust completely.

Yet she couldn't brood for long. For whenever her attention was not closely engaged with work or conversation, her mind turned back to that constant, nagging need to go north, to go upriver, to find relief from the urgent pressure of her body's desire.

River's hawk circled, swooped down to the boat. She turned to watch as it tore open a dove, ate its gut, and dropped the body, feathers and all, into the jar. The monkey was playing with itself; this was a calm, slow reach of the river, so the pilot didn't need a voice for a while.

The balance of River's ecology was a marvel and a mystery to her. River himself, he was fairly easy to understand; like all heads, he was somewhat insane, living for the journey up and down Cranwater. As long as the boat was sailing, he was well rewarded. But the monkey and the hawk—what did they get? The monkey ate with the humans, and seemed content enough. Besides, he had nowhere else to go. Monkeys were a species humans had brought with them to this world; they had no natural habitat here, and could survive only as pets. So maybe, at some primitive level, the monkey knew that his slavery at the bellows was the only way that he could live.

But the hawk—she could not understand the hawk. It could provide for itself. It needed no one. What did it gain from its service to River? Why did it stay? River had no hands to restrain it, no power to reward or punish it. The hawk seemed to live for pure generosity.

Perhaps the hawk conceived River to be part of itself, feeding the head out of the same instinct that made parents feed their children. Or perhaps the hawk had been trained, folded into a pattern in which it could not conceive of leaving River to die. Perhaps the hawk did not long for freedom. Or perhaps, being free, this was what the hawk freely chose to do.

When Will called them to dinner at noon, Patience did not want to come. It was Reck's hand on her shoulder that brought her. "Whatever Angel said to you," whispered the gebling woman, "you're still the heart of all our futures. Come, eat."

Yes, thought Patience. Come, puppet. Come, folded paper. Dance your dance, hold the shape we gave you.

Until your usefulness is over. Then someone—the geblings, Unwyrm, perhaps some mad Vigilant along the way—someone will burn you up.

11 | HEFFIJI'S HOUSE

LATE ONE AFTERNOON THEY WERE TRIMMING SAIL AS THEY rounded a bend through a narrow channel between sandbars, when River clicked his tongue twice and the monkey began to screech. By now everyone knew this meant River wanted a quick change in course. They stopped all conversation and listened—River's voice was never loud.

"Hard port!" he said. Will, who was at the helm, heeled the lever toward the starboard side, and almost at the same moment Sken grabbed Patience and a gebling and ran to the left side of the boat. Patience only had time to catch a glimpse of what they were avoiding—a large buoy, big enough that if they had collided head on, with their speed from such a brisk wind, it would have done real damage to buoy and boat alike. As it was, they still bumped into it, but side-on and slower.

"That's supposed to be two mile upriver," said the pilot. "Last flood season must have dragged her anchor down here so far. Cast a line."

Sken didn't hesitate. She knotted a rope onto a grappling hook, swung the hook above her head, and cast it against the buoy, now bobbing some dozen yards behind them. The hook caught on the first throw, but Patience didn't know whether that was remarkable or just what a competent riverwoman would be expected to do.

"What are you doing with that!" demanded Ruin.

"Putting it back where it belongs," said Sken, as if it were a fact that should be obvious even to a child.

"None of our affair," said Ruin.

"There's too many on the river feels that way already," said Sken. "But River and me, we feel the same on this. When something's out of place that you can fix, then you fix it, so next pilot won't risk what almost got us."

They got back on course through the channel and then it was clear sailing for a while. Long enough to take a better look at the buoy. It had a sign on it, at such an angle that you could just read it if you leaned out from the stern on the starboard side. In Geblic, Gauntish, Dwelf, and Agarant—the language all traveling humans used, regardless of their native tongue—the sign advertised a single thing for sale:

ANSWERS

Angel laughed aloud when Patience told him what it said. "When have you seen such arrogance before?"

"Maybe they're not selling," said Reck. "Maybe they're buying."

Patience did not laugh. It was too ironic. If there was anything she needed right now, it was answers. And here they were, offered in trade.

Two miles on, they dropped anchor and hauled in the buoy. Sken and Will lashed it to the boat, then hauled up the buoy's anchor and added a bag of ballast to it. It was an hour's work at most, but Patience took no part in it, so she had time to look for the place on shore where the answers might be found. It wasn't a heavily settled area, so it could only be the house well up on a hill, perhaps a quarter-mile walk from the river.

If the house had been one of the common inns along the river, preying upon travelers with rigged games, indigestible food, and bug-ridden beds, Patience would not have had them put ashore. Instead, though, it was old and modest, and far enough back from the water that it couldn't be a money trap for travelers. If they hadn't anchored to fix the buoy, it would have been visible only for a moment in a gap between trees along the river's edge. To Patience, this suggested that the sign was sincere enough. It was a place for people who wanted truth enough to work to get it—out of the way, hard to reach, with only a single sign to tell them what it was, and only a single sight to tell them where.

Of course, the moment she thought of stopping, Patience felt the pressure of the Cranning call within her, urging her to go on, faster, faster. It was no stronger now than before; Unwyrm was not trying to get her to avoid this place in particular. But because the need to hurry on was so great, and because she knew that someone else was producing that need within her, she resisted for the sake of resistance, the way that she had deliberately endured extra suffering as a child, to inure herself to hardship.

When Will and Sken climbed aboard the boat and began unlashing the buoy, Patience spoke her decision. "Bring the boat ashore."

"At that place!" said Sken. "I will not! We'll pass a dozen better inns before nightfall."

Patience smiled and spoke to River. "The pilot sets the course, the captain rules the life aboard the ship, but the owner says what ports the ship will visit. Am I right?''

River winked at her.

Sken cursed, but instead of raising sail again, she and Will poled the boat to shore.

They touched the ragged-looking pier that ran out into the river and tied the boat fast. Leaving Sken to keep watch over Angel, Patience led Will and the geblings ashore. Angel demanded to be taken along. Patience ignored him. She didn't feel the same need to defer to him that she had felt before he started lying to her.

There wasn't much of a path up the hill. Patience let Ruin lead the way—he could find a trail on bare rock in a rainstorm, or so it seemed. Reck and Will fell into place behind her. It was as though she were truly Heptarch, with an escort before and behind; or a prisoner, with keepers to cut off all escape.

The hilltop house was even shabbier than it had looked from below. The windows were unglazed and unshuttered, and the smell of the yard out back made it plain that the pigs were responsible for washing themselves. "Could it be that no one lives here now?" asked Patience.

Ruin grunted. "Fire's lit."

"And there's fresh water in the kitchen," added Reck.

Patience turned to Will. "Is there anything they *can't* find out with their noses?"

Will shrugged. Not too bright, thought Patience. But what could you expect of the sort of man who'd live with geblings?

Their knock on the door brought a quick shout from inside. A female voice, and not a young one. "I'm coming!" The cry was in common speech, but the accent told Patience that it was not her native tongue. And sure enough, it was a dwelf, smaller than the geblings, with the half-size head that made them look spectacularly repulsive.

"From a dwelf we're supposed to get answers?" asked Ruin, with his usual tact.

The dwelf frowned at him. "To a goblin I'm supposed to give them?"

"At least she speaks in complete sentences," said Reck.

But it was Patience who reached out her hand for the dwelf to lick her fingers. Custom satisfied, the dwelf invited them in, and immediately led Patience to what was obviously the seat of honor near the fire. Will, as always, hung back to stand by the door. He never seemed to consider himself to be part of what was going on. Only a watcher, a listener. Or perhaps not even that, perhaps an accessory, like a horse, to be brought forward only when needed.

The dwelf brought them boiling water and let them choose the leaves for the tea. Patience inquired about the possibility of getting rooms with closable windows for the night.

"That depends," said the dwelf.

"On what? Tell us the price."

"Oh, the price, the price. The price is good answers for my questions, and good questions for my answers."

"You can never communicate with a dwelf," said Ruin impatiently. "You get more intelligent conversation from trees."

He spoke in Geblic, but it was obvious that the dwelf had at least caught the gist of what he said. Patience suspected that she actually understood Geblic, which would make her much brighter than usual for her kind.

"Tell us," said Patience, "what sort of question you have in mind?"

"Only the Wise stay here," said the dwelf. "The

Wise from all lands, and they leave behind their wisest thoughts before they go.''

"Then we've come to the wrong place," said Patience. "All the Wise left our lands before I was born."

"I know," said the dwelf sadly. "But I make do with what comes along nowadays. You wouldn't happen to be an astronomer, would you?"

Patience shook her head.

"You have an urgent need for one?" asked Reck.

"Oh, not urgent, not urgent. It just seems to be a lost art, which should surprise you, considering that we all came from the stars.''

"*She* did, and the big one at the door," said Ruin. "The rest of us are native born."

The dwelf smiled a little. "Oh," she said. "You think geblings are natives here?"

Now, for the first time, Patience began to wonder if she shouldn't take this dwelf seriously, not just out of courtesy, but because she might know something of value. Certainly her hint that the geblings were also starborn implied that her ideas would at least be interesting. Interesting enough that Angel ought to be here. She might be annoyed with him, might not trust him, but Patience was not such a fool that she would reject the possibility of profiting from what truth he *would* tell her. She turned to Reck. "Do you think Will would go down and bring Angel up?"

Reck looked annoyed. "I don't own Will," she said.

Since Will acted far more like a slave than Angel did, Patience thought Reck's pretense of not controlling him was ridiculous. Will never did anything unless Reck had given him permission first. Still, Patience offered no retort, but merely turned to Will and asked if he thought he could carry Angel up to the inn. Will said nothing, but left immediately.

"Why are you sending for more of your party," asked the dwelf, "when I haven't said that you could stay?"

"Because Angel is the closest thing to a wise man we have with us. He's a mathematician."

"He's a nothing, then. Numbers and more numbers. Even if you understand enough to ask the questions, the answers mean nothing at all."

This delighted Patience, who had said much the same thing to Angel on more than one occasion. She could have recited Angel's answer, too, since she had memorized it from the sheer repetition. Instead, though, Patience took the dwelf at her word. She offered answers, so why not ask the question that mattered most? "Let *me* ask you a question. Who and what is Unwyrm, and what does he want?"

The dwelf smiled in delight, jumped to her feet, and ran out of the room.

"If she has the answer to that," said Reck, "then she knows what no other living soul knows."

Soon the dwelf came bounding back into the room. "Unwyrm is the brother of geblings, gaunts, and dwelfs, and the son of the Starship Captain's possessor," she said. "His mother once had the whole world, and he wants it back." She beamed with pride.

Ruin cut in, impatiently. "Anybody could make up this kind of mix of truth and speculation—"

"Hush," said Patience. Then, to the dwelf, she said, "I'm sorry, I missed part of that, where you said—"

Before she could finish, the dwelf said it again. "Unwyrm is the brother of geblings, gaunts, and dwelfs, and the son of the Starship Captain's possessor. His mother once had the whole world, and he wants it back." Again she smiled the identical smile. It was as if they had seen the same moment twice. The dwelf was giving an answer that she had memorized.

Ruin looked at Reck, then smiled. "All right, now let us give you a question," said Ruin. "Where is the mindstone of the ancient gebling kings?"

Patience had little trouble guessing the answer to this question herself, but controlled her own misgivings and feigned ignorance. "What's the mindstone?" she began.

But the dwelf was already up and running out of the room. And while she was gone, Reck and Ruin kept touching each other's faces as if each were studiously forming the other's likeness in clay. Patience decided there was more to their question than a mere test. And sure enough, when the dwelf came back into the room, they turned to her and waited intently for her reply, showing more interest than Patience thought their stolid faces could ever show.

"The mindstone of the gebling kings, which became the scepter of the Heptarchs, is imbedded in the shoulder of Peace, the rightful Heptarch. It is just behind the collarbone, near the neck, and he will give it to his daughter before he dies." The dwelf nodded wisely.

Reck and Ruin turned to look at Patience, who said nothing, trying to keep her face a mask of polite bafflement. There was no way this dwelf could possibly have known about her father's secret.

Watching the silent tableau of geblings staring at the human girl, the dwelf began to giggle insanely. "And now you've answered *my* question, all of you."

Patience turned to her politely. "And what is your question?"

"My question of you is, who are you, and why do geblings and humans travel together this way?"

"And what was our answer?" asked Reck.

"Your answer was that you are the gebling king, the boy and girl of you, and you, human, are the daughter of Peace, the Heptarch, and he is dead, and you now have the mindstone and scepter. You're going into battle, but you aren't sure whether or not you're on the same side.''

This was no ordinary dwelf.

Patience drew the slender glass rod of her blowgun from the cross at her neck. She also took the loop from her hair. She spoke quietly to Reck and Ruin, in a tone of calm, sure intention. ''If you move from your places, you'll be dead before you take a step.''

''Oh, my,'' said the dwelf. ''You shouldn't ask for answers that you don't want to hear. Let's not have any killings here. This is a place where the only traffic is in truth. Let me have your oath, all of you, that you'll wait to kill each other until you get back to the river.''

No one volunteered to take the oath.

''What have I done? Trouble, trouble, that's what the truth is. You poor fools—you thought a dwelf could never know anything, and so you asked me the questions whose answer you thought no one could have. But I have all the answers. Every one of them.''

''Do you?'' asked Reck. ''Then tell us how to resolve our dilemma. However you knew the answer, Patience has as much as confessed that she has the most precious possession of the gebling kings. Now more than ever before in our history we must have it, we must know its secrets. We would gladly kill her to get it, and she would as gladly kill us to keep it for herself. When Will comes back, we'll have no difficulty killing her, so she'll have to kill us before he gets here.''

''I told you, take an oath,'' said the dwelf.

''We would never keep an oath about the mindstone,'' said Ruin, ''nor would we believe her if she made one.''

''I don't even know what it is,'' said Patience. ''I only know that Father said to keep it at all costs, and Angel said to ask you to implant it in my brain.''

Ruin laughed. "He thought that *I*, once I had it in my hands, would put it into *you?*"

Reck, still not moving, silenced him with a hiss. Then she said, "Patience, my fool of a brother doesn't understand. Though the mindstone by rights belongs to us, it's no good to us now."

"No good to us!" said Ruin.

"When the humans first thought to put it in their brains, it drove them mad. There was too much gebling in it. But now we could never put it in our own minds—there's too much human in it."

Ruin frowned. "There's a chance we could use it."

"And there's a better chance we could destroy ourselves trying."

Ruin looked furious. "After so many years—and we find it now at the time of greatest need, and you say we can't use it!" But his anger turned immediately to despair. "You say it, and it's true."

Patience was skeptical. This could be a trick to lull her into complacency. So she turned to the dwelf for the only help she could think to ask for.

"I have a question for you," she said. "Tell me what the scepter does when it's connected to the brain."

"If I leave to get the answer," said the dwelf, "you'll probably kill each other before I get back, and then I can never ask you anything more."

"If they don't leave their chairs, then I won't kill them," said Patience.

"We won't leave our chairs," said Reck.

"But don't be too sure you could kill us," said Ruin.

Patience smiled. The dwelf shuddered and left the room. There was no spring in her step this time.

She came back in muttering to herself. "It's long," she said.

"I'm listening," said Patience.

The dwelf began to recite. "When implanted above the limbic node in the human brain, the organic crystal called the scepter or mindstone grows smaller crystals that penetrate to every portion of the brain. Most of these are passive, collecting important memories and thoughts. A few of them, however, allow the human to receive memories previously stored in the crystal by prior occupants. Since many of the memories belong to the first seven gebling kings, in whose brains the crystal originated, this can be most disorienting to the human. If the human is not able to gain control of the crystal, the alien memories can impinge on the mind in unwelcome and unmanageable ways, lending to confusion of identity, which is to say, madness. The safest way to use the crystal is to implant it in a protected place near a fairly important nerve. One or two chains of crystal will make their way to the brain, collecting memories but almost never supplying any to the human host. But there's bloody little chance that you'll ever meet anyone who needs this information, Heffiji."

All of them laughed at the last sentence.

"Whoever gave you that answer, dwelf, wasn't as wise as he thought."

"I know," said the dwelf. "That's why I left it in, so you could see that I asked him a good question after all, even though he thought I didn't."

"And what happens when it's implanted in a gebling's brain?" asked Patience.

"But why would anyone do that?" asked the dwelf. "All a gebling has to do is—"

"Silence!" whispered Ruin.

"No," said Reck. "No, let her tell."

"All a gebling has to do," said Heffiji, "is swallow it. The gebling body can break the crystal into its tiniest pieces, and it will form again exactly where it ought to be in the gebling's brain.''

"How could that happen?" asked Patience. "Why can geblings use it so easily, when humans—"

"Because we're born with mindstones," said Ruin, scornfully. "We all have them. And we eat our parents' mindstones when they die, to carry on the memories that mattered most to them in their lives." He looked at Reck with bitter triumph, as if to say, Well, you said to tell her, and now I have.

Patience looked from one to the other in growing understanding. "So all those stories that geblings eat their dead—"

Reck nodded. "If a human saw it, though it's hard to believe a gebling would ever let them see—"

"Dwelfs too," said Heffiji. "And gaunts."

"There are mindstones of some sort, much smaller than ours, too small to see, in all the animals of this world," said Ruin. "Except humans. Crippled, fleshbound humans, whose souls die with them."

Our souls die, thought Patience, except those whose heads are taken. It was a question she had thought of more than once. How did the taking of heads begin? Why did human scientists every *try* to keep a head alive? Because they knew, hundreds of generations ago, they knew that the native species had a kind of eternal life, a part of their brain that lived on after death. They were jealous. Taking heads was the human substitute for the mindstones of the geblings, dwelfs, and gaunts. Instead of the crystal globe of the mindstone, for us it was gools, headworms, and eviscerated rats dropped by a hawk into a glass jar.

"Only the Heptarchs, among all humans, have taken their parents into themselves," said Reck. "And that was only by stealing our noblest parents from us. Your ancestor killed the seventh king and stole his mindstone, so that the kings of the geblings have no memory now of how the kingdom began. Ruin is of the foolish opinion that it would be of some advantage to us to have it now. I, however, understand that it would only have been to our advantage if we had had it all along.''

"I must have it," said Ruin. "If I'm to know what I must know—"

"Unwyrm wants you to do it, Ruin." Reck seemed to enjoy forcing her brother to bow before her superior understanding. "It would please him, to have half the gebling king a babbling lunatic. Fool. If it drove humans insane, with their incomplete coupling with the stone, what do you think it will do to you, to be utterly and perfectly bonded to more than three hundred human minds? No gebling is strong enough to endure *that*."

Patience could see that Ruin was not pretending now; he was yielding to his sister's arguments. If she said nothing, it was clear the dispute would be settled with the scepter left peacefully in her possession, perhaps even implanted in her brain. Yet if it was so dangerous that Ruin would not use it, she had to know more of what it would do to her.

"Are human and gebling minds so alien to each other?" she asked. "We speak each other's languages, we—"

"You don't understand the beginning of the gebling mind—" began Ruin.

"It's our strength," said Reck, "and our weakness. We're never alone, from the moment of our birth. Isolation is a meaningless word to us. We can feel other geblings on the fringes of our consciousness, awake and asleep. When we swallow a mindstone, we *become* the person whose stone we swallowed, for days, sometimes weeks and months, until we can sort out all the memories and put them in their place. If Ruin had to *become* human that way, three hundred times over, the isolation would probably be unbearable, like the death of half himself. You, though, a human being—you're used to loneliness because you never know anything else. And the mindstone doesn't bond so perfectly with you. A strong human—like you—"

"You want me to implant it in her, don't you," Ruin said.

"I think so, yes," said Reck.

"It may make her even more subject to Unwyrm's will," he said.

"But what does that matter? At worst, it would make her a helpless pawn to Unwyrm. Since that's how she'll probably end up anyway, what difference does it make?"

Patience shuddered inwardly at their utter lack of sympathy for her. Even she, a sometime assassin, still felt some understanding, some elementary kinship with the people that she killed. Now, for the first time, she realized that they regarded her as a beast, not a person. They assessed her as a man might assess a good horse, speaking of its strengths and weaknesses candidly, in the horse's presence. The difference was that Patience could understand.

Ruin, still angry despite having to admit that his sister was right, turned to Patience. "I'll implant the mindstone, on two conditions. First, that you give it back to me or Reck or our children when you die."

"Why, when you can never use it?" asked Patience.

"When all this is over," Ruin said, "and my work is done, then I *can* use it. If it mads me, then it's no worse than death, and I'm not afraid to die. But if I succeed in mastering it, then all we lost will be restored to us, and I can pass it to my heir."

"I'll make you a different oath," said Patience. "Implant it, and if I die in the presence of the king of the geblings, I'll make no effort to stop them from taking it, whoever they are."

Ruin smiled. "It amounts to the same thing. Only you must promise to make every effort to die in the presence of the king of the geblings."

"If you promise to make no effort to hasten that day."

"I hate politics," said Heffiji. "You don't need any oaths. You'll implant it in her because it's no use to you, and you'll get it back when she's dead if you can." She snorted. "Even a dwelf with less than half a brain can tell you *that*."

"What is the second condition?" asked Patience.

"The first gebling king," said Reck. "He was Unwyrm's brother. His memories of Unwyrm are in the stone. You must tell us what Unwyrm is. You must tell us everything about him that you can remember, when the mindstone is in place."

"So the Heptarchs *remember* Unwyrm," she whispered. "They have known who the enemy is, all these years."

"Only the ones with courage enough to put it in their brains," said Reck.

"And strength enough to keep their sanity when they did," said Ruin.

Reck asked again, "Will you tell us?"

Patience nodded. "Yes." And then, deciding not to be the careful diplomat, she let Reck and Ruin see her fear. "Do you believe that I'm truly strong enough to bear it?"

Ruin shrugged. "If you aren't, *we're* no worse off than before." She was still an animal to him.

But Reck noticed her vulnerability this time, and answered with sympathy. "How many times has this been done in the history of the world? How can we know how strong a human has to be, to hold geblings in her mind, and still remain human? But I'll tell you what I know of you. Many humans, *most* humans, cringe in their solitude, frightened and weak, struggling to bring into themselves as many things and people as they can. To own so much that they can feel large and believe, falsely, that they are not alone. But you. You are not afraid of your own voice in the dark."

Patience put the loop back in her hair, and slid the tube into its wooden sheath. The geblings visibly relaxed. "You said your name was Heffiji?" asked Patience.

"Yes. A scholar gave it to me once, long ago. I forget what my name was before that. If you ask me, I'll tell you."

"A gaunt, wasn't he? The scholar who named you? Heffiji is a Gauntish word."

"Yes, she was. Do you know what it means?"

"It's a common word. It means 'never.' Never what?"

"Mikias Mikuam Heffiji Ismar."

"Never to Lose the Finding Place."

"That's me," said Heffiji. "I don't know anything, but I can find everything. Do you want to see?"

"Yes," said Patience.

"Yes," said Reck.

Ruin shrugged.

Heffiji led them back into the rest of the house. Every room was lined with shelves. On the shelves, in no apparent order, were stacks of paper. Rocks or pieces of wood served as paperweights in the rooms where the glassless windows let in the wind. The whole house was a library of papers scattered in a meaningless order.

"And you know where everything is?" asked Reck.

"Oh, no. I don't know where anything is, unless you ask me a question. Then I remember where the answer is, because I remember where I set it down."

"So you can't lead us to anything unless we ask you."

"But if you ask me, I can lead you to everything."
She smiled in pride. "I may have only half a brain, but I
remember everything I ever did. All the Wise came by
my house, and they all stopped and gave me every
answer, and they all asked me every question. And if I
didn't have the answer to their question, I kept asking
others the same question until one of them could answer
it."

Patience started to lift a rock from a stack of papers.

"No!" screamed Heffiji.

Patience set the rock back down.

"If you move anything, how will I find it again?"
shouted the dwelf. "Anything you touch will be lost
forever and ever and ever! There are a hundred thousand
papers in this house! Do you have time to read it all, and
remember where each scrap of it is?"

"No," said Patience. "I'm sorry."

"This is my brain!" shouted Heffiji. "I do with this
what humans and geblings and gaunts do with your large
heads! I let you dwell in it because you will add to my
memories. But if you move anything, you might as well
burn down the house with me inside, because then I'll
be nothing but a dwelf with half a brain and no answers
at all, none at all!"

She was weeping. Reck comforted her, the long, many-
jointed fingers stroking the dwelf's hair in a swirling
pattern like a bird's wing closing. "It's true," said Reck,
"humans are like that, they stumble into other people's
houses and break and destroy without any thought of the
havoc that they wreak."

Patience bore the abuse; she had earned it.

But Ruin took her silence to mean that she hadn't got
the point of Reck's remark. "She means that you humans
came to this world and ruined it for all of us who were
here before you—geblings and dwelfs and gaunts."

Suddenly Heffiji was no longer weeping. She pulled away from Reck with a broad smile on her face. "It's my best answer," she said. "Ask me the question."

"What question?" asked Ruin.

" 'All of us who were here before you,' " she said. "Ask me."

Ruin tried to decide what question she meant. "All right, who was here before the humans?"

Heffiji jumped up and down with delight. "Wyrms!" she shouted. "Wyrms and wyrms and wyrms!"

"What about geblings, then, if we weren't here when humans arrived?" asked Reck.

"What about them? Too vague—you have to ask a better question than that."

"Where did geblings come from?" she asked.

Heffiji jumped up and down again. "My favorite, my favorite! Come and I'll show you! Come and you'll see!"

She led them up a ladderway into a low and musty attic. Even the geblings had to stoop; Patience had to squat down and waddle along to the farthest corner. Heffiji gave her lantern to Ruin and took a sheaf of papers from a roof beam. She spread them along the attic floor. Taking back the lantern, she began to read the explanations of the drawings, one by one.

"There is no such thing as a native life form left on this world, and no such thing as Earth life, either, except for human beings themselves," she said.

"That's insane," said Ruin. "Everybody knows that the domesticated plants and animals came from Earth—"

Heffiji held the lantern up to his face. "If you already know all the answers, why did you stop at my house?"

Abashed, he fell silent.

Heffiji recited. "Comparing the genetic material of any plant or animal with the records concerning similar plants or animals preserved from the knowledge brought with mankind from Earth, we find that the original genetic code is still preserved, almost perfectly—but as only a tiny part of a single but vastly larger genetic molecule.''

Heffiji pointed to a diagram showing the positions of the Earth species' protein patterns within the single chromosome of the present Imakulata version.

"Clearly, the species brought from earth have been taken over or, as is more likely, imitated perfectly by native species that incorporate the genetic material into their own. Since the resulting molecule can theoretically contain hundreds of times as much genetic information as the original Earth species needed, the rest of the genetic material is available for other purposes. Quite possibly, the Imakulata species retain the dormant possibility of adapting again and again to imitate and then replace any competing species. There is even a chance that the Imakulata genetic molecule is complex enough to purposefully control alterations in the genetic material of its own reproductive cells. But whether some rudimentary form of intelligence is present in the genetic molecule or not, our experiments have proven conclusively that in two generations any Imakulata species can perfectly imitate any Earth species. In fact, the Imakulata imitation invariably improves on the Earth original, giving it a competitive edge—shorter gestation or germination times, for example, or markedly faster sexual maturity, or vastly increased numbers of offspring per generation.''

Heffiji looked at them piercingly, one at a time. "Well?" she asked. "Do you understand it?"

Patience remembered what Prince Prekeptor had once said to her. "The genetic molecule is the mirror of the will.''

Heffiji scowled. "That's religion. I keep those in the cellar."

"We understand," said Ruin.

"You must understand it all. If you have a question, I'll say it again."

They had no questions. Heffiji moved on to a series of drawings of wheat plants and a strange, winged insect.

"Our experiments involved separating the original Earth-species genetic material from common wheat, to see what was left when the currently dominant Earth-genes were gone. The experiments were delicate, and we failed many times, but at last we succeeded in separating the genetic material, and growing Earth wheat and the species that had absorbed and replaced it. The genetic structure of the Earth wheat was identical to the records passed down to us from the original colonists, and yet when it grew we could see no difference in the plant itself from the Imakulata wheat. However, the leftover genetic material from the Imakulata wheat did not produce a plant at all. Instead, it produced a small insectlike flier, with a wormlike body except for three wing-pairs. It was completely unlike anything we could find in our catalogues from Earth, but possibly similar to what the earliest colony records refer to as 'gnats,' which seemed to disappear from the first colony of Heptam after a few years."

"What does this have to do with geblings?" asked Ruin. "I know more about plants than any human scientist ever did."

Heffiji glared at him. "Go away if you don't want the answers that I give."

Reck touched her brother's cheek. "It isn't that he doesn't understand," she said. "It's that he already understands too well."

Heffiji went on. "We introduced a single Imakulata

gnat into a glass box containing a sample of pure Earth wheat that was ready for fertilization. Without a mate, the Imakulata gnat soon began laying thousands of eggs. The wheat also ripened and dropped seed. But the Imakulata eggs hatched first. A few of them produced gnats, which began attacking each other savagely until only one was left. Most of the seeds, however, produced an incredible array of strange plants, many of them wheatlike, many of them gnatlike, and most of them hopelessly maladaptive. Only a few grew more than a few centimeters in height before they died. Those that thrived, while they were generally somewhat wheatlike, were still easily distinguishable from the Earth species. By the time the next generation of Earth wheat germinated and grew, they had already gone to seed, and showed every sign of being new and vigorous species. We immediately began several other experiments to see if the results were identical.''

On to the next drawing. ''In the meantime, the sole surviving second-generation gnat mated, not with the new Imakulata species, but with the second generation Earth wheat. This time, most of the gnat's offspring were similar to what we call wheat today—completely indistinguishable from Earth wheat, except for the presence of a single immense genetic molecule which contains all the genetic information from the original Earth wheat. We repeated these results at will. When the second-generation gnat was allowed to reproduce with second-generation—or even tenth- or twentieth-generation Earth wheat—the result was always outwardly identical Imakulata wheat, which reproduced faster and grew more vigorously than either the Earth wheat or the new Imakulata plant species. In fact, the Imakulata wheat seemed particularly inimical to the new Imakulata nonwheat species. They were destroyed as if by poison within two generations.

The Earth wheat sometimes lingered as long as six generations before being utterly replaced. However, when the second-generation gnat was not allowed to reproduce with later Earth wheat, the Imakulata wheat never appeared. Instead, the new Imakulata species and the Earth wheat continued to breed true to form, with no further cross-breeding between species. This process of complete replacement within two generations may have repeated itself many times with every Earth species brought with the colonists except, of course, humankind itself, which has shown no changes in its chromosomal patterns."

And that was all.

"You never got to the geblings," said Ruin triumphantly. "We asked you about geblings, but you never got to them."

Heffiji stalked off with the lantern. Of course they followed. But she did not lead them down the stairs. Instead, she found another few papers and laid them out. There were four drawings, each drawn and labeled by the same hand. One was labeled "Human Genetic Molecules." The other three were labeled "humanlike sections" of gebling, dwelf, and gaunt genetic molecules.

In each case, the human genetic patterns were all imbedded within a single long molecule, just as the Earth wheat patterns had been incorporated in the single genetic molecule of all the Imakulata plants.

Heffiji could hardly contain her delight. "They didn't know it! I was the one who put it together, I was the one who knew that both of these were the answers to the same question! And when I saw humans and geblings together, I knew that you were the ones who needed to have this answer." She grinned. "That's why I cheated and gave hints."

"It isn't true!" shouted Ruin. "We are not just failed copies of humans!"

He flung out his hand as if to throw Heffiji's brass lantern to the floor. Both Reck and Patience caught his arm before he could do it.

"Are you trying to burn down this house?" demanded Reck.

"We are the original inhabitants of this world, and they are the interlopers! We are not descended from humans! They have usurped our world from us!"

Patience spoke to him quietly. "Ruin, you're right. Even if half your heritage is human, the other half is not. The other half is native. To imitate us was part of your nature. Whatever your ancestors were before humans came to Imakulata, it was their nature to absorb and adapt. What you are today is the fulfillment of what your ancestors had to become, if they were to be true to themselves."

"And what were we before?" asked Reck. The question was rhetorical. But again Heffiji ran off with the lantern, this time clattering down the ladder. They had no choice but to follow as she ran through the house, shouting, "I know I know! I know I know!"

They found her in the great room, where Will once again stood by the door, while Angel sat in the seat by the fire. Heffiji was holding a large paper, which contained four versions of the same drawing. She kept reciting the words written at the top of the page: "Most likely reconstruction of large segmented animals found at Rameling and Wissick sites."

It was a large wormlike animal with vestigial wings that fanned out just like geblings' fingers, with a head as proportionately tiny as the head of a dwelf, and with a body as long and lithe as a gaunt. Its belly looked loose and open, as if loose sections of bowel were protruding.

When Heffiji at last quieted down, Angel spoke softly from his place by the fire. "Wyrms," he said. "The earliest colonists called them that, and killed them all, even though there was evidence that they lived communally and buried their dead. They were too frightening, they awakened too many human fears. And now they're extinct."

"Except one," said Patience. "That's what Unwyrm is, isn't he? The last of the wyrms."

"Not quite," said Ruin, who looked exhausted and defeated. "We geblings named him, didn't we? Unwyrm. Not-wyrm. Not our father; our brother. We didn't remember that he looked like this, didn't remember what a wyrm was. But now it's clear enough. Just like the second-generation gnat that killed off the other gnats and waited to mate again with the Earth wheat. That's what Unwyrm is doing. Waiting to mate again with a human being."

"The seventh seventh seventh daughter," murmured Angel. "I told you not to come."

"A new human species to replace the old," said Reck. "And to destroy the others—gaunt, dwelf, and gebling."

"Why did he wait so long?" asked Patience. "The gnat finished the process in the very next generation. Why did Unwyrm wait 343 generations for me?"

Heffiji was crestfallen. "I don't have the answer to *everything*, you know."

12 | THE SCEPTER

RUIN CAREFULLY SHAVED PATIENCE'S HAIR FROM BEHIND the ear almost to the middle of the back of her head.

"You'll *have* to wear your wig now," said Angel. "This new hairstyle might attract some attention."

Ruin chewed a leaf, then licked the shaved area with his rough tongue. He jabbed her skin many times with a dry needle. Patience did not feel it except as a tiny pressure—the nerves of pain had already gone numb.

"I won't care how my hair looks," she said. "I'll be lucky if I come out of this remembering I'm a girl." She was trying to show her confidence by joking, but she surprised herself by sounding frightened instead. "Or even a human."

Reck touched her hand. Patience vaguely remembered that only a month ago, if a gebling had touched her it would have taken concentration to avoid showing revulsion. Now the touch came as a comfort to her. Beware of liking her too much, she told herself. Beware of affection, the great deceiver.

"Patience," whispered Reck, "it isn't good if you

189

aren't sure who you are. You'll have the memories of hundreds of men and women in your mind when this is done. Some of them are very strong—especially the geblings. The gebling kings have always been very, very strong."

"I know who I am," Patience whispered. But it was a lie. If she knew who she was it was a secret even from herself. A secret she would at last discover, she hoped. Having the mindstone would unfold her, back to what she was before she learned the roles assigned to her in life. If she was blank, if she was nothing but her roles, then the mindstone would fold her back again, and she would disappear in a storm of memories and selves long dead. But if she had a real self deeper than the faces painted on her by others, she would find her way out, she would keep control, she would survive.

Either I am someone, and I'll live, or I am no one, and my self dies.

She felt Ruin lift a flap of her skin and pin it out of the way. From the grinding sound, he was cutting at her skull, but she felt no more than if her head were a slab of stone. He was a stonecutter, turning her own brain into a sort of heads hall, with all of the heads alive and staring down at her, yammering at once from their jars of gools and headworms. She shuddered.

"Hold still," murmured Ruin.

Angel began a steady monologue to calm her. "Obviously, Patience, this information about Unwyrm and the origin of the geblings and dwelfs and gaunts was not discovered for the first time by whoever left these answers here. The prophecies themselves, the very name of Unwyrm, the traditions of the nonhumans that they are descended from a prehuman ancestor and that Unwyrm is their brother—these all imply that this information has been known before, perhaps many times."

Ruin pried out a section of skull and set it on the table. It made a little clunking sound.

"But knowledge comes and goes. For instance, what happened the first time a human and a gebling met? Had the geblings already developed a language? A society? Or did they fashion their social patterns after those of human beings?"

Ruin held the tiny scepter in his hand. "This is my heritage," he whispered. "No human being could have made this. It belongs to me and Reck, and you have no right to it."

For a moment Patience thought he was reneging on his agreement, that he would put it in his mouth, swallow it, and himself walk along the brink of madness. She was relieved, for just a moment, not to have to do it herself. But then he set it at the base of her brain and she trembled to know it was her ordeal after all. His tongue pushed it through the small incision he had made, until it rested where he wanted it, exactly on the middle of her limbic node. Then he withdrew his tongue, licked a small dish covered with a fine powder, and reinserted it to smear the powder into place.

"And another question that intrigues me," said Angel, going on as if Ruin had not spoken, as if Patience were not now irrevocably committed to a journey that could destroy her. "How does the crystal relate to nonhuman intelligence? The geblings, of course, have humanlike brains, but the dwelfs don't. You all have the crystals, but the gaunts have no will, no sense of identity—the mindstones can't be the seat of personality. And you geblings, you and Unwyrm have in common your means of communication that transcends anything possible to human beings. And yet Unwyrm can use it to call to humans—there must be something in it that is at least latently possible to us."

"You're such an ass when you try to talk like a scholar," whispered Patience.

Angel ignored her. "And the wyrm that originally called the Starship Captain—it had that same ability, and perhaps more."

Ruin spoke without looking up from his work. "No doubt the wyrms used their ability to lure their prey and repel their enemies. One wyrm used it with your Starship Captain, but no doubt it doesn't depend on any intelligence on the part of the victim."

"And instead of eating the captain, they mated," said Reck.

"I wonder which he would rather have done, in the end, mate or die," said Angel. "I wonder how much abasement a human being can bear, and still desire to live." He sounded sad.

"With his right hand he drew what the wyrm wanted him to draw," whispered Patience. "With his left hand he warned us. He still had some part of his human will, even though the wyrm controlled most of his actions."

"Yes, a fragmentation, that's it, a breaking down. Part of the will carried in the brain, created and shaped by memory, by experience. The conscious mind, the controllable mind, the mind of words. And part of the will carried—where? In the genes? Certainly the genes are the only part of us that has any hope of surviving our death—what more appropriate place for a seat of a part of the unconscious mind . . ."

Patience's vision suddenly focused. She had not realized it was blurred before. But it was not Angel speaking at all, it was old Mikail Nakos. Whose voice had she thought it was? She couldn't remember. Mikail, he was the one who had taken it upon himself to study these creatures, the geblings. I thought it could do no harm. But now he wants to implant this organic crystal in someone's mind. He doesn't understand the implications of it.

"What if the crystals actually enhance human mental abilities, make it possible for human beings to communicate telepathically, the way the geblings seem to?"

Then another voice. "It might be possible." It was her own voice, she knew, but not what she expected. For some reason she expected it to be a girl's voice, trained to be mellifluous, soothing; instead it was harsh, commanding, male. Why not male? Am I not a man? The Heptarch listened to himself, trying to remember why his own voice didn't sound right to him.

"I suspect, though, that the telepathic communication has more to do with the molecules than the crystals. The crystal is more likely to be memory. Incredibly well-ordered, clear, and powerful memory." He did not doubt his ability to converse intelligently with a brilliant scientist. But then the old Heptarchs had been scientists, in the beginning. But why am I calling him an old Heptarch? It's not me, then. Not really me talking, though I remember it as being myself. "I'm guessing—but the little ones, you see, the ones they call dwelfs, they can remember with absolute perfection everything that they've ever done, even though they can't hold an idea more complex than their name for very long. They store millions of items of data, but have no organizing principle."

"Not implausible, sir. Not at all. The crystal would be the data storage. The brain, the systematizer. But the telepathy—it might be in the crystal."

"I'm not even sure I believe there *is* any telepathy. It's only speculation. The geblings are certainly not telling, bless their murderous little viper souls."

"Still, sir, combined with a human brain, the crystal could provide a great enhancement of mental abilities."

"If it can combine. If it actually has anything to do with mentation."

"Difficult to answer. But the geblings aren't answering —and they probably don't know, anyway. Ignorant little devils."

For some reason the Heptarch wanted to correct him. To tell him the truth about geblings. But he couldn't remember why he thought he knew geblings so well, so he said nothing.

"You see, sir, if the geblings weren't so dangerous, so deadly, we might be able to leave it alone. But they're cannibals—we saw how they eat each other's brains— and they've murdered almost a dozen of our people already. We have to understand all we can about them. What they want, where they come from—"

"So you need a little white mouse to test the crystal."

"Unfortunately, it needs to be a highly intelligent white mouse. I intend to have it implanted in my own brain, sir."

"Nonsense. If you implant it in anyone, implant it in me."

"You're the Heptarch. I can't do that."

"I'm the Heptarch, so you *must* do it. There is no duty so difficult or dangerous or unpleasant that one of my people can do it, and I cannot."

Patience was suddenly aware that she was not the man who chose to have the mindstone placed in his brain. That was long ago, another person. But how could the crystal contain a memory of an event that obviously took place before the crystal was implanted?

No sooner had the question occurred to her than the answer came, a mother speaking to a daughter; she was the mother *and* the daughter, hearing the conversation from both sides, speaking both sides of the conversation herself. It was confusing, but exhilarating.

"When the scepter first enters your brain, it searches for your most potent memories and copies them and keeps them."

"You won't know my memories, will you?"

"No, darling, but you'll know mine. You'll know what I'm thinking at this very moment, how much I love you, to give you this gift while I'm still alive."

"I'm afraid."

"The first thing you think of is always our great ancestor, who first chose to bear the scepter. He is our courage, and part of him becomes part of you."

Why didn't Father help me, as this mother helped her daughter? Then she couldn't remember who Father was, or who she was, except the mother, except the daughter.

"You're safe as long as you don't think of certain things."

"What things?"

"If I tell you what they are, my foolish child, then how will you stop yourself from thinking of them?"

I know what they are, thought Patience. They are the gebling kings in whose brain the crystal first grew. They are the wyrm-hearted gebling kings that I mustn't think of.

And that very thought brought her to the memories most to be feared, a terrible alien viewpoint. She knew at once that she had taken the step into the abyss. She could feel a faint buzz of feeling, like peripheral vision, like background noise, like a metallic taste in her mouth, like a smell redolent of sweet and bitter memories, like the touch of a thousand tiny flies upon her skin; gradually she realized, as the gebling whose mind now dwelt in hers realized, that these were her brothers, her sisters, the life of them speaking to the firstborn, the gebling king, myself.

The other geblings are still tearing their way out of

their soft-skinned shells, their hair curled and matted. I am curled by my mother's exhausted body, her black segments trembling from her labors. Beside me lies my father, his poor, weak, hairless body covered with sweat. Come to me, Father, open my mouth—

"Full-grown. Whatever it is, it's no baby." The voice is soft. "Haven't you heard of babies around here?"

His mouth moves and the sounds are beautiful. Teach me how to make these sounds.

Father's face is twisted as he looks at me. "Full-grown little apes." He touches me. He pushes me. "You brought me here so you could give birth to *these!*"

Another egg opens, but with something black inside. Black like Mother. The tiny tiny head like Mother. It's hungry. I can feel it being hungry. It wants to kill Father. It wants to kill me. It wants to kill everybody and eat all the world.

Father taught me what to do. Already he saved me. Father taught me pushing. I push the black one, I push him but he hurts me very much. I cry out with my fear. Mother, help me. Father, save me. I hear a terrible frightened sound and it is my own sound coming out of my own mouth like Father. I scream and scream.

They fight, Mother and the black one. Father is shouting and shouting—

"Stay here and die, all of you stay and for God's sake eat each other!"

The sound of his voice says fear and I am also afraid. Father goes through a hole in the wall of the birthing place. Father knows the way. Father we are coming! Come with Father I shout with my silent voice and they hear me with their othermind. I go and so all the others go, all those who look like me, and some of the littler ones and taller ones, all who can move, all who do not writhe on the ground dying because their bodies don't work. We cry out to him We're coming, Father, but he doesn't hear us because we don't make a sound and in the silence he is deaf. I see it in his eyes when he looks at us, he doesn't understand our cries, he only hears our screaming.

Behind us the black one that looks like Mother is eating her belly out and he will eat us all if he can. Hungry, hungry, he pushes his hunger out into all of us, Come to me, says his hunger, come and fill me, and I can feel my brothers and sisters yielding to him, stopping, going back toward the birthing place. No! I cry! No! Come with Father, come away. With Father with Father tell everyone to come with Father.

And the strongest ones take up my call, they call also, Come with Father, and we are stronger as we call together, stronger and stronger until we have overcome the Mother-eater's hunger.

Down into the black tunnel, all of us in the black tunnel, where are you, Father? Where are you?

I see you, bright sisters and brothers, I feel your path in the darkness, I know where you are, every one of you, in so many different tunnels. From Father's footsteps splashing ahead of me I know the path outward. Follow the water. Follow the running water. It goes away from the birthing place, follow the water—

Patience cried out with joy as she saw the light of the world for the first time. From a cavern's mouth in the face of a high cliff she looked down on a vast forest, with the heads of the River Cranwater joining to form a single river flowing away from Skyfoot. Even as she remembered she was Patience, she could also remember being the first gebling king, feeling the presence of every other gebling as each came out of his or her own tunnel to find the sky, the water leaping out from each cavern mouth. Again she saw through the gebling's eyes.

We all stand here, looking at the bright light, like-me and bigger and littler, I can feel us all here at the edge of the world. And beside me is Father, I have found him, there is water on his face. "I sold my soul for you," he says. "All I wanted was that wyrm back there. How could I want her." He shudders. "It was eating her. What kind of monsters—"

I try to feel him, too, like I can feel all the others, but he isn't there, my eyes see him, my nose smells him, but my othermind can't find him. I touch his cheek and taste the water on his face. It is salt, not like the clear water of the cave. He sees my tongue and wrinkles his face. Then he reaches to me and touches my cheek and his mouth says, "You're not a wyrm, though, are you? It's not your fault, is it."

Then he stands and takes my hand and leads me to the edge and holds out his hand to point to the bright blue dazzle that blinds me and all the children of man and wyrm.

"Sky," he says.

"Sick. I." I speak. I am like him, not like Mother. She was eaten by the wyrm in the birthing place, but Father lives and I am like him.

"Born an hour ago, and already you can talk. What have I made here? What can you become?"

Patience watched the time flow faster. The babies born, the Starship Captain teaching them everything. To build houses, to hunt for food, to tend their children and teach them. Language came easily, all learning came easily to these new people who never forgot anything once they had done it a single time. They invented their own words faster than Father could teach them, until they hardly came to him for learning anymore.

The gebling king, who never had a name for himself, he came to Father often. "Wyrm," Father said. "Your mother is the wyrm, and I am your father, but most important of all is the monster that ate your mother and drove us from the birthing place. He looks like a wyrm but he isn't a wyrm. He's your brother and he'll kill you all if he can, and if he ever comes out of the mountain you must kill him first.''

So the gebling king was the first gebling who learned to kill, and he used the secret knowledge of murder just as human beings had used it from the start—to gather power to himself. I have the terrible secret. I can kill you if you disobey. But if you obey me, I can share the secret with you and you, too, can have power—

Until Father says one day, when he finds me covered with blood, "I wish Unwyrm had killed you that day in the birthing place, I wish he had killed me and eaten me rather than let me live to make you what you are. I'm sorry that I taught you, any of you."

So I kill him and eat his brain in front of the others, even though I find no mindstone in it; I don't tell them that he had no stone. And now my power is perfect, even greater than Unwyrm's power, because he has no one to obey him and I have all of these.

Patience screamed at the memory, at the taste and smell of Father's blood, at the look of horror and awe and admiration in the other geblings' eyes. I couldn't do this, I never could have done this, she cried out in revulsion. And yet this is what I was raised for, to kill in order to get power, to devour anything that threatens to block me from my will—

"It's maddening her," said Angel.

"Give her time to find herself," said Reck.

The voices meant nothing to Patience. For all she could see was the bloodshed through the years. The murders of the gebling kings, the murders of the Heptarchs. Wars and assasinations, tortures and rapes, she remembered committing all the crimes of seven thousand years of power and she hated herself for all that she had done—

Nothing in my life except death and terror, she thought.

And then her own mother's face (or was it her mother? She had three hundred mothers) smiling at her, touching her, saying, "Broken heart, don't cry. Don't cry at the things that have been done in your name. For every life that was taken, there were ten thousand who lived in peace with your protection. Do you think your power would last for a moment if all you had was the power to kill? They would rise up and strike you down. You have the power to draw them together, to make them act as one. You have made the weak strong by the sound of your voice, and they love you forever."

Patience clung to the message of that voice. I have made the weak strong by the sound of my voice. They love me forever.

And at last, having found a thread to cling to so she would not fall into the abyss, she slept.

13 | TRUE FRIEND

SHE AWOKE LYING IN A BED, COVERED WITH THREE FEATHER-
beds. A cold breeze from a broken window whipped past
her face. The trees outside the window were golden with
autumn. Are you really the trees of Earth? she asked
them silently. Or are you strange alien creatures that have
captured the trees and hidden them deep inside, so you
can wear their mask?

She thought of all the children she had ever had in her
hundreds of lives, pictured them smiling up at her, good
children every one; but then something dark, a dark
worm crawled into their mouths and now when they look
out at her it is the wyrm with the tiny head and the
fanlike fingers—not a wing at all—and the hundred fleshy
organs of tearing and digesting and reproducing—Unwyrm,
do you know the difference between eating and mating?
Or is there a difference to you? All hungers are the same
hunger.

She opened her eyes. She saw him before she saw
anything else, standing there half lit by the dim autumnal
light through the window. Will. His face watching her in

his utter silence, his unreadable stolidness, like an animal; or no, like a mountain, like the face of living rock. Why are you watching me?

She did not speak; he did not answer. He only noticed that her eyes were open, nodded, and walked from the room. He closed the door gently behind him. It was the tenderness, the gentleness of the closing of the door that told her that he was not, after all, made of stone. It wasn't lifelessness that made him still, it was peace. He had made his peace with life, and so his face had no more to say, no silent pleas to make between speeches, and his mind had no speeches to make between silences. He isn't hungry. He is already satisfied.

And as she thought of hunger, she felt again the Cranning call, as powerful as ever, gnawing at her womb. I am hungry to have his babies, she thought. It came to her as the memory of a hundred nightmares during the time she slept. He will make me hungry for his seed in me, just as his mother made the Starship Captain yearn for her. He will make me think that it is ecstasy.

She shuddered. But now that she had dreamed Unwyrm a hundred times, his writhing as he devoured his mother and slaughtered his helpless deformed brothers, now that it was so familiar to her it did not make her lose control of herself and scream, as she had done in all the dreams. She was too tired of it to cry out against it anymore. I'll just have to see to it that it doesn't happen, that's all. He'll die before he has me, or I'll die. His children will not be born from my body.

But even if I live, will I ever want a man as I want Unwyrm? What if he dies while still calling me? Will that need be with me then forever, always unsatisfied?

Thoughts like that made her angry with herself. She sat up, swinging her legs over the edge of the bed. At once she was almost overcome with dizziness. The door to her room opened, and Angel came in. Angel, looking strong and healthy, no longer weak from the wound in his throat.

"Your wound has healed and the trees have turned colors," she said. "How long have I slept?"

"Forty days and forty nights, like Moses in the mount, like the rain of the deluge, like Elijah fasting in the wilderness. If you can call it sleeping. You've done a lot of shouting and kept us all awake. Even River has complained that you frighten his monkey. How are you?"

She reached up and touched the side of her head that Ruin had shaved. The hair had grown several centimeters.

"Weak," she said. "Unwyrm is calling me."

"We were afraid the scepter was too much for you."

"It wasn't the scepter, really. It was all the terrible things I had done."

"You didn't do any of them."

"But I did, Angel. No, don't argue with me. I didn't kill my own father and eat his brain, the way the first gebling king did, or kill my own wife, as *my* father did. But I *have* killed. Obeying you or father, or to save my own life, I have killed easily, with pleasure, with pride. That made it hard for me to—separate myself from all their crimes. I could only find and follow a very slender hope running from life to life throughout my past, Angel. A hope that it all works together for good. That out of the blood I've poured into the ground, life can grow again."

"Many people who've just awakened from a sound sleep think they're philosophers," Angel said.

"Don't make fun of me," said Patience. "This is important. This is my—my contribution to the scepter, if I have one to make. All the children will look to me, gebling children and human children, they all will look to me and I have to keep them safe. From Unwyrm's children. And yet sometimes I think—Unwyrm's children would not be murderers. They would all be bound together with óne heart and mind, the way the wyrms were before the coming of humans to this world. Before human genes made us strangers to each other. Unwyrm's children would never be alone. And I could be their mother.''

"Don't say that, Patience," said Angel.

"It's just that I finally understood the thought he sends to me, Angel. I know what Unwyrm did to his own mother. He's the devourer, not me. I'll kill him if I can.'' But she knew she didn't sound convincing. It didn't matter, though. It wasn't Angel she had to convince, it was herself.

"He *is* a wyrm, then? A descendant of the ones the first colonists killed?"

"He is *the* Unwyrm, Angel. The very one. The only one. Alive for all seven thousand years of the world's history.''

"To live so long—''

"We're strangers here. The native life can adapt itself, make changes in a single generation that we take a million years to make. Unwyrm is more intelligent than all of them. In him are combined the most powerful of the native gifts, and he called the most brilliant of human minds, and they must have taught him all they knew. What's to stop him from repairing himself genetically, when he finds any part of him becoming weak, decaying? What's to stop him from living until he's ready to mate?''

"Why would he wait so long?''

"I don't know. I only know how humans looked to the first geblings. The machines that let our ancestors fly, that made pictures in the air, that chewed up forests and spat out wheatfields. What did the wyrms see, when a

new star appeared in the sky and metal birds skittered
above the surface of the world? They weren't gnats,
replacing safe and stationary wheat. They were at the
peak of the ecological system, these wyrms, but we were
more powerful than they. And if they were to replace
us—"

"They had to know all that we knew."

"The wheat sits there, passively waiting for its enemy
to destroy it. But the wyrms knew that human beings
weren't passive. We were the most deadly competitor for
life that this world had ever seen. To overpower us, the
wyrms' grandchildren not only had to be identical to
human beings—they had to excel at the things that human beings do best. They had to know more, to be more
beautiful, more brilliant, more powerful, more dangerous. How could a single wyrmchild, Unwyrm, hiding in
his ice cave in Skyfoot, how could he learn enough to
prepare his children?"

"An ice cave? That means he's high in the mountain,
where the glaciers are."

"Don't you understand, Angel? He couldn't defeat us
if we built machines. The wyrms knew it from the start.
When they captured the Starship Captain, before they
even brought him down, they first made him destroy all
the metal that was easy to mine. But there was still
metal—I remember my ancestors who pursued it, who
mined it, who tried to build machines with it. They might
have succeeded. But always the geblings came, a flood
of geblings out of Cranning."

"I'm reasonably familiar with the history of the world."

"Angel! I'm telling you what no one ever knew. I'm
telling you the *why* of it. I've seen the pattern in it,
remembering it all at once like this. Unwyrm sent the
geblings to stop mankind from making the machines that
would have made us irresistible. He waited all this time

to keep us weak while he gathered wisdom to himself. He gave himself seven thousand years. And then fulfilled his own prophecy by causing my brothers to be killed and me to be—"

He touched her head gently, to soothe her. His hand felt cool and loving on her forehead, on her cheek. "River tells us that Cranning is only a week away, and the autumn winds are strong for getting there. But we have to go *now*. The winter winds will beat us back. It's good you came to yourself today—we'll bring you to Cranning in your right mind."

There was an artificiality in his tone as he spoke; his heart wasn't in what he said, and she couldn't think why he was lying to her. But that was no surprise, she could hardly think at all. So she let it go, didn't try to discover what it was he was concealing. "Tell Reck and Ruin that I also know the map of Cranning."

"They know you do. You've told us much in your sleep. We've been writing down the stories you shouted out, and Heffiji has been storing them away here and there. I've tried to figure out what her system is."

"She doesn't have one."

"That was my conclusion. A true dwell. But no one else could have done this. Unwyrm was calling all the people who knew things. He would have called her, too, if she had actually known anything. The only way the knowledge could stay in the world was with someone like Heffiji who knew nothing of any value, but could lay her hands on everything that mattered. It's all here. All the learning of the world. Reck and Ruin have called geblings out of Cranning to guard the place. They're going to glaze and shutter the windows, put on a new roof. Whatever it takes to protect this house."

"Do the geblings accept Reck and Ruin as their king?"

Angel shrugged. "Who knows what goes on in their

minds? They say one thing, but something completely different might be going on under the surface. The fact remains that for the time being, these kings can't go more than a few dozen meters away from *you,* or they start being driven away from Cranning by Unwyrm. They can't exactly claim their right to lead the geblings while they're still chained to the human Heptarch, can they?''

"We've wasted enough time," Patience said. "Take me to the boat."

"We'll go as far as Cranning, but no deeper into the mountain until you're stronger."

"I wasn't sick, just crazy," Patience said. "Crazy people can be amazingly strong."

"Is the call—any different now?"

"Only because I know who it is that's calling me."

"So he doesn't control you—"

"Or if he does, he controls me so thoroughly that I don't know I'm controlled."

"That puts my mind at ease."

"Angel, I've become a terrible person."

"Have you?"

"If the scepter had been given to me before I knew the things we learned here in this house, I could never have coped with it. If I had been brought to Cranning without understanding all the things I understand, I would have been helpless when I faced him. I look back on all that you and father did, all that I did and the geblings did and—it was right, it was necessary."

"Why does that make you terrible?"

"Even Mother's death, Angel. Even that."

"Ah."

"What kind of person am I, to agree that my own mother had to die? I have lived through that so many times, all my life, only this time through Father's eyes. He never forgave himself for it. Yet I forgive him.''

Angel bent down and kissed her forehead. ''My Heptarch, only you are fit to rule mankind.''

''What kind of person am I?''

''A wise one.''

She didn't argue, though she knew it wasn't true. Wise she was not. But strong—she *was* strong. She had mastered the mindstone. There was a true self before all the folds of her life. She knew that much, but the rest of her self was still elusive, out of reach, out of sight. So let Angel call her wise, she cared nothing for that. ''But am I *good*, Angel?''

''As Heptarch, your choice is no longer between good and bad. Your choice is between right and wrong.''

She had been his student long enough to understand the difference, and agree that he was right. At least in her role as Heptarch, she could no longer live by the same moral code that others lived by. Her decisions now were the decisions of a larger community than just herself. But what community? ''Right for whom?'' she asked.

''For humankind, Heptarch.''

She knew at once that he was wrong. ''No. The King's House is all the world. I am a gebling, too. All the life that speaks, and all the life that doesn't speak, all the life of the world except one.''

''And that one wants you. But I'll die before I let him have you. He thinks I'm too weak to save you, but I can, and I will.''

His fervor as he spoke was no pretense. Whatever lies he was telling, this was not part of it. He *did* love her. She touched his cheek. ''Serve me as a free man, Angel.''

''Slave or free, I serve you the same. What difference does it make?''

''I ask you now, as a free man, to help me.''

Angel gently dressed her and led her from the room.

To her surprise, the house was busy with geblings, hundreds of them. Her room had been off limits to them, but through the rest of the house they were busy glazing, patching, repairing, making it whole again. Patience sat in the common room by a scant fire, a fall of sunlight catching her chair to help keep her warm, and watched the ladders going up and down, moving along the walls, the geblings scattering here and there. River's monkey scampered underfoot—a dozen times he was kicked, nearly stepped on, or knocked off some high perch. Always he got up, screeched a string of unintelligible obscenities, and bounded back into the thick of the fray. Patience could not help but notice that Heffiji was much like the monkey, almost frantic with delight and worry, scurrying in and out of the house, up and down the stairs. "Don't touch that!" she'd cry. The geblings would laugh and mock her, but they would also obey.

In his jar on the mantlepiece, River slept. Away from Cranwater, the world did not exist for him.

Patience found herself trying to feel the geblings' silent communication, the speechless call of the othermind. She remembered so clearly how it felt, when she was each of the first few gebling kings. Yet now she felt nothing. It was like reaching out with her hand, only to discover that her hand had been cut off. She watched them wistfully, grieving that she could never know them except in the vicarious memories that came to her through the scepter. And the geblings went about their business, not knowing who she was, not guessing that she was the one living human who knew what it was like to be a gebling, who could understand the constant fellowship that gave them their anchor in the world. How did I find the courage to live before, when I never knew what it was to know another person?

"Patience," whispered someone behind her. She knew the voice, knew that Reck's hand was reaching for her shoulder, and reached up her own hand to touch. And yes, it was there, the soft fur of the gebling hand. For a moment she thought that perhaps she had felt Reck's proximity through the othermind. But no; it could only be her instinct as an assassin, to know when a hand was reaching for her. She could not hope ever to take part in the gebling community.

"Reck," she said.

"We were afraid we'd carry a madwoman with us into Cranning."

"A madwoman should stay here. After all, this is a madhouse."

Reck laughed. "Not really. These geblings came to rebuild Heffiji's house, to keep the learning of human-kind safe."

"How did you call them?"

"Oh, the gebling king is known. Not by face or name—no, when they see us here they think we're just two more geblings who were summoned and came. But in the othermind, they know the call of the gebling king."

"Do they come from Cranning?"

"I don't think so. We called, and the nearest geblings heard it and passed on the call. As more and more took it up, it got stronger, until we knew we had enough. We're not Unwyrm. Our own call, alone, could never reach from here to Cranning."

"It's good of you to keep this house alive."

"This house has done the impossible. It has humbled my beloved brother Ruin. All the ideas that Heffiji has saved here. Ruin's made a pest of himself, questioning her, dogging her heels from answer to answer. He's hardly known a human in his life, and for obvious reasons he's never known any of the Wise. Now, though, he's seen what human minds can do at their best.''

''If he ever wants to know us at our worst, he has only to take the scepter,'' said Patience.

''Not likely,'' said Reck. ''We used to pity you humans for your solitude. Well, *I* pitied you, and he despised you. But now, well, he keeps telling me that solitude is the foundation of true wisdom, that all the brilliant thoughts in this house come as the desperate cry of one human being to another, saying, Know me, live with me in the world of my mind.''

''It's a very poetic thought.''

''I told him he's lovesick—he's fallen in love with the human race. But you know how it is. I've never hated humans the way he has, and so I'm not quite so impressed when I find out that not all humans are worthless.'' Reck walked to the chair on the other side of the fire.

''It's funny,'' said Patience. ''I kept dreaming about houses. Different houses that I needed to take care of. Sometimes Heffiji's house and sometimes my father's house, and sometimes Heptagon House. Sometimes the house where my mother was killed.''

Reck looked thoughtful. There were footsteps on the stair. Ruin padded into the room. Patience noticed at once that he was no longer naked. He wore short trousers. A step toward accepting human civilization.

''Why did you call me?'' he asked.

Reck turned to him, beckoned him closer. There was no one else in the room, but still it was better not to talk too loudly, not when they were saying things that could reveal who they were before they wanted to. ''She heard our call,'' said Reck.

Ruin looked at Patience, as if analyzing a strange new

herb he had just noticed on the forest floor. "The need to come fix a very important house? And where it was?"

"I saw paths sometimes, I never knew where from or where to. But always in the distance I could see the house burning, and I knew I had to hurry—"

Reck shook her head. "There was nothing about fire in our call."

"We don't even see images," added Ruin. "The othermind isn't that precise."

But Patience was excited at the thought that she might have experienced the gebling othermind in her own body. She wouldn't let these small objections disprove it. "I'm not a gebling, and my brain may translate things into images that I can understand. I may be more of a gebling than you think. I remember the othermind. I remember feeling all the other geblings, and the map of Cranning. And besides, I have the scepter now. Maybe that lets me feel your call."

Reck stroked her tongue with the long nail of her thumb. "No," she said. "Heptarchs have borne the mindstone before, but they have never heard the call of the king to the people."

Ruin cocked his head, studying Patience's face. "If it isn't the mindstone, then perhaps Unwyrm's call has made her more sensitive, so she hears what no human could hear before."

Reck raised a finger. "Remember, though. No Heptarch has ever worn the mindstone so close to Cranning. When the other geblings took up the call, to pass it on, perhaps it grew strong enough for her to hear."

"It was nothing like Unwyrm's call," said Patience. "That is so clear and powerful."

"Unwyrm is much better at it than we are. Our human nature. It weakens us." Reck sounded a little resentful.

"Do you wish that you had no human parent?"

Reck laughed bitterly. "Do you think the wyrms look any prettier to us? Nobody gave us a choice of ancestors."

"I saw it," said Patience. And she told them of the birth of the first geblings. Ruin made her slow down, tell every detail. He listened with his eyes closed, as if by concentrating on the sound of her choice he could conjure up the memories that the geblings had lost forever when they lost the mindstone of the kings.

When Patience told how the infant Unwyrm killed his mother, Ruin nodded. "Yes, yes," he said. "It wasn't murder. He had to eat the crystal, you see. To know all that she knew."

"We're more discreet now," said Reck. "We're more human. We wait until our parents die naturally. It means we have more life on our own before becoming our parents. But there's nothing unnatural about a child eating its parent's memory, not on Imakulata."

Patience went on with the story, with all she could remember of the life of the first geblings. And ended when the last of the gebling kings to bear this mindstone found the corpse of the last living wyrm. Humans had burned it to death.

"Of course," said Reck. "If it's strange and frightening, kill it. The human credo."

"Humans do what they have to do," said Ruin. Reck grinned wickedly and winked at Patience, as if to say, See how my brother has become a humanophile! "The wyrms did what they had to do," said Ruin. "They knew the humans could and would kill them all, with their machines. What do you do when the enemy is too strong to destroy? You become the enemy."

"Oh, yes, everybody's doing what their genes tell them to do," said Patience.

"If they hadn't chosen to mate with humans," said

Reck, "we wouldn't exist. We can hardly condemn the choice they made."

"But you see, Heptarch, we geblings are not what they decided to become," said Ruin. "We're the castoffs of the second generation, the failed experiments, the doomed hybrids, the pitiful grotesques. Dwelfs with no brain. Gaunts with no will. We geblings, we came close. But not a perfect match. It's the next generation that will be the perfect match, while we are meant to die."

"It's not as if anyone planned it," said Patience. "It's he way life evolved here on Imakulata."

"When you put it that way," said Reck, "it makes you want to bound up to Unwyrm and have his babies, doesn't it?"

"With all due respect to the wisdom of our most ancient forebears," said Ruin, "the gebling king has decided not to go along with the plan."

"We are wyrm enough to feel the life of every other gebling," said Reck, "and human enough to have an individual will to survive. As far as we're concerned, the adaptive process went far enough when it produced us and the gaunts and dwelfs."

"We are the heirs of the wyrms," said Ruin. "Different from humans, but enough like you to live alongside you. The genes of the wyrms are best preserved in us. Not in the perfect copy that Unwyrm means to make."

"We *are* allies in this war," said Patience. Impulsively she slid from her chair, sat on the floor before the fire, leaning against Reck's legs, her head resting on the gebling's knee. "I remember living gebling lives. I want you to survive as much as I want human beings to live."

Reck stroked her hair. "I have come to know you as I've known no other human being but one. I would regret it if the only way to stop Unwyrm were to kill you, too."

"But you would do it," said Patience.

"If there be no other way, I will."

"And if there be no other way," said Patience, "I want you to."

She happened, as she said it, to look back to the door. Angel stood there, his hands on the jambs on either side. The look on Angel's face said that he had overheard their conversation and that he would not consent to Patience's death.

And for the first time it occurred to Patience that Angel might have no intention of obeying her when it came to the final battle with Unwyrm. Angel had his own plans, and however much he might call her Heptarch, he still thought of her as a child under his tutelage.

A chill swept over Patience as she thought, What if I have to kill you, Angel, in order to do what I must do?

He could not have seen what she thought in the expression of her face, but weak as she was she could not hide the shudder. He saw it. Wordlessly he went back outside, closing the door behind him.

If Reck and Ruin noticed the momentary byplay, they did not comment on it. Perhaps it was because Reck felt her shudder that she asked, "Are you strong enough to go on?"

"What strength does it take?" asked Patience. "I'm sane, I think, and so we can go as soon as the work here is finished."

"Then we can go now. There's no need to wait here for the house to be done. It will be finished whether we're here or not. Besides, we can supervise it, in a general sort of way, without being here at all."

Reck got up.

"Wait," said Patience. "I wanted to ask you. Will. He was watching at the foot of my bed when I woke up."

Reck shrugged. "Will does what he wants."

"How long had he been there?"

"I don't know. Whenever I've noticed him, he was either coming from or going to your room."

Ruin chuckled. "He's a human male, after all, and you only came out of your boy disguise when I operated on you. Perhaps he likes looking at you. He's been celibate for a long time."

Patience was disconcerted for a moment, to think of Will perhaps desiring her as a woman. Then she realized Ruin was joking. She laughed.

"Don't laugh," said Reck. "I gave up trying to decipher Will's mind long ago, however, so my guess is almost worthless. He does what he wants. But I doubt he thought of having you, Child. I've never seen him want anything for himself. His life is nothing but service."

"A natural slave," said Ruin.

"No one could ever own him," said Reck. "He serves, but only where he thinks service is needed. I think that secretly he believes he's Kristos. Isn't that what the human god is supposed to be? The servant of all?"

"I'm a Skeptic," said Patience. "I don't pay attention to religion."

"Well, like it or not, religion pays attention to you," said Reck. "If you come out of this alive, you'll be lucky if they don't claim *you're* the Kristos."

"She's as good a choice as anyone," said Ruin.

"Or why not you?" said Patience. "That would stand them on their ear, to have a gebling savior."

Ruin laughed. "Why not? The goblin Kristos."

Patience laughed with him. As she did, she felt the Cranning call strengthen within her, as if it had been holding back, during her long madness, but had now awakened with the sound of her laughter. Lust for Unwyrm burned within her. She called for Sken, and Sken and Will readied the boat that afternoon. And in the morning,

Patience herself took River's jar from the mantlepiece. "Wake up," she said to him.

He slowly opened his eyes, then clicked twice and made a kissing sound. The monkey scampered into the room almost at once, and began pumping the bellows frantically. "About time," River said. "About bloody time, what do you think I had them save my head for, to watch while a bunch of goblins redecorate a dullfish house? Get me down to the boat, and you may rest assured that I'll remember this as the worst, the stupidest voyage of my life!"

He scolded all the way down the hill. Only the rocking of the boat in the water stilled him; then he sang the most curious song to the river, a song without words, without even much of a melody. The song of a man returned to his body at last, the ecstasy of once again wearing his own arms and legs, of once again being himself. River restored to the river.

They cast off from Heffiji's ramshackle dock and sailed north on the last of the autumn wind. Patience could feel Unwyrm rejoicing that she was coming to him once again. This month of waiting must have been hard for him, not knowing what it was that kept her, not knowing if she was injured, or had gained strength to resist him, or had been captured. Now she was coming to him once again, and he made her body tremble with the pleasure of it.

14 | VIGILANT

PATIENCE KNEW THAT THE SCENERY UPRIVER OF HEFFIJI'S house was identical to the scenery they had already passed. The same massive oaks, the same beech and maple, ash and pine. But she knew more now. She *was* more. She could remember some of the earliest Heptarchs as little children, learning long catalogues of flora and fauna, all neatly split between native and Earthborn.

Oak and maple are Earthborn, so are ash and pine. Beech and palm and fern are native, but were named for similar Earth species. Scrubnut, hotberry, glassfruit, and web are native; walnut is from Earth.

Like many of her earliest ancestors, Patience now saw clear divisions between Imakulata's native life and the life brought in the starship, and she began to understand the origin of the ancient enmity between humans and the intelligent natives they despised. They were ugly, strange, dangerous from the human point of view, while humans and the plants they had brought with them were safe and beautiful.

Yet Patience could also see what none of her ancestors

had seen. Even though she could remember the world as it was seen by the fifth Heptarch, she had no memory of an alien world. The forests of Imakulata, by the fifth generation, had become exactly as they were today, almost entirely Earthborn.

And yet not Earthborn at all. The native species had not been replaced. They had merely put on disguises and become, in appearance, the Earthborn plants that the humans nurtured. What was the oak before? A little flying bug, a worm, a seaweed, an airborne virus on a fleck of dust? The whole world was in disguise, every living thing pretending to be homely and comfortable for the humans who supposed themselves masters of the world. Everything that truly belonged to human beings had been kidnapped, murdered, and replaced with mocks and moles. Patience imagined she could see through the disguise of the deer that drank at water's edge and bounded lightly away at their noisy approach. She pictured the secret self of an oak as a hideous, deformed baby leering wickedly at her from the heart of the tree. Changelings, a world of changelings, all conspiring against us, lulling us into complacency, until the moment that they finally begin to replace us, too.

She shuddered. And she imagined that Unwyrm whispered to her with the desires of her body. Come to me, come and bear my children, my children, my changelings, we'll steal into every house in the world, you and I, and creep to the children's beds. We'll lay our little wyrmling into the cradle, and watch as it changes shapes to look just like the human baby lying there. Then we'll take the human baby, carry it outside, slit its throat and toss it in my bag.

A thousand bags, each emptied into a garden, where the leering oaks suck the last dregs of life from the dessicated flesh. Patience thought she walked through the garden, brittle bones crackling under her feet, watching where her husband emptied another bag, then looked at her with his tiny wyrm's head and said, "The last. That's the last of them. There's only one human child left in all the world." He took a living baby out of his bag, its terrified eyes looking hopelessly up at her, and graciously offered to let her dine.

Instead, she ran away, to a place where the ground was soft and forgiving to her feet; to a small hut in the forest, where she could hear a mother crooning to her child. Here is a place we missed, she thought. A child that lives on. I'll protect it, I'll hide it from Unwyrm, and he'll grow up and thrive and kill the changelings—

She peered into the window and saw the baby, and he was beautiful, his delicate fingers wrapped around his mother's thumb, his mouth making sweet sucking motions. Live, she said silently to the child. Live and be strong, for you are the last.

Then the child winked at her and leered.

Angel shook her awake. "You screamed," he said.

"Sorry," she whispered. She held to the gunnel and looked across the water at the trees. None of them seemed any different. Her dream had been nonsense. If it looks like an oak, if it cuts like an oak, if you can build with it like an oak, what does it matter that it has one immense genetic molecule, instead of many small ones? What does it matter if the deer is only half deer, and the other half of its bloodline is some strange creature of Imakulata? Life is life, form is form.

Except my life. My form. That must be preserved. Unwyrm's improved version of humanity is the death of the old, flawed, lonely, but beautiful Earthborn people. My people.

Come, hurry, hurry, come, spoke Unwyrm's passion.

"Look," said Angel. "River sent Ruin up the mast,

and he saw it at the last bend of the river. Skyfoot. For a few minutes, we can see it even from the deck.''

Patience got up. Despite what she'd been through on this journey, her body still responded quickly. She was alert and strong in a moment. My body doesn't know I'm three hundred generations old, she thought. My body thinks that I'm a young woman. My body still thinks I have a future of my own.

Skyfoot was a shadow just topping the distant trees on a long, straight stretch of river.

''If the forest weren't so tall,'' said Angel, ''we would have seen it a week before we reached Heffiji's house, instead of three days after leaving it.''

''It's very close,'' said Patience.

''Not really. Just very high. Seven kilometers from base to ridge.''

''And now hidden again.''

It was too brief a glimpse, and too far away to make out any features. But each sight of it seemed longer than the one before. Two days later they dropped anchor in another bend, and as the dusk hid the mountain itself, the lights of Cranning began to dot the sky like a low-hung galaxy.

The lights went as far from east to west as they could see through their alley between the shores of tall timber. That night Reck and Ruin climbed the rigging in the darkness, to perch together on the mast and watch their patrimony come alive with light.

River grew surly. Cranning meant nothing to him but the end of the voyage. It was the journey that he lived for, and each arrival was like a little death.

The next day the river began to break up into many wide and slow-flowing streams passing among wooded islands. ''What we have here,'' said Angel, ''is an ancient tectonic collision of massive proportions. We are on a plate that once was sliding down under the huge up-thrust of Skyfoot. Now the two have joined, and the ground is stable, but once there must have been terrible earthquakes. From here on, the land actually falls toward the base of Skyfoot. The water from the melting glaciers atop the mountain piles up in the sunken area, making a lake that runs along the entire base of the mountain. The original colonists saw it and wrote that there was nothing like it on any habitable planet in the universe.''

"So far," said Patience.

"Well, one assumes that anything that can happen once, can and will happen again, eventually, on some other world."

They could make out clusters of buildings on the mountain's face now. All day Ruin clung to the mast or sat in the bow, rapt, watching the face of the mountain as though it were a beloved supplicant coming to him.

"He's useless to anyone," Sken complained. "We ought to tie a rope on him and throw him overboard as an anchor."

Reck's reaction to the mountain was the opposite of Ruin's. While he grew silent, she became talkative.

"I've heard the stories since I was little," she said. "The soil and water of the ten thousand cavern mouths of Cranning are so rich that never a stick of wood or morsel of food has ever been imported here. The foot of Cranning is a moist and humid rain forest. The mountain rises through all the weathers of the world. Anything that can live and grow anywhere in the world grows here."

She told of the kingdoms of men that had risen and fallen on the mountain's face, some of them only three kilometers wide, fifty meters deep, and twenty meters high, yet with their own dialects, armies, cultures. "And behind them all, in the deepest caverns, in utter darkness, we geblings carry on our lives. Ten million geblings, more than half the geblings in the world. While men and dwelfs and gaunts have their wars and intrigues on the face of Skyfoot, we hold its heart. They build their boundaries and walls, so that none can pass—but the geblings pass, because we know all the hidden ways.''

"Don't you rule on the surface, too?" asked Patience.

"When we want to," she said, smiling. "When we decide to rule, then we rule. Everyone there knows that. We don't have to be officious about it.''

Patience felt no rapture at the sight of the mountain. Somewhere near the top he was waiting for her, sensing her coming closer, getting more eager for her arrival. She found herself longing to turn the boat around, drift downstream and never think of Cranning or the Heptarchy or anything else again. She dreamed more often, and woke up sweating in the night, trembling from the desire that ruled her sleep.

One such night she got up from her bed and left the cabin. Ruin was keeping his watch toward the bow, but she moved quietly and if he noticed her, he did not show any sign of it. He faced the mountain lights, now dying out one by one as the hour grew later. She went to the stern of the boat and curled up beside a thick rope coiled on the deck. River was asleep in his jar, swaying gently as the current rocked the boat. The air was cold, but she liked the discomfort; it distracted her from the Cranning call.

She wasn't aware of having been asleep, but when she opened her eyes, Ruin was not at the bow. Someone else's watch, then. Whose turn was it? There was no light yet in the sky. Sken? Will?

She heard splashing in the water near the boat. Immediately she became alert. She knew all about the river pirates on the lower reaches of Cranwater; she had never heard of any this near Skyfoot, but it was possible. She silently withdrew the glass blowgun from her cross and eased herself to a sitting position. The splashing moved along the port side of the boat, and sure enough, a hand reached up onto the gunnel. As the other hand appeared, the boat dipped slightly, for now it was taking the weight of a very large man.

Then Patience relaxed a little. She knew those hands, knew only one man that large. Will slowly lifted himself waist-high above the gunnel. Then he swung his legs one at a time onto the deck, stood up, and began to walk toward the stern. He was naked. And Patience, perpetually aroused from the passion of her unendingly erotic dreams, gasped in spite of herself.

He froze immediately. Patience was ashamed of having so little self-control that she would make an involuntary sound; Will showed no shame about his nakedness. He saw her, shook his head, and then walked toward her a few steps before rounding the cabin wall to where his clothes were waiting.

In the moonlight, Patience clearly saw the wide white hairless scar tissue that formed a dimpled and puckered cross from his navel to the root of his groin, and from stem to stem of his hips. From the width of the scars, it was plain he had been branded long ago, as a child. But it was still a shock to her. Only one sect chose to disfigure themselves with the sign of the cross in the hidden places of their bodies. Will was a Vigilant.

He did not try to conceal it. He faced her as he pulled on his shirt first, then his trousers. His hair still dripped with water; he left his stockings and boots aside. In two steps he was before her, as tall as Skyfoot from her perspective. Then in a single swift motion he sat down and looked in her eyes. "A Vigilant was once my master," he said softly.

She did not know why she was afraid of him now.

When she had served Oruc, the Vigilants were dangerous because they paid no heed at all to law or government, and when they spoke there was revolution in their words and the courage of madness in their eyes. They were dangerous because the common people believed that they held some special power from God, and came to visit them in their solitary huts, bringing food, clothing, and above all, an eager audience for their sedition.

That was no risk to her now. With what the Vigilants believed about *her*, she was in less danger from a Vigilant than anyone alive.

But she *was* afraid.

"Vigilants don't brand their slaves," she said. "Not against their will."

Will nodded. "I was a Vigilant, too. As a child."

"Did you renounce the vows?"

"No."

"Then you're a Vigilant still?"

"I think of my life—as a vigil. But most of the hermits in their little huts would think I am a blasphemer."

"And why is that?"

"Because I don't believe that Kristos will come to unite all humans to rule the world in perfect peace and harmony."

Already this morning he had said more to her than in all the weeks before. Yet his speech was as simple as his silence had been, as if speech or silence made no difference to him. She could have asked him these questions at any time, and he would have answered. "What is your vigil, then?"

"What all vigils are—for the coming of Kristos."

"You go in circles."

"In spirals. Closer to the truth on each pass."

She thought again about what he had said, trying to figure out the answer to the problem he had posed. Then she realized that he was testing her, just as Father and Angel had always tested her. She shook her head. "Just tell me. Or don't tell me. I don't care."

"I believe that Kristos will come to unite geblings, dwelfs, and gaunts. And humans, too, if they can humble themselves enough."

"Vigilants don't believe that geblings have souls."

"I told you I was a blasphemer."

"And what of me?" she asked.

Will shook his head and looked down at the deck. She studied his face, the open simplicity of his look. She had once thought him stupid, from this visage. Now she saw him as a man at peace with himself, open-faced not because he was naive and trusting, but rather because he was wise and trustworthy. A man without guile. If he did not want to answer, he did not lie; he simply said nothing. It was the only situation her diplomatic training had never prepared her for: an honest man.

Finally he lifted his gaze to her face. His expression changed again. What was it? Despair and hope, struggling together?

"What do you hope for?" she whispered.

He did not speak. Instead, he reached out his massive hand and brushed the backs of his fingers against her lips. It was the gesture of obeisance to the Heptarch. She went cold inside. Another one who had plans for her.

But then he shook his head. "It's a lie," he said. "Once that was all I wanted for you."

"And now?"

His hand passed behind her head, covering the stubble of the part of her hair that had been shaved, gripping her firmly and yet without violence. He leaned his face toward hers, kissed her on the cheek, and pressed his cheek to hers for a long moment.

No one had ever embraced her like this. Since her

mother died she could not remember anyone really embracing her at all. Her control slipped away, and she trembled. After all the pent-up yearning of the Cranning call, she could not help but know that this was what her body wanted. She turned her face, kissed his cheek.

And then cried out in pain.

He quickly pulled away from her, studied her face. Could he see the terrible wave of revulsion that swept over her body?

"I'm sorry," he murmured.

"No," she whispered, struggling to say words at all. "No, it's Unwyrm, he forbids it, he forbids—" But Patience did not wish to be forbidden. Impulsively she took Will's shirt and pulled herself to him, pressed her face against his shoulders; she felt his tentative hands touch her back, her shoulders, and his breath was warm in her hair.

But the longer he held her, the more agonizing the punishment from Unwyrm. Even though she was breathing, she felt a terrible, urgent need to breathe, as though someone had pressed a pillow over her face. I *am* breathing, she told herself, but her body panicked in spite of her will. She pushed Will away and hurled herself down to the deck, gasping.

"You *are* Kristos," Will said. "Don't you see? You're the hero to face the wyrm in his lair. You're the one who will save or destroy us all, man and gebling, dwelf and gaunt."

The punishment eased, now that he wasn't touching her. She began to breathe more calmly.

"He doesn't touch your deepest place," said Will. "He can only force your passion, not your will. All the Wise who went to him, they were weaker than their passion. They had spent all their lives increasing their understanding, building their stories of the world. Their

memory, their identity, that part of the triune
honed to perfection, sharper than any sword I eve
into battle. But when Unwyrm came, he came i
passion. It was unfamiliar territory to them, a plac they
had not conquered in their soul, and so they went to him,
thinking they had no choice.''

"He made me think I couldn't breathe, even though I
was breathing.''

"If you had wanted to stay in my arms," said Will,
"you would have stayed.''

"I couldn't.''

"If you had wanted to, completely, without any reser-
vation of your own, you could have stayed.''

"How do you know what I can or cannot do?''

"Because he has called me, and I know the limits of
his power.''

She studied him as well as she could in the moonlight.
As far as she could tell, he spoke the truth. This hulking
giant was one of the Wise? This man who had pulled on
his own plow in Reck's field, who never spoke, who had
lived as a slave and believed at least some of the doctrine
of the Vigilants—was one of the Wise?

"You and I," said Will, "we have learned the same
strength. We both grew up under strong masters, and we
both obeyed. But we learned to turn our obedience into
freedom. We learned how to choose to obey, even when
others thought we had no choice. So that even though we
gave the appearance of having no will of our own, all our
actions all our lives have been free.''

She thought of Father's and Angel's tests, the rules of
protocol, the rituals of self-denial. Sometimes it was as
Will said. Sometimes she chose freely. But other times,
no. Other times she was not free at all, and chafed at the
bonds of slavery.

"Did he ever take away your breath?'' she asked.

"I went into battle one day. My master was the captain general, and his banner drew the enemy to us. I stood between them and him, as I had always done. Only this day, Unwyrm called to me. He put terrible fear in me, but I stood my ground. He made me so thirsty and hungry that my head ached and my mouth went dry, but I stood my ground. He made the need of my bladder and bowel so great that my body released all that it held, but I paid no attention and stood my ground. And then, as the enemy reached me, he made me feel as if I were suffocating. The need to breathe is the one irresistible need, and I knew that I would not find ease from that agony until I left the field of battle and began my trek Cranningward."

"What did you do?"

"What you would have done. I made sure I really was breathing, and then went ahead and did what I wanted, regardless of the pain. I killed forty-nine men that day— the flagbearer kept count of it—and my master offered me my freedom."

"Did you take it?"

"How could he offer me what I already had? I was free. As you are free. If you had not secretly doubted that you wanted to love me, you would have had me here on this deck."

"And would you have given yourself to me?" she asked.

"Yes."

"Because I am Heptarch?"

"Not because you are *Heptarch*, but because *you* are Heptarch."

"I'm not as strong as you think."

"On the contrary. You're stronger than you know."

She turned the conversation; she did not believe him, and wanted to, and feared that if she listened any longer he would lead her to overconfidence. "You're one of the Wise? What secrets do you know, which Heffiji could put in her house?"

"She asked me her question, and I gave her my answer," said Will.

From his tone, she knew not to ask directly what the question or the answer might have been. Instead, she asked her own question. "What did you learn, as a slave?"

"That no one can ever be a slave to another man."

"That is a lie."

"Then I learned a lie."

"But you believe it."

Will nodded.

"There are people who do things for fear of the lash. There are people who do things for fear they will lose their families or their lives. There are people bought and sold. Are they not slaves?"

"They are slaves to their passion. Their fear rules them. What power do you have over me if I am not afraid of your lash? Am I your slave, if I am not afraid to lose my family? I obey you, faithfully, completely, because I choose to; am I your slave? And when you come to hate me for my freedom, which is greater than yours, and you command me to do what I will not do, then I stand before you in disobedience. Punish me, then; I choose to be punished. And if the punishment is more than I am willing to accept, then I will use such force as is necessary to stop the punishment, and no more. But never, for a moment, have I done anything but what I choose to do."

"Then no one is as strong as you."

"Not so. I've given my obedience to God, and use my best judgment to carry out his purpose, when I have some understanding of it. But those who have chosen to give their obedience to their passion, or to their memory, they freely choose to obey. The glutton freely overfills his belly, the pederast feeds on innocence, and the fearful man obeys his fear—freely.''

"You make it sound as if our desires were separate from ourselves."

"They are. And if you don't know that, then you might well become Unwyrm's slave after all."

"I know something of the doctrine of the Vigilants."

"I am not talking about a school of doctrine. I'm talking about the answer I gave Heffiji. The reason Unwyrm calls to me."

Now she could ask him outright. "What question did Heffiji ask?"

"She asked me whether dwelfs have a soul."

"Then it *is* theology."

"What she really was asking—and it's a question you'd better answer before you face Unwyrm—she was asking what part of her was herself."

Patience studied Will's placid face. How could he have known the question that so haunted her? "My father taught me to listen to everything and believe nothing."

"The dead do that much," said Will.

"The dead don't listen."

"If you believe nothing, then you are listening exactly as much as the dead."

"I'm not dead," Patience whispered.

Will smiled. "I know," he said. He reached out as if to touch her cheek; she recoiled from him and shook her head. So he sat back, making no effort to conceal his disappointment, and began to teach. "Each part of the triune soul has its desires. The passion has the desires of pleasure and survival and the avoidance of pain. Those who are slaves to passion are the ones we see as hedonists or cowards or addicts or drunks, the ones we pity or despise. And these slaves think that their passion is themself. I want this drink. I want to breathe. Their identity is in their needs. And to control them is easy. You simply control their pleasure or their pain."

She smiled. "I learned this in the cradle. People who are that easy to control, though, aren't worth controlling."

"So," he said. "They're the weakest. Are you one of them?"

"When he calls me, I can hardly think of anything else but the need for him. Even when I remember what he looks like, from the gebling memories within me, even when I should loathe him, he makes me want him, want his children."

"You came through Tinker's Wood when he didn't want you to."

"If he had really wanted to stop me, he could have."

"I say he couldn't. Because you long ago separated yourself from your body's desires."

She remembered the cold breeze from the unglazed window of her room. She nodded.

"So." He did not teach as Father did; there was no sense of triumph when she bent before his argument. He merely went on. "The second part of the triune soul, the memory—it's more difficult. It has another kind of desire, one that is born in us as surely as the need to breathe, but because it is never satisfied, we don't know that it exists. For a moment, between breaths, we don't need to breathe, so we recognize the need to breathe when it returns."

"But this one is never gone, so we never notice it."

"Yes. Yes, you see—our memory can't hold everything. Can't hold every vision we see, every sequence of events that happened to us, everything we read, everything we hear about. It's too much. If we actually had to do that, we'd be insane before we left our infancy. So we

The things that are important. We remember only what matters. And we remember it in certain orders, in patterns that mean things together. In daytime, the sun is up; and all daytime becomes one day, and all nighttime becomes one night—we don't have to remember every day to remember the idea of day. But we don't just remember this—we remember the *why*. It is daytime *because* the sun is up. Or the sun is up *because* it is daytime. You see? We don't remember randomly. Everything is connected by threads of cause."

"I'm not one of the Wise," said Patience. "Maybe the Wise understand the cause of everything, but I don't."

"But that's just it, that's just where the hunger comes. Every shred of experience that we remember comes as a story—a series of events that are connected by the pushes and pulls of cause. And we believe this story, of how everything is causally connected, without questioning it. I did this *because*. I did this *in order to*. And this is the world we live in, this pattern of events that cause each other. It becomes the framework by which we remember everything. But some things come along that *don't fit*."

"Not just *some* things."

"The weak-minded never notice it, Lady Patience. Everything fits for them, because they simply don't remember the things that don't belong. They never happened, the memory is gone. But for those who live in the mind, the places that don't fit, they don't disappear. They become a terrible hunger in the mind. Why, they shout. Why, why, why. And you can't be content until you know the connection. Even if it means breaking apart all the network that existed before. Once there was a time when mankind was locked on a single planet, and they thought their star circled that planet, because that was all they saw. That was the evidence of their eyes. But there were some who looked closely, and saw that it didn't fit, and the *why* pressed upon them until they had an answer. And when it all fit, they were able to send starships to worlds like this.''

"Every child asks why," said Patience.

"But most children stop asking," said Will. "They finally get a system that works well enough. They have enough stories to account for everything they care about, and anything their stories can't handle, they ignore.''

"The priests say that the self is in the memory—that we are what we remember doing.''

"That's what they say.''

"But I remember doing the acts of hundreds of Heptarchs, and a few geblings, too. Are they part of myself?''

"You see the problem as few people see it," said Will. "The self isn't in the memory, only the story we believe about ourselves. It can also be revised. It's constantly being revised. We see what it was we did, and we make up a story to account for it, and believe the story, and think that we understand ourself.''

"Except the dwelfs, who can't hold long memories in their conscious minds.''

"Yes.''

"So what did you tell Heffiji—that she had no soul?''

"Only that her soul had no story. Because ourself is something else.''

She knew what he would say; it was clear to her now. "The will, of course. It's strange, Will, that you're named for the thing that you think is most important. Or did you decide it was important because it was your name?

"Will wasn't the name I was born with. I took that name the day Reck looked at me and said, 'Who are you?' ''

"What's the desire of the will, then? You said all three parts of the soul had their desire."

"The will makes only a simple choice, and it's already made. Your whole life is nothing but acting out the choice that defines who you really are."

"What's that?"

"The choice between good and evil."

She let him see her disappointment. "All this talk, and we come to *that?*"

"I'm not talking about the choice between killing people and not killing people, or between stealing and not stealing. Sometimes killing a person is evil. Sometimes killing a person is good. You know that."

"Which is why I decided not to care about good and evil a long time ago."

"No. You decided not to care about legal and illegal."

"I decided there wasn't any absolute good and there wasn't any absolute evil. You just said the same thing."

"No I didn't," said Will.

"You said sometimes killing is good and sometimes it's evil."

"So. Killing isn't absolute. But now, when you go to Unwyrm, what's wrong with doing what he wants? What's wrong with you having his children?"

"Because I don't want to."

"Why? You know he'll give you pleasure. And your children—they'll be human, perfectly human, only stronger and smarter, wiser and quicker, and they'll no doubt have a perfect connection between their minds, all of them like Unwyrm combined with the best human traits. You'll be the mother of the master race. The most magnificent intelligent beings ever created. The next step in human evolution. Why don't you desire it?"

"I don't know," she said.

"If you don't know, then at the crucial moment, when

you are with him, and all your desire is for him, won't know. You'll still refuse, but perhaps not ... all your strength. And it'll take all your strength to resist him, I promise you."

"Come with me," she said. "Kill him for me."

"I'll come with you, if I can. And I'll kill him, if I can. But I think I won't be able to. I think there's only one person who'll ever come close enough to hurt him, to stop him."

"Then tell me. What is it I need to know?"

"It's simple. Nothing exists except in relation to something else. An atom is not an atom. It doesn't exist, except in relation to other atoms. If it never responded to anything else, it would not exist. All existence is like that—utterly isolated pieces that only come into existence in their interaction with other pieces. Human beings too. We don't exist except in relation to the other events of the world. Everything we do, everything we are depends on our responses to other events, and other events' responses to us."

"I knew that."

"You didn't know that. It's so obvious that no one knows it. If nothing you did caused any change in the world outside, and nothing in the world outside caused any change in you, then you wouldn't know there was a world outside, and it wouldn't know you existed, and so it would be meaningless to speak of your existence at all. So your existence, all our existence, depends on every piece, every person in the universe behaving according to certain set patterns. The system. The order in which everything exists. The laws that bind atoms and molecules are very firm. They have no freedom to vary, because as soon as they vary, they cease to be. But life—ah, there the freedom begins. And we who think we are intelligent, we are the freest of all. We make our own patterns and change them as we like. We build systems and orders and tear them down. But you'll notice that none of our choices have any effect whatever on the way that atoms and molecules behave. Just as we have no idea what any particular molecule is doing, they have no notion of what we're doing. We can't change their order at all. We can use it, but we can't break down their system and cause them to wink out of existence."

"I suppose that's true. We can burn wood, but the atoms that are torn from certain molecules combine again with others, and the system hangs together."

"Exactly. So we can't do good or evil to most of the universe. Only to other living things. Mostly to each other. Because the systems of human beings are ours to control. They're every bit as real as the universe itself, and they are what gives us our existence—but we can manipulate them. We can change the systems that create the terms of our life. And we do change those systems, according to the single simple choice of our will."

"What's the choice?"

"It arises from the desire of the will. And the desire of the will is simple. To grow."

"I don't want to grow."

"Every living thing has this same desire, Patience. Angel touched on it, in his childish way, when he spoke of people who own things. That's the most pathetic way people have of growing. The way Sken makes this boat part of herself—it makes her larger. Eating also makes her larger."

Patience smiled. "You're being ridiculous now."

"I'm not. Kings also make themselves larger, because their kingdom is part of themself. Parents make themselves larger through their children. Some few people, though, have such a powerful hunger that they can't be satisfied until their self includes everything alive."

"The King's House is all the world," n
Patience.

"What did you say?"

"Something my father taught me."

"Oh."

"So, is it good or evil to desire to be larger?"

"Neither. It's *how* you choose to grow larger. The system lives on sacrifice. No order could exist in which every person in it received everything he desired all the time. The system that gives us our existence depends on people making sacrifices. I give up something I desire, so that others can receive some of what *they* desire. In turn, they give up something they want, so I can have some of what *I* want. Every human society depends on that simple principle."

As always, her mind raced ahead, trying to solve the problem before it had to be explained to her. "So you're saying that good people sacrifice everything, and evil people sacrifice nothing."

"Not at all. I'm saying that good people sacrifice anything that is necessary in order to maintain the order that allows all others to exist, even if they have to sacrifice their own life. While evil people manipulate and force the sacrifice of any and every other person in order to wholly gratify their own hunger. Do you see the difference?"

"This is theology. Kristos was good, because he sacrificed his life."

"Don't speak foolishly, Patience, not to me. Everybody dies, and some have been martyrs in stupid causes. Kristos is Kristos because we believe he sacrificed himself for the whole world. For the largest order of all. He would not have died for anything less. Because his self had grown to include all the systems of mankind, and he acted to protect them all."

"Now I see how you became a heretic."

"Of course you do. These fools who think their Kristos will come to unite humans in perfect peace, without including the millions of geblings, gaunts, and dwelfs—it would not be *good*, because such a Kristos would be forcing the sacrfice of half the people of the world, to serve herself. So if Kristos is to be Kristos, she is willing to sacrifice anything to maintain the order that gives life to all."

"I'm no Kristos. I don't believe any of this."

Will looked sad. "Oh, you believe my story," he said. "But you won't know that you believe it until after, looking back. If either of us is alive then."

"It's a pretty philosophy," said Patience. "It makes sense within itself. You'd have a sure career in the School."

He let the insult roll off him. "When you face him, Patience, you'll remember. A tiny part of your memory will hold on to my story, and you'll remember who you are, and who he is, and you'll doubt your own desires and believe my story. You'll destroy him, even though at that moment you'll love him more than all the world. You'll destroy him, because you know he's evil."

"If I can destroy him, it will be to save myself."

"Yourself is the world, and all the worlds. How long before his children, after they've replaced all other intelligent life on this world, build starships and go out to conquer every other world that humanity has visited? There was once a philosopher who said that there could never be war between the worlds of different stars, because there'd be nothing to gain. But he was a fool. There is greatness to be gained, largeness of self, to have every world filled with your children. It's the most powerful urge of all life. Questions of profit or politics are trivial beside it."

"When I face Unwyrm," said Patience, "it won't be a grand question of good and evil. It'll be me, my body, my wit, such as it is, against his. Nothing more."

"His house against the King's House. The prize is the world."

"I don't want the world."

"That's why you'll have it."

She laughed in frustration. "Will, what can I do with you? You see me larger than I am. I can never be what you imagine me to be."

Will shook his head. "I imagine you to be a girl, fifteen years old, sometimes frightened, always brave. I imagine you to be unaware of your beauty, which makes you infinitely beautiful; unaware of your power, which makes you dangerously powerful. I have had many masters in my life, but you are the only master I could follow until I die."

"You see? How can I bear that? I can't be perfect."

"If *I* can be perfect, you can be perfect." He showed no sign that he was aware of how boastful he sounded.

"You're *perfect?*" she asked.

"I made myself perfect, so I could serve you when you came. You are skilled in all the skills of government but one: war. I made myself perfect in that, so I could serve you in it. My masters were all generals, but I served each one the same—I made them all victorious."

"You? A slave?"

"A trusted slave. They all learned that when they took my counsel, they won. I prepared myself so that you would find me ready when you needed me."

"How did you know that we'd ever meet? There on your farm with Reck and Ruin. What were the chances I'd ever find you?"

"There's no chance in this. From the time I discovered the truth of the soul, the Cranning call was always with me, Lady Patience. Then one day we marched along a road, from Waterkeep to Danswatch, and for a brief moment, as we passed a hut at the north end of the village, the call faded. And was replaced by a repulsion, a powerful desire not to go toward Cranning. And then we went a little way, and the Cranning call returned to me. I knew at once that something in that house—"

"Reck and Ruin."

"I didn't know that geblings lived there. I certainly didn't know they were the gebling king. But I knew that whatever was there, Unwyrm feared it, and if Unwyrm feared it, it was good, and I must ally myself with it. So I escaped and went to Reck. With her and Ruin, the Cranning call disappeared, so I was at peace. But that wasn't why I went to them, and it wasn't why I stayed. I stayed waiting for you."

"How could you possibly know that I would come there?"

"For the same reason that I went there. Because if you didn't, Unwyrm couldn't be defeated."

"That's not the reason."

"Nevertheless, it *is* the reason."

"You're too mystical for me."

"I don't think so," said Will. "I think I'm exactly mystical enough for you."

"I liked you better when you were silent," she said.

"I know," he said. "Endure me." He reached out his hand. With the tips of his fingers he stroked her cheek, her hair. His fingers traveled down her body, her neck, her shoulder, her breast, her waist. Finally he rested a hand on her thigh. "When you want me to speak again," he said, "I will. As slave to master. As subject to king. As Vigilant to Kristos. As husband to wife."

Then he leaned down and kissed her lips. Unwyrm again filled her with revulsion at his touch, but this time she ignored it, put it behind her, and accepted the agonizing gift he gave. When the kiss was finished, he stood and walked across the deck to where his boots waited for him. "Time for me to clump around," he said, "and wake the others."

It was true. Light was coming in the east, over the trees; the stars were fading. And the high wall of Skyfoot rose in the northern sky, topped with eternal snow, where Unwyrm waited for her, hungered for her. Will has told me stories, and some of them I believe, but what will it matter when I come to you, Unwyrm? You're the only husband that was prophesied for me.

Even Unwyrm couldn't stop her from wishing for Will's hand to touch her again, his lips to invite her. After all Will's philosophy, she suspected that the only thing he had given her that might help her at all when she faced Unwyrm at the end would be the dream of a human lover. She could not hold on to a mystic view of good and evil. But she could hold on to the memory of the touch of a living man.

She turned around, just to look downstream, just to be turning, and happened to see River's face. His eyes were open, gazing at her. Tears had tracked their way down his face.

"Did we wake you?" she asked inanely.

His lips answered, silently: The river is all the life I need.

But she knew it was a lie. For a few minutes in this early morning, she and Will had reminded him of life.

15 | STRINGS

THE CLOSER THEY GOT TO SKYFOOT, THE BETTER THEY COULD see that it wasn't a sheer cliff at all. It was steep, but a slope nonetheless, with occasional deep ledges that were thick with orchards or farmland. Large reaches of the mountain were terraced for farming, while houses and buildings clotted and clumped in towns and villages and vast cities on the mountain's face. There were horizontal roads high up the mount, with carts that had been built on the mountain passing back and forth. There were hanging platforms that were constantly rising and lowering to carry passengers and cargos to towns hundreds of meters above or below. The whole face of the mountain as far and as high as they could see was a hive of activity.

Clouds hung only a few hundred meters above them when they came at last to the clear and seemingly bottomless lake that fronted the mountain like an apron many kilometers wide. Dozens of bustling harbors thrust wharves out into the water. River muttered his commands, and Sken worked the helm as they picked their

246 | ORSON SCOTT CARD

way skillfully among the boats and jetties, finding an
empty slip in the harbor River picked out for them.

To everyone's surprise, Will jumped ashore almost
before an aging portboy had finished tying their line to
the dock. Will elbowed the old man aside, then retied the
line himself.

"Why did you do that?" demanded Angel as Will
carefully stepped back into the boat. The portboy was
muttering curses behind him.

"Because this is Freetown, and if you fall in with the
jackals at the beginning you're lost."

"What do *you* know of it?" asked Ruin.

Will looked at him steadily for a moment, then turned
to Reck. "I've been here before," he said.

Reck raised her eyebrows.

"I had a master once who brought me here as his
bodyguard."

Patience saw that Will spoke with the same openness
that she had seen a few mornings before, when they
talked in the predawn darkness, lit only by the moon. It
was the same in daylight. He did not lie. It was impossible not to believe that he believed what he said. Yet in all
their journey, he had not given her or anyone else the
slightest hint that he had ever been to Cranning before.

"*You've* been to Cranning?" asked Ruin.

"Why didn't you say so before?" demanded Angel.

Will considered a moment before he answered. "I
didn't know you'd dock right here. This is the only part
of Cranning I've visited." He smiled. "My master thought
there were some secret whores in some of the houses
higher in Freetown. Some whores who could do things
that no one had ever imagined."

"Was he right?" asked Sken.

"He didn't have much imagination," said Will. "So
he was easy to satisfy." He tossed a small coin to the old

portboy, who was still wailing on the dock. The man caught it with a quick, snakelike strike of his hand and grinned. "Now he'll fetch us someone who has the money to buy our boat. Instead of pretending that he's willing to guard it for us."

From the back of the boat, they heard River's voice. "I'm known here," he said. "I fetch a fair price."

"I daresay," said Patience. "But you didn't much care whether *we* got that price, or that old portboy's cronies."

"I can't spend it," River admitted freely. "What's money to me? But when they steal me, they put me back on the downstream voyage much faster."

Sken was furious. "I ought to break your jar."

"If I still had my body," River retorted, "I'd teach you what a woman ought to do to a man."

"You were never man enough for me," said Sken.

"You were never woman enough to know a real man when you saw one."

Their quarrel went on; the others paid no attention. In a matter of moments, the whole hierarchy of authority aboard the boat shifted. Sken and River, the autocrats of the voyage, were now mere background noise. The others simply transferred to Will the trust they had placed in Sken. The tyranny of knowledge.

Will did not embarrass himself with authority as Sken had done. Patience watched as he deftly took charge of their expedition. In all these many days and weeks of travel, he had never once asserted himself, except on that single morning with her, when no one else could see. But now he stepped easily and naturally into command. He did not have to order people about or raise his voice. He listened to questions, answered them, and made decisions in a quiet way that admitted of no discussion. She had seen many men who were accustomed to command; most of them wore their authority defiantly, as if someone had just accused them of being powerless. Will took his authority as if he didn't have it, and so the others obeyed him without resentment, without noticing they were subjecting themselves to him.

If he were my husband, would he expect me to obey him? Almost at once, she was ashamed of the thought. For he was using his authority solely for the good of the group. That's why he was equally content to follow and to lead. For whether he gave the command or someone else did, if it was a good command it should be obeyed. And so if he were her husband, if he ordered something that was right and good, she would do it, and have no doubt that if she ordered what was right and good, he would easily obey.

"You can't take your eyes off him," Angel whispered to her.

She had no desire to tell Angel why. "He's not the silent oaf we thought him to be."

"Don't trust him," said Angel. "He's a liar."

She could not believe that Angel would say such a thing. "How can you hear him and see him and think he says anything he doesn't believe?"

"All you're telling me," said Angel, "is that he's a very good liar."

She moved away from Angel to conceal how flustered she was. Of course Angel could be right. It hadn't occurred to her, and it should have, that Will's openness and honesty could be as much an illusion as her own. After all, hadn't she schooled herself all her life to speak so she would be believed? Couldn't he have done the same?

Or had Angel sensed how much she was beginning to center herself on Will? Could he be jealous of the man's influence on her? But no. Angel had never acted out of jealousy in his life. She had trusted Angel from her earliest memories. If he doubted Will, it would be dangerous for her not to doubt him, too.

Yet she couldn't doubt him. In that one night, he had moved to the very center of the story she saw unfolding for herself. She couldn't thrust him into the background again. Whatever Angel thought of him, Will's abilities were real enough, he was proving that. And she did love him, she was sure of that—

The doubt was there, though. Now Angel stood on the dock, talking with Will, paying no more attention to Patience; but his words had been enough to put a doubt in Patience's mind. Her trust of Will was no longer complete, as it had been. And she resented Angel for it, though she knew she ought to thank him. Trust no one, Father had said. And she had forgotten it, with Will. But what a fool she had been, a religious fanatic like that, a Vigilant, and she had trusted him completely. Wait and see. That's what she would do. Wait and see.

Will sold the boat almost at once, and for a low price. River was included in the price—and he cursed Will for valuing him so low. Will only laughed. "I sold you fast to get you on the river sooner," he said. "I thought that was all you cared for."

River clicked his tongue, and his monkey turned his jar around to face downstream, so River couldn't see his former owners anymore.

Speaking to Patience, Will had another explanation for the low price. "We're better off if they think we care nothing for money. They'll take us for rich visitors who have come to play. In Freetown there's no official government and no written law. But as long as they think we're here to spend money, our lives are absolutely safe. We could drop a purse of steel on the open street and come back a week later and find it untouched."

"People are that honest?" asked Angel.

"The robbery is more organized. The big thieves make sure that little thieves don't interfere with their profits. Street crime? Just keep to the main streets, the well-lighted streets and walkways and stairs. We'll be safe. The thieves will be waiting for us indoors, at the gaming tables and in the whorehouses. No one leaves with much more than the price of passage back home."

"What happens when they find out we're just passing through?" asked Patience. "That we aren't here to lose a fortune and then go away and tell other people what a wonderful time we had?"

Will smiled. "We may leave some corpses behind us when we leave. Angel told me you were good at that." His words, his expression gave no hint that he remembered their conversation. He *was* a deceiver, then, a concealer; either he was hiding his love for her now, or he was wearing it as a false mask then. Either way, Angel was right—he *could* lie.

They called good-bye to River, who ignored them; then they left the wharf and took rooms at an inn three levels above the river. Patience and Angel passed as a rich young woman and her grandfather, with Will as bodyguard, Sken as servant, and Reck and Ruin as gebling merchants who had traveled with them as their guides. The surprise was Ruin. Will insisted that he dress the part, and when he appeared on the dock bathed, brushed, and finely attired, with his sister elegantly at his side, Patience saw that his previous undress and uncivility were from choice, not ignorance. Together they were king of the geblings, and could look the part if they needed to.

All this time that we traveled together, thought Patience, I believed I was the only one in disguise. But we were all in disguise, and are in disguise again. When we reach Unwyrm, if we're still together, will the last disguise be gone, and the truth of all of us be known?

If there *is* any truth. Perhaps we are what we pretend to be, taking on new identities with each change of costume.

She knew that she, at least, would have no disguise when she faced Unwyrm. No hiding place. No protection but her wits and what strength she could muster. It made her feel naked, as if everyone could see through her clothing to the thin and white-bodied girl that Unwyrm called.

"You must come down to the gaming tables," said Angel.

"I have better things to do with my time," said Patience. She sat at the window, looking out over the harbor and the forests beyond.

"Sit and brood? Feel his fingers close in on your heart?"

Sken piped up from the bed. "If I can bathe every day, you can go down and play Kalika."

"Sken is right, you know. We're here pretending to be pleasure-seekers. We therefore must seek some pleasure. Whether it pleases us or not."

"Visit the whores for me, Angel. Do double duty." But she left the window and walked to the mirror. Her hair was still cropped short, and deeply marred by the surgery. Still, the stubble was now a good two centimeters long. "Angel," she said, "cut the rest off, will you? To this length."

"It's not your most attractive style," said Angel.

"I may need to shed my wig somewhere along the way. Be a good fellow." She smiled flirtatiously. Since Angel was the one who taught her how to smile that way, she knew he would see it as a joke. And, indeed, he smiled. A trifle late, though. He was preoccupied. It was harder for them to pretend to be calm when they were here in Cranning, with Unwyrm's lair somewhere above them.

Angel took the shears from his trunk and began to cut. It gave her a severe look, to have her hair almost gone.

"Where is the nearest tunnel from here?" asked Patience.

"Reck says we'd be insane to try the tunnels from here. It would take three times as long, and there are robbers who live in the shallow caves."

"I didn't ask if we should use the tunnels, I asked where the nearest tunnel entrance was."

Angel sighed. "There's probably one in the back of this place. Somewhere. Along this cliff, though, the houses are built half on top of each other. Who knows which ones touch the mountain face at a point where a tunnel comes out?"

"If I could once step inside a tunnel, I'd know where he is. I have the geblings' memory of the labyrinth. I'd have a sense of where we're going, then."

"And what's to stop him from forcing you to go through the tunnels? He can keep *you* safe enough, Lady Patience, but *we'll* have no protection. I imagine he'd be just as glad to have us all dead somewhere in the tunnels, and bring you safe and sound—and alone—to meet him."

"If I want to step into a tunnel for a moment, Angel, I don't see why I can't do it."

"Do you want to?"

"Yes, I think so."

"Do *you* want to?"

Or was the idea coming to her from Unwyrm? She frowned into the mirror. "Are you trying to make me doubt everything?" she asked.

"I just want to make sure you're doing what's best."

Patience kept silent. Everyone seemed so eager to give

her advice. As if the presence of Unwyrm's urging in her mind made her incapable of making decisions on her own. Or was her resentfulness coming from Unwyrm, in his effort to separate her from her companions? She wondered if she could trust her own judgment. It would be so comfortable to concentrate on keeping Unwyrm at bay, while letting Angel lead her up the mountain. Angel could keep her safe. Perhaps she should have been taking his advice all along. She thought about Will and Reck and Ruin in the next room, and wondered if she had been wise to take the road through Tinker's Wood after all. They were just an added complication. Angel was enough, with Sken to help them where brute strength was needed. Reck and Ruin were too unpredictable—when had human and gebling interests ever coincided? And Will—what insanity, his religion. With Patience as deity, a love goddess, a sacrifice; that morning on the boat was a dream, a deception. How could she go up the mountain with these strange people tagging along? Who knew what they might do?

She almost suggested to Angel that they ought to leave now, without telling the gebling king, just disappear into the crowds. As soon as she was far enough from Reck and Ruin, Unwyrm would repel them from Cranning again; they could never follow her.

But she felt uneasy about that. A fleeting memory of lips on her cheeks, fingers touching her body. Am I such an adolescent, to be held by such meaningless stirring in the blood? But it held her. And something else, too: the memory of being the gebling king herself. She felt the pressure of that, too, the sense that Cranning was herself, that all the millions of geblings who lived their busy lives here were her responsibility, hers to protect, hers to command. She remembered clearly that she had ruled here once, when only a few thousand geblings inhabited the place. She couldn't cast aside that responsibility, not easily, anyway. So she said nothing.

Angel set aside the shears. "Lovely," he said.

"You look like a prisoner just getting out of Glad Hell," said Sken.

"Thank you," said Patience. "I find the style becoming, myself." She put on her wig and became a woman again. "What's the game of the house?"

"Actually, this is more of a show house." Angel smoothed the back of her hair. "There's a theatre here, with a company of gaunts. But they do have worm-and-slither fights, and the betting gets quite intense sometimes."

"I've never actually seen a worm-and-slither," she said.

"Not pretty," said Sken.

"We ought to bet something, or they'll think we aren't gamblers, and they'll worry about whether we're worth keeping around." Angel tossed a heavy purse into the air and caught it. Sken's gaze never left the bag.

"Still. The show sounds better. What is it?"

"I don't know. In this place, probably a scat show."

"Maybe we can look for a show somewhere else."

Angel frowned. "If you want theatre, there are better places than Freetown."

"I'm here on business," said Patience. "So I don't have much choice."

A knock on the door. Will stuck his head in. "We're ready when you are."

"We're ready now," Angel answered.

There was a fair-sized crowd in the worm-and-slither room. Angel led them to the pens first, to size up the evening's competitors. The slithers all clung to the front of their glass cases, colors shifting like ribbons inside them, new arms and legs growing in various directions as others retreated. They weren't more than five centimeters across. "I thought they'd be bigger," said Patience.

"They will be, during the fight," said Sken. "They starve them down to low weight for transportation. Slithers are all pretty much the same, anyway. What matters is the worms."

The worms were kept in swarms, as many as a dozen to a case. They drifted slowly and aimlessly through the water. Patience quickly lost interest in them and looked around the gaming room.

It was strange to see how easily humans and geblings intermingled here. There was no sense of separation, no hint of caste. There were even a few dwelfs who were not servants, and gaunts who might not have been prostitutes, though it was hard to tell about that. Gaunts wouldn't do very well in a game of chance—they'd take too many bad bets. Surely the people here weren't so unsporting as to steal from creatures with no resistance.

Everyone was beautiful, or at least wanted to seem so. Dozens of thick women and paunchy men wore clothing tailored to emphasize this sign of wealth; jowls and chins abounded. Brocades tumbled from padded shoulders; velvets flowed from uncontainable hips. But the gaunts who stood here and there among the crowd made a mockery of human attempts at beauty. The human ideal was massive and strong for men, rounded and fertile for women; good breeding stock, it was called, and it was high praise. But men and women both had a way of thumping when they walked, as if beneath their clothes they wore bronze plate. The gaunts, on the other hand, seemed to glide. Not ostentatiously, the way a dancer might do it, isolating the legs from the trunk, so that the head stayed on an even, unmoving horizontal plane. Rather they moved like a ripple in the earth itself, as if they grew out of the floor like the graceful, purposeful pseudopodia of the slithers in their cages.

When they move, their bodies are the song of the earth.
When they speak, their voices are the song of the air.
When they love, ah! the pleasures they give
Are as strong as the pulse of the sea.

So said the "Hymn to Gaunts," a half-satirical, half-insane paean by an ancient poet who was too eccentric for his name to be remembered or his poetry to be forgotten.

And Father had said, Humans don't miss their machines on Imakulata because the gaunts are almost as obedient and far, far more beautiful.

One gaunt in particular, a young boyok, white-blond and, though small, too tall for his weight: Patience noticed him as he bobbed in and out of the front row of the crowd that gathered around the current game. His hand sometimes, and sometimes his shoulder, had a way of brushing ever-so-gently across the crotch of a rich-looking customer. A catamite? No—when he had their attention, he handed them a thin paper. Selling something, then, but something that sold better with a sexual approach.

It was inevitable: in his passage through the crowd, the young gaunt did his brush-against-the-crotch routine to Angel. But then Patience noticed a curious thing. Angel acted exactly like all the others: a moment of startlement, a look of pleasant surprise at the beauty of the gauntling, a smile of recognition at the sight of the handbill, a look of wistful disappointment when the boyok moved away. To Patience, though to no one else, this clearly showed that Angel was *not* surprised. For if he had really been surprised, he would have shown no emotion at all for a few moments, until he was certain what the encounter meant. Then he might have imitated the natural response, but not so perfectly. Obviously, then, he had been aware of the gauntling, but did not want anyone to notice that he had been aware. It disturbed Patience deeply, because no one in the gaming room would have paid the slightest attention except Angel's traveling companions, including her. For some reason, Angel had been aware of the boyok, and yet did not want her to know he had been aware.

So Patience walked over to Angel, who now was watching the slither being prepared for the next game, and whispered, "What was he selling? The little whore with the advertisement?"

Angel shrugged. "I dropped it somewhere—"

Patience saw the curl of paper on the floor, picked it up. It was written in glyphs instead of alphabetics, which explained why it was written on the single vertical strip. The glyphs were easy ones, though, enhanced with graphic drawings. "Lord Strings and His Wandering Wonder Machine at the Melting Snow. Private Boxes. By Invitation Only."

"Just a sex show," said Angel. "Nothing worth seeing."

"You've been abroad in the world," said Patience. "What's tedious to you might be interesting to me."

"You're only fifteen."

"With a lover," she said.

He frowned.

"Waiting for me on ice," she added. She put enough insistence in her voice that he would know she was serious.

His frown faded. "If you want to."

And she knew that this was what he wanted. Had he intended her to see his deceptive response before? Or was he planning some more indirect maneuver? For some reason, Angel wanted to go to the Melting Snow to see whatever entertainment Lord Strings had prepared. As so often before in her life, she was puzzled. What had he seen in that little gauntling that made him decide to go?

Angel placed bets—large ones, but not large enough to attract undue attention—on the upcoming game. He bet on the slither by five centimeters. It was daring to give such a wide margin, but the payoff would be so much the greater if he happened to win. Patience had never seen Angel gamble, though she had watched Father often enough. She had never figured out, in Father's case, whether he really enjoyed playing, or merely pretended to enjoy it for diplomatic purposes.

The slither was dropped through a dekameter of open air into the fighting tank. The shock of the air shriveled it; once in the tank, its body immediately began to expand as it took on nutrients from the surrounding culture. It was a fast one; in the three seconds before the worms' release, it more than doubled in size.

The worms were slow and stupid at first, swimming languidly and aimlessly. The instant that the first of them bumped into the slither, however, all of them became purposeful and quick. They fastened to the surface of the creature and began to eat their way in.

The slither noticed them, too, of course, and in its eclectic fashion it considered the worms to be as welcome a meal as any other. The slither walls grew out around the worms, enwombing them in the semirigid gel of its interior. The worms immediately began to twist and corkscrew in agony as the slither's digestive fluids ate into their bodies. Yet their writhing was not directionless. They moved from the edge of the slither inward, toward the yolk that included its primitive intelligence and all its reproductive system. If they reached it, the worms would deposit their own genetic molecules, which would take over the slither's body and make it a device for reproducing worms. But this slither had grown too quickly, and its yolk was by chance quite far from the side where all the worms had penetrated. The worms were all dead before any had reached the yolk. However, the nearest worm had come within four centimeters.

Angel showed no reaction at all. He just reached out his hand in a grandfatherly way and said, "Come along, little lady. We'd better eat before I lose everything." A few people chuckled—it wasn't likely that anyone would actually say such a thing unless there wasn't the remotest possibility of bankrupting.

They ate at a place with glass walls that looked out over the lake and forest on one side, and faced a delicate and beautiful cliff garden on the other. The food was as good as anything Patience had eaten in King's Hill, though many of the fruits were dwarfed and surprisingly tart, and the meat was flavored with liquors that she didn't know.

And then, when dinner was over and darkness had come, Angel made a show of inquiring where to find the Melting Snow. The master of tables cast a long and disapproving glance toward Patience—the Melting Snow was apparently a place where decent people, even pleasure-seekers in Freetown, did not take virginal girls. Angel was unabashed.

"Why are we really going?" she finally asked him. They walked along wooden runways that hung precariously over rooftops and gardens three stories down. The geblings were close behind, but not close enough to hear. Will and Sken were too large to walk abreast of anyone; they filed along to the rear.

"Didn't you see?" asked Angel. "The little fellow sought us out. From the time he came into the gaming room. As soon as he gave me the message, he left."

"What does it mean, then?"

"Gaunts have no will, Patience. They sense the desires of the people nearest them, and try to satisfy whatever desire is strongest. They make notoriously undependable messengers, since they can be distracted so easily. But this one was unwavering."

"Unwyrm?"

"It occurred to me that he would be able to keep a gaunt focused on a single purpose."

"Then we should avoid this place."

"As I have futilely tried to tell you before, Unwyrm is trying to get us into his lair, and we are trying to get there. It isn't until we arrive that our purposes diverge."

It was a hopelessly stupid answer. Unwyrm wanted Patience there, but he didn't want anyone else. Obviously, then, the danger was not to Patience, but to everyone who accompanied her; if Unwyrm could, he would strip them all away so that she would come unaccompanied into his presence.

She didn't have time to find out why Angel had said such nonsense, however, for they arrived at the Melting Snow and Angel at once began to arrange a table. Patience supposed that he still thought her so childish he could fob off a stupid answer while he kept his real reasoning to himself. After all this time, he still underestimated her. Or did he? Perhaps the reason for what he was doing was obvious, and only Unwyrm's pressure kept her from understanding. She would not notice if Unwyrm impaired her thinking, but Angel would, and perhaps he had already seen that her judgment was unreliable. It frightened her, and Unwyrm's joy surged within her.

The show was just ending as the boxmaster seated them in a grill-fronted box overlooking the circular stage. The boyok from the gaming room was there, along with two tarks and an unusually tall, sad-looking gaunt with long, grease-gray hair. They were all naked, all fragilely, ethereally beautiful as gaunts were supposed to be. But in the final minutes of the dance, Patience realized that this was no mere sex show, designed to warm the couches in the boxes around the stage. There was a story being enacted through the dance. The sad-looking gaunt was not even aroused. He just stood, tall and straight, yet with his head hanging limply to one side, hair falling unkempt across his face, as if his shoulders were suspended by taut wires from the ceiling, but nothing held up his head at all. The boyok was trying to reach the old gaunt; the tarks, just as young as he, and almost as boyish, tried to hold him back with touches and strokes that were at once violent restraint and gentle provocation. The boyok was aroused—the customers were paying for it, weren't they?—but he seemed uninterested in what the tarks were doing. Finally, as the music climaxed, the boyok reached the old gaunt. Patience steeled herself for some unpleasantly coarse pornographic climax, but instead the gauntling climbed the old fellow as if he were a tree, knelt on his shoulders—his balance was precarious and yet he did not so much as waver—and then lifted the old gaunt's head by the hair, until it was upright and alert as the rest of his erect body.

Silence. The end.

The audience applauded, but not with enthusiasm. Obviously, they had noticed what Patience had seen: that this was not a sex show at all, but rather dance with an erotic theme. The climax had been aesthetic, not orgasmic. The audience was, quite properly, disappointed. They had been cheated.

But Patience did not feel cheated. It had kindled in her, in those few moments, a longing that defied her self-control and brought tears to her eyes. It was not the sort of passion that Unwyrm put in her, not a compelling, coercive urge. It was, rather, a melancholy longing for something not physical at all. She wanted desperately to have her father back again, to have him smile at her; she longed for her mother's embrace. It was love that the dance had aroused in her, love as the Vigilants spoke of it: a pure need for someone else to take joy in you. And almost without thought, she turned to look at Will, who stood near the door at the back of the box. She saw in his guileless face a perfect mirror of the longing that she felt; and she rejoiced, for he was also looking at her, searching for the same thing in her.

Then she turned back to look at the stage. The applause had died, but still the four gaunts held their final pose. Wasn't the show over, after all? The music was gone; there was only silence, except for the breathing and murmuring of the audience in their boxes and in the cheap open seats on the floor. For a long few seconds, the pose remained perfect. Then, slowly, the old gaunt began to sag. The boyok pulled upward on his hair, as if trying to hold him up, but the gaunt sank from the shoulders, as if the boyok's weight were too much for him.

As he sank, he turned, so that when he finally stretched full length on the floor, propped barely on an elbow, with the boyok supine across him, still gripping his hair and pulling his head up, the old gaunt's face was directly toward the box where Patience sat. Indeed, his eyes seemed to see her, and her only, looking at her with supplication. Yes, she said silently. This is the perfect ending for the dance. In silence, in collapse, and yet with the boyok's effort unabated, the head still up, the face still skyward.

Then, as if her unspoken approval were the cue, the lamps were snuffed out all at once. The darkness lasted

only a second or two, but when the lamps were rekin-
dled, the stage was clear. Patience applauded, and some
in the audience joined her; most had lost interest. "I
want to meet them," said Patience. "Gaunts or not, that
was beautiful."

"I'll go get them," said Will.

"I will," said Angel.

"Then give the money to me," said Will.

"I won't be robbed," said Angel.

"I've been here before," said Will. "You're safe on
the open street, but not in the passageways of a house
like this."

Angel paused a crucial moment, then gave two purses
to Will. Patience knew that he had probably kept most of
the money anyway, but it was a compromise, and there
was no point in arguing over something stupid.

If the show had been a success, there would have been
little hope of getting even one of the gaunts up into their
boxes, not without a serious effort to bribe the boxmaster.
But since it had failed, only the two tarks had been
spoken for—a tark was a tark, after all. Both the old
gaunt and the boyok from the gaming room followed
Angel when he returned to their box.

Another, more predictable show was beginning on the
stage; Patience drew the curtain to shut out the sight of it
and muffle the sound. Will opened the candle-window all
the way, so they could see each other.

"Did you like it?" asked the old gaunt.

"Very much," said Patience.

"Yes, yes, you're the one I felt. You're the one who
needed to see the real ending. So many were disappointed, but I felt you, stronger than any.

"How does it usually end?" asked Sken.

"Oh, with an audience like this, we usually tup each
other three ways each. Scum. No sense of art." He

smiled at Patience. "That was the best the ending has ever been. The collapse, with my head still up—ah, thank you, lady."

It had not occurred to Patience, though she should have realized it. Gaunts always respond to the strongest desire. No wonder they had pleased her so perfectly. Unwyrm's intrusion had made all her passions so much more intense that of course she was the most dominating person in the theatre.

Yet even though the impulse for the ending had come from her, the execution of it was theirs. "You were beautiful," she said.

"You don't even want a taste of Kristiano here, do you?" said the old gaunt, pointing to the boyok. His surprise was obvious.

"No," she said.

"Or me. But you're hot as a bitch in heat, lady. I could feel it before you came in the building."

"Never mind," snapped Angel. Patience saw just a flicker of movement from Will, too, as if he had been prepared to stop the conversation even more abruptly than Angel.

"Who are you?" Patience asked.

"Strings," he said. "Not really *Lord* Strings, of course. I never heard of a gaunt being a lord, did you? Just— Strings. And Kristiano, my dear boyok, best I ever had."

"The finest artist from ice to Cranwater," said Kristiano. It was a slogan, of course, but the gauntling believed it.

"We travel," said Strings. "Where are you going? We'll go with you, and perform for you every night. Your need is very strong, and you guide us into beauty we crave to create."

Reck and Ruin had remained silent throughout this human entertainment. It was well known that geblings felt contempt for the human fascination with sex. Their own couplings were informed by empathy, so that each knew when and how the other was satisfied. They didn't hunger, as humans did, for some relief from isolation, for some reassurance that what one felt, the other felt.

So it was not surprising that Ruin immediately spoke against the suggestion. "We have companions enough for our purposes."

Angel coldly corrected him. "We have *more* than enough companions, sir."

At once Strings looked a bit ill. "I really don't enjoy disputes, if you please."

"It was a pleasure to watch you," Patience said. "But my gebling friend is right. We're here to sample the pleasures of Freetown, and then be on our way."

Strings laughed.

Kristiano touched her knee. "Lady, great lady, Strings can't be deceived, not by someone whose need shouts so clearly."

"I know where you're going," said Strings, "and I know the way."

Will spoke softly. "Let's leave here. Now."

Patience was uncertain. Obviously this gaunt was unusually adept at empathy. Yet how could empathy tell him her destination? There were no words in it, no images.

As if in answer to her question, Strings let his head rock backward at an impossible angle, as if all the muscles in his neck had gone slack. Then he began to murmur, his words an incantation. "I'm not so old now that I can forget the taste of the need like a knife in your heart. I've tasted the hunger, the yearning to climb to the ice where he waits, where he waits, where he waits. And the lady he calls is the one that he waits for, he calls you more strongly than any before you, but under the layers of pain that he sends you I feel something stronger than ever before. You are his enemy. You are his lover. And I am your guide to his lovemaking chamber.''

During the speech, Kristiano had almost unconsciously begun to move, as if the words were lyrics and he the visual music. Even in the confines of the box, the shape and movement of the boyok's body were exquisite. He oriented himself, perhaps instinctively, so that the light from the candle-window played off his arms and hands, profiled his face, and made shadows that became part of the dance.

How can one so young be so experienced already in the most difficult of arts? No sooner had she asked herself the question than Patience saw an answer to it: Kristiano was enacting the dance that Strings gave him. Strings—and Kristiano his puppet. But that would mean that Kristiano was responding to a gaunt as if the gaunt were a human or gebling, with a powerful will.

"How does a gaunt put a dance into a gauntling?" she asked.

Strings came out of his trance, looking confused. "Dance?" Then he looked at Kristiano, as if he had been unaware the boyok was dancing. "Not now," he said. Kristiano at once relaxed his pose.

"You gave him a dance as you spoke to me," she said. "How can you do it, when you have no will?"

He was preparing to lie; she could see that. But if he was indeed Unwyrm's guide up the mountain—for the Wise who had come before her, and now for the seventh seventh seventh daughter—then she had to have the truth from him, and for some reason she knew that this was the question that mattered.

His face contorted. "Lady, you torture me with your desire."

"Then ease yourself, and answer me."

"I am a monster among gaunts," he said.

"Because you *have* a will, after all?"

"Because I wish I had one. I wish. I take them up the mountain—from the time I was little I find these men and women with the hunger on them, and I take them up the mountain to the yellow door. It's where they want to go, but they never come down. And you, such beauty you gave me, do you think I can forgive you far being such a lifegiver? Like the water down the mountain out of his palace, a lifegiver, and I'll take you up the mountain like all the others and you'll never come down and what am I to do then? How are we ever to dance again, now that we've found the audience that can bring us to life?"

Again, Kristiano danced during Strings' recitative, giving a strangely separated life to his words.

"I'm old," said Strings. "The boyok here, he is my child-self. What dance can I do now, except to stand and give the others their movements around me? Not until you came, not for years have I done anything but stand in the middle of my dance."

"Then you *are* powerful," said Patience. "Enough to control the others, anyway."

"I have no will, great lady, but I have desires, as strong as yours are, hot as fires, cold as the bedchamber waiting for you, and perfect, yes, I know the perfect shapes. I desire the shape of perfection from them, and they answer me, they follow me. Let me follow you, lady." His eyes pled with her.

She tried to understand the pleading look he gave her. All that he had told her was true. But something more. She had to know even what he kept back from her. She let the desire grow within her, pushed into the background her desire for Will, her fear of this place; she even subdued, for a moment, her need to rise to where Unwyrm waited.

His face twisted. His breath came in labored heaves.

And then, suddenly, out of a mask of agony he spoke again. "Don't go up the mountain, lady, he'll have you then, all alone, there'll be no help for you."

"I'm not alone," she said.

"You will be, you will be, except for the liar, except for his puppet, except for the wise man who went and came back, the traitor who—"

As he spoke, Patience thought of the one man who claimed to be Wise and who admitted he had been to Cranning and returned. She looked at him, and so the others did, too. Will, ready to betray her for Unwyrm's sake.

And she would have gone on believing that, if she hadn't glanced back at Strings just before his speech petered out, and he went limp and collapsed on the chair, his breath a thin whisper of exhaustion. Kristiano gasped, and immediately felt him for a pulse; relieved that Strings was not dead, the boyok held the old gaunt against him.

But even in the dim light, Patience had seen. Strings had not collapsed from exhaustion. Angel's hand had reached out, had touched the gaunt in the places that Angel had taught her could make a man lose consciousness. Just when Strings had said enough to incriminate Will, but before Strings had said all he meant to say, Angel had silenced him. Had silenced him at the moment when all were looking at Will. She was the only one who could have noticed. Had silenced him before Strings had actually named a name or pointed a finger or looked at anyone.

"You," said Angel. He was looking at Will. "You're the one he meant. You've been here before. And I heard you tell Patience the other morning on the boat, I heard you tell her that you had felt the Cranning call. That you are one of the Wise. Do you deny it?"

If she had not seen Angel's fingers at their work, she

would have believed his words. But she knew that the traitor was Angel. Even as he accused Will, he confirmed the truth to her. He had been a young man when he heard the Cranning call. He came to Cranning as all the Wise had come, no better able to resist the call than any other. But Unwyrm needed one task performed. The daughtering of Peace. So Angel had come back down from the mountain, armed with the knowledge of how to repair what had been done to Peace. Soon Unwyrm's bride was conceived and born, and Angel then devoted his life to bringing her up, preparing her. And finally bringing her here. All the time, he had been in Unwyrm's service. All the time. And my father trusted him. She wanted to tear at him with her hands, reach in through the soft places of his face and rip him to pieces. Never had she felt such rage and shame as now, knowing that all her childish love had been given to a man whose show of affection was all a mockery. He is a pigherd, and I am his only swine. Now he leads me to the slaughter, and I, blind to what he truly is, love him.

Not blind now, though. And because she could hide anything when she needed to, she let nothing of her rage show.

Ruin was laughing at the thought of Will being one of the Wise, but Reck was alert. Patience caught her eye and gazed steadily at her for a moment, while Angel continued his accusation against Will. Did she understand? I will act, and you must watch me if you mean to stay with me up the mountain.

Still her thoughts raced, putting everything together now, revising all her past memories to fit the present reality. Angel was the enemy. He had tried his best to keep her from meeting Ruin and Reck, and now he meant to get rid of them before she reached Unwyrm. He was too good an assassin for her to believe the gebling king would reach the top of the mountain alive, if Angel were with them, and Will not there to protect them. So Angel would not be with them.

"Will," she said. "With what has happened, you can see that I can't trust you anymore." She hoped that he, too, could read in her steady gaze a plea for him to understand, to play along with her. "But I don't want Angel to kill you."

"Not kill him!" whispered Angel.

"So I'll bind you here, and leave Sken to watch you, and we'll bribe the boxmaster to leave you undisturbed for the night. Don't try to follow us, or I'll kill you myself."

Will said nothing. Did he understand?

"This is insane," said Angel. "He's a dangerous man, and you mean to leave him alive?"

"There's no harm in him," said Reck. But she looked confused, as if she was not sure whether to believe that Will was a traitor or to cling to her long belief in the man.

"We can argue later," said Patience. "Outside this box." She glanced toward the curtain that was the only barrier between them and the audience. "Or do we want to be part of the show?"

Patience had Sken tie him with the cord she had worn around her waist. It was long and strong enough to hold. Patience carefully maneuvered herself between Angel and Will, for fear Angel would slip a knife into him or poison him and then apologize for having done what he thought best. Patience wasn't sure yet how to get through this crisis without bloodshed. But she knew that she could trust Will, and wanted him alive. Will never took his gaze from Patience's face; he never denied anything, either. She hoped this meant he trusted her, too.

Every word that Angel said now, every move he made

filled her with anger and dread. Hadn't she looked up to him as the master assassin?. Everything she knew of attack and defense she had learned from him; she had come to rely on these skills, had believed she could defeat anyone, but now she wondered what Angel had kept from her. She could try this, or that, but he had taught it to her—a thrust with a needle, a dart in the throat, a pass with the loop, he knew every move she could make, while she could not guess what he might have hidden from her.

Did he notice that she kept herself between him and Will? Did he notice that she maneuvered so that he would leave the box first, giving him no chance to separate her from the geblings? Did he know that she no longer trusted him? She hoped he was too worried, too distracted by how close Strings had come to unmasking him, to realize from her actions that she knew the truth about him. The fact that she had even seen him silence the gaunt was proof that he was not at his best right now. This alone gave her a chance to defeat him, to escape.

Angel led them out into the hallway. Sken stood in the doorway after the others passed through, watching them.

"We should take the gaunt," Angel said softly. "Even if Unwyrm controls him, he *does* know the way."

"Angel," she said. "I'm so frightened. I trusted Will, and he was Unwyrm's creature all along." She put her arms around him, clung to him as she had when she was little. But before her fingers could reach the places she had to touch to render him unconscious, his fingers had found hers. She knew, then, that he was not deceived. That he was perfectly aware that she no longer trusted him. She had a fleeting vision of herself, collapsing unconscious in his arms. He would tell them she had fainted; they would believe him. And without her there to protect them, Reck and Ruin would not last long. It was over.

But his fingers did not press. "I loved you," she whispered, letting the agony of betrayal sound in her voice.

And still he hesitated. Now her fingers found the places; she did not hesitate. He fell at once to the floor.

"Let's go," she said to the geblings.

"What's happening?" asked Ruin.

"Angel is the traitor."

The others looked at her for a moment, uncomprehending.

"I saw him silence the old gaunt before he could name names. It's Angel who is Unwyrm's man."

"Then we must set Will free," said Reck.

Sken turned around to go back into the box and untie him. But just then the boxmaster appeared at one end of the corridor. "What are you doing!" he shouted. He could see Angel's body lying on the ground. "What have you done! Murder! Murder!" He ran back the way he had come.

"This is stupid," Ruin said. "He isn't even dead."

"Stupid or not, if he brings the police, and they arrest us for questioning, they imprison humans and geblings in separate jails, where Unwyrm can push you away while he pulls me on," said Patience.

The boxmaster was still shouting, and soon he would be back. They could hear the audience, too, becoming alarmed. Patience wanted to wait for Will and Sken, but there was no time. Ruin tugged at her arm. Reck and Ruin led her quickly toward the far end of the corridor.

"What makes you think this is a way out?" asked Patience as they ran. "It's right against the mountain face."

There was a spiral stairway leading upstairs to the actors' rooms, where the pleasures of the performance were often continued through the night, with improvisation and audience participation. Since there was nowhere else to go, they climbed. Patience, between the geblings, stumbled and fell against the stairs.

"Unwyrm knows what I've just done," she said. "I can feel it—he's trying to punish me for leaving Angel." She tried to climb, but could hardly take a step. Unwyrm was pounding at her; she was a storm of conflicting passions; she could not think.

Ruin ahead of her and Reck behind, they dragged and pushed her up the stairs. There were rows of dressing rooms here, with naked gaunts and humans busy cleaning themselves up from the last show or preparing for the next. The geblings held her by the arms and led her down the corridor. Step. Step. The movement gave her something to concentrate on. Unwyrm's surge began to weaken—he couldn't maintain such a powerful call for long. Gradually her self-control returned to her, and she began to walk faster, without the geblings' help.

"Are there windows in the dressing rooms on the outside wall?" she asked.

"This one," said Ruin.

A naked young gaunt was glittering his crotch when they came in and tried the window.

"It's cold out there," he said mildly.

"Lock the door, please," said Patience.

"I'm sorry," he said. "It doesn't lock."

"Pretty far down," said Ruin, looking out the window. "And the walkway isn't very wide there. A lot farther down if we miss."

Patience looked out the window. "Child's play," she said. She swung out the window, hung from her hands, and dropped. The geblings had no choice but to follow her. Reck ended up sprawled on the walkway. "We geblings are not wholly descended from apes," she said.

"We don't have your instincts for jumping out of windows."

Patience didn't bother to apologize. The night was dark, with clouds only a few meters above them, and it was hard to see where they were going, but they broke into a run. Suddenly Patience felt very tired. It was a long way up the mountain. She hadn't slept since last night on the boat; why couldn't she just go back to her room and rest? She wanted to rest. But she shook off the feeling; she knew where it came from. Unwyrm was not going to make anything easy for them. As long as Angel had been with them, Unwyrm hadn't had to put obstacles in their way. But now, if Unwyrm was to keep the geblings from arriving with Patience in his lair, he would have to use other people to try to pry them from Patience. Or kill them. Patience had no desire to face Unwyrm alone. She knew his strength, and needed help; if the geblings were all the help she could get, then she certainly didn't want to lose them. She could trust no one else. Everyone was her enemy.

They stopped at their rooms in the inn long enough for Reck to get her bow and Ruin his knife, and to take cloaks for the climb upward into winter. There was no human conspiracy working against them, only Unwyrm sensing the nearest people and arousing them against the Heptarch's party. So there was no particular danger in going to their rooms—only in staying for more than a few minutes. They did not separate: the geblings stayed with her in the room she had shared with Angel and Sken, and she in turn went with them to theirs. Someone knocked on their door as they were preparing to leave.

"It's probably just the innkeeper," said Reck.

"It's death," said Patience. "Unwyrm will see to it that we meet nothing but death on our way up the mountain."

Ruin thrust open the window. Patience climbed out. The window hung over a thirty-meter drop. It was too much even for her. But she had always been a good climber, and she saw it would be easy enough to get to the roof. "Trust your human half," she said. "You'll need all your ape ancestry for this." She stood on the sill, reached up to the rain gutter, and pulled herself up. Reck followed right behind her. Ruin had barely joined them on the roof when they heard a roaring sound. Flames leaped out of the window of the room they had just left.

"We'll have to be quick about this, won't we?" said Ruin.

"Up," said Patience. They ran along the rooftop to where a ladder connected it to the walkway of the next level. How many kilometers to the glacier at the top of Skyfoot? Patience didn't want to remember. She just set her hands and feet to the ladder and climbed.

16 | ANGEL

Sken struggled to untie Will, until he said to her, "Wouldn't it be faster to cut it?"

"Oh, now he can talk. Why didn't you say anything before?" She sawed with her dull eating knife. "When I was tying you, why not a word about how you were innocent?"

"Because somebody *wasn't* innocent, and I didn't know who."

A cord finally separated. "It was Angel."

"I gathered that." His hands and feet came free, once the central knot was cut. He got to his feet quickly—he hadn't been tied long enough to become stiff.

Just as he reached the door, the boxmaster ran by, waving a cudgel and leading a group of highly irregular soldiers. Certainly not the official guard, just a spur-of-the-moment mob gathered to serve Unwyrm's purpose. Real soldiers would be summoned soon enough. Will decided to make no effort to follow them. He knew Patience and the geblings well enough not to fear for their safety yet. And he had another matter to attend to.

"Is there enough of that cord left, Lady Sken, to bind this fellow before he wakes up?"

Sken stepped into the corridor and joined him beside Angel's unconscious body. "They left him?"

"Unwyrm was urging them on. He doesn't let his people have many distractions."

She prodded Angel with her toe. "Are you sure nobody's home? He's a crafty one."

"Poke him long enough and he's bound to wake up. I don't want his hands free when he does."

Sken tied him—Will knew from experience what an admirable job she could do—and together they carried the old man back into the box. Only then did Will pay any attention to Kristiano and Strings. The old gaunt was awake again.

"What happened to me?" asked Strings.

"Angel thought your story was getting too personal."

"Story? Oh, yes. Yes, my story. I tried to lie. I could feel how much Angel wanted me to lie."

"But you told the truth anyway?"

"The girl. She wanted the truth more than he wanted the lie. It was very distressing. I think I fainted."

"You were helped along."

"I knew him," said Strings. "I knew them all. But Angel—he was a good one, a bright one. When I took him up the mountain, there wasn't a trace of evil desire in him."

"I couldn't even guess what a gaunt thinks is evil," said Sken.

"We think the same as everyone else thinks," said the gaunt. "And like everyone else, our actions have no relation to our opinions of good and evil. I wasn't chosen accidently as the guide for the Wise. I'm very clever."

"Your dance was beautiful."

"Clever. Merely clever. It's the best a gaunt can hope

to achieve. Yes, Kristiano?" He tousled the hair of the beautiful gauntling beside him. "I am the peak of gauntish ambition. But don't grieve; we are the ultimate innocents. We are never the cause of our own actions. It allows us to reach a ripe old age untroubled by guilt."

Will thought he heard irony in the old gaunt's tone. "You knew what you were leading them to?"

He shrugged eloquently. "They all wanted to go."

"I also want to go," said Will. "Will you take me?"

"*He* doesn't want me to take you," said Strings. "And he makes the most urgent requests of me. I have never denied him."

"He isn't paying attention to us right now."

Strings looked thoughtful for a moment. "You're right. It doesn't mean anything, though. He left me alone for ten years. And then three days ago he came to me again. I've never hurried so fast. I was on the other side of Cranning, playing in a decent place, a palace filled with people of breeding and discernment. Then he made me leave everything and come here, to take a booking like this—I don't like working in this kind of place. The crowd has deplorable tastes. Why do you want me to keep talking?"

"I like the sound of your voice."

"No, you want more than that from me. You want to know—ah. Yes. Well, how can anyone know who a gaunt really is? Am I good or evil? Can you trust me or not? Can you tell him, Kristiano?"

Kristiano smiled. His face had the peaceful sweetness of a saint. Or an idiot.

"How strong are your passions, man? You have the size and strength of a horse, but that's nothing to me. It's the dimension of your lust, your gluttony, your ambition. You can trust me if your desires are strong and never waver."

"In your list of desires, you mention only evil ones."

"In my experience, they're the ones with vigor. Except the fanatics. I once fell in with a Vigilant, when I was a child. He made me whip him until he bled. And one day such a religious fervor came over him that he died of it. Give me the lust of the sinners before the austerity of the holy men."

"What about your own desires?" asked Will. "You said you have them."

"Oh, I'm a man of passion, all passion, and no achievement. I have done shameful things. I have led my brothers to the wyrm's maw. Unwyrm isn't kind to his servants. He doesn't stop us from regretting what we do."

"Until regret is the taste in your mouth in the morning, and the last painful noise in your ears at night."

Will and Strings looked at Angel, who was awake now.

"I know what it is to be a gaunt," said Angel. "Unwyrm makes gaunts of us all."

"You shut up," said Sken. "That little girl believed in you."

Will looked at her, and at the look on his face she fell silent.

"Except you," said Angel. "Except Will. Strings, can you believe it? Will is one of the Wise. Only he never came to Unwyrm. He was even here in Cranning once, and he never came to Unwyrm."

Will shook his head. "I never felt the Cranning call when I was here. It was only later. When I learned enough to be worth calling."

"I can't untie you," said Strings, regretfully. "This one is so much stronger."

Angel sighed. "Yes, very strong. I tried, you know. All the way from Cranning to Lord Peace, I tried to disobey. I even tried to kill myself. And later, many times, I wanted to warn Peace, to tell him about the snake that he kept in his own house. But above all that came the desire to stay with Patience, to protect her, to bring her safely to him. I would have killed you if you had tried to sleep with her."

"And now? When he no longer pulls you?"

"Is he truly gone? No wonder I feel so empty. Like a head with an empty air bladder, nothing to say and no breath to say it. I can hardly remember who I was before. But is he gone? I still love her."

"You tell *me*."

Angel smiled. "I'm an excellent liar. You can't believe me, especially when I'm most believable. I warn you. Kill me now. It's the only way you can trust me not to stab you in the back."

"There's another way," said Will. "I can keep you in front of me."

"He's gone from me," said Angel. "And I still love Patience. I was so afraid that I wouldn't, that—she's been my life. All I cared about. She's my child—as surely as her father or her mother, I caused her to be alive. *I* did. Unwyrm can't put knowledge in a human brain—I had to learn it, with my own mind, to understand it. What the Wise before me said could never be undone, I undid. And if I discovered that I had never cared for her, that it was all from Unwyrm, then what was my life, who was I?" Then, to Will's surprise, Angel began to weep. "And all the time, I hoped that I would hate her, that when he—took her from me, when he finally left my mind, I'd find that she was loathsome, and I hated her, and she deserved to be betrayed."

Then his weeping overpowered his speech.

Strings nodded wisely. "That's the way it is, for us. We know what we're doing. We know it, and we don't want it, but we can't choose otherwise. We're very sad creatures, actually."

Sken looked at him with surprise. "You said you felt no guilt."

Strings sighed. "It makes people feel better when I tell them that. But it's a lie. We remember doing everything that we have done. We even remember wanting to do it. How can we absolve ourselves of *that?*"

Kristiano began stroking Strings's forehead, his gentle fingers making a graceful dance on the old gaunt's face. Will wondered how it would feel, to have those fingers touching him. And then, almost before he was aware of having the thought, Kristiano came to him and touched him, just as he had caressed Strings. Will felt ashamed; Kristiano quickly moved away, cowered in a corner, hid his face.

"I'm sorry," said Will.

"Oh, Kristiano's very sensitive. And you're very powerful." Strings smiled. "When you want something, when you *decide* something, why, it's decided, isn't it?"

Will shrugged.

"Where is she?" asked Angel.

"Gone. With the geblings. To face him."

"She can't. She doesn't understand—he's much stronger than he's ever shown her. Stronger than the geblings, stronger than she is. And with only three of them, his attention won't be divided, he'll have his way with them—"

"So," said Will. "That's why Strings is going to take me and Sken up the mountain."

"And me. You're a Vigilant, aren't you? For God's sake, then, let me redeem myself."

"You misunderstand the doctrine. It is Kristos who will redeem you."

"There'll be no Kristos! Her children will be monstrous parodies of human beings!"

"I understand that," he said. "But I'll never let you

up the mountain with us. A moment ago you asked me to kill you. It *was* a good idea."

"No it wasn't," said Angel. "You need me."

"Unwyrm doesn't even need you now."

"You can't kill me. As a Vigilant, you gave up murder, didn't you?"

"I also vowed never to let an unbeliever use my belief against me."

"I can help!"

"Unwyrm knows all the paths into your brain, Angel. How many years now? He has crawled through every passage in your skull and knows secret doors you've never found."

"Do you think so? I had my hands on her head and neck, I was ready, I could have made her sleep. I could have said she had fainted, and gone off with her and the geblings, and killed them both so easily, and we would have been free to go to him then, Patience and I—and he wanted me to do it, he made *me* want to do it." He smiled triumphantly. "I didn't. I didn't. I held on, I held out just long enough that she could put *me* to sleep. It wasn't long, Will, it wasn't a heroic resistance like yours has been, never to succumb to him. There'll be no epic poem about it. But Unwyrm could have won, right in that moment, and I resisted him just long enough." His voice became an intense whisper, a plea, a prayer. "I do love her, Will, and even if you kill me, you have to remember that I saved her, I did, I saved her—"

"He's stronger than he looks," said Strings.

"What do *you* know about it?" said Will. "All you can feel is desire. And what he lacks is what you lack—a will of his own."

"I know what I know," said Strings. "You tell me I'm wrong, but you want me to speak on. Because you do want to forgive him. I know you do, because I want to forgive him."

"That's *his* desire you're feeling."

"No," said Strings. "*He* wants me to kill him. And I would, too. I have my little ways."

"What's stopping you?" said Angel.

"This one." Strings pointed at Will. "He's a monster of compassion. He pities you."

"It's very hard to conduct a delicate bargaining session," said Will, "with you telling him what I really want."

"But you want me to tell the truth. I promise you, Will, that the minute you really want me to shut up, I will."

Will laughed. "For years I kept my silence and no one knew anything about me. Now my conscience has found a voice."

Angel moved uneasily, straining at his bonds.

"Don't try to get loose," said Sken. "It won't do you no good."

Angel slowly sat up and moved his hands out in front of him. He was completely untied. "Fools," he said. "There was never a cord that could hold me, when I want not to be held."

Sken reached for her knife, but then she saw that Angel had it. "I swear I tied him," Sken protested. "And my knife, how did he—"

"I could kill you all," said Angel. "But you see? I don't. Because I'm not what I was. He doesn't rule me now. I want to go with you, to have a chance to help her. I love her more than any of you, and I've harmed her more and must repay her more. And if we all face him together, if we all—he won't be able to take command of me, then. I can stand with all of you, and fight him—"

"You couldn't answer for yourself for a second," said Will.

"I could. I'm stronger than you know."

"And so am I," said Will. As he wanted, Strings had moved behind Angel, silently, slowly. Now, at Will's unspoken wish, Strings flipped a loop out around Angel's neck and drew it close. "Drop the knife," said Will.

Angel dropped the knife. Kristiano picked it up. Strings removed his loop from around Angel's neck. Angel touched a spot where the loop had broken his skin. "No one has ever done that," Angel said. "No one has ever surprised me."

"I'm a dancer," said Strings. "I'm very good at this."

"I wasn't going to hurt anyone," said Angel. "I just wanted you to see that I *could*, but chose not to."

"And I just wanted to show you that you *couldn't*," said Will.

"You're all insane," said Sken. "I wish I was back on the river."

"Before you kill him," said Strings to Will, "would you let me ask him a question?"

Will nodded.

"I led so many to him, but none of the others has ever returned. Tell me—what did he do to the others?" His face was eager; then, suddenly, it wasn't. He looked at Will through tired eyes. "Can't you leave my desires alone, even now, Will? You have made it so I don't want to know the answer to that queston. But I know that I *want* to want to know. As soon as you take away this compulsion, I'll want to know again, it will obsess me again as it does whenever I'm undistracted. So I beg you, give me back the desire of my heart, and let me want to know."

But Will did not think it would be good for Strings to know the fate of the humans he had led up the mountain. If he was consumed with guilt, to a point where he could not function well, he might not be able to guide Will to Unwyrm's lair.

"Will," whispered Strings, "if you don't let me ask this question now, then you're no different from Unwyrm, changing people's desires to whatever is convenient for you."

It struck Will hard, to hear himself compared to Unwyrm. And Strings smiled. "Tell me, Angel," he said.

"You *are* sly," said Angel. "You have some tricks to manipulate human beings, too."

"We gaunts *do* have a will, you know. It's weak and not well-connected. It drys up like old cake and crumbles into dust whenever a human or a gebling or even, disgusting as it is, a dwelf desires something of us. But when we're alone, we don't just sit staring into space until another human comes. Alone, we have strength enough to think and scheme and, sometimes, act. My question, please, even though you don't want to tell it."

Will nodded to Angel. "I want to know, too."

"It's nothing—painful," said Angel. "He implants in them—in us—in me. He implanted in me a seed, a virus of some sort, I believe, that caused a crystal to grow within my brain. That's all. Most of them he kept there for a year or two, to give the crystal time to penetrate, to gather memories and wisdom from every part of the brain. Then he—took it out."

"He killed them, then," whispered Kristiano.

"No," said Angel. "No, they're humans, they're not from Imakulata. They can live without the mindstone. The crystal steals their memories, but it leaves them shadows. They don't die when the crystal is gone. They just—forget. Everything. But it's still there, the shadows are there in their brains, and as long as they live, they stumble now and then over some of the old information, quite by chance. They may even find some of the pathways, recover some of their identity. I don't know. It doesn't kill them, though. He lets them all die a natural death."

"Prisoners, till they die?" asked Will.

"No. Not really prisoners. They love him."

"Thank you," said Strings. "I've done evil, but not as evil as I feared."

"Never evil," murmured Kristiano. He touched Strings's hand. "Good heart," the boyok whispered. The old gaunt smiled and nodded.

"You were different," said Will to Angel. "He didn't take your mindstone."

"He needed me to go back out into the world. To cause Patience to be born."

"What was your wisdom?" asked Will. "What was it you studied, that made him call you?"

"I studied new life. The way young organisms grow, from the genetic cells in the parent's body to the final maturation of the living child."

"Not just organisms. You studied humans."

"All there is to know about the growth of the human infant, fetus, embryo, egg, and sperm—I know it. I knew it then."

"He didn't take your mindstone—but you taught him."

Angel shook his head. "No."

"Yes," said Will. "If he wanted to gather information vital to destroying the human race, he'd have to know what you knew."

"Oh, yes," said Angel. "But I didn't *teach* him. I *studied* him. I examined the cells he had developed within himself. Ready to combine with the vigorous new human genes that Patience would bring to him. He wanted to be sure that he was ready. He wanted to know that his offspring would do all he wanted them to do."

"And what does he want them to do?"

"Oh, I don't mean their careers, or anything like that.

I only studied them to predict their growth patterns. He has done marvels. His incredible genetic molecule—it can change itself. His own body makes new hormones, and those pass into his gametes and cause them to change. They lack the human component as an active feature. But they're there, anyway, though no human traits are dominant. I was able to stimulate artificial growth, cloned life from his sperm alone. It never lived longer than a few minutes. I don't work miracles.''

"What did you learn?"

"In those few minutes, they did what human zygotes do in six months. It's why they died. He had jiggered them so the individual cells reproduced at an incredible rate. My nutrient solution was too poor for them. I pumped it into them; they grew visibly in front of my eyes, and then they withered and died. It frightened him. For a moment he made me want to kill myself.''

"He's sterile, then?" asked Will. "His children will die in the womb?"

"No. Not now."

"What do you mean?"

"I told him what they needed. To grow slower, that's what I told him first, but he said no. He wants his children to be adults within hours, minutes—then they can eat his mindstone, you see, and know all that he knows, and walk out of the birthing place knowing everything.''

" He talked to you?"

"I dreamed of it. He made me desire it, too. To see them grow so fast, and live. So I told him that his children must have a yolk. A source of material and energy so rich that they'll have enough to grow at that incredible rate. He can't have as many children as he would have, but they'll be adults within an hour. He's afraid for them, he knows he can't protect them. So from his own body he'll produce a very dense, very rich yolk, which he'll implant along with his sperm—"

"In Lady Patience."

"Do you believe in God? Pray for her, Vigilant."

"So the children will be few."

"The children had better never be conceived," said Angel. "Or they'll come down out of the mountain in an hour, able to communicate with each other as the wyrms always did. Not the feeble thing the geblings do. The ancient wyrms were one self. No matter how many bodies his mate brings forth, Unwyrm will have one child. And if they do take over the earth, they'll be a single entitity, knowing all things that each one knows. If any survive at all—"

"None will," said Will.

"I'll see to that," said Sken. "I'll see to the little monsters."

"Monsters?" said Angel. "Yes, you see to the monsters."

"Strings," said Will. "How fast can you get us up the mountain to Unwyrm's lair?"

"Outside Freetown, the Miserkorden have platforms that rise most of the way. If Unwyrm doesn't try to stop us, we could be there in twelve hours or so. If we leave here at dawn, we'll be there by nightfall."

"You can bet the others won't have it so easy," said Will. "It won't do to face Unwyrm unrested. Strings, is there somewhere here that we can sleep? Just for a few hours?"

"You've paid for this box," said Strings.

"I suppose we wouldn't be the first to stay all night."

"You'd be the first who slept." Strings smiled. Kristiano laughed.

"Sken," said Will, "I'll stand a two-hour watch. Then you wake for the next two."

"I had hoped for more sleep than that," she said.

"It's all we'll get. And you, Angel—you might as well sleep straight through. You may think you're an invincible assassin, but I've been a soldier in my day, and my body count is at least as high as yours."

"I told you, he isn't in me anymore."

"I just warned you in case he came back." Will smiled.

"You mean you're not going to kill him?" asked Sken.

"That's right," said Will.

"And will you take me with you?" asked Angel.

"I've known Unwyrm's call," said Will, "and I feel no contempt for those who succumb to it. God has some good purpose in mind for every soul that's born. You have a right to try to redeem yourself. But I promise you, I'll kill you in a moment if I see that Unwyrm has you again."

"I know," said Angel. "I want you to."

"He does," said Strings.

"Four hours," said Will. "At dawn we'll head for the top. We're not much of an army, but with God's help we'll be more than Unwyrm can handle."

"How do you know God doesn't want Unwyrm to win?" asked Angel.

"If he wins, we'll know God wanted him to." Will smiled. "Reality is the most perfect vision of God's will. It's discovering God's will in advance that causes all the trouble."

"The fate of mankind is in the hands of a fanatic," said Angel. "As usual."

17 | THE HOUSE OF THE WISE

"YOU SHOULD HAVE GOT MORE EXERCISE ON THE BOAT," said Ruin.

Patience could hardly speak for panting; Reck was doing scarcely better. Only Ruin seemed tireless as they ran along the narrow street.

Despite Ruin's greater endurance, it was Patience who had chosen their route so far, dodging among the buildings, climbing over roofs and scrambling up ladders and trellises. Reck and Ruin had little experience with urban scenery; they had no sense of where blind alleys might lead, or what buildings could serve as inadvertent highways to the next level. Patience, however, had spent years climbing over, under, and through the many palaces and public buildings of King's Hill, which in some areas was as densely populated and overbuilt as Cranning.

The soldiers were shouting behind them, but a curve in the road that skirted a jut in the cliff's face hid them from the soldiers' view. Patience saw an open gate into a small garden on the cliff side of the road. She quickly scanned the area for possible escape routes. The garden was beside a two-story house, which led upward to a stone retaining wall built against the cliff face. The wall no doubt supported a road on the next level up. A sewer pipe protruded a couple of meters below the lip of the retaining wall; to avoid having the waste from above pollute them, the builders on this level had connected it to a thick masonry drainpipe that carried the wastewater down to a collector barrel. Until now, there had always been ladders or stairs or elevators connecting the different levels, but apparently these two states were feuding, and the sewer connection was the best they had seen so far. To Patience, it looked like a highway to safety.

The problem was that during the climb they would be hopelessly exposed. But if they hid in the garden, the soldiers might pass them by. It would give them a few moments until Unwyrm realized what had happened and began to guide them back. Powerful as Unwyrm was, he couldn't see through his minions' eyes, or even understand their conscious thoughts. He could only shove them in roughly the direction he wanted them to go, by making them want desperately to go that way. It gave Patience some time, some room to maneuver; it was the only reason Reck and Ruin had not yet been killed, or Patience separated from them.

All this thought took only a moment; Patience drew the other two through the garden gate. It had been open slightly, jammed in place by debris and built-up dirt that showed that the owner never moved it. Patience left it undisturbed. She had the other two move well into the garden, behind some barrels, out of sight. She waited near the entrance, her loop in hand. Only one person at a time could get through the gate. With luck, though, no one would try.

They heard the soldiers run by. Their captain was shouting orders to them. Then there was silence, except for their distant running footsteps as they ran farther and farther away.

Patience turned to leave the gate and join the geblings, but Ruin was waving to her frantically: get back, get back. She turned around just as a soldier, his sword leading, stepped through the gate. It was a reflex, with no thought at all, to lariat his head with the loop and snap it tight. By chance the loop fell right where cartilage connected two vertebrae of his neck; the force and speed of her attack were so great that the loop gave only a moment's hesitation in cutting right through the spine. The man's head twisted and spun off his shoulders; both his own forward movement and the pull of the loop made the head tumble toward her, striking her chin and rolling down across her chest.

Angel said I couldn't do this, she thought. Said I couldn't cut off a man's head with a single pass of the loop.

And at the same time, she thought: The blood will never wash out of this gown.

The soldier's body still stumbled forward, his arms reaching out to break his fall. Then the last instructions of the head to the body were exhausted; the body collapsed.

Patience quickly dragged the body inside the gate, where it couldn't be seen from outside. Then she put the head back on the neck and propped it in place with rocks and a small keg. Let them not see at once that he was dead. It might be a useless gesture, but Angel had taught her to do that, since it usually bought more time than it cost; and because the person who discovered the body was the one whose action would make the head separate from the neck, it was all the more horrifying—and therefore demoralizing.

Ruin and Reck had already guessed the next move, and were climbing up to the roof of the house. After climbing dozens of similar buildings this morning, they had mastered the basic routine. They stayed behind chimneys and did their best to be invisible from the street. Patience quickly joined them—she was a more practiced climber than either of them. In moments she was leading the way again.

There was a boy, about ten years old, working on the roof. He had a hammer, which he had been using to repair shingles. At the moment, however, he had a murderous glint in his eye. Unwyrm was in him, and all he wanted was to use his hammer to stop them. Patience knew *she* could get by him; already his gaze went past her, as he looked with loathing on the geblings behind her.

"I don't want to kill you," said Patience.

"Go back," he said to the geblings. "Go back, you filth!"

Behind her, Reck fitted an arrow to her bow.

"He's a child!" Patience shouted. "He can't help himself!"

"Neither can I," said Reck.

Before Reck could get off a shot, Patience kicked out, catching the boy in the belly and knocking the wind out of him. He fell back against the stone wall of the cliff face behind him. He didn't drop the hammer. So she had to do it again, and this time she could feel ribs break. "Live!" she shouted at the boy. "Live and forgive me!" Then she ran on, leading the geblings to the base of the sewer line.

"All Unwyrm needs to do to defeat you is send an army of children," said Ruin. "Save your compassion for a time when we're not fighting to survive."

"Shut up, Ruin," said Reck. Then she pushed on the sewer pipe. It wobbled. "We're supposed to climb *this*? It's pottery. It'll break."

"The frame is wooden," said Patience. "And there are gaps in the stone wall. Easy." She proved it by climbing up *beside* the sewer pipe, using only the crevices in the stonework. Reck and Ruin scrambled up behind her.

Shouts below; the soldiers had come back, and Patience and the geblings were clearly visible now. There was no possibility of hiding; they were as visible as roaches on a whitewashed wall, and could not scurry nearly as fast. Patience knew the only escape was to climb as quickly as possible, getting higher and harder to hit before the soldiers came within bowshot.

"Maybe I could get some from here," Reck said. The gebling woman was obviously frustrated at not having been able to use her weapon all day.

"If you killed five, there'd still be fifteen shooting at us," said Patience.

She reached the place where the sewer pipe stuck out from the stone wall. Unfortunately, the wall was newer here; it had not weathered as many years, and there were no crevices to which she could trust her weight. Using the last of the cracks below the sewer line, she was able to get up on top of the pipe. It was a precarious balance, not helped at all by the fact that the pipe was not firmly cemented in place; it wiggled slightly. Her face pressed against the stone, she carefully raised her arms above her head.

It occurred to her that if she really wanted to thwart Unwyrm, she had only to lean backward just a little, and it would be over. But as soon as she felt that desire, she was filled with a desperate urge to survive. Her fingers touched the top of the wall, with a few inches to spare. The stones were firm; she began to lift herself. It was harder than hoisting herself onto a tree branch; she couldn't swing front-to-back in order to give herself momentum.

But slowly, with growing pain in her arms, she was able to lift herself till the wall was at waist height; then she toppled over to safety beyond the wall.

On this side, the road was half a meter below the level of the wall, so that the wall formed a sturdy curb to keep carts from toppling over the edge. Almost as soon as she was behind the wall, the arrows started flying from below. Of course Unwyrm hadn't been willing to let anyone shoot when there was a chance of hurting *her*. Now, though, only the geblings clung to the wall, high and difficult to shoot, but open targets nonetheless. A chance arrow was bound to hit one of them sooner or later.

"I can't reach!" shouted Ruin.

Of course. The shorter geblings couldn't possibly climb as she had done. And she doubted she had the strength left in her arms to reach over and pull him up.

At the same moment, Unwyrm increased the urgency of the Cranning call. Leave them. She felt a sudden revulsion for the geblings. Filthy creatures, hairy and crude, imitating human beings but planning only to betray and kill her. It took all her strength not to do as she desired, to run from the wall and proceed alone to where Unwyrm waited, her lover, her friend.

She clung to the memory of Will's voice, telling her that her desires were not herself. She pictured the passions that Unwyrm sent as though they stood outside her, while her passionless self remained inside the machine of her body, making it do what it so desperately desired not to do.

She pulled her gown off over her head and knotted it to her cloak. Then, clad only in her chemise, with a cold wind whipping along the road, she sat with her feet braced against the wall, passed the cloak behind her back, and flipped the gown over the wall. She held the knot in her left hand, the other end of the cloak in her right; the friction of the cloth against her back would allow her to support far more weight on the gown than her arms could have managed alone.

"I'm supposed to climb *this?*" shouted Ruin.

"Unless you can fly!" she shouted back. Unwyrm raged at her, tore at her in her mind, but she held, despite the impulse to let go, to let the gebling fall. I will do what I decide to do, she said silently, not what I want to do, and she felt the emotional part of herself become smaller, recede as if it were rushing away from her. This is Will, she realized. This is his silence, his strength, his wisdom, that he can send away all his feelings when he doesn't want them.

The cloth of the gown gave and tore slightly, then more, but in a moment Ruin scrambled over the wall. Then he leaned over and shouted encouragement to Reck. Suddenly there was a cry from the other side.

"She's hit," said Ruin. He shouted, "It's nothing, it barely hurt you, come on, come on!"

From the weight on the makeshft ladder, Patience knew that Reck was climbing now. Ruin leaned over, caught his sister under the arm, and helped pull her up. The arrow protruded from her left thigh, but Ruin was right—the head had not buried itself, and he easily pulled it out. Reck was gasping, her eyes wide with terror. "Never," she said. "I could never stand heights."

"And you think of Cranning as home?" asked Patience. She was examining her gown. It was shredded where it had scraped on the wall. It pulled apart in her hands. "I'm glad there aren't three of you. The third one would have fallen."

She unknotted the cloak from the gown. A spent arrow dropped beside her. She flipped it back over the wall. "Hope it lands in someone's eye."

Ruin was looking at her. Studying her. "Why didn't you go off and leave us?"

"I thought of it," she said.

"I know—we get the shadow of what he says to you."

"Well, if I'm going to be a bride, I need a wedding party. Have to have you along." It was a bitter joke. She wrapped the cloak around her waist to protect her legs from the cold wind that whistled down the unprotected road. "I also need a warm fire."

"At least we don't have to run for a few moments." Reck tried out her injured leg. "Hurts," she said.

Ruin looked around. "If we find the right herb—"

"They say everything that grows anywhere grows in Cranning," said Reck.

"*Somewhere* in Cranning," said Ruin.

"There are trees that way," said Patience. "And if we're lucky, we won't run into anybody that Unwyrm can set to chasing us."

The houses, which were several streets deep for a while, thinned out and finally gave way to gardens and orchards. Soon they found themselves on a road that led along the rim of a large flat orchard area. The trees were stunted, for only dwarf trees could live at such an altitude. Ruin wandered among the trees, which had long since lost leaf and fruit; finally he called to Reck and jammed a furry leaf against her wound.

"We can't rest here for long," Reck said, holding the leaf in place. "He'll have someone after us soon."

"I've never worked so hard in my life," said Patience. "And I'm so tired."

"We haven't slept since we left the boat," said Ruin. "But Unwyrm couldn't be happier. We've got to sleep sometime."

"Now," said Patience.

"Not now," said Reck. "We have to get higher. Where there's no human or gebling to send after us."

Patience could see heavy clouds moving in from the west, at their level. "There'll be fog. We can hide in the fog."

"It won't be fog, it'll be snow," said Ruin. "We need shelter. And we need to get higher."

"Can't we use the tunnels *yet?*" asked Patience. Tunnels would be shelter *and* a passage to Unwyrm that they could follow easily.

"Oh, yes, of course," said Reck. "But the entrances are pretty rare up this high. We're nearly at the top of the inhabited area now. We'll just have to find another way up."

The herb acted quickly, taking away enough of Reck's pain that she could keep up, though she kept losing blood in a thin trickle as a scab formed and broke, formed and broke. Finally they found a stairway along the surface of the steep and polished wall that led up to the next level. The gate at the bottom was wide open. The gate at the top was less cooperative.

"They could at least have had the decency to lock the gate at the bottom, too," said Reck.

But Patience had been trained as a diplomat, and among his other lessons, Angel had taught her that a simple lock like this meant that the owner wasn't really serious about wanting privacy. Using a short stick and a dart, she had it open in a few moments.

They emerged in another garden, this time without trees. Behind the garden Skyfoot rose steeply again. This time, however, it was no polished wall. It was the raw mountain, with a few caverns yawning in its face. They had not seen natural rock like this since they reached Cranning. It looked as though no human hand had ever cut into it.

"Is this the top?" asked Patience.

Reck shook her head. "The top is a glacier, but the city may not go any higher than this. At this point, anyway."

"Do you know where we are?"

"I would if I could stand in that cave," said Ruin. They began to trot toward it, between two low hedges that seemed to lead in that general direction. Then the clouds moved in, and a few seconds later they couldn't see at all.

They stopped at once and touched each other, held hands so they wouldn't be separated.

"You're cold, Heptarch," said Reck. "You're trembling."

"She doesn't have fur," said Ruin. "We'll have to hold her until the cloud passes."

"He doesn't want me to wait," murmured Patience. "He's waited so long already."

They lay on the ground, Reck in front of her, Ruin behind, shielding her as best they could from the snow that now fell heavily from within the cloud.

"Are you all right?" Reck asked her once.

"All I can think about," said Patience, trembling, "is how much I want him." Then she laughed slightly. "All I can think about is sleep."

They held her tighter, and in the warmth of the geblings' embrace she slept.

The cloud was gone and the stars were out, but the snow half-covered them and the air was thin. Reck felt the wound in her thigh throbbing. The pain was not intense, but it had been enough to wake her. Reck felt no breath on her back from the human girl that slept behind her. She called her brother silently.

Ruin opened one eye and looked at her.

"How is she?" Reck whispered.

"She's weak. But then, I think he wants her weak."

"The caves won't help much. They're colder than outside."

"Stand up and see if there are any lights," said Ruin. "I'll hold her."

Reck pulled herself away from the sleeping human. There were some lights twinkling far away. A long walk in the darkness.

"A long way," said Reck. "But we can't go for help. So we'll have to take her, cold as it is." Reck knelt and stroked Patience's cold bare arm, then shook her lightly. "She won't wake up."

As if in answer, Reck suddenly felt what she had not felt in all the time they had been with Patience: the repulsion of Unwyrm. But here, so close to his lair, it came with such power that she could not breathe. She cried out with the pain of it. "We're too close to him!" she cried. With Patience asleep, Unwyrm could focus on them, on pushing them away.

"Wake her!" Ruin gasped.

Reck hardly heard him. She could hardly think of anything at all now except her urgent need to run to the wall of the garden and throw herself over the cliff, downward, all the way through the air down to the water at the base of Skyfoot, to sink into Cranwater. She got up and started staggering toward the wall.

"No!" screamed Ruin. He clutched at her feet. Strong as the repulsion was, he was more practiced at resisting it; her wound had weakened her a little, too, and so he held on to her. "Wake up, damn you!" he screamed at Patience. "Wake up, so he'll have to call you again!"

In answer, Patience began to tremble from the cold. She whimpered. She called her father softly. She did not wake up.

"Let go of me!" shouted Reck. "Let me fly!"

"He's trying to kill us!" cried Ruin, though he, too, felt the need to leap.

"What is it!" called someone in the distance.

"Where *are* you, ta-dee, ta-doo!" sang someone else.

"It's kickety cold!" cried someone else. Obviously the group was in a good mood, whoever they were.

"Here!" shouted Ruin. "Help!"

"Let go of me!" cried Reck.

The would-be rescuers bounded up to them. Ruin saw only that they were humans. "Let go of her!" said one of them. "Help him," said another.

They were old, and they sounded either drunk or stupid. Ruin doubted they could hold Reck if she wanted to get away. There was only one hope. "Wake up the one that's lying there! She's lying there, the girl in the snow—wake her up!"

"Look at this! She's not very warmly dressed—"

"In the snow—that's not very wise."

"Good thing we came. We know what's what."

They pulled Patience upright.

"Slap her!" Ruin shouted.

He heard several slaps. Then the sound of Patience crying. "Stop it," she said.

And suddenly the need to die faded. Reck stopped struggling.

"Take this frozen young thing into the house—"

"No," said Ruin. "Not without us! Keep her near us—"

"Do we want geblings?"

"Oh, they're quite all right. This is a gebling city, after all. Very nice geblings."

"Yes. Keep us together," said Ruin.

Many hands lifted him, helped him stand. They were carrying Reck, who was too exhausted to walk. Patience walked ahead of them, murmuring, "I'm coming, I'm coming, this isn't the way—"

"Of course it's the way. We know the way, don't we? Isn't this the way?"

Fires at both ends of the long, low room kept it almost hot. Ruin and Reck sat on either side of Patience, holding her hands as they faced the fire. The old men surrounded them, commenting inanely.

Patience tried to ignore them. She was worried about how they could go on from here. The snowstorm was none of Unwyrm's doing, of course. But he had been able to use it well enough. And now she was afraid to sleep, for fear that Reck and Ruin could be made to kill themselves or run away while she wasn't there to protect them. It was so complicated—they needed her to protect them so they could get to Unwyrm; she needed them to kill Unwyrm before he could mate with her. And Unwyrm was too strong, they were no match for him. No one was a match for him.

"No," said Reck.

"Is he doing it to you, too?" asked Ruin.

"Despair. We can't do it," said Reck.

Patience nodded.

The old men changed their babbling a little. "What are these little ones talking about? Buck up, children, don't despair. This is a happy place, don't look so mournful. Maybe a song, what?"

A few of the old men began a song, but since no one could remember the lyrics, it soon petered out.

"We need Will," said Reck.

"What for?" asked Ruin. "There's nothing to plow here, and Angel's the only one of our party who's been this high before."

"We need him," said Reck again.

It was Patience who told him why. "We've been blown by the wind that Unwyrm can blow, and it's too much weather for us. We need the man who has never bowed to Unwyrm."

"Unwyrm!" shouted one old man, and the others took up the cry. "Unwyrm! Unwyrm!"

Patience had been trying to ignore the old men till now. "You know about him?"

"Oh, we're *old* friends!"

"We came here to visit him, and he lets us stay as long as we like."

"No one ever goes home."

"Till they die, of course. Lots've done that."

"We all will, you know."

"Did Unwyrm invite you, too?"

Bald and gray and white-haired heads bobbed up and down around them. Like little children, they could hardly stand still. Their obvious senility had lulled Patience. Now she began to remember that she had followed a path that others had walked before. "Yes," she said. "Unwyrm invited us. But we got lost in the snow. Can you tell us where he is?"

"Behind the golden door," said one. The others nodded solemnly. "But you can't go all at once. Only one at a time."

"He wants us all at once," said Reck.

"Liar liar," said one of the men.

Patience glared at Reck, as if to tell her, I'm the diplomat and you're the recluse. Leave this to me. But in fact Patience had no idea how to deal with these men. They seemed harmless enough. Still, they knew Unwyrm and Unwyrm knew them, and they might have strength enough to make things difficult.

"Right now we have to rest," said Patience.

"No tricks," said the youngest of them, a man whose

hair had not yet turned white, though his plump face was sagging badly.

"You," said Patience, "sir, could I know your name?"

"Trades," said the man. "You tell us first."

"My name is Patience," she said.

"Patience, you shouldn't walk around with such thin clothing in snowstorms." Then he giggled as if his advice had been a masterpiece of wit.

"And your name."

"I cheated," he said. "I don't have a name."

"I thought you said no tricks."

He looked crestfallen. "But Unwyrm took our names and he won't give them back."

Patience wasn't sure what game they were playing, but she tried to play along anyway. "You must be very angry, then, to have lost your name."

"Oh, no."

"Not at all."

"Who needs a name?"

"We're very happy."

"We have everything we need."

"Cause we don't need anything." This last was said by the youngest one. He was nodding wisely, like a child. But his eyes were no child's eyes. They were heavy with sadness and loss.

It occurred to Patience that these men, for all their cheerful babbling, might indeed be trying to communicate. We have everything we need because we don't need anything. Therefore we have nothing. She began to pry, as delicately as she could.

"What other good things has Unwyrm done for you?" she asked.

"Oh, he takes away our worries."

"We never worry about a thing—"

Suddenly Ruin interrupted. "Makes me sick," he said.

The men fell silent.

Patience looked at him and smiled with murder in her eyes. "Maybe Unwyrm will help you feel better for the next few minutes, so you won't feel obliged to say anything."

Ruin got the hint and returned to glowering at the fire.

"What did he do with your worries?" asked Patience.

"Took them all away."

"Took them out of our heads."

"Put them into his own head."

"No more worries about . . ." But he didn't finish his sentence. They all waited stupidly for someone else to speak.

"What did you worry about?" asked Patience.

"Old bones," said one. "But I'm very sleepy."

"Got to sleep," said another.

"Oh my. About to yawn."

"Good night."

The youngest man also yawned, but he leaned close to Patience, smiled, and whispered, "The capacity of long genetic molecules to carry intelligence." Then he smiled and toppled to the floor.

All the old men lay in heaps on the floor, snoring.

"The Wise," said Patience.

"Funny," said Reck.

"I'm not joking. These are the Wise. The ones that Unwyrm called, who stopped at Heffiji's house to answer her questions. Unwyrm ate out the kernel of their minds, and these are the husks he threw away."

She knelt by the man who had made the effort to tell her what he really was. "I know you now," she said softly. "We've come to give you back what he's taken, if we can."

"Why would he do this?" asked Reck.

"Gathering all the knowledge of the human species, so

he could replace it, mind and body both,'' Ruin held his hands between his legs to warm them. "What I don't understand is why he left them alive.''

"These can't be all the Wise in the world,'' said Reck.

"Unwyrm's call began sixty years ago,'' answered Patience. "These must be the ones who were young, who were brought most recently. Even they will die soon, and if it weren't for Heffiji's house, all that they knew would be lost.''

"But there *is* Heffiji's house,'' said Reck. "And you *did* come to our village, despite Unwyrm's best efforts. And when Ruin and I were in danger out there in the snow, Unwyrm's own cast-off manflesh saved us. Why?''

"Luck,'' said Patience. "It can't always go against us. Chance.''

"I hate chance,'' said Ruin. "I hate believing that the future of my people, of the whole world, depends on an accidental coming-together of events.''

"Come away from the fire,'' said Reck. "You'll singe your hair.''

He turned, silhouetted against the hotly burning fire. "What kind of majesty is there in a victory like that?''

"Maybe,'' said Patience, "with all the patterns of life on this world set against us, maybe a little luck is the only way we'll win.''

"I'll take luck,'' said Reck. "I'll even take acts of the gods. Just so we win.''

"Will would say that it was the hand of God that got us this far,'' said Patience.

"If God's hand is in the game, and on our side,'' said Reck, "why doesn't he just snuff out Unwyrm himself?''

"God doesn't have the power to act except through our hands,'' said Ruin. "He can only do what *we* do for him.''

Reck laughed aloud. "What! Are you secretly a Watcher, my gebling, my sibling? In your wanderings through the forest, did you find religion?"

"What do humans know about their god? They want him to have power over earth and sky. But all he has power over is the human will. Because he *is* the human will—and a weak, feeble god he is. Not like the god of the geblings. We've seen it, haven't we? Together, all the geblings are one soul. We ignore it most of the time, but at a time of great need we act together, we do the thing that consciously or not we know must be done for the whole of us to survive. That is the god of the geblings—the common, unspoken and unspeakable will. The othermind. Even the humans have a faint touch of othermind that lets Lady Patience hear a dim echo of our call, that lets Unwyrm speak to them. Together they create a god, which is the good of them all, and it rules. Weakly, pathetically, in fits and starts, but it rules." Ruin twisted the hair of his cheek. "It rules even Unwyrm. Just like a gebling, he's half human, too. The human god lies like a root in his path; he doesn't see, he stumbles."

"I can't think of many priests who would like your theology," said Patience.

"That's why I'm not putting it up for sale," said Ruin. "But it's more than chance that helps us. We aren't lonely creatures trying to save our people. We are the instrument of our people, which they unconsciously created to save themselves."

Patience connected Ruin's view to something spoken to her on the boat not too many days before. "Will says that geblings—"

"What do I care what *he* says?" said Ruin. "It's his *strength* that we need now, not his ideas. We need the strength that let him stand against the Cranning call."

"He says that geblings and humans all have souls, and the same god means to save us all."

"If he does, then I adjure this god to bring us Will, to stand before Unwyrm and resist him for us." Ruin was mocking, but not to amuse them. His mockery was a mask for desperate faith, Patience could see that. He had invented for himself a god he could believe in, and now he prayed to that god.

And was answered.

Outside, during a lull in the wind, they could hear the high, sweet sounds of Kristiano and Strings singing harmony. And another voice calling Patience by name.

"Angel," said Patience.

"He killed the others," said Reck. "Unwyrm has brought him to us."

There were footsteps crunching in the crisp dry snow outside.

"Patience!" cried Angel again. He knocked on the door.

"Go away!" shouted Patience. "I don't want to have to kill you."

Reck was nocking an arrow, and Ruin had his knife ready.

"Patience, I'm free of him!" shouted Angel. "Let me in, I can help you!"

"Don't believe him," said Reck.

"Go away!" shouted Patience. She held the blowgun near her lips. "I'll kill you!"

The door crashed open and swung back to bang against the wall. Immediately an arrow trembled in the door at belly height; Reck was preparing to shoot again, as soon as anyone entered.

Patience knew, however, that Angel hadn't the strength to kick in the door. "Will," she said. "You can come in, Will."

Will came in, followed by Angel, who was tightly bound and tethered to Sken. Strings and Kristiano came after. They were warmly dressed against the cold.

"Here we are," said Strings cheerfully. "The House of the Wise. And the Wise, as you can see, are asleep."

It was true; even the shouting and the banging of the door hadn't aroused them. It was a sign of Unwyrm's presence here, that he could keep them asleep through anything.

"Will," said Reck. "Why didn't you speak! We were sure Angel had—"

"He didn't speak," said Angel, "because he didn't know whether *you* were under Unwyrm's power. The arrow in the doorway was quite convincing."

Patience looked at Angel. His bonds were a joke, of course—she knew that Angel could easily slip the knots, if he wanted to. It was his face she studied.

"I know why you look at me that way," said Angel. "Do you think I haven't thought ten thousand times, what will she think of me, when she learns the truth?"

But Patience was not thinking of his betrayal now. She was thinking: the fire is gone from behind his eyes. He is weak and alone, and he was never alone before. Even though Unwyrm is your enemy, Angel, it strengthened you to have him always with you. And now, you have the look of a child whose parents have wandered off. You are waiting for him to come back. You think you can carry on alone, but you wait for him all the same, to bring you back to life.

"But I'm not who I was," said Angel. "I don't need bonds now. I was young when he took me, young and unprepared. But I know him, and now that he's gone, I'll never let him back."

"Why did you bring him?" demanded Ruin of Will. "Why didn't you just kill him down below?"

Will only glanced at Ruin, as if to say, Who are you to expect an accounting from me? Then he turned to Patience. "My Heptarch," he said, "I brought your servant to you. He wanted to redeem himself."

"After Unwyrm is dead," said Patience, "then he can become himself, and my true servant. But as long as Unwyrm is alive, Angel is the wyrm's slave, and not the Heptarch's."

"No," said Angel. "I've faced him before. I know where he's weak—"

"You know nothing of the kind," said Ruin, "or you would have killed him before."

"All he's thinking about now is you, Patience," said Angel. "All he cares about is to stay alive long enough to impregnate you. He's waited seven thousand years, constantly renewing himself, until he hates the taste of his own life, but when you come, then he can achieve all he waited for. He cares nothing for me, or Will, or the geblings—"

"He leaves you free," said Ruin, "so we'll trust you and bring you with us. Then he'll rule you again and you'll betray us in our moment of greatest weakness."

"These bonds won't hold me," said Angel. "Either take me with you, or kill me now."

Patience shook her head. "You did me no kindness, Will, to bring him here."

"Kindness was never my purpose," said Will.

"What *was* your purpose?"

"My purpose is God's purpose."

Ruin laughed aloud.

"And what is God's purpose?" asked Angel scornfully.

"*We* are his purpose," said Will. "Our life, we who create and discover and build and tear down, we who love and hate, who grieve and rejoice, we are his purpose. His work is for our kind to live forever, human and gebling, dwelf and gaunt, rising up from the womb and lying down in the grave."

"Very lovely," said Ruin. "But right now our job is to lay Unwyrm in his grave, and the only way to have a chance at that is to put Angel there first."

Patience drew the loop from her hair and let it hang, limp, from one hand. "The more of us who go there to face him, the better. He'll be calling to me, and it'll be hard for him to concentrate on destroying you."

"We hope," said Reck.

"He won't let anyone come close but me," said Patience. "It's the bow that will kill him, if anything does. Reck."

"Of course," she said. "It's what I was born for."

"But no one understands his body, or where he must be shot to be killed. Ruin, you're the one who has lived with the life of this world. Your intuition is all we have to go on, in knowing where to strike him so he'll die."

"I know," said Angel. "I know where to strike—in his eyes, piercing through to—"

"You know nothing now," said Patience. "He could have lied to you a thousand times, and you would have believed him because you wanted to believe." She walked around Angel, stood behind him. "I think that Unwyrm controls best the minds that he knows best. Angel he would control most easily. But scarcely better than Reck and Ruin and me. He has held us in his grasp so many times that he knows all our pathways as surely as the geblings know the tunnels of Cranning. It will take all our strength just to stand against him. But you, Will, and you, Sken—he doesn't know you. Not the way he knows us. Will can resist him, and Sken—forgive me, but he must not hold you in high regard or he would have called you before now. So you must come last, and stand behind us. Keep the geblings from running away, force them to stand against him, so they can concentrate all their strength on killing him. And in the end, if they fail, then you must kill me before Unwyrm's children are born."

"I'm not a hero," said Sken.

"We aren't here for heroics," said Patience. "We're here for murder. Unwyrm's, if we can manage it. Mine, if we can't."

"They'll begin by killing you, if they can," said Angel. "It's the easiest way to stop his children from being born. You'll have Reck's arrow in you before the end. You can't trust them."

"And you, Angel, my teacher, my friend, my father," said Patience. "How can I leave you behind me, when Unwyrm has only to think of you, and you flinch and cower and obey?"

She whipped the loop around his neck and gave it a quick twist, a slight, delicate pull. Blood flowed from all around his neck. Angel's face held a look of surprise, of wonderment, perhaps even of gratitude. Then he toppled forward off the chair. Patience bent over him, carefully unwinding the loop from his neck. The others looked away to give her a moment of grief. She had done what must be done, and had not put the terrible duty on anyone else. She was the stuff Heptarchs were made of, they all saw that.

"I'm so sorry," said Strings. "So sorry. He was so very very good. And he wants to kill Unwyrm, he truly does."

"Enough," said Will. "It's done."

"He's calling me," said Patience. "It's stronger than I can bear."

"You know," said Ruin, "when it comes down to the truth of it, Heptarch, you are the least reliable of us all."

"I'm going now," said Patience.

"He knows his way through your mind better than anyone's but Angel's, and he cares more about you. He can do what he wants with you. And yet you're the one who made our plan for us."

Patience walked to the door. "Now," she said. She

opened the door and walked out into the moonlit snow. The wind whipped a white dust behind her, like a cowardly shadow retreating into the warm room. Will snatched a lamp from the wall and followed right behind her, with Ruin, Reck, and Sken trotting close after.

Sken was enthusiastic. "Now I finally get to see what this Unwyrm looks like."

The others ignored her. Will was holding Patience's arm; she struggled against his grip, trying to run to Unwyrm. "Slowly, calmly," whispered Will. "I'll hold you back for now, Lady Patience. Remember that none of this is you. All of us face him in you. You aren't alone against him."

The mouth of the cave waited for them in the distance. "I'm coming," whispered Patience.

Back in the House of the Wise, the old men awoke, yawning and stretching. One of them stumbled over to where Angel lay. "Nasty cut there," he said. He busied himself untying the knots that held Angel's arms together.

Angel opened his eyes. Then he sat up and gently touched his neck. "She cut it close, there. Cut it close."

"Why were we asleep?" asked the man who had untied him.

"It's time," said Angel. "And he has her now." He got up and tore open the lining of his cloak. Three throwing knives were hidden there.

"What happens now?" asked the man.

"You'll see," he said. "You'll see." And then he spoke quietly, to someone who could not hear his words. "Call me all you like. I'm coming."

18 | THE BIRTHING PLACE

IT WAS EARLIEST DAWN WHEN THEY PASSED INTO THE CAVern, the first light shimmering in the east. They did not wait for sunrise; the lantern was the light they'd live by now.

Patience led the way, Will's hand gripping her arm with the strength of a tree root. Their passage wound upward through the rock, with an icy stream of water coming down the tunnel. The walls were covered with ice, and so was the tunnel floor; they soon found that if they walked on the frozen ground, their feet slipped, and if they walked in the stream, their feet froze. After half an hour they came to the golden door.

It was just a wooden slab that had once been painted yellow. There was no lock. There was no handle. Dozens of names were scratched in it, and in the ice-slick rock beside it. The door could not have been more than a hundred years old. The names in the rock might have been there for millennia.

Patience was calmer now. Headed toward Unwyrm, she could feel the pressure ease, and she gained some control of herself. The door was the last barrier between them. Even as she longed to pass beyond it, she could feel, like a distant memory, a desperate wish for it to stay closed.

"Resist him as much as you can," said Ruin. "Go as slowly as you can."

Patience just nodded. She was gasping with the effort to stay and listen.

"I'll look at him, try to figure out where the arrow has to go. We know almost nothing about his body, and what parts are vital. We know he has no brain, though. Probably no heart. In the end, we may have to pierce him as often as we can, till he loses enough fluid to die. That's why you have to be as slow as possible. To give us time."

Again Patience nodded.

"All of you," said Will. "All of you listen. We don't know how many of us will be left alive at the end of this. But whoever lives, if we're too late, and he fathers children on Patience—Angel told me that the children will grow quickly. They must be killed. There may be dozens of them, and they must all be killed because if any of them lives, we've lost."

"They'll be *my* children," whispered Patience. "Mine."

"God help us," said Sken. "Will they look like worms?"

"Human infants," said Will. "And killing them will feel like murder."

Reck saw how Patience was sweating, steam rising from her body in the bitterly cold tunnel. Reck remembered all too well the terrible need that Unwyrm had forced on her, how little she had been able to think, to remember that throwing herself from the mountain was certain death. When Unwyrm commanded with that much strength, there was no denying him. She spoke to Ruin.

"We're asking too much of her. She's sheltered us all this way, and had no shelter for herself. When she's with him, she'll have no thought for any plan."

Patience began to sob and struggle against Will's hold on her. Now that she was stopped again, the call began to build an unbearable pressure within her. "Let me go, Will," she begged.

"Patience!" The cry rang through the tunnel. Reck and Ruin whirled to look down the tunnel they had just traveled. "Patience! I'll go! I'll go first!"

Will handed the lantern to Sken and gripped Patience by the shoulders with both hands. "You didn't kill him!"

"Unwyrm wouldn't let me!" she sobbed.

Angel appeared in the dim light their lantern cast at the far end of the tunnel, where it curved down and out of sight. He brandished throwing knives in both hands. The clotted blood still made a ghastly pattern on his neck. "Out of my way!" he shouted. "I'll kill him, I can do it! Let me by! You can't, none of you can do it, let me by!"

He forced his way past them, knocking Will to one side, shoving the door open with his shoulder. Patience came free of Will's grasp then, and began to run after Angel. Ruin and Reck stumbled after her. But she had gone too far ahead. Almost immediately they began to move slowly, as if they were pushing through stone.

"Help us!" cried Ruin.

Will came after them, seized their clothing in bunches from behind, and shoved them brutally forward through the tunnel. Sken ran after with the lantern.

The birthing room was ablaze with light. Sunrise had come while they were in the tunnel. The icy ceiling was so thin in places that the light burst through. It showed them Angel dead on the ice in the middle of the floor. His knives had slid away from him when he fell. A slender dart arose from the back of his head. Patience was still holding her blowgun. Then she cast it away. It skittered across the ice and slid into a swift-flowing stream that carried it away, out of the birthing room, down through one of the tunnels that led from here to the farthest reaches of Cranning.

"She's *his* now," said Will. "She'll do nothing to help us."

"Where is he?" whispered Reck.

As if in answer, the black wyrm slid rapidly down into the birthing room from a white tunnel near the ceiling. Where is he weak, thought Reck desperately. Where can I put an arrow and end his life?

"My bow," said Reck. "Tell me where to shoot him."

His back was made of hard segments that formed an impenetrable wall. "I don't know where," said Ruin, "I don't know, there's no place."

"That's Unwyrm speaking."

"No place," he said.

Unwyrm came near to where Patience waited. Then he rose up, exposing his belly. It was not the soft, smooth belly Reck had hoped for. Instead it was alive with appendages that alternately thrust forward like soft swords, then went limp and receded. They were wet and dripping. Unwyrm's feeble hands fanned out across his side, trembling.

"Look how he's shaking," whispered Reck. "He's old."

"That isn't age, it's passion," said Ruin. "We can only bleed him. It's the only hope."

Patience whirled to face them. "There is no hope!" she howled. She was an animal, her eyes darting from one of them to another. "Not for you!" And she hurled the loop at Reck.

Before the spinning wire could reach her, though, Will

thrust Reck down on her face. The loop took him above the wrist of his right arm, cutting through to the bone. The skin of his wrist and hand sloughed downward, like a glove suddenly pulled half off; blood gouted from above the wound.

Will screamed in pain, but almost at once acted to save what he could. Since there was no hope now that he could hold both Reck and Ruin, he shoved Ruin down, placed his foot on the gebling's leg, and then with his left hand he pulled the gebling up. Ruin cried out with pain as his leg snapped. He would stay in the room. "Sken!" cried Will. Sken hurried forward, slipping on the ice and nearly falling; she caught herself against Will, who still had the strength to take her weight without falling over.

"Hold Reck, keep her here!" cried Will. Then he dropped to his knees and fell forward, thrusting his arm into the crystal water that flowed in a stream across the middle of the cavern. "Patience!" he shouted. His arm cast a bloom of blood ribbons into the water. "Patience, he doesn't rule you!"

Reck felt Sken's powerful arms around her waist just as Unwyrm urged her to run, to fly away, to escape this place. But she could also feel Ruin calling to her in her othermind. Stay. Kill. With shaking hands she took her bow, nocked an arrow, and shot. Unwyrm dodged easily; the arrow fell harmlessly behind him. She nocked another, tried to concentrate. He pounded at her mind; her eyes blurred—

And Patience saw this, saw it all. There was no hope in her of resisting him, her lust for him was all she could think of. Yet at the same time, she could remember Will's story of who she really was, of that small and forgotten self masked by memory and desire. I must help, came the thought. She could not resist Unwyrm, but she could distract him.

She stepped forward, crying out to him. "Unwyrm!" She pulled her tunic off over her head and knelt naked before him. "Unwyrm!" Her knees slipped smoothly across the ice and she leaned back, offering herself to him.

Reck felt the pressure on her ease. In a swift movement Unwyrm's body arched forward and lunged onto Patience. He rooted one of his appendages in her groin. Patience cried out in her inexpressible relief. Weeks of longing were finally fulfilled.

Unwyrm's upper body began a rhythmic swaying. For a moment he had forgotten them; he, too, had a need that was too long unfulfilled to be put off. Reck fired two quick arrows. One struck him in the eye. Another spiked his tongue to the roof of his mouth.

"His head is nothing!" screamed Ruin. "His belly! His belly, where the blood is!"

Reck took another arrow, but this time, instead of nocking it, she had a powerful urge to eat the arrow. To bring it to her mouth and jam it down her own throat. She raised the arrow above her face and smiled at the death that pointed at her.

Suddenly Sken's fist came down savagely on her belly. The pain drove Unwyrm's command from her mind. It also made her realize that she could not possibly do enough damage to Unwyrm's belly to kill him. Only Patience was close enough. The Heptarch now lay on her back, her hand within easy reach of one of Angel's knives. She was shuddering and writhing in ecstasy beneath him. Somehow, Reck knew, she had to be distracted from the delight that Unwyrm gave her, forced to remember what was really happening. A sudden pain might break the hold that Unwyrm had on her mind, make her forget the pleasure long enough to take the knife and disembowel him.

So Reck readied the arrow and aimed, not at Unwyrm, whose belly was pressed against Patience, but at the girl herself. Reck shot for the thigh, and in a moment the arrow trembled in the Heptarch's flesh.

Patience tossed her head back and forth from the pain. Did she see the knife?

"Kill him!" cried Ruin.

She saw it. She reached it easily, brought it up to kill, then suddenly cried out again in ecstasy. She knew what she had to do, and yet her body could not respond. I am a gaunt, now, at the end, Patience realized. I have no will before him. She struggled to raise her hand against him, but all she could think of was a great aching love for him as she could feel her womb filling. Gradually her arm dropped back down. But her fingers clung to the knife. She did not let go, though now she couldn't even remember why she held it, or what it was.

"She's still holding it," said Ruin. "She's not gone!"

Sken raised her voice to taunt them. "King of the geblings! Why did you come alone? Where are your armies when you need them most!"

"Geblings," whispered Reck. And in that moment she and Ruin both knew that they had one tool that might free Patience's mind from Unwyrm's control.

"We must call the geblings—" murmured Ruin.

"The geblings must call *her*," said Reck.

They cried out with their silent mind. Feel and repeat this urgent need—to kill Unwyrm, to kill the child-killer, the mother-eater.

Geblings in the highest reaches of Cranning fell the urgent call in their othermind. They stopped what they were doing; it was the king, they knew who called them, it was the king and all unknown to them the final battle had already been joined. Kill Unwyrm! They echoed the silent shout, passing it on to the other geblings farther down the mountain.

Cart drivers let their oxen walk on unattended; geblings in conversation fell silent; workers let their tasks slip from their hands. All joined in the fervent call: Kill Unwyrm.

In moments, the message passed silently to every part of Cranning. It was echoed by ten million gebling minds. Every other time that Cranning had cried out together, the geblings had gathered from every part of the world to join battle against the human kingdoms and strike them down. This time, the message was much simpler. Death to their brother, their enemy, their satan, the wyrm.

And in Patience's mind that same cry also arose, stronger and stronger, making its way against the perfect pleasure that Unwyrm gave her. She felt the knife in her hand again, knew that the desire to kill him was her true self even though her body cried out against it. She felt his blood spill almost before she felt the knife enter his body. Unwyrm arched backward, then slapped himself forward on top of her. She screamed in pain, then jabbed at him again. He whipped away, slithered toward his upper chamber, then writhed out his dance of death, smearing himself across the ice as he whipped to and fro. All that he desired in the last moments of his life Patience felt, for the bond was still firm between them. She screamed his scream for him. At last he was still, and her voice was her own again.

Except for their labored breathing, the room was silent. Patience curled up on her side and sobbed quietly, Unwyrm's blood slowly freezing on her.

Sken let go of Reck and leaned back against the ice behind her. Reck fell forward, gasping for breath. ''Will,'' she whispered.

Ruin crawled to Will, dragging his broken leg behind him. He pulled the large man over onto his back. His face was blue from the cold, but the icy water had slowed the bleeding of his arm. "Save him if you can," whispered Reck. Ruin at once drew a threaded brass needle from his kit and began feverishly sewing the severed arteries and veins together.

Reck looked back at Sken. "Help the Heptarch, can't you?" She did not wait to see if Sken would obey. She slid across the ice to where her brother labored over Will. "He held us here, he got us here when no one else could have—"

"Get me a leather pouch," said Ruin. "Not that one, no, sniff it, like krisberries, yes, that's it." Reck opened the pouch and Ruin dipped his tongue into it, then smeared it on the severed surfaces. It would make the cells of Will's body grow again; it would stimulate the living nerve ends to grow out and find new connections.

Then Patience cried out. Softly. Reck looked up. Patience had rolled over and was lying on her stomach, her head toward the others. Her body heaved twice.

"What's happening?" whispered Reck.

Ruin looked up in time to see the head of a half-developed fetus rise up from between Patience's legs. "The wyrm's child!"

"We were too late!" shouted Sken.

Reck reached for her bow and arrow, but Sken was stumbling along the ice, her hatchet in hand, blocking a clear shot. And by the time Sken got there, Patience was standing up, holding the infant, shielding it. "I'm going to kill it!" Sken shouted.

Patience nodded, but she still held the child out of Sken's reach. Was it an illusion, or had the child grown? Yes, it was larger, and it was no longer fetal—it was a fully developed infant.

"Take the baby!" shouted Reck.

"It's going to die anyway!" Patience cried. "Can't you see? I killed his father too soon, he's going to die."

It was true. They could almost see that as the child grew taller, feebly wiggling its limbs, the skin tightened, grew tight around the bones, like a victim of famine. The baby opened its mouth, and spoke its only words: "Help me." They were grotesque, coming from a body so young. It was clearly Unwyrm's child, clearly a monster, yet from the sight of him he was any infant, helpless, demanding their compassion and getting it.

The baby died. Patience felt it, the sudden slackness of the body. She relaxed her protective posture. Only then could Sken reach the body, tear it away, cast it to the ground, and raise her hatchet to hack at it.

"It's dead!" shouted Patience.

"It was growing!" Sken cried. "It spoke!"

"But it's dead!"

Sken lowered her hatchet. Reck took Patience's garment from the cave floor and carried it to her. "Only the one," said Reck. "And Unwyrm didn't have time to give it strength to live. We did it. In time."

Paience turned away and pulled the chemise over her head.

There were shouts and footfalls in the tunnel leading up from the golden door. Armed geblings rushed a few steps into the room, then stopped to take in the scene. The corpse of Unwyrm, split open and spilt on the ice; the starved, skeletal body of a human infant. A few of the old men came in, not looking half so doltish now.

"Behold," said Sken bitterly, "the gebling kings. Behold the Heptarch!" Her face worked to keep from crying. She flung out her hand toward the baby lying on the ice. "Behold the child of prophecy!"

Reck hushed her. "The baby was no Kristos. It was a wyrm, it was death to humans and geblings, and if it hadn't died I would have killed it with my own hands."

The old men walked toward Unwyrm's body. One of

them took Angel's other knife, the one that Patience hadn't used, and sliced Unwyrm's head from snout to crown. The skin burst apart as if it had been under pressure, revealing the shining facets of a green crystal.

"His mindstone," whispered Reck. She walked toward them, looked at the crystal.

It was not a single mindstone, but many hundreds of them, fused together. The old men pulled the flaps of skin farther apart, and the crystal toppled forward onto the ice.

"Here," said one of them.

"This is where he kept all the gifts we gave him," said another.

"Everything we knew."

The old men knelt, touched the crystal, as if to find where in the living jewel their own knowledge lay. The youngest one lifted his head and cried out like a dog baying. "Give it back to me!"

Reck turned from the old men and walked slowly, wearily to Patience. They embraced, and Reck helped the exhausted woman walk across the ice, out of the room. Geblings were already helping Ruin, preparing to carry him out. Others were binding up Will's arm and wrapping him in blankets.

Sken looked up when Patience passed. "Heptarch," she said. "Did we sin?"

Patience stopped, stood before the fat woman with her twisted, tear-stained face. She touched Sken's cheek with her bent fingers.

"Did I raise my hatchet to murder God's own son?" Her voice was high and weak, like a child's. "Am I damned forever?"

In answer, Patience pulled her close, embraced her. "No sin," she whispered. "This day's work honors us all forever."

19 | CRYSTALS

THE FIRES ROARED IN THE HOUSE OF THE WISE. IT WAS afternoon, but outside it was dark with clouds and falling snow. The cold seeped in through the shutters and under the door, but the fires in the two hearths fought it back to the edges of the room.

Sken, stark naked, was up to her neck in a huge and steaming tub, occasionally bellowing curses at Strings, who was scrubbing her back. Strings endured it calmly enough; Patience, listening, knew that he only served Sken because Reck and Patience wanted him to. Sken cursed again, but then began to tell him—for the third time—how she had killed Tinker's men in the battle in the woods, months before. Strings listened, the perfect audience, responding exactly when she needed to hear him say, "Yes," or "Bravely done," or "Remarkable."

Patience knew that Sken was telling of the battle with Tinker because she could bear to think of it; she had little to say of the battle in Unwyrm's cave, and did not tell the tale of the baby who died only moments before Sken would have murdered it. We'll all choose the stories we

327

can live with, and forget the rest, thought Patience. I hope so, anyway.

She walked to the east fireplace. Many of the old men were watching as several geblings carefully worked on Unwyrm's huge mindstone. Reck was directing the work of separating the hundreds of mindstones that had grown together. The geblings poured a solution over the crystal, then carefully pried the surface crystals away. Many small mindstones, the size of the one that Patience bore within her brain, lay in a tray before the fire, drying.

"What are you looking for?" asked Patience.

"These are all the crystals of the Wise, which he took from them and ate," said Reck. "But in the center there'll be the crystal that was his own. Himself. That's the one I want."

"What can you do with it?" asked Patience.

"We'll know what to do when we find it." Reck led her away from the fire. "See how the old men watch? They know where those mindstones came from, and they want them back."

"Can't you do it? Give the mindstones back? They came from their brains in the first place."

"Which one do we give to each of these men? They have so little memory left—just their memory of life in this house, with vague shadows of the past—that whatever stone we give them will take them over and become them. It would be no favor. And besides, these stones have lived as long in Unwyrm's head as they ever lived in their original human hosts'. Do these men look strong enough to endure Unwyrm's memories?"

Patience shook her head. "But it's tragic. This great treasure of learning, useless."

"This?" asked Reck. "These stones are the way that wyrms passed their wisdom from one generation to the next. You humans brought another way. And that way still lives."

"Heffiji's house," said Patience.

"What was learned once can be learned again," said Reck. "Ruin is already babbling about a university there, administered by geblings whose whole purpose is to protect Heffiji and catalogue her house. I think nothing will be lost."

"Except these old men."

"What's the tragedy there, Heptarch?" asked Reck. "How is what happened to them any worse than death? And that's how all lives end. Their works live on at Heffiji's house—it's more immortality than most people get. And these old men live. No matter what you might think of it right now, life is good and sweet, even with the memory of great loss and terrible grief."

"I have lost both my fathers," Patience whispered, "and I killed them both with my own hands."

"You were Unwyrm's hands when Angel died."

Patience shook her head, then walked toward the other hearth.

Will lay on a pallet stretched before the fire. Kristiano knelt by the giant man, wiping his naked, sweating torso with a wet cloth. Patience knelt beside the boyok.

"He likes this," said Kristiano. "But he's afraid."

Patience took the gauntling's hand in hers. "May I?"

Kristiano relinquished the cloth with a sweet but enigmatic smile. Patience saw herself, for a moment, as the gauntling saw her—this human woman would come and serve Will for a moment, but the gaunt would serve him hour after hour, unfailing. If love was giving the gift most desired, then only gaunts in all the world truly loved. But Patience shrugged off the silent criticism of the beautiful child. You are what you are; I have other work to do, and I can only give a few gifts to anyone. Maybe none at all.

Will's eyes were open, but he said nothing. Patience

had no smile for him, nor he for her. They were alive, weren't they? And Unwyrm was dead. That was victory. But it had been Patience's hand that threw the loop that nearly cut off Will's. And it had been Patience also who killed Unwyrm and held Unwyrm's only child as it died. There was much murder and pain in Patience's memory, and she had not yet discovered whether any love remained.

Ruin sat nearby, his broken leg heavily splinted, his face glum as he stared into the fire. Reck soon came with a carafe of water and gave Ruin a draught of it. He drank long and deep, then touched her arm in silent thanks. Reck gave the carafe to Patience, who took it, lifted Will's head, and let water into his mouth. Will lapped it gratefully. Gently she lowered him to the pallet again.

Finally, now, Will spoke. "How did you find strength to do it?" he whispered.

"It wasn't my strength," said Patience. "It was lent to me. The geblings called me. Together, with one voice. It gave me just enough freedom within myself to find myself. So I did what I was born for."

"Saved the world."

"Murdered an enemy who trusted me. I remained the consummate assassin to the end."

"You did what God wanted," whispered Will. Then he closed his eyes.

Ruin spoke. "He's right, you know. About what God wanted. The kind of god I believe in, anyway. Humans and geblings and gaunts and dwelfs, we all wanted to live more than Unwyrm wanted us to die. It all worked together. You couldn't kill Angel, and he lived to bring into the birthing place the knives you killed Unwyrm with, after he thought he had left you weaponless. Reck's arrow saved you; Will broke my leg to save me; Sken, useless and stupid and foul, kept Reck from killing herself under Unwyrm's control. Every bit and piece of it, an intricate and impossible network, a web that could have failed at any point." Ruin nodded, almost angry in his insistence. "We are god, if there is a god, and Unwyrm fell before us."

Patience remembered again the unbearable joy she had felt under Unwyrm's body. And felt again the way his ichor spilled over her, the way her knife tore through his tender organs. It was not what she had felt with her body that most affected her now. It was what she had felt with her mind. For as the death agony came, he cried out to her with his silent voice, the one that had ruled her for so long; he cried out: I live. I want to live. I must live. It was the desperate cry of her own heart, too. He had wanted nothing more than any human wanted. To live, to pass on his genes to his children, to keep death at bay for as long as he could. His people—for such the wyrms were, to each other—his people had lived for centuries, but he had lived longest of all, waiting to be the salvation of all his race. And his death was the death of ten thousand generations of wyrms.

His death was the death of the miraculous child she had held in her arms, the new shape a dying species had tried to adopt in order to save themselves. They saw us coming, and they knew we would be the disease for which there was no cure. They did all that they could do. The last breath of their struggle grew in my womb, shaped like a human in tribute to the human gods who had come to destroy them. But we did not accept the offering, no; I killed Unwyrm before the child's yolk was complete, and when the child was born I let it die in my arms.

What is so much better about my kind of life, that we should survive, and they should die? She could think of no standard of judgment that made sense, except this one: I am human, and so humans must live. It was not a struggle for justice. It was a battle of savages. The cruelest won. I was the perfect savior for mankind.

"Unwyrm held in his mindstone the memory of this planet," said Reck. It was as if she had read Patience's thoughts. "His root was back to the first wyrm that had a thought. And in his mindstone, the stories of his kind, forever. Of our kind. We have as much wyrm ancestry as he had."

"You favor the human side," murmured Will.

"See how beautiful it makes us," said Ruin.

"You *are* beautiful," said Patience, looking at Reck. "I remember being a gebling myself. I remember the way it felt, inside my body; I remember the voice of my siblings in the othermind. And something else, too. The loneliness of never knowing my father, and then, when the scepter came to me, finally remembering his life as he knew it."

"It nearly drove you to insanity," Ruin reminded her.

"I wish that every human could have such madness. Or a taste of it, just for a moment, to know their mother or father. It would be a great gift."

"To know them, but not to *be* them," said Will. "You are very strong, Lady Patience. Few can endure having other people's memories live in their minds. I couldn't."

"You?" said Patience. "You're the strongest of all."

His eyes went distant, rejecting the praise. "Will I keep my hand?" he asked.

"It will dangle as beautifully as ever at the end of your arm," said Ruin. "As for using it—I've done all I can to encourage the nerves to grow."

"I won't be much use to anyone without my right arm," he said.

Patience touched his forehead, drew her finger along his cheek, and finally let her fingertips rest on his lips.

"We're all looking for new careers," said Patience. "There aren't any prophecies about what I'll do *after* Unwyrm is dead. I'm not seventeen yet, and everything I was born to do is done. Does this mean that I'll have to learn a trade?"

Reck laughed softly, and Will smiled.

"You're Heptarch," said Ruin.

"There's a man in King's Hill who would disagree," said Patience. "And he's not a bad man, and not a bad Heptarch."

"He's a caretaker," said Will. "Ruling only until your work here is done."

"When an army of a million geblings stands at his border, he might give thought to abdication," said Ruin.

"No," said Patience.

"What, do you think we'd do it for you out of altruism? The geblings are best served by having a Heptarch who remembers being a gebling. We aren't subhumans to you, now."

"Not a drop of my people's blood will be shed in my name," said Patience.

"There you are," said Ruin. "You're right. Your life work *is* over."

"Shut up, Ruin," said Reck.

Sken walked up to them, buttoning a clean gown that fit her like the draping of a warhorse. Her ruddy face gleamed in the firelight. "Heptarch, the geblings have brought the body of your former slave out of the birthing place. They want to know what you want done with it."

"I want him buried with honor," said Patience. "Here, among the Wise. The graves here are all honorable ones."

"I'm sorry we didn't take his head in time," said Reck. "We know that's how you humans preserve the counsel of your wise ones, since you don't have mindstones to eat."

"We were busy," said Ruin, "and the moment passed."

"But he *does* have a mindstone," said Sken. "Doesn't he, Will? Isn't that what he said? He had a mindstone, just like these other old coots. Unwyrm just didn't take it from him, that's all. That's why his mind isn't at the low-water mark. Isn't that right, Will?"

Will closed his eyes.

"Angel had a mindstone?" asked Ruin.

"Let it die with him," said Will.

"Bring his body in here. Bring him to me!" shouted Ruin. The rest of the room fell silent. Ruin stood, leaning against the chimney, his face flickeringly lit by the fire below and beside him. "The gebling king will have his mindstone."

"No," said Reck. "You can't."

"When the ancient king of the geblings died, a human Heptarch took his mindstone and had it placed within his brain. Some Heptarchs were so weak that it maddened them, but some were not. Do you think I'm weak, Sister?"

"But you're the gebling king," she said. "You can't take the risk."

"You're also the gebling king," he answered.

She looked away from him.

"Do you think I didn't know what you were planning?" said Ruin. "And I understand it, Reck. I understand, I agree, and I know you're strong enough to bear it, and to pass it whole to your children. But what will I be then? The feeble gebling king, a pale shadow of the human Heptarch who can hold both races in her mind, an even weaker shadow of you? What will they call you, Mother Wyrm? There'll be no name for me, if I'm too weak to do as you do, as she did."

"What are you planning?" asked Patience.

At that moment, the geblings who had been working

on Unwyrm's mindstone came toward them. One of them held a single crystal in the palm of his hand. "This is the one," he said. "It was in the center, and it's the oldest of all."

"I've never seen a larger one," said Reck.

"Much larger than your own," Ruin reminded her.

She lifted the stone to her mouth and swallowed.

"You can't!" cried Patience.

"She already has," said Will.

"He was so strong! How can she endure—"

Reck smiled. "It wasn't right for our ancestors to perish utterly from their own world. So I will remember, and my children after me. Not particularly Unwyrm, not above any other—what was he, compared to the thousands of generations before him? They're all in here, all in me. And now I will come to know them, and speak in their voice."

Will spoke from his pallet on the floor, his voice thick with grief. "And what of my friend Reck? Will she have a voice left, when this is done?"

"If she does," said Reck, "it will be a wiser one than before."

Ruin insisted that they make a bed for her. Reck laughed lightly, but then, when it was ready, she lay in it, for the crystal was already beginning to work its influence on her.

Then they brought Angel's body from the snow outside and laid it on a table in the middle of the room. Patience went to him, and looked down into his stiffened face, forever locked in the same neutral, undecipherable expression he had cultivated in life. "You never had a chance to discover who you were," she murmured to him. "Nor had I."

They carried Ruin to a stool beside the table where the

body lay. "He was your slave," said Ruin. "I should have your permission."

"He was Unwyrm's slave, and he won his manumission before he died," she answered. "Still, if you must have a human memory to join with your own, why his? Why not any of the others—there are five hundred mindstones there."

"They've all been tainted with Unwyrm's mind," said Ruin. "I want no part of him—that's my sister's sacrifice. I hated him too long; she never did. And Angel—if I'm to understand human beings, why not this one? Strings says that he was good, before Unwyrm had him. Wouldn't you rather the gebling king became human through the memories of a good man?"

The geblings rolled the body over on its side, and they brought Ruin a knife, to cut into his brain and retrieve the mindstone that had grown there. Patience did not watch. She returned instead to Will, who lay by the fire. She reached across him and took his left hand, his whole hand, and held it tightly.

"We have unfinished business," she said.

"I'm not the man for you now," he answered.

"If I'm to be Heptarch in fact, and not in name, I need a man who can lead armies."

"I'll serve you however I can."

"And not just lead them, but create them. Out of whatever rag-tag of volunteers and rebels I can raise, I need a man who can train them into a force that can put me in my place."

"So you want that place now?"

"I can see what Reck and Ruin want to do, and they're right. The time has come for all of humanity to be united in fact under one king, as the geblings are. A king who remembers being a gebling, as the geblings will be ruled by a king who remembers being a human.

And both kings able to speak with a woman who remembers being a wyrm. Being every wyrm that ever lived.''

"Then I'll serve you."

"And more," said Patience. "I want more of you."

"What more can I give? All my wisdom is in the ways of war."

"My womb has borne a child, but it was a monster, and it's dead. I need heirs to my kingdom. Unwyrm doesn't watch now, to make sure that the line of the Heptarchs doesn't fail. So I need a consort who can create children who are large and strong, keen of mind and quick of hand. I need a consort who can teach my children what strength and wisdom are."

He said nothing, and his open eyes stared at the ceiling.

"And more," she said. "He's gone from me. The desire that burned in me for so many weeks is gone. On the boat when you touched me, and I wanted you then, I feared that it was my desire for Unwyrm. But now he's gone from me, and still when I see you I love you. Surely God will let his Vigilant answer the need of a weak and frightened girl."

He smiled. "Weak and frightened."

"Sometimes," she said. "Aren't you?"

"Terrified. Of you. I never thought to marry a woman who could kill me with a little piece of string."

"Then you'll marry me?"

"I'll serve you as I can," he said.

She bent to him and kissed his lips. Behind them, now, Reck and Ruin lay in torment, sweating and tossing and ranting on their beds. Strings and Kristiano bent over them, bound them so they did not scratch out their eyes, wiped their brows to cool the fever, sang softly to them to soothe away the terrible dreams.

Will and Patience watched, and spoke to them in the moments of sanity. Sometimes Ruin became Angel, and

Patience could talk to him; a hundred times, it seemed, he begged for her forgiveness, and she for his. I betrayed you, he would say; I killed you, she would answer. Then they forgave each other until the memory returned afresh.

Reck had no words in her madness, except, now and then, the learning of the Wise that had dwelt in Unwyrm's mind. She would lie staring at the ceiling, at the fire, at the wall, whichever way her head happened to face. Kristiano and Strings sang the ancient geblings songs of mighty deeds in battle, of terrible and forbidden love, of the sins of fathers remembered by their daughters, of the great gebling kings and their battles for the soul of the world. No one knew if Reck even heard the music, or if it helped her follow some thread out of the darkness; until one day in deep winter, when the snow was three meters deep and they brought in food through the second-story doors, Strings turned away from Reck after an hour's song and then, suddenly, turned back. "She wants me to go on," he whispered. Will and Patience came, then, and listened as Kristiano joined in the song; they wept in relief when Reck smiled in her troubled sleep. She was not lost. The songless wyrms had not stolen her utterly away.

Late in the winter, when the snow was grey from coal fires, Will regained some feeble use of his right hand. He could curl the fingers into a grip—not enough to wield a sword, but enough to help his left hand. It was enough of a triumph for him to be willing to do what Patience had asked him to do; as Heptarch, she proclaimed him her consort, and they loved each other in the cold sunlight through the upstairs window.

Not long after, Kristiano called to them to come; Ruin was awake. When they came into the room, he was kneeling beside his sister's bed, his face grave. He saw them, and held out his arms, embracing Will, then Patience, and looking at them with new respect. "You bear it all your lives," he said. "Alone."

But Will's hand was touching her shoulder, where Ruin did not see—Patience knew that the solitude was not as complete, not as unbridgeable as Ruin thought. He knew only Angel, good and grief-stricken Angel, whose isolation from humankind had been more complete than any other man she could think of. But it was not inappropriate, Patience decided, for the gebling king to have the memory of human life at its most tragic; she did not tell him that not all humans were so utterly alone.

And then, when the wind turned southerly and warm, and the snow melted, and the first shoots brought green back to the forest below, Reck awoke. Her eyes were distant, her thoughts remote, and often she would startle, as if she had only just come awake. She had thoughts she could not put into words; she could not tell them stories of her lives among the wyrms, because there was no language for it. But as they made their plans for the future government of the world, she listened, and from time to time spoke quietly and unknotted the tangled threads of the future.

They did not call her Reck anymore; she did not remember the name, for wyrms had no names, and had never needed them. Yet even though she had lost her name in the labyrinth of her mind, she had not forgotten them, and loved gaunt and gebling, dwelf and human, with the compassion of mother for child. They began to call her Mother Wyrm, and though Ruin had some hours of grief, longing for his sister, he also loved this new soul that dwelt in his sister's body; she comforted him for his loss, as she comforted them all.

They all soon realized that Mother Wyrm had grown stronger, with Unwyrm's memory within her; Strings and Kristiano reported that she was always with them, and they could do nothing without her consent. Oddly, though, she wanted nothing from them; the result was a freedom they had never known before. They still felt the needs of the others there in the House of the Wise, but they were not compelled to obey. Instead, there was Mother Wyrm within them, awakening their own will, strengthening it. "We're free," said Strings, "in bondage to her."

Hearing that, Ruin spread the word through Cranning that gaunts should be brought to the House of the Wise. The warm weather brought them like petals on the southern wind, coming into the house in slavery, and leaving it in freedom. And not just gaunts; soon geblings, dwelfs, and humans also came. Mother Wyrm no longer belonged to the little group that had come with her to Skyfoot, and they knew that when they left Cranning to begin their work in earnest, Mother Wyrm would stay behind, for her work was already begun, and would never take her away from this house.

The cherries were in full blossom in the orchards of Skyfoot when the Gebling King, the Heptarch, and Will, her consort and captain, came down out of the mountains.

20 | THE COMING OF KRISTOS

THE RUMORS HAD BEEN COMING ALL WINTER, AND INTENSI-
fied in the spring. King Oruc began to hear whispers, and
finally open speech. Agaranthemem Heptek, they called
her, and her husband was Lord Will, who had been slave
to dozens of great generals, and now was the greatest
general of them all. Other rumors called her Kristos, and
said she had killed the great satan with her own hands;
God would now give the world to her, and King Oruc
would die an agonizing death, after witnessing the torture
and death of all his children.

There were also stories of the geblings. How all the
geblings in the world had stopped at one moment, their
faces twisted with murder and hate, while the daughter of
prophecy worked her miracle in the heart of the world.
Now the gebling king had become an angel, and was
coming to destroy all human life on Imakulata. Behind
him was Mother Wyrm, a great dragon who had been
resurrected from a corpse as ancient as the time before
the starship; she was calling for the purification of
Imakulata, the final battle between human and gebling.

341

In the spring the rumors became reality. A gebling army gathered; the spies confirmed it. And Patience had been seen, had even spoken to one of them. He brought back her message:

"Lord Oruc, my friend," the messenger quoted. Oruc trembled at the way she did not call him King, and at the bitter irony in her condescension. "I come to you at last, to thank you for your good care of my kingdom. You will be well rewarded for the excellence of your regency, for I have not forgotten anything you ever did." She signed it with her dynastic name, and then with the signature he had so often seen: "Patience."

He knew then that she meant his death, and he prepared for war. He called on the other human kings and rulers to stand with him against the gebling invasion and the traitor Patience. This was one more in the long history of gebling invasions, and it would be the most terrible of all; if humankind was to survive, they would have to stand together.

Most of the kings agreed with him, and brought their armies, uniting under the banner of the Heptarch. But he knew that in every camp, in every tent, the men and women muttered the name of Agaranthemem Heptek, and remembered the prophecies of the seventh seventh seventh daughter, and wondered if they were not blaspheming and fighting against God and his Kristos. How can I defend humanity, when my people are not even sure they want to defeat their enemy?

He gathered his children and grandchildren around him, and told them the danger that was coming. They all chose to stay with him, knowing well that if the geblings won, there would be no hiding place.

The armies camped in sight of each other in the last afternoon of spring, before the solstice. There were no banners in the gebling camp. The grey-furred bodies seemed to stretch from horizon to horizon; the spies said that what they saw was only the vanguard of the gebling host. His own army, the largest ever assembled by any human king, looked pathetic as a pebble before a flood. Oruc had chosen his ground as well as he could—a hill to defend, with open ground before them and wooded land behind. But he could not hope for victory against such an enemy. That night he withdrew into his tent, alone, and wept for his children and grandchildren, and the death they would suffer on the morrow.

When dawn came, however, his generals brought the incredible news. The gebling army was gone.

Oruc came down himself to the field where he had expected his blood to flow, and found that only the trampled ground gave proof that the gebling army had been there the day before. Only a single tent remained of all his enemies, and a single banner.

As he stood there, the tent flap opened, and she came forth: Patience, as he remembered her, scarcely changed by the year that had passed. To her right walked a giant of a man, whose right arm hung limp and useless at his side; to her left, a small furry gebling carried himself with the ease and dignity of power. Lady Patience, Lord Will, and King Ruin, alone, at his mercy. He had wept in grief the night before. Now he did not understand at all.

Lord Will called out, and his voice could be heard clearly by the soldiers in the front ranks; they passed along his words to those behind. His declaration was simple.

"Here is the daughter of prophecy. By right of blood and prophecy, she is your King. She will not shed one drop of human blood to claim her right. If you refuse her, she will gladly die. If you receive her, she will forgive you."

And when he was sure that every man in Oruc's army had heard his words, he cried:

"Where are the soldiers of Agaranthemem Heptek! Where are the Vigilants of God!"

Oruc's soldiers did not hesitate. Their voices swelled like the rising voice of the wind over the sea, and they threw down their weapons and came to her, crying her name at first, but then changing the cry into the simple chant: "Kristos! Kristos! Kristos!"

Oruc gathered his family about him, preparing to die with courage. But when she had him brought to her, she smiled kindly at him, and he could detect no savagery in her face or vengeance in her voice.

"You stood in a hard place, and did well," she said simply. "I have come as Heptarch of all humankind. I ask you to rule Korfu as my viceroy, a title to be conferred on your heirs as long as one of your blood is found worthy."

He bowed before her then, as she gave his children back to him, and his life, and his kingdom. He ruled as always in King's Hill, and she visited him only once every year; he served her loyally and well, and she honored him above all other human kings.

But the center of the world was no longer Heptam. It had moved to a new city, only a few days downriver of Cranning. The city was built around a university, and the university was built around a house on a hill overlooking Cranwater. The city took the name of the school, and the school was named for the house, and from this new city called Heffiji's House the Gebling King and the Heptarch ruled. This was the place where all the humans and geblings and dwelfs and gaunts of the world looked for justice, for wisdom, for mercy, for peace.

And every year, King Ruin and Agaranthemem Heptek left Heffiji's House and made the voyage up Cranwater to Skyfoot; every year they climbed together to an ice cave at the base of the glacier that roofed the world. There they sat with Mother Wyrm, and told her all that had happened in the world, and like any other supplicants to that holiest place in all Imakulata, they listened to her wisdom and received her love and joy. So also did their children, and their children's children, through all the ages of the world.